DANGEROUS SEDUCTION

THE REYES CARTEL
BOOK 1

M. S. PARKER

Copyright © 2024 Belmonte Publishing LLC

Published by Belmonte Publishing LLC

ONE

NATALIA

I was a sucker for romance and the idea of forever, but getting ready for tonight's date felt like prepping for a showdown with El Chapo himself. My heart was racing, but my hands were steady as I applied my lipstick. The color "On Fire" was ironically appropriate for the evening I hoped to have.

I slipped off the hair tie, letting my dark waves cascade freely over my shoulders, and studied my reflection. The red dress, a snug number I swiped from Valentina—my best friend and confidante—clung to my curves in all the right places, transforming me into someone I barely recognized.

The last few weeks had been rough on the job, but tonight, I wasn't Special Agent Natalia Ramírez. I was a young woman madly in love, excited for a special evening with the man I spent the last year of my life with.

My fingers quivered ever so slightly as I secured the

intricate clasp of the gold necklace. The heart-shaped locket nestled perfectly, just grazing the swell of my chest. Within it, a miniature portrait captured Jason and me, beaming at the lens, our faces intimately close. The snapshot was a souvenir from our January getaway, a snowy escapade on Colorado's ski slopes.

I glanced at the clock, the hands ticking to 6:45. It was time to move. Jason texted earlier, saying to meet him at Bella Notte's at 7:30. Bella Notte was my favorite, and one of the most exclusive restaurants in Miami. With its crisp white tablecloths, flickering candles, and calm, intimate atmosphere, it was the kind of place people went to propose.

"You look nervous," Valentina said as she leaned against the doorframe of my bedroom. Her sharp eyes took in my dressed-to-impress appearance.

"Nervous? Me? Ha. As if," I forced a laugh, hoping to convince us both. "I'm just... eager. It's been a while since Jason and I had a proper date night. I'm hoping tonight's the night he—"

"Pops the question?" Valentina finished with a knowing grin.

"Something like that," I muttered, feeling my cheeks flush. "I mean, we've been together for over a year. It's not crazy to think Jason might be ready to take things to the next level, right?"

"Not crazy at all, Natalia. It's about damn time if you ask me. That man better propose, or I'll have to pay him a visit."

I threw my lipstick at her, but she dodged it with a laugh.

"Easy there, tiger. You don't want to mess up that gorgeous face. Now, go knock Jason's socks off."

I grabbed my purse and keys, shot my friend an air kiss, and headed for the door.

The Miami sun hung low, blinding me as I emerged into the humid heat. I slid my sunglasses on, savoring the shield they offered, and inhaled deeply, a cocktail of anticipation and jitters swirling within me.

The cab ride was seamless, the cityscape blurring past until Bella Notte came into view. Inside, the air was alive with the hum of conversation, clinking glasses, and a sultry dance of soft jazz, the kind that wrapped around you like a velvet ribbon. The rich, heady scent of garlic and basil teased my senses, promising a night of indulgence.

The maître d' greeted me with a polite smile as I approached his podium. "Buona sera, signora. Do you have a reservation?"

"Yes, it should be under Jason Crawford for 7:30," I said.

He scanned his list and nodded. "Ah yes, here it is. Signore Crawford is already waiting at the table. Right this way."

Butterflies danced in my stomach as I followed him across the dimly lit dining room. Jason stood as I approached, looking devilishly handsome in a navy suit that brought out his piercing blues.

"You look stunning," he said, pulling out my chair like the perfect gentleman.

"Thanks, you don't look so bad yourself," I said, feeling my cheeks flush. He gave me a quick peck, not as long as I'd hoped.

We ordered our usual—fettuccine Alfredo for me, chicken Parmesan for him—and made small talk while we waited for our food. Jason looked a little nervous, his eyes darting around the room, but I attributed it to his planned surprise.

After the waiter poured our wine, Jason cleared his throat and reached into his pocket. My heart skipped a beat as I realized this was it. The moment I'd been waiting for. My hands froze on my wine glass as I held my breath, waiting for him to speak.

"Natalia, you know I care about you, right?" he began, his voice soft and a little hoarse.

"Of course," I said, my heart beating so hard I could barely hear my voice.

He took a long breath and then blurted out, "I think we need to take a break."

A sudden chill ran through me. I must have heard Jason wrong. "What?"

He looked down at his hands, twisted together on the table. "I care about you, but I think we need some space. I've been feeling a little smothered lately. Honestly, it's not you, it's me..."

As I tuned him out, the pieces started clicking into place. The way he'd angle his phone away from me whenever a notification popped up, like he didn't want me to see who was texting him. And then there was the bracelet in a fancy gift box I'd found in his apartment last week - a delicate silver chain with a charm that was definitely not my style. I had chalked it up to a gift to his sister or mom, but now I realized how naive I'd been.

My training as a DEA agent had taught me to trust my instincts and pick up on even the smallest details of a crime scene, but apparently, I was a lot less clever in my love life.

"You've been cheating on me," I said flatly. It wasn't a question. Jason finally looked up, his face a pathetic mix of guilt and resignation, telling me all I needed to know.

"Who is she?" I demanded. My mind raced through the possibilities. It had to be someone I knew for him to look this uncomfortable. Then it hit me. "Oh, my God. It's Melissa, isn't it?"

The flash of panic in his eyes confirmed my guess. "Natalia, I didn't mean—" he started, but I held up a hand to silence him.

"Don't," I hissed. "Just don't." I felt like I'd been sucker-punched, the air rushing out of my lungs. Of course it was Melissa. That conniving, backstabbing bitch. I should've known something was going on between them, the way she'd been eyeing Jason whenever we ran into her in the hallway or by the pool.

Tears stung my eyes, but I blinked them back furiously. I refused to give Jason the satisfaction of seeing me cry. "How long?" I demanded, my voice hard and brittle.

He had the decency to look ashamed. "A few months."

A few months. The realization hit me like a ton of bricks. All the times Jason had claimed he was working late - he'd been with Melissa, betraying me, lying straight to my face.

"I can't believe this," I said, shaking my head in disbelief. "I thought...I thought you were going to propose tonight."

Jason at least had the good grace to wince. "I'm sorry, Nat. I never meant to hurt you, but...I just don't think I can be the man you need me to be."

I let out a humorless laugh. "The man I need you to be? How about just a faithful, honest partner? Is that too much to ask?"

Jason spewed some bullshit, but I no longer gave a rat's ass what lame excuse he had up his sleeve.

"Shove it," I spat, getting up from my chair. "Go fuck up your life with Melissa. See if I care."

I marched my ass out of the restaurant, chin up, determined not to give that prick the satisfaction of seeing how badly he'd fucked me up inside. But the second I hit the sticky summer night, the floodgates opened, and tears of rage poured down my face. I swiped at them, pissed at myself for wasting precious tears on that two-timing, lying sack of shit.

I must've been blind not to see Jason's true colors from day one. Seriously, what kind of asshole plans a breakup at the same place you had your six-month anniversary? The kind who's got "DOUCHE" fucking tattooed on his forehead, that's who.

I hailed a taxi and barked my address at the driver, a wiry man with a graying beard and eyes that had seen too many drunken tourists.

"Rough night, huh?" he asked, glancing at me through the rearview mirror.

I glared at him. "You could say that."

"Look, sweetheart, it's none of my business, but any man who makes a woman look like she's ready to spit nails must've done something pretty stupid."

Despite my mood, I snorted. "That's the understatement of the year."

He chuckled. "Well, you're a looker and have fire in your eyes. You'll find someone who deserves you."

I managed a half-smile. "Thanks, but I think I'll stick to battery-operated companions for a while."

The driver laughed hard as we pulled up to my apartment building, but just as he brought the cab to a stop, a muffled ping came from my purse. I pulled out my phone to see a text from Jason.

I'm sorry. I never meant to hurt you. I hope we can still be friends.

I barked out a sharp, bitter laugh. Of course, Jason would try to pull that line—a lame attempt to assuage his guilt. I angrily flipped to my contacts list to block his number.

Just as I was about to drop my phone back into my purse, it lit up again with a call. I frowned as I saw my partner, Agent Matt Bennett's, name flashing on the screen. He knew I was supposed to be having a romantic night with Jason, so it had to be important for him to interrupt.

I cleared my throat before picking up. "Ramirez," I said, trying to keep my voice steady.

"Nat, you will not believe this," Matt's voice crackled with urgency through the phone. "We've got a nibble on the Reyes cartel. A snitch just crawled out of the wood-work, ready to spill his guts. He says something's going down tonight. This might just be our golden ticket."

His words sent a jolt through me, the sting of Jason's bullshit evaporating in an instant. The Reyes cartel–our Moby Dick–had slipped through our fingers repeatedly, a ghost in the drug trade we'd been hell-bent on exorcizing. If this tip paid off, we could strike a crippling blow to the coke flooding Miami streets.

"I'm en route," I said, my resolve solidifying with every syllable. "I'll be there in ten."

I instantly morphed back into Special Agent Natalia Ramírez as I turned to the driver with the address. The sting of Jason's betrayal faded into the background as the adrenaline of the mission surged through my veins.

TWO

DANTE

My eyes were fixed on the ocean, its deep blue expanse stretching toward the horizon, but my mind was elsewhere. I stood on the balcony of my penthouse apartment, the warm Miami sun on my skin, but a sense of unease lingered in my thoughts. The tranquil view before me usually brought a sense of calm, yet today, it did little to soothe the restlessness within me.

The buzz of my phone startled me from my reverie. Glancing at the screen, I saw Marco's name flashing. An instinctive wariness washed over me, knowing that Marco's calls were rarely social.

"Dante, where are you?" Marco's voice held a sharp edge, cutting through the quiet of my home. "Get down to the warehouse. Your father's requested your presence for the drop tonight."

I frowned, a surge of confusion coursing through me. "The drop? Why the hell would he want me there? You know I haven't been involved in the drug operation for over a year. This is Tony's territory now."

There was a brief pause on the other end, and I imagined Marco weighing his words carefully. "Look, I don't know, okay? Your father just said he wanted you there. Said it was important. And he's... expecting you."

Disdain laced through me at the mention of my father, Ricardo Reyes. Our relationship was strained at best, and his demands rarely boded well for anyone involved. I ran a hand through my hair. "Fine, I'll be there. But this better be good, Marco. I have a club to run."

Hanging up, I reluctantly left the serenity of my balcony and made my way to the warehouse, an old building nestled in an industrial part of the city. As I drove, questions swirled in my mind. Why was my father summoning me, and what did he want with me at a drug drop? It had been well-established that I wanted no part in the cartel's drug activities anymore, preferring to focus on my night club in South Beach.

Upon my arrival, I spotted Marco standing by the loading bay doors, his posture taut with anticipation. He exuded an air of unease, which did little to ease my own reservations about this unexpected gathering.

"Took you long enough," Marco muttered as I approached, his gaze darting around the deserted parking lot.

"Couldn't be helped," I replied, my eyes scanning the area for any signs of trouble. "Why the sudden interest in having me present at a drop? You know I'm not usually invited to these family reunions."

Marco shrugged, his jaw set in a tight line. "Your father's orders, not mine. He wanted all hands on deck. Must be a big shipment."

I snorted. "Or a big show of force. He loves his theatrics."

Marco didn't argue with that. We both knew Ricardo Reyes relished demonstrating his power and control over the cartel, and this was likely just another way for him to exert his dominance.

As we moved inside, I got the feeling that something was amiss. My senses were on high alert, attuned to even the slightest hint of danger. The warehouse was quiet, too quiet, and I felt a tingle at the base of my spine, a warning that something was about to go down.

Marco must have sensed it too because he whispered, "This doesn't feel right. We should be prepared for anything."

"Always am," I said, my hand instinctively going to the gun holstered at my waist—a constant companion in my line of work.

As we made our way further into the warehouse, I spotted Tony Gutierrez, one of my father's loyal soldiers, standing near the loading bay. His presence only added to my unease, and I found myself walking over to him, unable to quell my curiosity any longer.

"Tony," I called out, my voice echoing slightly in the vast space. "Why am I here? You know I haven't been involved in this part of the business since I took over Club Diablo."

Tony turned, a smirk playing on his lips. He ran a hand through his greasy black hair and took a deliberate drag on his cigar, blowing the smoke casually in my direction. "Ah, Dante. It seems your father wanted to make sure you haven't become a soft, pampered prince, running a strip club and drinking fancy cocktails all day."

His words stung, and my jaw clenched. I took a step forward, my hands balling into fists, but before I could unleash my anger, voices drifted from the main entrance, halting me in my tracks.

Marco's hand snapped out, grabbing my arm and pulling me back just as a flurry of movement caught my eye. Tony reached for his weapon, his smirk transforming into a snarl. Instinctively, I drew my own gun, my body tensing as I prepared for the unknown.

Marco wasted no time, pulling me behind a towering stack of wooden crates marked with the cartel's insignia. Peering around the edge, I saw a team of people in tactical gear, guns drawn, slowly making their way into the warehouse. My heart hammered in my chest as I realized what was unfolding—a raid.

The cartel members, including Tony, quickly engaged, gunfire erupting across the warehouse. Marco and I remained hidden, surveying the situation. We were outnumbered, and with Tony and the others occupied, we knew we had to act quickly.

I turned to Marco, my eyes fierce. "We need to get out of here. Now."

He nodded, his eyes scanning the chaotic scene before us. "Let's split up. We'll have a better chance not getting caught. I'll meet you outside."

As I watched Marco disappear into the darkness, I realized just how much I hated my life. Being Ricardo Reyes' son meant I was born into the cartel, a life I could never escape even if I wanted to.

THREE
NATALIA

I PUSHED THROUGH THE GLASS DOORS OF MIAMI'S DEA headquarters, the sharp report of my footsteps punctuating the hushed atmosphere of the building. Heads turned as I strode through the bullpen in my form-fitting red dress, a stark contrast to my fellow agents' utilitarian suits and tactical gear. I ignored the raised eyebrows and curious glances; my mind focused solely on the task at hand.

I spotted Matt hunched over his desk, his brow furrowed as he pored over a stack of documents. His eyes lifted to meet mine, and for a moment, they widened, drinking in the sight of me. "Damn, Ramirez," he breathed out, a whistle slipping through his teeth. "Tonight was the night, right? Where's the sparkler? What the hell went down?"

His question stung, and I cringed, the ache inside my

heart flaring up. "Plans changed," I managed, my voice a thin wire about to snap. "What's the update?"

The humor drained from his face, replaced by a knowing look. He'd always been able to read me like a book, and right now, he could see the heartache I was barely keeping under wraps.

"Our snitch hit the jackpot," he said, sliding a folder across the desk to me. "He handed us the cartel's drug stream on a silver platter. They're expecting a mountain of blow in less than two hours at a warehouse. If we swoop in fast, we can catch them with their pants down and snatch a fortune in dope. Cripple their entire operation."

I could hardly believe it. Months of dead ends and false leads had us chasing our tails, and now, the universe dropped this bombshell in our laps tonight of all nights? It felt like we'd just won the lottery on a whim.

"This is also your operation, Nat. What's your take?" Matt's voice cut through my thoughts, laced with an urgency that matched the pounding of my heart.

I flipped through the file, my pulse quickening as I read the intel. Warehouse location, guard rotations, entry points - it was all there. This really could be the break we'd been waiting for.

"Let's rally the troops," I told Matt, returning the file. "Let's get everyone locked, loaded, and ready to kick down doors in 30." I looked down at my dress. "Shit, I need to go change into something I can actually run in."

Matt nodded, his eyes lingering on me for a second.

"You sure you're up for this, Nat? I mean, after what just—"

I cut him off with a sharp look. "I'm fine," I said, my tone brooking no argument. "My fucked up love life stays at the door. We have a job to do."

I turned and strode off towards the lockers before he could argue, my hips swaying and drawing stares from every guy in the room. Fuck 'em. My head was already in go mode, gearing up for the high-stakes operation ahead.

I quickly removed my dress and heels in the locker room, trading them for tactical pants, a black T-shirt, and sturdy boots.

Fuck romance. Fuck heartbreak. I've got a city to save and a cartel to bury. My personal life could wait.

The next half hour passed in a blur of controlled chaos as our team prepared for the raid. I strapped on my Kevlar vest with practiced efficiency, double-checking my weapons and equipment. The familiar rituals helped calm my nerves, pushing away all thoughts of Jason's betrayal.

The ride to the warehouse was tense and silent; each agent was lost in their mental preparation. When we arrived, I signaled for the team to take their positions. We surrounded the building, weapons drawn, waiting for my command.

"On my mark," I whispered into my radio. "Three, two, one - go, go, go!"

We burst through the doors, flashbangs and smoke grenades creating a disorienting haze. Shouts and gunfire erupted as the cartel members scrambled to react. I moved swiftly through the chaos, my gun raised.

"Ramirez, watch your six!" Matt yelled over the din. I spun just in time to see a cartel thug emerging from the smoke, his gun aimed right at me. I dropped to the ground, rolling behind a crate as a spray of bullets slammed into the concrete where I'd just been standing.

Adrenaline pumping, I popped up and returned fire, catching the thug in the chest. He crumpled to the ground, his weapon clattering uselessly beside him—no time to catch my breath. I pushed forward, clearing room after room, securing evidence, and taking out hostiles.

Just as it looked like we had the upper hand, a devastating explosion rocked the building. I was thrown off my feet, my ears ringing, and vision blurred. Dazed, I stumbled to my feet, trying to make sense of the sudden turn of events.

"Ambush!" Matt's voice crackled over the radio. "They fucking knew we were coming!"

How could they have known? My stomach dropped when the implications hit me. Someone in the DEA must have given them a hint, willingly or by accident.

But there was no time to dwell on that now. The warehouse had turned into a kill box, cartel reinforcements swarming in from all sides.

I fought through the smoke and debris, desperately trying to regroup with my team. A bullet whizzed past my head, the near-miss a stark reminder of my mortality.

Suddenly, a cry of pain cut through the din of battle. My heart seized as I recognized the voice.

"Matt!" I screamed, sprinting towards the sound. I found him crumpled behind an overturned table, clutching his abdomen as blood seeped between his fingers. "Hang on, Matt. I've got you."

I dragged him to cover, pressing my hands against the wound to stem the bleeding. But it was no use. The bullet had torn through his vest, ripping into his gut. His face was ashen, his breath coming in short, wet gasps. If they were using Kevlar-piercing bullets, they didn't just know we were coming. Somebody was deliberately trying to kill us.

Tears blurred my vision as I gripped his hand, slick with blood. "I'm not leaving you," I said fiercely. "We're going to get you out of here, get you patched up. Just hold on."

But even as I said the words, I knew it was a lie. The light was fading from Matt's eyes, his grip on my hand weakening. "It's okay," he whispered, a faint smile ghosting over his lips. "It's been an honor serving with you, Ramirez. Give 'em hell for me."

Then he was gone, his body going slack in my arms.

A ragged sob tore from my throat, grief, and rage threatening to consume me. I gently closed Matt's eyes, my hand trembling as I smoothed back his hair

As I knelt there, swallowed by sorrow, a cold, hard circle of steel pressed against the nape of my neck. "Freeze," a voice, deep and authoritative, commanded. "Lose the gun. Hands in the air."

My pulse spiked, adrenaline flooding my veins as I carefully placed my weapon on the ground and lifted my hands skyward. My assailant came into view as he moved in front of me—a towering figure with an athlete's grace, his hair a dark shade of blonde, and eyes of piercing blue that seemed to strip me bare. I knew him. Dante Reyes, the cartel's golden boy.

Dante took a moment to survey me, his eyes roaming over my tactical gear and the shield lying forgotten beside me. "A woman," he remarked, the faintest note of surprise lacing his tone. "Didn't peg the DEA for sending a lady to a suicide raid."

The threat hanging in the air should've iced my veins, but his voice—a sultry, honeyed melody—sent an unwelcome surge of heat through me. I silently chastised myself, corralling my thoughts back to the difficult reality of the moment.

"Well?" I challenged, my voice a mask of calm over the tremor of adrenaline. "What's stopping you? Do it. Kill me."

A smirk played on Dante's lips, his eyes alight with mischief. "Kill you?" he repeated, the idea seemingly unthinkable to him. "Where's the fun in that?"

He leaned in, his breath a searing whisper against my skin. "I've got a better idea. I'll let you walk away. Consider it a nod to your... dedication."

Before I could respond, the sound of approaching sirens pierced the air, signaling backup and first responders. Dante's eyes flicked toward the entrance, and he stepped back.

"It appears our time is up," he said, his voice low. "But, Agent... this is not over. Not by a long shot."

And with that, he turned and disappeared into the smoke and chaos, leaving me alone with my swirling thoughts and a burning desire for answers.

I swallowed hard, my brain churning as I tried to make sense of the night's events. My personal life was in shambles, my partner was dead, and now I had a cartel kingpin playing mind games with me. I felt a stream of frustration and a deep-seated need for revenge.

I took a steadying breath, my fingers tightening around my gun. Whatever Dante Reyes was insinuating, I would get to the bottom of whatever was going on. I owed it to Matt, and I owed it to myself.

FOUR
DANTE

I MARCHED DOWN THE GILDED CORRIDORS OF OUR palatial family mansion, my gut tying itself in knots. The closer I got to the old man's study, the more last night's shitshow pushed to the front of my mind, demanding attention.

What was supposed to be a routine drug delivery at the warehouse had turned into a disaster. One minute, we were prepping for a massive shipment; the next, all hell broke loose. The DEA hit us hard, their tactical teams breaching the building with a ferocity I hadn't seen in a long time.

Gunfire erupted, chaos took over. Our men rallied, fighting back with everything they had. Amid the commotion, I spotted her—the female agent—moving to her partner's side with lethal grace. He'd been shot, already gone by the time I'd sneaked up behind her. Our eyes locked for a split second, and something stirred deep within me, a primal curiosity I couldn't quite place.

I could have ended her life right then. But instead of pulling the trigger, I let her live—a decision that both intrigued and unsettled me. My father would likely give me hell for it if he knew.

Breathing heavily, I pushed open the doors and stepped inside.

"Ah, Dante," my father's voice boomed, surprisingly jovial. "Come in."

Ricardo Reyes cut an imposing figure, even when seated behind his massive desk. His broad shoulders filled out the expensive suit he wore, and his salt-and-pepper hair was slicked back in a manner that exuded power and authority.

"You wanted to see me, Father?" I asked, my voice even despite the unease that churned within me.

"Indeed, my son." He gestured for me to take a seat, his piercing gaze never wavering. "I trust you've recovered from last night's... unpleasantness."

I bristled at the memory, my jaw clenching involuntarily. "The DEA caught us off guard. It won't happen again."

Amusement danced across my father's features. "Oh, but it's not a problem, Dante."

My brow furrowed in confusion. "What do you mean?"

Ricardo leaned back in his chair, steepling his fingers as a sly grin tugged at the corners of his mouth. "Let's just say I had a hunch and made the arrangements. Made sure the product was safely stored elsewhere."

Realization dawned on me, and I felt anger rise within me. "You knew the DEA was coming, and you still sent me?"

My father's grin widened, his teeth gleaming like a shark's. "They had to believe we were clueless about them coming. With you there, they assumed we had no idea. And it worked like a charm, did it not?"

I clenched my fists, struggling to rein in my fury. "People died in that raid, Father. And for what? Some twisted game to...one-up each other?"

Ricardo waved a dismissive hand. "Casualties are inevitable in our line of work, Dante. It could happen to you and me tomorrow. You know that better than anyone."

He was right, of course. Death was an ever-present specter in the world we inhabited, a constant companion that never strayed too far. Still, the casual way he brushed off the loss of life left a sour taste in my mouth.

"As for the game," my father continued, "plans are in motion. The DEA is getting closer, but we'll stop them."

I shook my head, still trying to understand his tactics. "But how? Unless we scale back our drug trade, we'll end up either in prison or dead. I don't see the endgame, Father."

Ricardo's expression grew somber, his eyes taking on a steely glint. "The endgame, my son, is survival. The DEA has been snapping at our heels for far too long. It's time to turn the tables and put them on the defensive."

A slow, sinister smile spread across his face, and I saw the depth of my father's brutality. He was playing a long game that would undoubtedly leave a trail of bodies in its wake.

I fucking hated this life.

"What about the female agent?" I asked, unable to shake the memory of her defiant eyes.

My father's brow arched ever so slightly. "The one you let live?"

My jaw dropped. Papi knew. Somebody must have seen me.

"An interesting choice, Dante. Perhaps you saw something in her that piqued your curiosity."

I said nothing, unwilling to play into his games. Ricardo studied me for a moment, then chuckled.

"No matter. She's inconsequential in the grand scheme of things. A pawn to be sacrificed when the time is right."

His words sent a ripple of unease through me, but I kept my expression neutral. The female agent may have been an adversary, but something about her stirred a sense of... fuck, I didn't have a clue.

"Anyway, I need your help, my son. I know you have your little pet project going, but can you spare me half your time? Oversee a couple of deliveries. Take Marco with you if you must."

"Of course," I said and nodded, a fake smile plastered on my face.

"Wonderful, now if you'll please..." My father lifted his hand to dismiss me, but last night's raid wasn't the only topic on my mind. Something, or rather someone, bothered me.

"Father, on another matter, we can't ignore the Cruz situation any longer," I began, keeping my voice level despite the simmering frustration. "Javier keeps harassing the club, threatening our staff. He's getting bolder and more aggressive. It's only a matter of time before he makes a serious play for power."

Ricardo fixed me with a look that could freeze lava. "You can't touch Javier Cruz," he said, his voice dangerous.

I felt my eyebrows shoot up in surprise. "What? Why the hell not?"

"That's not your concern, Dante," he said, his tone brooking no argument. "I need you to focus on keeping our operations running smoothly. The last thing we need is fighting between the cartels."

I clenched my jaw, feeling the muscles twitch with the effort of holding back a torrent of words I knew I'd regret. "With all due respect, Father, ignoring Cruz will not make him disappear. He's a threat, and it's only a matter of time before he—"

"Enough!" Ricardo slammed his fist on the desk, the sound echoing off the walls of his opulent office. "I have my reasons, and you will abide by my decision. Do I make myself clear?"

I stood up, the chair scraping against the marble floor. "Crystal," I ground out, my hands balled into fists at my sides.

"Anyway, enough talk," my father said, rising from his

chair. "Go take care of that silly club of yours. I'm sure there's something that needs to be done."

I nodded, recognizing the blunt dismissal for what it was. My father had always hated the idea that I wanted an actual business. He didn't grasp that it made the cartel look more legit. Instead, he called it a waste of money.

As I turned to leave, my father's voice stopped me in my tracks.

"Oh, and Dante?" I glanced over my shoulder, meeting his piercing gaze. "Don't let your... curiosities cloud your judgment. We're at the brink of a war with the DEA, and in war, there can be no room for weakness."

His words hung in the air like a lingering threat, a reminder of the consequences that awaited me should I stray from the path he had laid out. With a curt nod, I exited the study.

My life was fucking complicated. One foot in my father's gruesome world, the other in my dream of a curated fleet of establishments, clubs, bars, and hotels in South Beach. Away from the violence and politics among the cartels and their leaders. What was their goal, anyway? More money? More power? Was it worth the price we paid, the pieces of our souls we chipped away with every brutal act?

I shook my head. Now was not the time for contemplating and daydreaming. Even if I wanted to, I couldn't abandon my father. I was born to one day replace him as the head of the cartel. I couldn't afford to look weak, not now, not ever. I had a job for my father—and a club to run for myself.

I caught sight of my sister, Sofia, in the study, pacing back and forth, her phone pressed to her ear. She was engrossed in conversation, her free hand gesturing animatedly as she spoke. Curiosity peaked, and I moved closer.

"I know, right? And it'll be fine. Don't worry!" she gushed, her voice filled with excitement. "I can't wait for you to meet him."

Suddenly, she looked up and noticed me standing there. Her eyes widened, and she quickly wrapped up the call. "Hey, listen, I've got to go. My brother just walked in. I'll call you back later, okay? Bye!"

She hung up the phone and turned to face me, her brow furrowing with concern as she took in my expression. "Dante? What's wrong? You look upset."

I sighed, running a hand through my hair. "It's nothing, Sof. Just got out of a meeting with Dad, that's all."

Her eyes softened, and she nodded in understanding. "Ah. I see. One of those meetings, huh?"

A humorless chuckle escaped my lips. "Yeah. You could say that."

Sofia knew better than to press for details. Growing up in the Reyes family, we learned early that certain things couldn't be discussed openly. The family business was a complex web of secrets and lies; the less she knew, the better.

"I'm sorry, Dante," she said, squeezing my arm. "I

know how much pressure Dad puts on you. But you know you can always talk to me, right? Even if it's just to vent."

I smiled, grateful for her support. "I know, Sof. And I appreciate it. But trust me, you don't want to know the details of this one."

She held up her hands in mock surrender, her perfectly manicured nails glinting in the soft light of the hallway. "Say no more. I know the drill. But now that I have you here, I need a small favor."

I raised an eyebrow. "Oh? And what might that be, dear sister? Another one of your schemes?"

Sofia grinned, her eyes sparkling with the kind of mischief that had gotten us into trouble more times than I could count when we were kids. "Well, I was thinking... how would you feel about a dinner date with me and Allen?"

I groaned, shaking my head. An evening of forced conversations with some random guy, likely looking to take advantage of my sister, was my least favorite way of spending a night. Her guys never last more than two weeks tops, anyway. "Sofia, I'm sorry, but I don't have time. With business going crazy, you know. By the way, who's Allen?"

She pouted, her lower lip jutting out in that infuriatingly adorable way that always got to me. "Allen is new in town, and I really like him. I want you to meet him to ensure he's good enough for your little sister. Plus, you gotta eat!"

I sighed, feeling my resolve crumble in her pleading gaze. Sofia was always my weakness, the one I could never say no to. Even when we were kids, she had a way of wrapping me around her little finger with just a bat of her eyelashes and a well-timed "please."

I looked at her, taking in her face. Her dark hair was pulled back into a messy bun, and her brown eyes were wide and pleading.

"Fine," I relented, throwing up my hands in defeat. "If you guys are still together in a month, I'll think about it. This Allen dude better be a nice guy to you, or–"

Sofia squealed with delight, throwing her arms around me in a tight hug that nearly knocked the wind out of me. "Thank you, thank you, thank you! You're the best brother ever, you know that? And don't worry, I can take care of myself. But it's sweet of you to be so protective."

I chuckled, hugging her back and ruffling her hair affectionately. "Yeah, yeah. Just remember this the next time I need a favor from you. And for the record, I'm not being protective. I just don't want to deal with you moping around the house if things don't work out."

She laughed, punching me lightly in the arm. "Please, as if I would ever mope. That's more your style, Mr. Broody."

I clutched my chest in mock offense as Sofia's words hit me. "Mr. Broody? Ouch, little sis, you wound me."

She rolled her eyes, a mischievous grin playing on her lips. "Oh please, don't be so dramatic."

I laughed. Sofia was the one person who could remind me not to take life too seriously.

"Alright, alright. I'll leave you to enjoy your evening," I

conceded, affectionately ruffling my sister's hair. "Just don't do anything I wouldn't do."

She batted my hand away, sticking her tongue out at me. "That doesn't leave much out, does it?"

With a wink and a laugh, I headed for the door, leaving Sofia to her devices. As I stepped outside into the hot evening, I loosened my tie and inhaled deeply, savoring the brief respite from the heavy burden of my responsibilities.

I made my way across the expansive grounds to the garage, where my pride and joy awaited—a sleek, gunmetal gray Maserati Quattroporte. The purr of the powerful engine roared to life as I slid behind the wheel. Something about the thrill of speed never failed to invigorate me.

As I peeled out of the driveway, I felt some tension from my meeting with my father dissipate. The city blurred past my window, a kaleidoscope of color and sound, and for a fleeting moment, I allowed myself to get lost in the rush of adrenaline.

But the reprieve was short-lived. As I merged onto the highway, my mind drifted back to the previous night's events and the chaos that had unfolded at the warehouse. The female agent's eyes, their defiance smoldering even as my gun loomed before her, scorched a permanent place in my mind.

I felt that there was more to her than met the eye. Something about her had sparked a curiosity, a desire to unravel the mystery behind those piercing eyes.

Shaking my head, I pushed the thought aside. Now was not the time for such distractions. I had a club to run, and with my father's latest machinations, the stakes were higher than ever.

Reaching into my jacket pocket, I pulled out my phone and hit the speed dial for Marco. After a couple of rings, his gruff voice crackled through the speakers.

"Yo, what's up, man?"

"Marco, it's me," I said, my tone all business. "I need you to meet me at the club. We've got shit to discuss."

There was a brief pause before he responded. "Roger that. I'll be there in twenty."

I ended the call and tossed my phone onto the passenger seat, my knuckles tightening around the steering wheel. Marco had been my right-hand man for as long as I could remember, the closest thing I had to a brother outside my blood family. If anyone could help me figure out the next step, it was him.

FIVE

NATALIA

THE SOLEMN NOTES OF TAPS HUNG IN THE HUMID Miami air, a final salute to my fallen partner. I stood rigid beside Valentina, watching as the honor guard meticulously folded the crisp American flag that had draped over Matt's casket.

My chest felt like a hollowed-out cavity, raw and gaping, as they presented the tri-cornered emblem to Matt's mother, Barbara. She accepted it with trembling hands, her face a mask of quiet anguish. Guilt consumed me, intertwined with the scorching acknowledgment of my shortcomings. I should have been there for him; I should have taken that bullet instead.

Val must have sensed the torrent of emotions raging within me because she slipped her hand into mine and squeezed tight—a silent gesture of support that grounded me, if only for a fleeting second.

When Barbara stepped up to the podium, I steeled

myself, swallowing hard against the lump in my throat. Her eyes were rimmed red from crying, but her voice sounded clear and strong.

"My son was a hero," she began, her gaze sweeping across the sea of sad faces. "He lived to protect and serve, to make this world a little safer for all of us. And in the end, he made the ultimate sacrifice, giving his life in pursuit of justice."

A strangled sob escaped my lips, and I clamped my jaw shut, determined not to break down completely. Not here, not in front of everyone. Barbara's eyes found mine in the crowd, and the faintest of smiles ghosted across her lips.

"Matt loved being a DEA agent," she continued, her words quivering with the intensity of her feelings. "And he loved his partner, Natalia. She was like family to him, and I know he thought the world of her."

My vision blurred with tears as Barbara's words washed over me. Matt had been more than just my partner; he'd been my brother-in-arms. We'd had each other's backs through thick and thin, and now Matt was gone, leaving a gaping hole in my life that could never be filled.

When the service concluded, I drifted through the crowd of mourners like a ghost, accepting condolences with numb nods and vacant stares. That's when I spotted Chief Reynolds standing off to the side, conversing with a cluster of high-ranking officials.

A sudden surge of determination flared within me, and before I could think, I strode towards him.

"Chief," I said. "I want in. I want to go undercover and take down the Reyes cartel. For Matt."

Reynolds's eyes widened, and he glanced around quickly to ensure no one had overheard. "Agent Ramirez, this isn't the time or place—"

"I don't give a fuck," I hissed, stepping closer. "The Reyes Cartel killed my partner, and I'll be damned if I let them get away with it."

He sighed, pinching the bridge of his nose. "My office. One hour," he muttered through clenched teeth. "We'll discuss this properly then."

I opened my mouth to protest, but he'd already turned his back on me, dismissing me. A muscle twitched in my jaw as I fought the urge to argue with him right then and there.

A gentle hand on my arm made me cringe, and I whirled around to find Agent Morrow eyeing me with a blend of concern and curiosity.

"Everything okay, Ramirez?" he asked, his voice a soft murmur.

I forced a tight smile, keenly aware that we weren't alone. "Just peachy, Morrow. The chief and I are discussing...operational matters."

Morrow's brow furrowed, but he didn't press further. With a curt nod, he melted back into the crowd, his gaze lingering on me for a beat too long. Morrow was a veteran, all knuckle and sneer after decades of navigating the seedy underbelly of law enforcement. I felt a prickle of unease but pushed it aside, my mind already racing ahead.

An hour. That's all I had to compose myself before my showdown with Reynolds. I scanned the dwindling crowd until I located Valentina standing beside the refreshments table, a paper cup of stale coffee clutched in her hand.

"Val," I said, closing the distance between us. "I need you to cover for me. I'm going to see Reynolds, and I feel it will get ugly."

She eyed me warily, no doubt taking in the fire burning in my eyes. "You're not going to do anything stupid, are you, Nat? Because I don't want to go to another funeral next week."

I shook my head, mustering what I hoped was a reassuring smile. "Have a little faith, would you? I'm just going to get some answers. That's all."

The lie tasted bitter on my tongue, but I had no choice. If Val knew I wanted to go undercover, she would have a fit.

Val's lips pressed into a thin line, but she reluctantly nodded. "Fine. But you'd better loop me in after, you hear me? I've got your back, partner."

Her words sent a pang of gratitude through me. Despite the maelstrom of grief and anger swirling within, I knew I could count on Valentina. She was my rock, my anchor in the madness that had become my life.

"You know it," I said, squeezing her shoulder. "I'll catch up with you later."

I STORMED INTO CHIEF REYNOLDS' office, the door slamming shut behind me with a resonating thud that echoed the pounding of my heart. He looked up from his paperwork, his eyes narrowing as he looked at me.

"Ramirez," he said. "This better be good."

"I want in," I declared, my hands curling into fists at my sides. "I want to go deep undercover into the Reyes cartel. I owe it to Matt."

Reynolds sighed, setting his pen down with deliberate slowness. He leaned back in his chair, his gaze sweeping over me with an infuriating mixture of sympathy and condescension. "Agent Ramirez, we've been over this. You're not ready for such a high-stakes operation. Not after what happened."

My jaw clenched, frustration boiling over into my words. "I'm more than ready. I've been training for this my entire career. Matt was my partner, and it's my responsibility to bring his killers to justice."

"It's not about what you owe," Reynolds retorted, his voice firm. "It's about making smart decisions. You've been through a traumatic event and need time to heal."

I shook my head vehemently, the movement whipping my loose hair around my face. "I don't need time. I need action. I need to do something."

"You will," he said, his tone softening ever so slightly. "But not now. Not like this."

I stared at him in disbelief as he delivered the crushing blow. "You're forcing me to give you a leave of absence. Six weeks," he stated as if there were no arguing.

"Six weeks?" I echoed, my voice rising in pitch. "You can't be serious. I'm fine, Reynolds. I can handle—"

"You're not fine, Ramirez," he interrupted, his eyes hardening. "You're running on fumes and adrenaline. You need to step back, clear your head, and return when you're at full strength."

My mind raced, searching for a counterargument, a way to change his mind. But he was unyielding, a fortress of bureaucratic bullshit that I couldn't seem to penetrate.

"I'll file an official protest," I threatened with a growl.

"You do that," he said, leaning forward to meet my gaze. "But it won't change a thing. This is for your own good, whether or not you realize it."

Defeated, I turned on my heel and stalked out of his office. The door slam made a hollow sound that seemed to mock my helplessness. As I stepped into the hallway, I nearly collided with Morrow, who was leaning against the wall, his arms crossed over his chest.

"Rough meeting?" he asked casually.

I glared at him, my anger still simmering. "He's benching me, Morrow. Six weeks. Can you believe that?"

Morrow's face remained impassive, but there was a flicker of something—interest? Curiosity?—in his eyes. "I can help you," he said, glancing around to ensure we were alone.

"Help me?" I scoffed. "What are you going to do? March into Reynolds' office and tell him he's making a mistake?"

A ghost of a smile tugged at the corner of Morrow's

mouth. "Not exactly. Listen, Natalia, I have some experience training undercover operatives from... let's call it an unofficial department. I could help you prepare for your mission."

I eyed him suspiciously. "And why would you do that for me?"

"Because I believe in you," he said. "And because I owe it to Matt to see this through. He was one of us; we don't leave our own behind."

My throat tightened at the mention of Matt's name, but I forced myself to focus on Morrow's proposition. "What do you need me to do?"

"First, we have to get you out of that DEA mindset," he said, leading me down the hallway toward the file room. "You must become someone else. Someone who can infiltrate the cartel without raising suspicions."

The file room was a dimly lit cave filled with rows of metal cabinets, each bursting with classified information. Morrow navigated the maze with practiced ease, stopping before a cabinet labeled 'Reyes Cartel.'

He pulled out a thick stack of files and handed them to me. "Study these. Memorize every name, every face, every detail about the cartel's operations. You need to know them better than they know themselves."

I nodded, flipping open the first file and scanning the pages. It was daunting, but I was determined to see it through. "And then what?"

Morrow reached into his jacket and produced another file, this one noticeably thinner. He handed it to me, and I opened it to reveal a dossier on a woman named Eva Morales.

"This is your new identity," he explained, watching my reaction closely. "Eva is a celebrity stylist who's just moved to Miami. She's glamorous, confident, and she has a knack for getting close to powerful men."

I raised an eyebrow. "Are you suggesting what I think you're suggesting?"

"If you want to get close to Dante Reyes, you're going to have to seduce him," Morrow said bluntly. "Eva's profession is the perfect cover. It gives you a reason to be in his orbit, to gain his trust."

My mouth went dry, the implications of his words sinking in. Seducing Dante Reyes wouldn't be just a job; it would be a dangerous game of cat and mouse with the highest possible stakes.

"I'll do it," I said, my voice steady despite the flutter of nerves in my stomach. "I'll become Eva Morales."

Morrow nodded, satisfaction in his eyes. "Good. You've got six weeks to transform yourself. Study these files. Work on a Spanish accent. You need to be flawless when you step into Eva's shoes. Oh, and there's one more thing you need to work on."

"What's that?" I asked, my brow furrowing in concentration.

"You'll find it in your new place. Let's take a drive."

I PAUSED as we approached the apartment building.

"Eva," he said, using my undercover persona. Are you ready for this?"

I met his gaze with a steely determination that matched the confident, alluring persona I would soon embody. "I'm ready," I said, my voice sharp and distinct. Let's get this show on the road."

Morrow nodded as he handed me a set of keys. "This is the key to your new identity. Your home away from home, so to speak."

I took the keys, letting their weight settle in my palm, a tangible symbol of the mission I was about to undertake. "What's this key fob for?" I asked, looking up at Morrow with curiosity.

A rare smile tugged at the corner of his mouth. "It's for your Porsche. Consider it a part of your cover. You must make an impression, and arriving in style will help."

I raised an eyebrow, genuinely impressed. "A Porsche? That's a pretty sweet ride."

Morrow chuckled, the sound surprising in its warmth. "You'll find it in the garage. Just remember, this isn't a joyride. It's a tool for your mission."

I nodded, my fingers curling around the key. "Understood. But I can't deny it. I'm a little excited to give it a whirl," I confessed, throwing in a playful wink.

The apartment was pure luxury, from the ornate crystal chandelier casting a dazzling glow overhead to the floor-to-ceiling windows showcasing a breathtaking view of the Miami skyline. Just when I thought it couldn't get any better, my eyes landed on the walk-in closet, its double doors standing ajar. My heart raced with excitement as I crossed the room and peered inside, my jaw dropping at the sight.

Rack upon rack of designer dresses, blouses, and skirts lined the walls, a kaleidoscope of colors and fabrics that would make any fashionista swoon. Chanel, Dior, Prada— the crème de la crème of haute couture filled every inch of space. It was like stepping into a dream, a fairy tale come to life.

I ran my fingers over the silky material of a crimson Valentino gown, marveling at the intricate beadwork that adorned the bodice. This was a dress that belonged on the red carpet.

A low whistle escaped my lips as I plucked a sparkling Judith Leiber clutch from the shelf, turning it over in my hands. "You went all out, didn't you?"

Morrow nodded with a smile playing across his lips. "We spared no expense. Eva Morales needs to look the part, doesn't she?"

The reality of the situation hit me. For the unforeseeable future, I would be Eva Morales, a glamorous enigma wrapped in designer threads, rubbing elbows with the crème de la crème.

"How did you pull this off so quickly? I mean, I literally just signed on for this gig."

Morrow took a step back, a cryptic smile on his face. "Let's just say I've got some 'business associates' eager to watch Ricardo Reyes and his cartel crash and burn. We've been biding our time, waiting for the perfect person to infiltrate their ranks."

"And who exactly are these mysterious business associates of yours?"

"Sorry, sweetheart. That's classified information at this point. But trust me, we wear the white hats in this scenario."

A chuckle escaped me. "You know, that's exactly the kind of line the villains always use."

Morrow laughed, heading for the door. "You've got a shitload of homework to do, Ramirez. I'll check back in a couple of days. Don't let me down."

For the next seventy-two hours, I barely left my apartment. I was drowning in the files Morrow had dumped on me, obsessively memorizing every goddamn detail. Names, faces, the tangled web of alliances and feuds that held the cartel together - I devoured it all, determined to become Eva Morales inside and out.

I practiced walking in high heels, experimented with different makeup looks, and watched countless hours of Spanish-language television to fine-tune my accent. Morrow even brought a stylist to teach me the fashion terminology and how to coordinate my outfits to reflect a woman of Eva's stature.

As the days turned into weeks, I felt myself slipping into Eva Morales's persona. She was bold and vibrant, a woman who commanded attention whenever she entered a room with her confidence and ability to navigate the treacherous waters of high society with grace and poise.

Morrow checked in regularly, offering guidance and feedback on my progress. He was a harsh critic, but his insights were invaluable, helping me refine my portrayal of Eva until it was second nature. One afternoon, after a particularly grueling training session, he pulled me aside, his expression serious.

"Luckily, you were wearing tactical gear during the raid, so Dante couldn't get a proper look at you, but your eyes could still give you away," Morrow said, handing me a box of blue contacts. "Start wearing these so you'll get used to them."

I took the box, nodding. "Got it. Thanks, Morrow."

───────

AFTER THE FINAL week of preparation and training, I was ready. My six-week leave of absence was over. Tonight, Eva Morales would enter Dante Reyes's world.

I sank into the bed, my mind wandering to the man who was my primary target—the cartel prince with piercing blue eyes and a voice like velvet sin.

I shivered at the memory of his intense gaze raking over me in that warehouse, the way his full lips had transformed into a wolfish smirk as he'd uttered those fateful words: "I've got a better idea. I'll let you live. Consider it a nod to your... dedication."

Even six weeks later, the recollection of that encounter sent a delicious shiver racing through me. Something about

Dante, raw and primal, called to my soul's darkest corners: the intoxicating thrill of dancing with danger.

But I couldn't afford to lose myself in those kinds of thoughts. Dante Reyes was the enemy, the kingpin I had sworn to take down, no matter the cost. Any lingering attraction I felt towards him was nothing more than a fleeting distraction, one I would have to bury deep within me if I hoped to succeed in my mission.

A soft chime from my purse snapped me out of my reverie. I reached for it, my heart skipping a beat, when I saw the name flashing across the screen: Val.

A rush of warmth flooded me as I swiped to open the message, my best friend's words lighting up the screen.

Hey, girl. I know you're gonna kill it as Eva Morales, but please, for the love of God, be careful out there. These cartel assholes are no joke, and I can't lose you too. Remember our code: if shit hits the fan, text me 'red velvet,' and I'll be at our usual spot with backup. Stay safe, Nat. I've got your back, always.

As I read the message, a lump formed in my throat. Val's unwavering support and concern shined through every word of her message. She was more than just my partner and confidante; she was my sister in arms, the one person I could trust implicitly in this dangerous game we were all playing.

I quickly tapped out a response, my fingers flying across the screen. *Thanks, Val. I'll be careful, I promise. And don't worry, I haven't forgotten our code. If shit goes*

---

sideways, you'll be the first to know. Love you, girl. Wish me luck.

With a heavy breath, I set my phone aside and rose from the bed, padding across the plush carpet to the floor-to-ceiling windows. The city stretched before me, a glittering tapestry of lights and life, pulsing with the energy only Miami could offer.

This was it, I thought, pressing my palm against the cool glass. No turning back now. From this moment on, I was Eva Morales, a woman of mystery and desire, a creature crafted to lure one of the most dangerous men in the world into my web.

SIX
DANTE

I tapped my nails against the town car's side window irritably, cursing under my breath as Pedro whipped around yet another corner. This detour was burning daylight, and the hairs on my neck told me we had unwanted company.

That sleek black Cadillac had been trailing us since we left the mansion, maintaining a discreet but unmistakable distance. At first, I'd chalked it up to a coincidence, but my instincts kicked into high gear after a few strategic turns failed to shake our pursuer.

"What do you think, Mr. Reyes?" Pedro's gruff voice crackled through the intercom, his eyes meeting mine in the rearview mirror.

"My hunch was right. We have a tail, Pedro," I said, my tone clipped.

He gave a curt nod, his knuckles tightening around the steering wheel as we merged back onto the thoroughfare. I leaned back in my seat, and thoughts flooded my mind as I contemplated the potential threats.

It could be the DEA, still trying to gain a foothold in our operation after the disastrous warehouse raid six weeks ago. Or one of our rivals, like Javier Cruz, was making a bold move to encroach on our territory. Either way, the situation needed to be handled.

When the familiar restaurant building came into view, I was fifteen minutes late, and Sofia would undoubtedly give me an earful for my tardiness. Not that I was looking forward to the evening's festivities–meeting her new beau held about as much appeal as a root canal. I'd been avoiding it for weeks. My sister finally gave me an ultimatum: show up tonight or prepare to be scorned forever. Even I didn't dare challenge that.

As the town car pulled up to the valet stand, I saw the Cadillac lingering a block away, its tinted windows concealing the occupants. A muscle twitched in my jaw as I exited the vehicle, straightening the crisp lines of my suit jacket.

"Pedro, stay close," I muttered under my breath. "And have Marco investigate that tail. I want to know who they are and what they want."

Pedro peeled away from the curb with a curt nod, leaving me alone to stride into the restaurant. Pedro was a good guy, solid and loyal.

The maître d' greeted me with a polite smile, his eyes widening as he recognized me.

"Mr. Reyes, welcome. Your party is already seated. Right this way, please."

I followed him through the dimly lit dining room, my gaze sweeping over the well-heeled patrons as they sipped their wine. Sofia spotted me first, her expression a concoction of relief and exasperation.

"There you are!" she exclaimed, rising from her seat. "I almost thought you'd stood us up."

"Fashionably late, as always," I quipped, leaning in to brush a kiss against her cheek. "You know how I like to make an entrance."

Sofia rolled her eyes, but her smile took any sting out of the gesture. "Dante, this is Allen Hawkes," Sofia said, her voice brimming with affection. "Allen, my brother."

My gaze shifted to the man sitting beside her, and I felt an immediate hint of dislike as he rose from his seat, extending a hand that I took with reluctance. His grip was firm, almost too firm, as if he were trying to assert dominance.

Allen Hawkes exuded an air of... I don't know; maybe it's arrogance and entitlement. His slicked-back hair and designer suit screamed "trust fund brat," and how he was eyeing Sofia made my protective instincts flare.

"Pleasure to finally meet you, Dante," he drawled, his voice dripping with false sincerity. "Sofia has told me so much about you."

"I wish I could say the same," I said coolly, holding his gaze in a silent challenge.

Allen's smile faltered for a moment before he recov-

ered, slinging an arm around Sofia's shoulders in a possessive gesture that made my hackles rise.

"Well, now that we're all acquainted, why don't we
order some drinks and get this party started?" he suggested,
overly cheerful.

As the evening wore on, Allen's true colors became
increasingly apparent. He dominated the conversation,
rarely letting anyone else get a word in, and was more
interested in impressing Sofia than getting to know her as a
person. But, judging by the occasional sideways glances
Sofia shot me, it was clear she was into the fucker.

During a lull in Allen's endless prattling, I felt my
phone vibrate in my pocket. After excusing myself from
the table, I stepped to the bar and answered the call, my
jaw tightening as Marco's voice crackled.

"We've got a situation, Dante," he said without
preamble. "That tail you noticed earlier? It's the DEA, and
they've been tracking your movements for the past few
days. Not sure what is going on, but they are up to
something."

I ended the call with Marco. My jaw clenched tight as
I processed the information about the DEA tail. Those
bastards were up to something, alright.

I slipped the phone back into my pocket and noticed
the presence beside me. A woman, her back turned as she
leaned against the bar, nursing a glass of red wine. Even
from this angle, I could tell she was stunning—the kind of
beauty that demanded attention.

I inched closer to get a better look, my curiosity piqued. The woman was wearing a dress that hugged her curves in all the right places, the deep crimson fabric a striking contrast against her sun-kissed skin. The neckline plunged just low enough to tease at the swell of her breasts while the skirt ended mid-thigh, showcasing a pair of legs that went on for miles.

As my gaze traveled upward, I took in the cascade of dark, glossy waves that tumbled down her back, the soft curls brushing against her bare shoulders. She had one elbow propped on the bar, her slender fingers wrapped around the stem of her wineglass, and her nails painted the same shade of red as her dress.

She must have sensed my stare because she turned then, her eyes meeting mine with an intensity that nearly knocked me off my feet. They were a deep blue, framed by long, dark lashes that fluttered enticingly as she regarded me with a blend of intrigue and amusement.

Her lips, a lush, berry hue, turned into a slow, seductive smile that made my pulse quicken. Her high cheekbones, delicate nose, and jawline that could cut glass came together to create a face that was nothing short of breathtaking.

But it was more than just her physical beauty that drew me in. There was something about her an air of confidence and mystery that was alluring and dangerous. She carried herself with the poise of a woman who knew exactly what she wanted and how to get it.

It was almost as if I'd met her before, but I knew that

was impossible. A woman like this? There was no way in hell I would've forgotten her.

As she tilted her head to the side, studying me with those mesmerizing eyes, I realized I was staring like a fucking idiot. I cleared my throat, trying to regain some semblance of composure, but she spoke before I could say a word.

"See something you like?" she purred, her voice sultry, with just a hint of a challenge.

Her voice was like honey, rich and smooth, with a whisper of teasing sending a tremor of desire rippling through me. I recovered quickly, flashing her my most disarming grin. "Maybe I do," I said, my tone equally playful. "But I haven't decided if you might be trouble."

She laughed then, a rich, throaty sound. "Oh, honey," she said, leaning in close enough that I could catch the scent of her perfume—something dark and exotic, with a bit of spice. "I'm definitely trouble. The question is, are you man enough to handle it?"

"Never met trouble I couldn't tame," I shot back, locking eyes with her, bold as brass.

She didn't so much as blink, holding my stare like it was a game of chicken she had no intention of losing. Anticipation buzzed through my veins—this woman was no delicate flower waiting to be plucked.

"Dante Reyes," I said, extending my hand. "And you are?"

She regarded me for a moment, those smoldering eyes seeming to strip me bare, before slipping her hand into mine. Her grip was firm and confident, her skin like silk against my calloused palm.

"Eva Morales," she purred, her lips curving into a smile promising delicious secrets.

Eva. Even her name rolled off the tongue like a decadent indulgence. My curiosity was piqued in a way it hadn't been in years.

"Well, Eva Morales," I said, holding her gaze. "It's a pleasure to make your acquaintance."

She tilted her head ever so slightly, her eyes sparkling with amusement. "Is it, now? And what makes you so sure of that?"

A chuckle escaped me, and I leaned in closer, invading her personal space in a way that would've had most women swooning. But Eva didn't flinch, didn't back down an inch. If anything, the challenge in her eyes only intensified.

"Call it a hunch," I said. "Something tells me you're... different, Eva."

Her full lips curved into a slow, seductive smile that went straight to my groin. "You have no idea, Dante Reyes."

The tension had me yearning to close the distance between us. But before I could act impulsively, a familiar voice cut through the haze of desire.

"Dante! There you are!" Sofia appeared at my side, looking furious. "I was beginning to think you'd ditched us."

I forced my gaze away from Eva's captivating presence,

offering my sister a sheepish grin. "Sorry, sis. Got caught up talking to this lovely lady."

Sofia's eyes widened as she took in Eva's striking look, and I could see the questions forming behind her gaze. But before she could voice them, Allen sidled up beside her, his arm snaking around her waist in a possessive gesture that made me want to punch him in the throat.

"Everything alright, babe?" he drawled, shooting me a look of equal parts disdain and challenge.

A bit of rage welled up within me, my protective instincts flaring at the sight of his pawing hands on my sister. But before I could spit out a clever line, Eva fixed those dark, smoldering eyes on me, and damn, it was like she lit a fire in my pants. "It was a pleasure, Dante. Who knows, our paths might cross again."

I composed myself and handed her one of our Club Diablo cards. "Let's make sure of that. Stop by my club tomorrow. I guarantee you'll have a good time." I smirked, cocky as hell.

She winked, took the card, and glided through the crowd. As I watched her sexy strut, the skirt hugging her curves, I knew I wanted to get her alone.

"Whew, bro, who's the bombshell?" Sofia asked, her eyes wide with curiosity.

I shook my head, still dazed from the encounter. "Eva Morales," I said, the name rolling off my tongue.

Sofia's brow furrowed. "She seemed... interesting."

"That's one word for it," I muttered, my mind still spinning. Eva Morales was not your average chick.

SEVEN

NATALIA

I BARELY RECOGNIZED MYSELF. THE PRACTICAL AGENT with the tidy ponytail and forgettable blazer was gone. In her place stood Eva Morales—a vision of sultry elegance with cascading dark hair, smoky blue eyes, and a dress that accentuated every single curve.

I'd almost dropped the wine glass when Eliza, my stylist, presented me with the dress for the night. It was a masterpiece—clinging to my body like a second skin, hugging all the right places. And the shoes... they were pure torture, but the way they elongated my legs were worth the pain.

I ran my hands over the curve hugging dress one last time, my heart pounding beneath it. Tonight was the night. Last night had been the opening act—a chance encounter, a meet-cute. But now, my acting skills would be truly tested, and weeks of preparation would come to a head. If I failed this evening, my undercover assignment would be over before it had truly begun.

For the past several days, the DEA had been tailing Dante, tracking his every move, searching for an in. And last night, at that upscale restaurant, an opportunity had presented itself—a chance for me to make an introduction.

I had been a bundle of nerves, sitting at the bar, nursing a glass of wine, trying to exude an air of mystique and confidence. When Dante approached, I knew I had to bring my A-game.

Portraying Eva Morales—the enigmatic, captivating woman meant to entangle Dante in her web—was more than just acting. It was a delicate dance of seduction and intrigue that I had to perfect if I wanted to gain his trust.

Trust... that was the key. I had to make Dante trust me. Hell, I needed him to trust me more than his own people. If I could seduce Dante, make him believe in my unwavering devotion, he'd willingly open the doors to the Reyes cartel's inner sanctum. I'd have access to intel, contacts, and evidence that could bring down their entire operation.

And scoring that invitation to Club Diablo was the first step.

Taking a deep breath, I slid into the sleek town car that would spirit me away to the club. I sank into the soft leather seat, the dress riding up my thighs as I crossed my legs—a subtle yet powerful weapon in my arsenal.

Tonight was for Matt. For all the victims who had gotten caught in the crossfire of the Reyes cartel's ruthless game. I was determined to bring them down, one step at a time, one cocky cartel member at a time, if I had to.

The car purred to a stop in front of Club Diablo, the neon sign flickering above the entrance like a seductive siren. A final glance in the mirror revealed a woman transformed—my hair cascading in sexy, dark waves over my shoulders, my lips a glossy red, beckoning temptation itself.

Showtime.

I stepped out of the car, the cool night air caressing my skin, and made my way to the club's entrance.

The bouncer was an imposing figure, all brawn and no brain. He eyed me with suspicion as I breezed past the desperate souls waiting in line. I offered him a coy smile, tilting my head.

"Private party, invite-only," he rumbled, his arms crossed defensively over his chest. "No exceptions."

I feigned surprise, tracing a fingernail down his muscular arm. "Oh, sugar, there's always an exception for me." My voice was a sultry purr, with a hint of underlying danger.

His eyes narrowed, daring to challenge me. "I don't care if you're the Queen of England herself. No invite, no entry. Now step aside before I have to get rough."

Adrenaline coursed through my veins, but I maintained a cool, amused facade. "Dante Reyes invited me. Tell him Eva Morales has arrived. Believe me, cariño, you don't want to keep him, or me, waiting."

The bouncer hesitated, a drop of sweat sliding down

his temple. Slowly, he reached for his walkie-talkie, his eyes never leaving mine. "I got a woman here claiming Dante invited her," he grunted. "Says her name is Eva Morales."

I noticed the security camera and stared directly into it, my expression confident, a challenge in itself.

A crackle of static, then—"Let her in, idiot."

I smirked as the bouncer reluctantly unhooked the velvet rope, granting me access. I could feel his gaze burning into my back as I sauntered past, my hips swaying with each step.

When I entered Club Diablo, the vibrant energy of the place washed over me. Pulsing lights, gyrating bodies, and the heady scent of debauchery filled my senses. Servers, clad in revealing attire, weaved their way through the crowd, balancing trays of expensive drinks and champagne bottles with practiced ease.

But this wasn't your average Florida strip club. Club Diablo was a beast of its own, catering to the rich, the powerful, and the depraved. Everything about the place oozed luxury and excess—from the crystal glassware to the exotic dancers on raised platforms, their bodies shimmering with sweat under the strobing lights. Even the air felt thick with the smell of money, power, and raw, unchecked desire.

I schooled my features into a mask of bored indifference, scanning the club as if I were used to such extravagance. My nerves tingled, but I wouldn't let it show. I was

Eva now—a woman who frequented these elite circles, exuding an air of sophistication and confidence.

A waiter approached, his eyes glittering with lust as he took in my appearance. "Can I get you a drink, mamacita?" he murmured, leaning in close, his cologne heavy in the air between us.

I arched a perfectly shaped eyebrow, meeting his gaze with calm intensity. "A glass of your finest red, cariño," I drawled, allowing the faintest hint of a smile to touch my lips. As he scurried off, my attention returned to the pulsing, neon-lit depths of the club.

And then I saw him—Dante Reyes, standing in a secluded VIP alcove, exuding an aura of smoldering confidence. Six feet and two inches of sheer masculine presence, dressed in an dark suit that accentuated his sculpted frame.

Steeling my nerves, I held his gaze, ready to unleash my acting prowess.

As I strolled towards the bouncer guarding Dante's exclusive domain, his eyes devoured me hungrily. I gave him a saccharine smile, my voice dripping with honeyed seduction. "I'm Eva Morales. Dante's expecting me."

The mountain of a man hesitated for a moment, then grunted and stepped aside, his eyes glued to my retreating form as I sashayed past. Success.

The moment I entered the VIP lounge, all eyes were on me. High-rollers in expensive suits, no doubt the cartel's inner circle, followed my every move. I recognized a few faces from DEA files, my heart twisting with nerves and determination. But my focus remained on one man—Dante Reyes.

His chiseled features were illuminated by the soft glow of the VIP lounge, those striking blue eyes locking with mine and capturing me in their electric intensity. I felt that penetrating gaze in the deepest recesses of my soul, anticipation coursing through my veins.

A slender blonde, barely legal by the looks of it, draped herself possessively over Dante, shooting daggers at me from beneath her perfectly mascaraed lashes.

"Eva." Dante's deep, rich baritone broke the charged silence, snapping my focus back to him. "Thought you might've stood me up."

I flashed him a mischievous smile, letting my gaze linger on his full lips. "Forgive me, Dante. I was... delayed. But I'm here now."

A glint of amusement sparkled in his eyes, and he gestured to the space beside him on the plush sofa. "Then, by all means, make yourself comfortable."

I sank onto the soft cushion, maintaining a tantalizing distance between us, acutely aware of the blonde's hostile glares. She dug her perfectly manicured nails into Dante's thigh, claiming her territory.

"Dante, darling," she purred, her voice oozing with disdain. "Aren't you going to introduce me to your... friend?"

Dante's gaze flickered between us, a hint of amusement playing at the corners of his mouth. "Ah, yes. Eva, this is Giselle. Giselle, meet Eva Morales."

Giselle's icy blue stare could've frozen hell itself, but her smile was sickly sweet. "Charmed," she bit out through clenched teeth.

I matched her grin with a challenging one of my own, letting my eyes roam over her with calculated disinterest. "Charmed is all yours, honey."

Dante watched the interplay between us with evident delight, his fingers tapping seductively on the couch. "Now, now, ladies. No need to get territorial. There's more than enough of me to go around."

Giselle draped herself over him possessively, her lips brushing his jaw as if marking her territory. I had to suppress the urge to roll my eyes at the desperate display. If this blonde bombshell was my competition, I pitied any man caught in her web.

Well, almost.

As the Barbie-esque woman clung to Dante, practically purring as she nuzzled his neck, I shifted my attention back to the man himself. Our eyes met, and the air thickened with a dizzying mixture of lust and unspoken challenges.

"So tell me, Dante," I cooed, my fingers lightly tracing patterns on his hand. "What gets a big, strong man like you off?"

His eyes darkened, a storm cloud of desire and something more, his jaw clenching beneath my intense gaze. "My tastes are quite... diverse, Eva."

Leaning in, I let my lips brush against the shell of his

ear, my breath teasing his skin. "Then you're in luck, Dante. I'm a woman of many, many skills."

Dante sucked in a sharp breath, his body tensing beneath my touch, and I felt a rush of dark satisfaction. I had him hooked, line and sinker.

The game had truly begun.

Bye-bye, Giselle. Time for the grown-ups to play.

EIGHT
DANTE

MY COCK THROBBED WHEN EVA LEANED IN CLOSE, HER warm breath caressing my ear, lush lips a hair's breadth from my tingling skin. "Why don't we ditch the third wheel?" Her voice was pure sex with sinful promise.

Everything about Eva tested my restraint, but I played it cool, shooting a grin her way. "And what's in it for me?" I kept my tone lazy even as I boldly dragged my eyes over to Giselle plastered against my side, her fingers drawing teasing circles on my inner thigh.

Eva's eyes flashed with the thrill of a challenge. "Normally, I'd be all for a little threesome action, but tonight, I want you all to myself."

Giselle's head snapped around so fast I feared whiplash, her meticulously styled hair whipping with the sharp motion. "Who the fuck do you think you are?" she snarled, eyes blazing hot with outrage. "Dante doesn't need your skanky ass. He has me, and I'm more woman than he can handle."

A laugh bubbled up as Giselle threw her predictable jealous fit. She was a stereotypical possessive wreck, but Eva stirred something in me—a part of myself I'd kept locked away for far too long.

"Enough," I said, holding up a hand. "Giselle, you know I like a little variety in my life." I shot Eva a wink, reveling in the way her features morphed into a slow, seductive smile.

Giselle bristled beside me, her nails digging into my thigh again, harder this time. "Dante, you can't be serious," she hissed. "This woman is nothing but a cheap tramp. She's not fit to lick the bottom of my Louboutin's."

Eva's laugh was rich and melodic, sending a shiver of anticipation down my back. "Oh, darling," she purred, her gaze locked on mine. "You have no idea what I'm fit for."

I felt the challenge in her words like a physical caress, resisting the urge to shift in my seat.

"Giselle," I said, facing the fuming blonde at my side. "Why don't you go powder your nose? Eva and I have some business to discuss."

Her eyes widened in outrage, her glossed lips parting in protest. But one look from me had her snapping her mouth shut, her jaw clenched tight. With a huff of indignation, she rose from the sofa, shooting Eva a venomous look before stalking off in a cloud of expensive perfume and wounded pride.

"Wow," Eva said, her eyes dancing with amusement as

she watched Giselle's dramatic exit. "That was... interesting."

I shrugged, unconcerned. "Giselle is... complicated," I said, shifting closer to Eva on the sofa. "But enough about her. I'm much more interested in you, Eva Morales."

Eva's dark, smoldering eyes pierced me, stripping away any pretense. "Is that so?" Her velvet voice caressed my senses, igniting a shiver.

"It is." I held her stare, my boldness enough to make most women melt. "You're different from the other women here, Eva. There's something unique about you."

Her eyebrow quirked upwards as the corners of her mouth curled into a coy smile. "And what makes you say that, Dante?"

I leaned in close, in a way that would make most women swoon. But Eva didn't flinch or retreat. The challenge in her eyes only intensified.

"Call it intuition," I rasped, my low voice sending a frisson of awareness through my body. "Your confidence and air of mystery intrigue me."

Eva tilted her head slightly, her gaze unwavering. "Maybe you're just not used to a woman who knows what she wants," she countered, her tone playfully teasing.

A slow grin spread across my face as a thrill of excitement coursed through me. "And what do you want, Eva?"

She leaned in, her lips nearly brushing against mine. "Pour us a drink, and I'll show you."

The air crackled with palpable tension and electricity between us. I nodded slowly and reached for the crystal decanter, pouring two generous glasses of the finest Macallan.

Our fingers grazed as I handed Eva her drink, sending a subtle spark through me. Our eyes met and held, the surroundings fading away as an electric awareness stretched between us.

"To new connections," Eva purred as she raised her glass.

I tapped my drink against hers, the whiskey sloshing. "And to all the delights we've yet to discover together," I said, my gaze unwavering as it held hers.

A slow, sensual smile spread across her luscious lips. She brought the glass up, eyes locked on mine as she took a leisurely sip. It was a sight of pure temptation that sent heat rushing straight to my cock.

"What secret desires does a man like you harbor, Dante?" Her voice was a silken purr that made my blood run hot.

Leaning in, I said, "Why don't you uncover them yourself, Eva? Something tells me you're a woman of many hidden depths."

She moved her head, her lips a hairs breadth from mine, and I could taste the sweet promise of sin on her breath. "Wouldn't you like to know?" she purred, her tongue darting out to moisten her full pout in a move that had my cock straining against the confines of my slacks.

I fought the urge to capture those luscious lips with my own, to lose myself in the intoxicating allure of this enigmatic woman. Instead, I let my gaze roam over the swell of her breasts, the tempting curve of her hips accentuated by the dress that clung to her body.

"You're playing a dangerous game, Eva," I rasped, my voice rough with barely restrained hunger.

Her eyes glinted with challenge. "Danger is my middle name, Dante."

The sound of her saying my name, the way it rolled off her tongue like a forbidden caress, sent my pulse racing. I was teetering on the edge, yearning to give in to the smoldering heat that crackled between us.

A flash of movement in my peripheral vision caught my attention. Giselle was stalking back towards us, her face twisted into a mask of fury and anger. I felt a flicker of annoyance at the interruption. Still, before I could decide how to handle the situation, Eva's hand landed on my thigh, her fingers digging into the muscle with a possessive grip that made me harden even further.

"It seems your... friend has returned," she said, her lips curving into a slow, wicked smile. "Perhaps we should take this somewhere more... private?"

The blatant suggestion in her tone sent a jolt of pure, unadulterated lust through me. I wanted her – God, how I wanted her – in a thrilling and terrifying way. This woman was like a force of nature, a hurricane of desire and sin that threatened to sweep me away if I let my guard down for even a moment.

But that was part of the allure, wasn't it? The promise of losing control and surrendering to the primal hunger that Eva seemed to stoke with every heated glance and whispered temptation.

"You read my mind," I growled, rising to my feet and offering her my hand.

Her fingers slid into mine, her grip firm and confident. This was happening – I was about to whisk this tantalizing creature away to one of the club's private suites, where we could indulge in delicious pleasures, free from prying eyes and interruptions.

As we exited the lounge, I caught Giselle's gaze, her eyes burning with jealous fury. Let her stew in her bitterness – tonight, I had no room for anyone but Eva in my world.

We approached the secluded hallway that led to the private suites, and I felt Eva's hand tighten around mine, her body pressing against my side in a way that had me gritting my teeth against the surge of desire that threatened to overwhelm me.

"Where are you taking me, Dante?" she breathed, her voice a husky purr that went straight to my groin.

I leaned in close, my lips grazing the delicate shell of her ear. "Somewhere we can be alone," I said, letting the promise hang heavy between us.

We finally made it to the door of the club's most bougie love nest - the kind of place where rich fucks like me go to let their freak flag fly. I swiped us in and watched Eva's reaction as we stepped into a porn director's wet dream. Wall-to-wall velvet, plush furniture you could drown in, and right smack in the middle, a bed straight out of a brothel, with sheets so shiny you could see your reflection.

"So? What's the verdict?" I inquired, my tone tinged with anticipation.

Eva's eyes flashed, taking in the whole fuck-tastic setup. "I'm thinking," she purred, her voice like honey, "this is the perfect spot to do some deep diving if you know what I mean."

Next thing I know, she's pressed up against me, all soft curves and scorching heat. Her fingers are doing a slow crawl up my chest, nails grazing my shirt, those come-fuck-me eyes locked on mine.

"Give me your all, Dante," she whispered, so close I could almost taste her. "I want to see how deep your freak goes."

I made this noise like a fucking animal and yanked her against me, attacking her mouth like I was dying of thirst and she was the last drop of water in the desert. Eva gave as good as she got, her hands fisting my hair as our tongues wrestled for dominance.

"Dante," she panted, my name like a prayer and a curse all rolled into one, and fuck if it didn't make me hard as a rock.

Tonight, I was going to fuck the hell out of this delicious woman.

NINE
NATALIA

I had Dante Reyes right where I wanted him. Literally, under me.

Within seconds, I ripped off his shirt, buttons flying everywhere, and I ran my fingers along his sculpted abs, my lips hovering over a tattoo—a serpent coiled around a sword. His body was a work of art, every muscle perfectly defined under a layer of ink.

The last time I'd been in such close quarters with this man, I'd felt the cold steel of his gun against the back of my head. Now, I was feeling an entirely different kind of gun, and this time—I hoped he would blow my mind.

I slid my tongue out, tasting the salty warmth of his skin, and he jerked beneath me, a deep, primal sound rumbling in his chest. His hands gripped my hips, his touch possessive. Desire pooled low in my belly as my thighs moved up and straddled his waist, my fingers tangling in his dark gold hair.

How he looked at me—intensity and need burning in those electric blue eyes—sent a thrill through me. I knew Dante would be easy to seduce, but I hadn't anticipated our raw, unchecked hunger. It was like our bodies had their own language, speaking in whispers and moans, each touch and taste unlocking a new level of pleasure.

"Fuck, Eva," he ground out, his hips arching off the bed. "You're killing me."

I gave him a sly smile, my fingers tracing the contours of his chest. "Hopefully not yet, babe. The night is young. We've only just begun."

He chuckled and hauled me against him, his mouth crushing mine in a hungry kiss. Our lips and tongues dueled, tasting, exploring, fueling the fire burning between us. His hand slid down my back, palms branding my skin through the thin fabric of my dress, until he gripped the curve of my ass, pulling me tighter against his straining erection through his pants.

"God, I need to be inside you," he growled, his voice raw and hoarse.

I shivered at his words, a pulse of longing deep within me. "Then take me," I whispered, my breath hitching as he rolled us over, his body pressing me into the plush mattress. "Take all of me."

His eyes blazed as he helped me from the bed, his hands trailing over my body with a reverence that belied the ruthless nature I knew lay beneath the surface. I bit my lip as he kissed his way down my neck, nipping and sucking at the sensitive skin, leaving marks that would remind me of this night for days to come.

His fingers found the zipper at the back of my dress and slowly pulled it down, baring my back inch by inch. Goosebumps prickled along my spine, desire coursing through my veins like lightning. When the zipper reached the small of my back, he paused, his breath warm against my neck.

"You're so fucking beautiful, Eva," he whispered.

I felt beautiful. Dante made me feel like the most desirable woman on the planet. An ache pulsed between my legs, an urgent need that demanded to be satisfied. I arched my back, silently encouraging him to continue.

Dante pulled my dress down with a delicate touch, unveiling the provocative lingerie I had meticulously selected for this moment. The red silk and jet-black lace accentuated my figure, showcasing my assets in a manner designed to make any man lose control. Dante was no exception, his eyes devouring every inch of my body with unrestrained desire as we tumbled back onto the bed, with him now pinning me beneath his muscular frame.

He savored every curve, his rough hands exploring my sensitive skin, his mouth igniting a blaze of passion with each kiss. Dante worked his way down my quivering body, teasing my belly button with his tongue until I writhed and laughed.

"Tickles," I gasped, my hands twisting in the sheets.

"Wait until I get lower," he said against my skin, his voice a sinful promise. "That's when the real fun begins."

His teasing lips trailed down, skating over my hips and the soft skin of my inner thighs. My breath quickened, my heartbeat thundering as anticipation curled in my belly when he gently removed my lingerie. Dante's hands slid up my thighs, pushing them apart and exposing the core of me to his intimate exploration.

"God, Eva," he groaned, his breath hot against my skin. "I'm dying to taste you."

His words sent a shiver through me, but I couldn't deny the thrill that coursed through me at the thought of being desired by him. I knew this was wrong on many levels, but I couldn't bring myself to care.

The second his tongue found my clit, I cried out, my back arching off the bed. Pleasure shot through me like lightning, and I tangled my hands in his hair, urging him closer and wanting more.

"Dante," I gasped, my head tossing from side to side. "Oh God..."

His name fell from my lips, a plea for him to keep doing what he was doing, to drive me out of my mind with pleasure. That's when I felt two fingers slide into my pussy.

"Holy fuck," I moaned, my hips bucking against his face. "You're gonna make me lose my fucking mind!" My pussy clenched around his invading fingers, my walls spasming as he teased my clit with his devilish tongue. His thumb found that spot, that magical spot that made me see stars, and I couldn't hold back a high-pitched moan that would've embarrassed me any other time. But right then, right fucking then, all I cared about was the pleasure he was dishing out like a goddamn pro.

"That's it, Eva," he said against my skin, his voice thick and husky. "Let me hear your fucking screams, baby."

His words pushed me over the edge, and I cried out, my body shuddering as wave after wave of pleasure crashed over me. I felt Dante's mouth on me again, his tongue laving and tasting, drawing out my climax until I thought I'd go mad.

Finally, I collapsed back against the bed, my limbs like jelly, my breath coming in harsh pants. Dante kissed his way up my body, his hands exploring, his touch gentle but possessive. I couldn't stop touching him, running my hands over his chest, shoulders, and arms.

He captured my mouth in a deep, possessive kiss, his tongue dueling with mine. I could taste myself on him, and it only fueled the desire simmering between us. My hands found the button of his slacks, and with nimble fingers, I worked it open, eager to feel what was underneath.

He groaned into my mouth as I slid my hand inside, grasping his cock, feeling his arousal throbbing in my hand. I ran my thumb over the tip, and he shuddered, a primal sound rumbling in his chest.

"Let me get a condom," he managed to gasp, his eyes hooded with lust.

I smiled, my fingers tightening around him. "Better hurry."

He rolled off me, rummaging through the drawer until he found what he sought. I watched as he ripped open the packet with his teeth, hissing out a curse as he struggled to roll it on.

"Here, let me help," I said, reaching for the condom.

I rolled it into place, my hand stroking him slowly, enjoying the feel of his rock-hard cock. He sucked in a harsh breath at my touch, his eyes closing. When he opened them again, the raw need burning in his gaze sent a thrill through me.

Dante moved on top of me, his body heavy and possessive. I ran my palms over his sculpted back, relishing the feel of his skin, the power in his body.

"Last chance to back out, Eva," he growled, his voice thick and raw. "You sure you're ready for this?"

"Yes," I breathed, my fingers digging into his shoulders. "Take me, Dante."

"Fuck, yes," he groaned, his hips thrusting forward, filling me in one smooth stroke.

I cried out at the overwhelming sensation, my nails digging into his shoulders. He felt impossibly large, stretching me wide as he filled me completely. Dante's eyes bore into mine as he started to move, his thick cock gliding in and out of my dripping pussy with deep, sensual strokes that had me ready to climb the fucking walls. He stared at me intensely, as if he was trying to sear this moment into his brain forever.

His pace picked up, hips slamming into me faster and harder, chasing that sweet release. I matched his rhythm, fingers clawing at his back, spurring him on. The pleasure was building again, a live wire of electricity shooting through my body that had me biting back screams.

Dante's hot breath tickled my ear as he panted, his voice a feral growl. "Fuck, you feel so good wrapped around my cock. So tight and wet for me," he rasped, his words dripping with lust and depravity. "I'm going to make you come so hard, mi amor. Going to fuck this sweet pussy until you're screaming my name."

His filthy promises set my body ablaze with desire, every nerve-ending sparking to life. I could feel the coil of pleasure winding tighter in my core, my inner walls fluttering around his thick length as he drove into me again and again. "Yes, Dante," I moaned, my nails raking down his sweat-slicked back. "Don't stop. I need to come on your cock. Please..."

Dante's hips bucked as he emptied his load inside the condom, the sensation enhancing my release.

I felt his hot breath washing over my neck, and for a second, we just stayed there, joined as one, panting in the dimly lit room.

Slowly, Dante pulled out of me, his eyes dark and intense as he reached to brush a stray lock of hair from my face tenderly. His thumb traced the curve of my jaw, his touch gentle despite the evidence of his raw need still pulsing between his legs.

"That was..." He trailed off as if searching for the right words, his eyes never leaving mine.

"Incredible," I finished for him, my voice husky. "Better than I could've ever imagined."

A slow, sinful smile curved his lips, his eyes lit with a dangerous heat. "We're not done yet, Eva. I plan to make you come so often that you'll lose count."

I shivered at his words, my body already responding to the promise in his eyes. I'd gone into this mission dreading the idea of intimacy with my enemy, but somehow, Dante had made it feel like anything but.

TEN
DANTE

The Escalade's engine purred as Marco and I cruised through the abandoned industrial district. My thoughts were elsewhere, though. Back to last night, to the scorching heat of Eva's naked body against mine, her skin tasting like a drug I couldn't get enough of, and the way she wailed my name when she came. Yep, that was one hell of a night.

"You seem...distracted, Dante." Marco's voice penetrated the fog of lust, hazing my mind.

Flashing him a naughty grin, I drawled, "Let's just say I had a fan-fucking-tastic night."

His eyebrow quirked. "The girl from the club?"

I chuckled, indulging in the memories again. Eva's wicked red lips, her body writhing under me, her flavor drugging my tongue. No woman had ever snared me so entirely in her sensual web.

"Her name's Eva," I muttered, the words spilling out. "She's, uh, something else." I shrugged, trying to play it cool but failing miserably.

Marco glanced at me before refocusing on the road ahead. "Something else, huh? In what kinda way?"

"Yeah, it's like... I don't know, man; I've never met a chick like her. She's... just... she's... fucking..." I shook my head, at a loss.

Marco didn't say anything for a while, looking thoughtful. When he finally opened his mouth, his words had an edge of worry. "Just watch yourself with her, Dante. We can't lose focus now."

We swung around the bend, and the dilapidated warehouse appeared, sticking out like a sore thumb next to the high-end buildings clustered around it. Marco killed the engine, and we sat silently momentarily, taking in the scene.

"You sure about this?" Marco's forehead creased with concern. "These Colombian fuckers have been acting sketchy lately. No telling what kind of bullshit is waiting for us in there."

I nodded, my jaw clenching. "No other options, man. My father needs this supply line, especially with the DEA breathing down our necks non-stop."

Marco let out a heavy breath but didn't push it. We were both aware of the dangers, but that was just another day in our line of work. With a final nod, we exited the car and moved toward the warehouse.

The vast interior was barely illuminated, the darkness

almost alive, undulating and shifting. Instinctively, my hand moved to the small of my back, finding solace in the familiar heft of my gun.

"Keep your cool," I said, low enough for only Marco to hear. "Let me do the talking."

Marco gave a curt nod, his jaw tightening, as a group of men emerged from the shadows, their faces hardened masks of grit and determination. At their center stood a figure I recognized all too well—Raul Moreno, the head of the Colombian gang.

Raul's dark eyes swept over us, his lip curling into a sneer. This man reveled in power, in the thrill of having others at his mercy.

"Dante Reyes," he drawled. "I must admit, I'm surprised your father let you off his leash for this little rendezvous."

I felt the insult like a physical blow but refused to let it show. Keeping my expression carefully neutral, I met Raul's gaze head-on. "My father knows I'm more than capable of handling our... business affairs," I countered, letting a hint of steel creep into my tone.

Raul's eyes narrowed, and for a tense moment, I thought he might push the issue further. But then, a wolfish grin settled on his mouth, and he clapped his hands together.

"Of course," he said, his voice dripping with a false warmth. "Let's not waste time on petty posturing, eh? We have matters to discuss."

I forced myself to remain impassive, even as my

muscles coiled with the urge to wipe that smug look off his face.

"You mentioned renegotiating our terms," I said, cutting straight to the chase. "What exactly did you have in mind?"

Raul's grin widened, his teeth gleaming in the dim light. "Ah, yes. My associates and I have been taking on additional risks lately. The DEA has been sniffing around, asking questions, making our operations increasingly hazardous. They're getting too close. If we are to continue doing business, we must account for this added danger. Double the original amount seems a fair solution to our problem."

Shit. There was no way in hell my father would agree to double. We all knew that, even Raul. This spelled trouble. I could feel Marco shifting restlessly beside me. One wrong move, one ill-timed word, and this situation could spiral out of control.

I drew in a slow, steadying breath. There was no use letting Raul's bravado get under my skin – that was precisely what the smug bastard wanted. With a casual shrug, I met his fiery glare head-on.

"You're not wrong, Raul," I admitted, keeping my tone even and dispassionate. "The DEA has been a relentless thorn in our side lately. A few... setbacks have forced us to rethink our operational strategies."

Raul's eyes narrowed to slits, but I held up a hand before he could interject.

"However, those setbacks are temporary," I continued smoothly. "My father has the situation well in hand. We're already implementing new contingencies to stop the DEA. Trust me, my father is on top of this."

It wasn't a complete lie – my father did have some twisted game in the works.

"In the meantime," I said, gazing over the assembled Colombians, "we understand the increased risks you're shouldering on our behalf."

A muscle ticked in Raul's jaw, but I could see the spark of greed flickering in his eyes—hook, line, and sinker.

"We're willing to offer a 25% premium over our current rates," I said, letting the words hang in the air like a baited hook.

Raul's nostrils flared, and for a heart-stopping moment, I thought he might spit in my face and call the whole deal off. But then, that wolfish grin stretched across his features once more.

"Twenty-five percent," he mused, rolling the words around like a fine wine. "I suppose that's a start."

The implication was clear – he intended to bleed us dry, one unreasonable demand at a time. But I couldn't let on that I saw through his ploy, not when we were in such a precarious position.

"I'm glad we could agree," I said smoothly, extending my hand.

Raul eyed my hand briefly, letting the tension build before clasping it in a grip that bordered on crushing. His smile was all teeth, a predator acknowledging the temporary submission of his prey.

As we left, Raul called, "Oh, and Dante?"

I paused, glancing over my shoulder with a carefully raised brow.

"Give your father my regards," he sneered. "Tell him the Reyes cartel had better get their house in order soon. We don't tolerate loose ends."

The thinly veiled threat hung in the air, but I refused to take the bait. With a curt nod, I led Marco out of the warehouse and back into the waiting Escalade.

I allowed the tension to bleed only when the engine rumbled to life, and we pulled away. Marco shot me a sidelong glance, his brow furrowed.

"You sure that was the right play, Dante?" he asked, his voice tinged with concern. "Giving in to Raul's demands like that? Dude's gonna keep squeezing us for all we're worth."

I let out a weary sigh, scrubbing a hand over my face. "We didn't have a choice, man. Not with the DEA breathing down our necks like this. We need that supply line, no matter the cost. At least I got him down from double the money."

Marco's jaw tightened, but he gave a reluctant nod. We both knew the score – in our world, survival often meant making deals with snakes like Raul Moreno.

"And it's only temporary," I muttered, more to reassure myself than anything. "Once we get this DEA bullshit sorted, we can cut those Colombian fucks loose and find a new pipeline."

Raul had been right about one thing—we needed to get our house in order fast. The DEA was closing in, and God only knew what other threats were waiting in the wings.

But dwelling on the risks would only drive me mad. I had to focus on the solutions.

A slow smile tugged at the corners of my mouth as my thoughts drifted to Eva and the memory of her body writhing beneath mine, a tempting oasis amidst the endless desert of violence and chaos that was my life.

I could find the time to seek her out again. To lose myself in her intoxicating embrace and forget this fucked up world.

MY STOMACH GROWLED, reminding me I hadn't eaten all day, consumed by the mountain of paperwork spread across my cluttered desk. I glanced at my phone as it buzzed insistently, the caller ID flashing my sister's name. Sighing, I reluctantly put down my pen and answered.

"What is it, Sof?"

"Dante, I need your advice," she said, her tone laced with concern. "It's about Allen. I think... I think he might be involved in something illegal."

My protective instincts kicked into high gear. "What makes you say that?"

Sofia hesitated for a beat. "I overheard him on the phone, talking about 'payback' and 'the cartel.' He got defensive when I asked him about it."

A muscle twitched in my jaw as I considered the implications. If Allen was involved in anything remotely connected to our world, it could spell disaster for Sofia. My father had kept her far away from our "activities" throughout her life. The thought of her getting caught up in the crossfire, of her innocence being tainted by darkness, fucking killed me.

"Stay away from him, Sofia," I said, my voice brooking no argument. "Just for the next few days. At least until I can investigate this further."

"But Dante, I –"

"No buts," I cut her off, my tone firm. "Promise me you'll steer clear of Allen until I give you the all-clear."

There was a long pause, and I could sense her reluctance, her desire to argue with me. But in the end, she relented with a heavy sigh.

"Okay, Dante. I promise."

"Bye, Sof."

I hung up and slumped back in my chair, rubbing my throbbing head. Shit, was this the life I wanted? All these power plays, backstabbing assholes, and blood on my hands that no amount of cash could scrub off?

Was there even a snowball's chance in hell for me to be more than another ruthless cartel kingpin? Some tiny-ass shred of hope for redemption, for a future without all the fucked up sins trailing behind me?

Hell, if I knew. The only thing I was sure of was that I had to keep Sofia safe, protect her from the cartel's dark shit that infected everything I touched.

My phone buzzed again. I scowled at the screen. Marco! I was just with him a few hours ago, and now he was already riding my dick about something.

"What?" I barked into the phone.

"I'm at Diablo. There's a problem," Marco said, rushing his words.

"Slow down, Marco," I said, pinching the bridge of my nose as I tried to make sense of his frantic words. "What's going on at the club?"

"It's Cruz, man," Marco said, his voice taut with tension. "He just rolled up with his crew."

Javier fucking Cruz, who'd been nipping at our heels for months, trying to muscle in on our territory, yet my father refused to do anything about it.

"I'm heading there now," I snarled, jaw clenched tight, already walking to my garage. "Keep that dickhead in your line of vision until I arrive. I'll personally toss his ass to the curb. Oh, and Marco?"

"Yeah, Dante?"

"Dig up what you can on Allen Hawkes, the schmuck dating my little sister. Something tells me he's wading into deep waters."

"You got it, boss. Consider it handled."

Already in my car, I put the phone down, and as I pressed the start button, the roar of the Maserati's powerful engine ignited a familiar thrill through my veins.

The city blurred into a neon river as I cut through the streets, my thoughts a high-octane reel of potential showdowns with Cruz, each more satisfying than the last. My dad may protect him, but one thing was carved in stone—I wouldn't let that arrogant prick step on my toes in my own goddamn backyard.

Tires screaming defiance, I skidded to a stop at the entrance to the club. The valet scrambled over, but I dismissed him with a flick of my hand, swinging out of the car with the grace of a prowling panther.

The bouncers stiffened as I strode up, their eyes wide with respect. A terse nod was all the acknowledgment they got before I swept past, my path unobstructed. They knew the drill; when I was on a mission, they stepped the fuck aside.

The club's heartbeat thumped deep in me as I crossed the threshold, the heady cocktail of sweat, booze, and forbidden pleasures filling my nostrils. I scanned the undulating sea of bodies on the dance floor, seeking Marco or any signs of Cruz's posse.

Spotting them was child's play—a tight knot of unfamiliar faces at a VIP table. Marco's gaze met mine from across the room, his face set in hard lines as he gave a subtle nod toward the group.

I made my way over, my jaw clenched tight as I prepared for the inevitable confrontation. Javier Cruz lounged in a plush booth like he owned the damn place.

"If it isn't the great Dante Reyes himself, gracing us

with his presence," he drawled, his voice loaded with contempt as his gaze met mine.

I came to a halt before his table, my eyes narrowing as I took in the assembled members of his crew. They were an ugly bunch, all sharp edges and predatory stares, their hands never straying far from the weapons concealed beneath their jackets.

"Cruz," I acknowledged, my tone clipped. "To what do I owe the... pleasure?"

Cruz's lips pulled back in a taunting sneer, his eyes glinting with malice. "Can't a man enjoy a night out on the town without being interrogated?" he countered, spreading his hands in a show of innocence that fooled no one.

I felt my jaw tighten as I fought back the urge to wipe that smug look off his face. "Cut the bullshit, Cruz," I growled. "You know damn well this is my club. What's your game here?"

Cruz leaned back in his seat, his gaze raking over me with a casual disdain that set my teeth on edge. "It's just funny, Reyes," he said, his voice mocking. "Seeing you, strutting around like you own South Beach, this entire city. News flash, pendejo – your reign is coming to an end."

I barked out a harsh laugh, shaking my head in disbelief. "Is that what you think, Cruz? That you can waltz in here and take what's mine? This club?"

Cruz's lips twisted into a cruel smirk, his eyes glinting maliciously. "Maybe not today, but trust me, Dante," he drawled, leaning back in his seat with smug arrogance. "You'll see soon enough."

Anger rose within me, my hands clenching into fists. Every instinct in my body screamed at me to wipe that condescending look off his face, to put this upstart in his place once and for all. But before I could act, Cruz rose from his seat, his crew falling into step behind him like a pack of mangy dogs.

"We're leaving to find a more welcoming place," he announced, his gaze sweeping over me with utter disdain. "But this isn't over, Reyes. Not by a long shot."

With those parting words, he turned on his heel and strode out of the club, his men trailing behind him like a dark cloud of menace.

My blood boiled, my fists clenching at my sides. I couldn't believe the nerve of that puto.

"Dante," Marco whispered. "Let it go for now."

I whirled on him, my eyes blazing with fury. "Let it go? Didn't you hear what he just said?"

Marco held up his hands in a placating gesture. "I did, but your father was clear – Javier Cruz is off-limits."

"He thinks he can just waltz into my place and threaten me?" I spat, gesturing towards the empty VIP booth where Cruz and his lackeys had been seated moments ago. "This is bullshit, Marco!"

Marco sighed and steered me towards the backstage area, away from prying eyes and curious ears. Once we were behind closed doors, he turned to face me. "I don't like it any more than you do," he growled through gritted teeth. "But until we know what's going on... Dante, you know we can't risk it."

I slammed my fist against the nearest wall, wincing as pain shot up my arm but welcoming the brief distraction from my boiling rage. "You think I don't know that? But this is bullshit! Why won't Papi tell me what the hell is going on?"

Marco shook his head, gripping his cropped hair in frustration. "I don't have a fucking clue, Dante."

ELEVEN
NATALIA

I sipped my wine, savoring the rich, fruity notes as they danced across my tongue. The dim lighting of the restaurant bar cast an intimate glow, the soft murmurs of conversation swirling around me. Being Eva, I wore my most seductive outfit, an emerald green dress that hugged my curves. The color was deliberate, meant to catch the eye and hold it. And I was hoping it would catch one eye in particular.

It had been days since my steamy encounter with Dante Reyes, and despite my best efforts, our paths hadn't crossed again. Going straight back to Club Diablo was out of the question. It would make me seem too eager. Meeting Dante again had to look like a coincidence. So, I'd been frequenting all the usual haunts, the exclusive clubs and upscale restaurants that were known playgrounds for Miami's elite, hoping to glimpse those piercing blue eyes and that devilish smirk.

But so far, no luck.

I was just about to signal the bartender for another glass of wine when I felt a presence at my elbow. Turning, I faced a stunning woman, her dark hair falling in glossy waves around a face that was all high cheekbones and full lips.

Recognition hit me straight on: Sofia Reyes, Dante's younger sister.

"Eva, right?" she said, her voice warm and inviting. "I remember you from the other night with my brother."

I forced a smile, my head abuzz, trying to think on my feet. I hadn't expected to run into any of the other family besides Dante, let alone be approached by one of them.

"That's right," I said, extending my hand. "And you're Sofia, if I'm not mistaken."

She grinned, taking my hand in a firm grip. "Guilty as charged. Mind if I join you?"

I gestured to the empty stool beside me. "Be my guest."

As Sofia settled onto the seat, I took a moment to study her. She was younger than Dante, probably in her mid-twenties, with a fresh-faced beauty that belied the darkness of her family name. From what I remembered from the files, she was the only Reyes not directly involved in the cartel's illegal activities.

"So, Eva," Sofia began, her eyes sparkling with curiosity. "I have to ask - what's the deal with you and my brother?"

I nearly choked on my drink, caught off guard by her bluntness. "I'm sorry?"

She waved a hand, laughing. "Oh, come on. I saw the way he was looking at you the other night. And he hasn't stopped talking about you. Dante doesn't get that...intense about just anyone."

I bit my lip, choosing my words carefully. "To be honest, I'm not entirely sure. We only just met."

Sofia nodded, a knowing smile playing on her lips. "Well, whatever it is, it's got him all twisted up. I haven't seen him this distracted in... well, ever. And I think it's good for him."

I felt some satisfaction at her words, even as I tried to tamp it down. Dante's interest in me was a means to an end for me, nothing more. But as I studied Sofia's face, I saw nothing but sincerity in her warm brown eyes.

"It's just refreshing, you know?" she continued, leaning closer as if sharing a secret. "Seeing Dante with someone like you instead of those escort women he usually hangs around with."

I raised an eyebrow, feigning ignorance. "Escort women?"

Sofia waved a hand, rolling her eyes. "Oh, you know the type. All flash and no substance. They are just arm candy. But you? You seem different. Real."

I fought back a twinge of guilt at her words. If only she knew the truth - that I was the furthest thing from real, that my entire persona was a carefully crafted lie designed to infiltrate her family's inner circle.

But I couldn't let my true feelings show. Instead, I offered Sofia a small, enigmatic smile. "I'm flattered that you think so, Sofia. But like I said, Dante and I barely know each other."

"Well, we'll just have to change that, won't we?" she said, a mischievous glint in her eye. "I have the perfect idea."

I tilted my head, curious despite myself. "Oh? Do tell."

"Every couple of months, my family gets together at our estate in Palm Beach. It's an entire weekend of sun, fun, and way too much tequila." She grinned, her excitement evident. "You should come with us!"

I blinked, taken aback by the unexpected invitation. A chance to spend an entire weekend with the Reyes family in the heart of their inner sanctum? It was an opportunity I couldn't afford to pass up.

But I couldn't appear too eager. I had to play my cards just right.

"Oh, Sofia, I don't know," I said, hesitating. "I wouldn't want to intrude on your family time. And I'm sure Dante wouldn't want me there."

Sofia scoffed, waving away my protests. "Nonsense! You wouldn't be intruding at all. And trust me, Dante would love to have you there. He's just too stubborn to ask you himself."

I hesitated, letting the moment stretch out as if I were genuinely considering her offer. My mind was jumping in excitement, already planning my next move.

"I don't know, Sofia," I said again, my voice soft and unsure. "It's a lovely offer, but..."

"No buts!" she declared, her eyes sparkling with determination. "I insist. You're coming with us, and that's final. Dante will just have to deal with it."

I let out a little laugh, shaking my head in defeat. "Well, how can I refuse when you put it that way?"

Sofia beamed, clapping her hands together in delight. "Perfect! I'll text you the details. Oh, this is going to be so much fun. You'll love Palm Beach, Eva. And I know you and Dante will hit it off."

I smiled back at her, letting her enthusiasm wash over me. If only she knew the actual reason behind my acceptance, the dangerous game I was playing.

But I couldn't dwell on that. I had to focus on the task at hand, on the opportunity that had just fallen into my lap. A weekend with the Reyes family, a chance to observe them in their natural habitat, to gather intel that could bring their entire empire crashing down.

I knew it was a risk, but it was a calculated one, a gamble I was willing to take.

However, getting close to Dante was one thing, but being invited into the family's private world? That level of intimacy raised the stakes in ways I wasn't entirely prepared for. I needed Agent Morrow to help me plan my next move.

I exchanged numbers with Sofia, her delicate fingers brushing against mine as she handed me her phone. "I'm so glad we met, Eva," she said, her voice soft and sincere. "I can't wait to get to know you better."

I smiled, feeling a genuine warmth beneath my carefully crafted persona. "Me too, Sofia. I have a feeling we're going to be great friends." With a final squeeze of her hand, I turned and made my way out of the bar.

The night air was thick with humidity, the distant chatter from the bar still buzzing in my head. I glanced over my shoulder, ensuring that no one was following me. Satisfied that I was alone, I walked to the corner and hailed a cab.

As I slid into the back seat, the driver met my gaze in the rearview mirror. "Where to, miss?" he asked, his voice gruff but not unkind.

I gave him the address Eva's apartment. "Thanks," I said, leaning back against the worn fabric of the seat and closing my eyes.

The ride passed in a blur, the city lights streaming past the windows as my thoughts raced with the possibilities and pitfalls ahead. The connection I'd forged with Dante was thrilling and terrifying, a high-wire act that could lead to the biggest bust of my career or send me plummeting into the abyss.

When the cab pulled up to my apartment, my nerves thrummed like live wires, my determination burning bright beneath the surface. I paid the driver and stepped out into the night, the key to my place – well, to Eva's place – clutched tightly in my hand.

The door closed behind me with a soft click, the lock sliding into place like a final barrier between me and the outside world. In the stillness of the room, I let out a shaky breath, my shoulders sagging under the pressure of the mission that stretched before me.

I wasted no time setting up the secure video link, my fingers flying over the keyboard as I entered the encrypted passcode connecting me to Morrow. This conversation couldn't wait.

As the screen flickered to life and Morrow's face filled the frame, I inhaled deeply, steeling myself for the briefing to come. I knew he wouldn't be thrilled about the risks, but he also trusted my instincts and abilities.

"You're playing a dangerous game, Ramirez," Agent Morrow growled, his grizzled face looming on the screen of my laptop running the Zoom session. "Infiltrating a family gathering at the Reyes vacation mansion? That's a whole new level of risk."

I sighed, running a hand through my hair as I paced the room. "I know, sir. But this is an opportunity we can't pass up. If I can gain Dante or Sofia's trust, get inside their inner circle-"

"You could also get made," Morrow cut in, his voice sharp. "And then where would we be? Down one agent and no closer to taking these bastards down."

I bristled at his tone, my jaw tightening. "With all due respect, sir, I know what I'm doing. I've been undercover before."

"Not like this," he countered, shaking his head. "The Reyes cartel isn't just another street gang or drug ring. They're a fucking dynasty with roots that go deeper than you can imagine."

Of course, he was right. The Reyes family had been

running Miami's underworld for generations, their power and influence stretching far beyond the city limits.

But I also knew that this was our best chance. With Dante's interest in me and Sofia's unexpected invitation, I had an opportunity that no other agent had ever managed to secure.

"I understand the risks," I said firmly, meeting Morrow's gaze through the screen. "But I'm willing to take them. For Matt and every other life these monsters have destroyed."

Morrow was silent for a long moment, his eyes searching mine. Finally, he let out a heavy sigh.

"Alright, Ramirez. You've got the green light. But listen up - you keep your head down and your eyes open, you hear me? The Reyes compound will be crawling with cartel muscle, and they'll be watching for any sign of trouble."

I nodded, my mind already racing with possibilities. "What should I be looking for, exactly?"

Morrow leaned back in his chair, his expression thoughtful. "Anything that could give us a lead on their operations. Shipping manifests, financial records, names, and locations of key players. Hell, even overheard conversations could be useful."

I made a mental note, committing his instructions to memory. "And if I do manage to find something? How do I get it to headquarters without blowing my cover?"

"Through me. Nobody else. This is the only way," Morrow said as if it were obvious. "If you find any physical evidence, I'll set up a secure location where you can leave the intel. But Ramirez - you can't tell anyone else about this. One wrong move, and it's game over."

I swallowed hard, the gravity of the situation sinking in. I was about to walk into the lion's den, armed with nothing but my wits and a flimsy cover story. If anything went wrong...

"I'll be careful," I promised, my voice calm despite the nerves fluttering in my stomach. "And sir? Thank you. For trusting me with this."

Morrow's face softened, just for a moment. "You're a good agent, Ramirez—one of the best. Just don't let those pretty boy looks of Dante Reyes distract you. He's a ruthless man who wouldn't hesitate to kill you the instant he learns your identity."

I felt my cheeks flush at his words. "I won't, sir. I know what's at stake."

"Good." Morrow nodded. "Now get some rest. You're going to need it. And Ramirez?"

"Sir?"

"Give 'em hell."

With that, the screen went dark, leaving me alone with my thoughts.

This was it. No turning back now.

TWELVE
DANTE

I leaned back in my chair, the seat creaking beneath me as I regarded the investor across the table. Alessandro Marconi was a powerhouse in Miami's real estate scene, with a portfolio that spanned luxury hotels, upscale restaurants, and prime beachfront properties— precisely the kind of player that could help legitimize my expansion plans.

"As I mentioned, Mr. Reyes," he continued, sliding a glossy brochure across the table, "this property on South Beach is prime real estate. With the right vision and invest- ment, it could become the crown jewel of your entertain- ment empire."

I nodded, flipping through the brochure and taking in the sleek renderings of the proposed development—a towering high-rise with a rooftop lounge, multiple restau- rants, and a state-of-the-art nightclub—a respected busi- ness venture to diversify the cartels' interests and potentially build a much safer future for the family without the drug trade.

As Alessandro droned on, extolling the virtues of the location and the profit potential, my mind began to wander. Suddenly, thoughts of a different kind of empire crept in, far more tempting than any real estate deal.

Eva. Stunning, delicious, mysterious Eva Morales.

I could almost taste her on my lips, a heady mix of sweetness and sin. Her heated skin against mine, our bodies entwined in a rhythmic dance of lust, each thrust and gyration etched into my memory.

I recalled the way her nails had raked down my back, the desperate noises she'd made as she unraveled beneath my touch. The memory alone was enough to make my cock twitch, hardening against my pants.

A soft touch on my arm jolted me back to the present, and I blinked to find Alessandro's assistant, Vanessa, if I remembered correctly, leaning in far too close. Vanessa was a leggy brunette with a predatory gaze that lingered a little too long on my body.

"Sorry, Mr. Reyes," she purred, her voice like honey. "You seemed... distracted."

I cleared my throat, shifting in my seat and putting more distance between us. "Not at all. Please, continue Alessandro."

But even as the words left my lips, my mind drifted again.

I had to discover Eva's darkest secrets, peel back the layers, and learn what lay beneath that sultry exterior. But more than that, I wanted to lose myself in her once more, to drown in the unexplainable sensations she had so effortlessly unleashed.

"Dante?"

The sound of my name snapped me back to reality, and I realized that both Alessandro and Vanessa were staring at me.

"My apologies," I said, forcing a smile that didn't quite reach my eyes. "I'm afraid my mind is elsewhere today."

Alessandro frowned, but Vanessa's gaze held a glint of understanding – or was it calculation? Her hand found my arm again, her fingers trailing along the fabric of my sleeve in a way that was clearly meant to be suggestive.

"Maybe we should take a break, Mr. Reyes," she purred. "Get you relaxed; work out all that tension. There's a plush suite upstairs. I could show you the way, make it worth your while…"

Her hand slid along my thigh, brazenly mapping the contours of my leg through the fabric of my trousers as she pinned me with a smoldering, fuck-me gaze, those sinful red lips parted in blatant invitation.

I bit back a scowl and removed her hand gently but decisively. She was a knockout, no question. But she was also here to sweeten the real estate deal with her dangerous curves and sultry pout, the sort of vixen I would've leaped to take six ways from Sunday not long ago.

Not today. Today, like yesterday and the day before, Eva consumed my thoughts. The silken slide of her skin against mine, the erotic symphony of her moans and sighs as I drove her to shattering orgasms, over and over...

"Excuse me a moment," I said, standing abruptly. "I need to make a quick call."

Alessandro nodded, a smirk playing about his mouth as he waved me off. "But of course. Take all the time you need."

I strode out of the restaurant, pulling my phone from my pocket as I stepped into the muggy Miami heat. I had no one to call, and there was no pressing business. I just needed a fucking moment to clear my head.

"Hey there, handsome."

I spun around at the sound of my sister's voice and spotted Sofia walking towards me with a quizzical look on her face.

"Hey, Sof," I said, forcing a smile. "What brings you to this neck of the woods?"

She shrugged, falling into step beside me as I started down the sidewalk. "Just running some errands. What about you? I thought you had that big investor meeting today."

I nodded, shoving my hands into my pockets. "I am. Just needed some air."

Sofia gave me a sidelong glance, her brow furrowing. "Everything okay? You seem... distracted."

I barked out a laugh, shaking my head. "That's one word for it."

"I hope you're not so distracted that you can't make it

to Palm Beach this weekend. Mami's been asking about you."

I groaned, running a hand over my face. The last thing I wanted was to spend an entire weekend trapped in conversations with my father and his endless lectures about the cartel's future.

"I don't know, Sof," I hedged. "I might have to stay in Miami for business."

She raised an eyebrow, a knowing smirk playing at her lips. "Business, yeah? Maybe only the woman from the other night could drag you away, then?"

I felt my cheeks heat and looked away, clearing my throat. "I don't know who you're talking about."

Sofia laughed, punching me lightly on the arm. "Oh, come on, Dante. Eva. I know you like her. And I may have invited her to Palm Beach."

My head snapped up, and my pulse quickened. "You did what?"

She grinned, her eyes sparkling with mischief. "I ran into her yesterday. We talked, and I thought it would be nice to include her in the family gathering. You know, since you two seem to have hit it off, kind of."

I gaped at her, my mind reeling. Eva, at a Reyes family dinner? The thought of her in the same room as my father, as the rest of the cartel's inner circle... Fuck, it was thrilling and terrifying at the same time. It could end up a fucking disaster.

"So?" Sofia prompted, nudging me with her elbow. "Are you coming or not?"

I hesitated for a moment, but as crazy as the idea was, the thought of seeing Eva again, of being near her, touching her, being deep inside of her...

"I'll be there," I said finally.

Sofia beamed, clapping her hands together in delight. "Perfect! I can't wait to see the look on Mami's face when she meets your new girlfriend."

"She's not my girlfriend," I said, but the words lacked conviction. Honestly, I didn't know what Eva was to me. All I knew was that I couldn't get her out of my fucking head.

"Sure, sure," Sofia said, waving off my protest with a flick of her wrist. "Just promise me you'll be on your best behavior. No talk of business, okay? This is strictly a family affair."

I nodded, my jaw tight. "I'll be the perfect gentleman."

Sofia snorted, rolling her eyes. "I'll believe that when I see it."

We parted ways soon after, Sofia heading off to finish her errands while I made my way back to the restaurant. But as I walked, my mind was already racing ahead to the weekend.

THIRTEEN
NATALIA

I DREW IN A LONG, DEEP BREATH, GATHERING MY thoughts, as I turned onto the long, winding driveway that led to the sprawling Reyes estate in Palm Beach. I watched the imposing, ornate gates as they parted, and I cautiously guided my vehicle forward, passing beneath the iron archway.

I had spent hours preparing for this family dinner, carefully selecting a figure-hugging red dress that accentuated my curves and a pair of sky-high stilettos that added an extra sway to my hips. My hair was styled in loose, sultry waves, and my makeup was flawless, highlighting my features perfectly.

But behind my sleek facade, my thoughts were consumed by the mission. I had mentally rehearsed every possible scenario, every potential conversation, and every subtle clue to look for once inside the Reyes' inner sanctum. Agent Morrow's advice echoed in my head as I slowed the car to a stop in front of the lavish mansion. "Listen up, Ramirez," Morrow had said, his voice gruff but tinged with concern. "You're about to step into a viper's nest. Stay sharp, trust no one, and always watch your back. These bastards won't hesitate to put a bullet in you if they smell weakness."

A young, sharply dressed male valet stepped up to take my car. He greeted me by name with a bow and said Sofia was expecting me. He told me he would park the car and have my bags delivered to my room in the house.

This was it - the moment of truth. I was about to face Dante's family, the people I had sworn to destroy. One wrong move, one slip of the tongue, and my cover could be blown sky-high.

As Eva Morales, I pushed those fears aside, channeling all my training and experience into a confident, alluring, and unflappable persona—someone who belonged in this world of wealth and power.

The door swung open before I could knock, revealing a smiling Sofia Reyes in a stunning cocktail dress. "Eva!" she exclaimed, pulling me into a warm embrace. "I'm so glad you could make it. Come on in. Everyone's dying to meet you."

I returned her smile, allowing myself to be swept inside the grand foyer. The mansion's interior was just as impressive as the exterior, with soaring ceilings, gleaming marble floors, and priceless works of art adorning the walls.

Sofia led me through the house, chattering excitedly about the dinner and the guests who had already arrived. I nodded and smiled at all the right moments, but my attention was focused on absorbing every detail of my surroundings, committing the house's layout to memory.

As we entered the sprawling living room, I felt several gazes land on me. Dante was there, of course, looking sinfully handsome in a tailored suit that hugged his muscular frame. His blue eyes widened when he saw me, heat passing between us before he quickly adjusted himself.

Beside him stood an older man with salt-and-pepper hair and a stern, aristocratic face. I recognized him instantly from the files - Ricardo Reyes, the patriarch of the family and the mastermind behind the cartel's operations.

Ricardo's gaze was assessing as he looked me over, his dark eyes seeming to strip away the layers of my disguise. For a heart-stopping moment, I feared that he could see right through me, that he knew exactly who I was and why I was there.

He smiled, a cold, calculating thing that didn't quite reach his eyes. His voice was smooth as silk as he welcomed me. "Sofia's told us much about you. It's a pleasure to have you here."

I forced a smile in return, extending my hand to shake his. "The pleasure is all mine, Mr Reyes," I said calmly, despite the nerves fluttering in my stomach. "Your home is stunning."

A waiter appeared with a tray of champagne flutes, and I quickly grabbed one for liquid courage. The introductions continued, and I felt Dante's gaze boring into me the entire time. I had to use every ounce of my willpower to keep my focus on the job at hand and not meet his stare.

The Reyes family certainly knew how to throw a dinner party, with no expense spared on the lavish decorations and free-flowing drinks. I was just about to head over to Sofia when a familiar presence appeared at my side.

"Eva," Dante said, his voice low. "Can I talk to you for a minute?"

I glanced up at him, his blue eyes making my heart skip a beat. "Of course," I said, keeping my tone light and casual.

He led me away from the crowded living room and into an empty adjoining space, closing the door behind us with a soft click. The sudden privacy was thrilling and unnerving, and I was acutely aware of Dante's proximity, his body mere inches away.

"I wanted to apologize," he began, running a hand through his dark golden hair. "For my sister's little matchmaking scheme. She can be a bit... enthusiastic when it comes to my love life."

"It's fine, Dante. I'm sure Sofia meant well. And maybe..." I paused, biting my lip as I met his gaze. "Maybe I didn't mind so much."

A rush of desire passed over Dante's eyes. He took a step closer, his hand brushing a stray lock of hair from my cheek. "Is that so?" he said, his voice rough with emotion.

I tilted my head up, my lips parting as Dante leaned in, his breath ghosting over my skin.

For a moment, I forgot about everything else - the

mission, the danger, the lies I had spun to get to this point. All that mattered was the man in front of me and the electric current flowing between us.

But just as our lips were about to meet, a sudden noise from outside the room made us spring apart, the spell broken. Dante cleared his throat, running a hand over his face as he took a step back.

"We should probably get back to the party," he said, his voice strained. "But Eva, before we do... there's something you should know."

I raised an eyebrow, my heart still racing from our near kiss. "What is it?"

Dante hesitated, his jaw clenching as he struggled with his words. "It's my father," he said finally. "Ricardo. He can be... intense. Suspicious of outsiders. It's just his nature."

I nodded slowly, unease curling in my gut. I had read the files on Ricardo Reyes and knew the kind of man he was and the ruthless empire he had built. But hearing Dante's warning made it all the more real; the danger I was walking into suddenly crystal clear.

"I'll be careful," I promised. "And Dante... thank you. For looking out for me."

He gave me a small, crooked smile, the kind that made my heart skip a beat. "Anytime, Eva."

We returned to the party and took our seats around the elegantly set dinner table. An undercurrent of tension set my nerves on edge.

"So, Eva," Ricardo said, his voice cutting through the

chatter like a knife. "Tell us a little about yourself. Where are you from? What brought you to South Florida?"

I met his gaze with a calm smile as I recalled the details of my cover story. "I just moved here a couple of weeks ago. I'm originally from New York," I said, my tone casual. "But I've always loved the sun and the sea. Miami just looked like the perfect place to start fresh."

Ricardo raised an eyebrow, leaning back in his chair. "Starting fresh, hmm? And what exactly do you do for a living, my dear?"

Dante tensed beside me, his hand tightening on my thigh beneath the table. "I work in fashion," I said. "Styling. It's a competitive industry, but I've been lucky to make good connections."

A calculating smirk settled on Ricardo's mouth, and I could tell he wasn't entirely convinced. "Fashion, is it? And how did you come to meet my son?"

I laughed lightly, placing my hand over Dante's on the table. "Oh, you know how these things go. A chance encounter at a club, a few drinks, and the rest is history."

Dante shot me a grateful look, but I could see the worry in his eyes.

The dinner progressed, and soon, I was in a deep conversation with Sofia, who sat across from me with a warm smile. "I've always dreamed of traveling the world, seeing new places, experiencing different cultures," she confided, her eyes sparkling with excitement. "There's so much out there beyond South Florida."

Seeing Sofia's face light up with her passion for

exploring the world tugged at my heartstrings. I knew the brutal reality: her family's criminal empire would suffocate those wandering dreams before they could take flight. Safety issues, for one. A mob kingpin's daughter would be a big target for rival gangs.

"Forget what anyone else thinks," I urged, my fingers entwining with hers across the table, "This is your life. Seize your dreams while you're still young."

Sofia beamed at me, and it was easy to see the woman she could become if she were free from the shadows of her family's criminal empire. The guilt gnawed at me, a constant reminder that my deepening bond with Sofia was built on a foundation of lies. But the affection, the need to shield her from the suffocating darkness of her family - that was real, undeniable.

Ricardo's voice sliced through my thoughts. "The Reyes family doesn't fuck around, Eva," he said, his casual tone barely masking the venom beneath. "We have expectations for those who run with us."

A cold dread crept down my back, but I met his stare unflinching, my voice never wavering. "Mr. Reyes, I understand. My intentions with Dante are heartfelt."

Ricardo's eyes turned to slits. "For your sake, I hope that's true, darling."

The menace hung in the air, suffocating. But I refused to let fear show in front of Ricardo Reyes.

I maneuvered through the rest of dinner with finesse, wielding my charm and sharp tongue to parry any more of Ricardo's pointed inquisitions. Dante's eyes locked on me, a potent cocktail of unease and desire swirling in their depths.

Despite the underlying tension, the evening began to take on a more relaxed atmosphere as the wine flowed and the conversation turned to lighter topics. Sofia and I engaged in a lively discussion about the latest fashion trends in Miami, and I was grateful for the momentary respite from Ricardo's scrutiny.

A sense of relief washed over me as the plates were cleared and the dinner party wound down. I had survived the first night in the lion's den and played my part perfectly.

Sofia caught my arm, her eyes sparkling. "Eva, I had the staff prepare a room for you," she said. "Come. Let's get you settled in."

As I followed Sofia upstairs to the guest wing, I felt Dante's gaze on my back, burning into me like a physical touch.

I could finally relax as I entered the luxurious guest room, the plush king-sized bed practically begging me to sink into its soft embrace. The en-suite bathroom was larger than my old apartment back in Miami.

I hoisted my suitcase onto the bed and stared at it sitting on the beautiful opulent bedspread. Sofia had been so genuinely welcoming, that I felt a pang of guilt for deceiving her. But I couldn't afford to let my emotions get in the way of my mission.

I unpacked and got ready for bed, and as I slipped under the silky sheets, cool against my skin, my mind wandered to Dante. The intensity of his gaze during dinner kindled a smoldering desire that threatened to consume me from the inside out.

I knew it was wrong. Dante was the enemy. But as I lay there in the darkness, listening to the distant crash of the ocean waves, I secretly and shamefully hoped that he would knock on my door tonight.

FOURTEEN
DANTE

I ADJUSTED MY JACKET AS I WATCHED EVA GO UPSTAIRS with my sister. Christ, looking at Eva in that tight little "fuck me" dress had my cock throbbing like a jackhammer all night, driving me out of my goddamn mind.

As I entered the library, my old man was already there, sipping a glass of Cognac with a grin on his face when I walked in. He waved me over, that smug-ass look never leaving his mug.

"That's one helluva piece of ass you landed there, kid," he said, half impressed, half giving me shit. "Eva's gorgeous, but watch yourself. Broads like that are a fuck-load of trouble."

His words pissed me off, even though a little voice in my head knew the old bastard had a point. There was definitely something dangerous about Eva, but no way in hell would I let my dad think I wasn't on top of it.

"I can handle her," I said, my voice firm and confident. "Even if she is quite special."

He raised an eyebrow, swirling the amber liquid in his glass. "Special, hmm?" He fixed me with a pointed stare. "Just make sure she doesn't become a distraction, Dante. We have our business to attend to, an empire to run." His voice lowered, a warning in his tone. "Don't let a pretty face make you lose sight of what's important."

I met his gaze unflinchingly, my jaw tight with resolve. "Of course, Papi. The family always comes first." I nodded, my words measured and firm. "I won't let anything or anyone jeopardize what you've built."

But even as the promise left my lips, I couldn't shake the image of Eva from my mind. The way her blue eyes had smoldered as they met mine at dinner, the secret smile that curved her lush mouth when no one else was looking. It was as if she had cast a spell over me, and I was powerless to resist her allure.

After a few more minutes of tense conversation, I drained the last of my drink and set the glass down with a decisive clink. "I'm gonna call it a night, Papi," I said, rising from my chair. "It's been a long day, and I'm tired."

He waved a dismissive hand. "Get some rest, mijo. We've got a lot of work ahead of us."

I nodded, grateful for the escape. I quietly left the library, and as I made my way to my room, I caught a glimpse of Sofia rounding the corner. For a moment, I considered stopping to talk to her to get her read on the situation. But the last thing I needed was more talk of Eva tonight.

Instead, I hurried to my room, closing the door firmly behind me and leaning against it with a heavy sigh. My eyes drifted shut as I replayed every moment of the evening in my head, from the first electric jolt of seeing Eva in that red dress to the way her hand had felt in mine as we said goodnight.

I couldn't deny the effect she had on me, the way my body instinctively responded to her presence. It was more than just physical attraction, though it was undoubtedly a big part. No, there was something else, a connection that ran deeper than I cared to admit.

I collapsed onto the bed with a groan, but sleep was a lost cause. Every time I closed my eyes, there she was - hips swaying, tits teasing, moaning like a porn star as I pounded into her at the club. My cock throbbed, hard as a fucking rock, begging for attention. I palmed it through my boxers, trying to resist the urge to jerk off like a horny teenager.

Screw it, I had to see her again. I knew it was a shit idea, showing up at her door in the middle of the night in my parent's house, but I couldn't help myself. Eva was an addiction, and I needed another hit, Dad's warning, and the consequences be damned.

I rose from the bed, purpose propelling me forward even as doubt kept whispering in the back of my mind. I tried to convince myself I was just checking on her, but I knew better. I was chasing the high only she could give me.

The mansion was silent as I navigated the shadowy

halls, the distant crash of waves the only sound. It was late, too late, but the promise of Eva just down the hall proved irresistible.

I hesitated outside her door, hand poised over the knob. This was insanity, and I knew it. But even as the thought registered, I turned the handle and slipped inside.

Holy fuck, there she was, looking like a goddamn wet dream come true, all tangled up in those fancy-ass silk sheets. The moonlight streaming in made her skin practically glow like some sexy alien goddess, and that dark hair was fanned out around her head like a work of art. I couldn't stop staring, my cock already straining against my boxers.

I stumbled to the bed, my heart about to pound right out of my damn chest. I reached out and barely grazed her arm with my fingertips, and she started to stir, those mesmerizing chocolate eyes fluttering open and locking right onto me.

"Dante? What are you doing in here?" Her voice was all husky with sleep and laced with this vulnerable confusion that made me want to simultaneously wrap her up in my arms and rip that flimsy nightie right off her sexy body.

"Shit, sorry. Didn't mean to disturb your beauty sleep." I yanked my hand back, trying to pretend I had a shred of gentlemanly decency left, even though all I could think about was diving face-first under those sheets with her.

She pushed herself up to sit, and god fucking damn, those sheets slipped down to her waist, drawing my gaze straight to her nipples poking at the silky little nightgown she wore. I think I actually forgot how to breathe for a second. She was warm, with inviting curves and soft skin, begging to be touched.

"Couldn't sleep. Just had to come see you," I confessed, gazing at her like a pathetic lovesick fool.

She hit me with this coy little smile, her eyes sparkling with mischief like the temptress she was. "Well, you found me. Now, what are you gonna do about it?"

I groaned, my self-control hanging by a thread. "You're playing with fire, Eva."

She leaned back, looking at me like she wanted to devour me. "Maybe I like it hot."

That was it. I pounced on the bed, my body over hers, hands on either side of her head. She gasped as I kissed her hard, leaving no question about what I wanted to do to her.

She kissed me back just as fiercely, her hands sliding up to grab my hair. I could feel how hot she was through that thin little nightgown, and it was driving me crazy.

I broke the kiss and started trailing my lips down her neck, biting and sucking. She arched her back, moaning, as I slid her straps down, exposing her perfect tits. I was ready to feast.

I groped her breasts, my calloused thumbs grazing over those hard nipples. She whimpered, nails clawing into my shoulders as I sucked one rosy peak into my mouth, my tongue doing dirty, unspeakable things to that sensitive little nub. Her body thrashed under me, hips grinding on my cock, desperate for some action.

I jammed my hand between her thighs, fingers prodding the soaked fabric of her panties. Shit, she was dripping wet and ready to go. Knowing I'd gotten her so fucking horny was like Viagra straight to my dick.

With a feral snarl, I shredded that flimsy lace off her body and plunged my fingers knuckle-deep into her slippery pussy. She screamed, body convulsing as I zeroed in on her magic button, rubbing and teasing until she was a thrashing, pleading hot mess pinned beneath me.

"Fuck, Dante, I need your cock in me like right now," she begged, eyes blazing with raw, primal lust.

With my heart beating, I peeled off my clothes in record time, revealing my engorged cock, as hard as a flagpole, pulsing with anticipation. I positioned myself at her slick entrance, the swollen, purple head of my thick shaft already leaking precum, begging for a taste of her scorching heat.

"Condom?" Eva gasped, her eyes wide.

"Fuck!" I swore, running a hand through my hair. The one thing I didn't have. "I didn't plan on...this."

"It's fine," she breathed, her face looking so damn sexy. "I'm on the pill, and I'm clean. And I need to feel all of you inside me, Dante."

"Fuck," I groaned. "Me too."

With her words, I couldn't hold back any longer. My cock, painfully hard, sank into her tightness, her heat clenching around me like a wet, hot fist. She felt so damn good, like a glove, like I had been made for this very moment, for her.

My dick slammed into Eva's drenched pussy with the

relentless pace of a jackhammer, our hips crashing in a wild tango of lust. She raked her nails down my back with the ferocity of a she-devil, marking her territory in a way that made me smirk for the coming bruises.

With each punishing thrust, the ecstasy coiled tighter in my balls, driving us both to the brink of insanity. I could feel her pussy flutter and grip around my cock, teetering on the edge of ecstasy.

"Give it to me, you ravenous nymph," I panted against her lips. "Cream all over this dick."

Eva let out an earth-shattering cry, her orgasm erupting like a volcano, her pussy convulsing and wringing every last drop of pleasure from me. Her climax hurled me into the stratosphere, and I drove myself to the hilt, unleashing a torrent of scorching cum into her depths with a growl.

We collapsed together in a sweaty, satisfied heap, panting like we'd just run a marathon. I rolled off and pulled her limp body against me, her head lolling on my chest as we caught our breath, totally spent.

I should've felt like a real shithead for being so goddamn reckless, but with Eva snuggled up against me, I was too fucking content to care. Holding her just felt...right, in a way nothing had for a long-ass time.

As the moonlight was creeping in, Eva was fast asleep, and it hit me - I was in some deep shit. Deeper than ever before. But, for once, I wasn't even sure I wanted to claw my way out. Except, tonight, I better not get caught here in her room.

I slipped out of her bed, tiptoeing like a ninja to avoid

waking sleeping beauty. I threw my clothes on and snuck one last peek at Eva before escaping.

Thoughts and feelings swirled in my head as I crept back to my room, all jumbled up. I'd always been a stone-cold badass, emotions on lockdown. But this chick...she'd gotten under my skin, stirred up parts of me I never knew I had.

Damn.

FIFTEEN
NATALIA

My eyes flew open, and I jerked upright, kicking the sheets off my legs in panic as the remnants of a vivid dream clung to the edges of my consciousness. For a fleeting moment, I was disoriented, the unfamiliar surroundings confusing me. But then, like a tidal wave crashing over me, the memories of yesterday came rushing back—the lavish dinner where I came face-to-face with the formidable Ricardo Reyes himself. And, of course, the late-night visit from Dante.

I recalled how Dante looked at me, his mouth on mine, his hands on my body, and then his lips trailed fire across my skin. His magnificent cock inside me.

Last night was anything but pretending. It was so real, so powerfully vivid, that I lost myself entirely in the experience.

But that's all it was – a fantasy, a carefully constructed illusion.

I untangled myself from the sheets, bare feet hitting the carpet.

After a quick shower, I dressed in a simple sundress and sandals, determined to make the most of my time in the mansion. Every room, nook, and cranny was a potential goldmine of information.

As I wandered out to the hallway, voices drifted up from below. Curious, I followed the sound to a massive library where Sofia and her mom chatted animatedly. They smiled as I entered.

"Eva, you're up!" Sofia jumped up to greet me. "We're planning the day. Have you ever ridden horses?"

"Horseback riding?" I said, masking my surprise. Of all the ritzy activities I expected at the Reyes estate, saddling up hadn't crossed my mind.

Sofia was excited. "Yes! It's one of my favorite things to do here. The trails wind through gorgeous scenery. And the stables are divine – you'll adore the horses!"

I forced a laugh, faking a self-deprecating smile. "Oh gosh, I don't know about that," I waved dismissively. "I'm no rider, really. More of a city girl."

Not a total lie – Eva Morales belonged among Manhattan's glitzy skyscrapers, not on a horse. But truthfully, I'd grown up riding, spending countless hours in the saddle on my dad's Texas ranch.

From the moment I could walk, Daddy had me on a pony, teaching me the land's ways and the value of hard work.

But that history had no place in Eva's meticulous backstory, so I buried those memories and focused on maintaining my cover.

"Nonsense!" Sofia exclaimed, waving away my protests with a flick of her wrist. "It'll be fun, I promise."

"Well, I suppose I could give it a try," I said, injecting just the right amount of nervousness into my tone. "But you'll have to promise not to laugh at me when I inevitably end up in the dirt."

Sofia clapped her hands together, her face alight with glee. "It's settled then! We'll have the stable hand prepare the horses after lunch."

As we chatted and made plans, I glanced around the room, taking in every detail: the artwork adorning the walls, the gleaming marble floors, and the expensive furnishings.

As Sofia and her mother excused themselves to prepare for our outing, I wandered the mansion halls, my steps taking me deeper into the heart of the Reyes domain.

I paused outside a set of heavy doors. I'd learned last night that behind those doors was Ricardo Reyes's study, the nerve center of his criminal empire. If there were any evidence to be found—any smoking gun—it would be in here.

With a furtive glance over my shoulder to ensure I was alone, I tried the handle. To my surprise, it turned easily in my hand, the door swinging open with a soft creak.

The study was decorated in masculine elegance, with rich leather chairs, floor-to-ceiling bookshelves, and a massive mahogany desk that dominated the center of the room. My gaze was drawn to the piles of papers and ledgers strewn across the desk, a veritable treasure trove of potential evidence.

Moving quickly but quietly, I crossed the room and began rifling through the documents: shipping manifests, financial records, and coded messages.

With trembling hands, I pulled out my phone and began snapping photos. Each click felt like a thunderclap in the stillness of the study, but I pressed on, driven by the knowledge that this could be the break we needed.

Suddenly, a noise from the hallway made me freeze. Footsteps, growing louder by the second. Someone was coming.

Panicked, I shoved the phone back into my dress and hastily rearranged the papers on the desk, trying to erase any evidence of my snooping. My heart was in my throat as the footsteps drew closer.

The door swung open, and there stood Dante, his brow furrowed in confusion as he saw me in his father's study.

"Eva?" he said, his voice tinged with surprise. "What are you doing in here?"

I forced a smile, willing my racing heart to slow, to regain some semblance of composure. "Dante, I... I was looking for the restroom," I lied, the words tumbling from my lips with practiced ease. "I must have taken a wrong turn."

He regarded me momentarily, those piercing blue eyes seeming to bore into my very soul. For a heart-stopping instant, I thought he could see right through me and sense the deception beneath my carefully crafted facade.

But then, to my relief, his features softened, and he offered me a crooked smile.

"No worries, babe," he said, crossing the room to take my hand. "Let me show you the way."

As he led me from the study, I released a shaky breath, my heart still pounding from the near-miss. The thrill of uncovering potentially crucial evidence was intoxicating, but a growing sense of unease tempered it. Dante's mere presence seemed to short-circuit my brain, leaving me fumbling and flustered, and I couldn't shake the feeling that my growing attraction to him was a dangerous distraction.

THE STABLES WERE A SIGHT – a sprawling complex of whitewashed stalls and gleaming tack rooms, with the scent of hay and leather hanging thick in the air. I tried to fake an air of wide-eyed wonder as Sofia led me through the grand archway, but the truth was, I felt more at home here than in most places I had been in years.

"Isn't it just beautiful?" Sofia breathed, her eyes shining with pride as she gestured to the immaculately groomed horses and the meticulous attention to detail. "These are some of the finest Arabian bloodlines in the country."

I nodded, letting out a soft whistle of appreciation.

"The horses are gorgeous," I said, my gaze lingering on a magnificent chestnut stallion who tossed its head, nostrils flaring. "Truly stunning creatures."

Sofia beamed at me, her enthusiasm infectious. "I knew you'd love it here," she said, looping her arm through mine and leading me towards a tack room. "Now, let's get you all set up with a horse, and we can hit the trails."

As we selected our mounts and began the process of saddling up, I fought to keep my movements slow and uncertain, playing the role of the inexperienced city girl to perfection. Sofia, bless her heart, was a patient teacher, guiding me through each step with infinite kindness and good humor.

"Okay, Eva," she said once our horses were ready. "Time for the real test – mounting up."

I took a deep, steadying breath, steeling myself for the performance of a lifetime. With a theatrical wobble, I approached the mare Sofia had selected for me, eyeing the stirrup with trepidation.

"Just put your left foot in the stirrup like this," Sofia demonstrated, her movements fluid and graceful. "Then grab the saddle horn and swing your right leg over."

I nodded, biting my lip in concentration as I followed her instructions. But just as I was about to hoist myself into the saddle, I let out a yelp and stumbled, my foot slipping from the stirrup as I landed on the ground with a dull thud.

"Eva!" Sofia cried, her eyes wide with concern as she slid from her mount and rushed to my side. "Are you alright?"

I groaned, clutching my lower back as I fought back a grin. "I think so," I managed, grimacing for added effect. "Just a little bruised pride, that's all."

Sofia shook her head, her brow furrowed with worry. "Maybe we should call this off," she said, biting her lip. "I don't want you to get hurt."

"No, no," I protested, waving her off as I staggered to my feet. "I'm fine, really. Just a little clumsy."

Sofia didn't look convinced, but I could see the disappointment flickering in her eyes at the thought of canceling our ride. With a surge of fake determination, I squared my shoulders and approached the mare again.

This time, I easily swung into the saddle, settling into the familiar leather with a contented sigh. Sofia's eyes widened in surprise, and I offered her a sheepish grin.

"Beginner's luck, I guess," I said with a wink, relieved I managed to fool her so effortlessly.

As we set off down the winding trail, the world fell away, and for a few blissful hours, I lost myself in the simple joy of riding. The rhythmic sway of the horse's gait, the gentle breeze carrying the scent of salt and sea grass, and the warm sun on my face were a slice of peace amid the chaos that had become my life.

Sofia was in her element, her face aglow with happiness as she led us through the lush landscapes of the estate. We talked and laughed, sharing stories and secrets like old friends, and for a moment, I could forget the lies that had brought me here.

As we crested a hill, the vast ocean expanse stretched

before us, sparkling like a million diamonds in the afternoon light. Sofia reined in her horse, her eyes shining with wonder.

"Isn't it breathtaking?" she said, her voice hushed with reverence.

I nodded, my gaze drinking in the beauty of the scene. "I can hardly believe it's real," I said, emotion choking my voice.

Sofia turned to me, her expression raw and unguarded. "Eva, can I confide in you about something?" Her voice was hushed, almost lost in the ocean breeze.

"Of course," I said, my heart clenching at the vulnerability in her eyes.

"It's Allen, my boyfriend. Dante's forbidden me from seeing him. He's convinced Allen's tangled up in some mob bullshit. That's why he's not here this weekend." She met my gaze head-on. "Sometimes, I feel like I'm suffocating. Like my family's expectations are a goddamn straight-jacket, and I'll never break free."

I reached out, my hand covering hers, offering solace through touch. "Sofia, you're a force of nature. So much passion and fire burns inside you. Don't let anyone kill that flame, you hear me?"

She smiled, unshed tears glittering in her eyes. "Thank you, Eva. I'm so glad you're here."

Guilt churned in my gut as we guided our horses back to the mansion, warring with the warmth of Sofia's friendship. She had bared her soul to me and entrusted me with her deepest fears and insecurities, and I was betraying that trust with every breath, exploiting her for intel on her brother's operation.

We returned to the stables, and I dismounted from the horse with a heavy heart.

"You alright?" Sofia asked, her eyes concerned as she handed over the reins to a groom.

"Y-yeah," I stammered, "Just a bit sore from the ride." Liar, Natalia, liar.

Sofia laughed, "Join the club," she said, rubbing her backside. "We should probably get back inside before Dante sends out a search party." She winked at me before turning away. "I'm glad we did this today."

"Me too," I said genuinely.

Sofia and I entered the house's foyer, and I forced a smile, determined not to let my inner turmoil show. "That was wonderful, Sofia. Thank you for sharing this with me."

She beamed, her eyes sparkling with happiness. "I'm so glad you enjoyed it, Eva." She paused, her head tilting to the side. "You know, I feel like I can be myself around you. It's...refreshing."

The words hit me hard, and I had to fight the urge to flinch. "I feel the same way," I said, my voice soft and sincere. "You're a wonderful person, Sofia. Never forget that."

She smiled, reaching out to squeeze my hand, and I had to resist the overwhelming urge to pull away. "Well, I'm going to go freshen up for dinner. Feel free to explore the grounds a bit more if you'd like. I'll see you in a bit!"

As she bounded up the stairs, I watched her go, my

heart heavy with conflicting emotions. Part of me wanted to call out, confess it all, and beg for her forgiveness. But I knew I couldn't. The mission came first, no matter the personal cost.

With a resigned sigh, I turned and headed outside, my feet carrying me towards the stables again. I needed a moment of solace to clear my head and regain my focus.

The familiar scent of horses enveloped me as I stepped into the cool, shadowy interior of the barn. I wandered the aisles, trailing my fingers along the smooth wood of the stalls, my gaze drawn to the powerful, graceful creatures within.

"Couldn't stay away, babe?"

I whirled around, my heart drumming a staccato beat, only to find Dante leaning against the doorframe with a crooked smile. "Dante," I breathed, cursing how my pulse quickened at seeing him. "I, uh, was just..."

"Enjoying the view?" he interrupted, pushing himself off the frame and strolling towards me. "Can't say I blame you. These horses are something else, aren't they?"

I nodded, forcing myself to meet his gaze. "They're magnificent. Your family has an incredible estate."

Dante's eyes darkened, a flash of something unreadable passing across his features. "That they do," he said, his voice rough. "Though I can't say I'm always a fan of the company that comes with it."

I tilted my head, intrigued despite myself. "What do you mean?"

He let out a humorless chuckle, running a hand

through his hair. "My old man, for one. He can be...a real piece of work. And his soldiers - they're not exactly the kind of people I'd invite over for a barbecue, you know?"

I forced myself to remain calm, to play the part of the curious, sympathetic lover. "I can imagine it must have been difficult growing up in that environment."

Dante's gaze searched mine, and I saw vulnerability in his eyes for a moment. "It was," he admitted, his voice barely above a whisper. "But I've learned to play the game, to keep my head down and my priorities straight."

I took a step closer, my hand reaching out to rest on his arm. "And what are your priorities, Dante?"

He stared down at my hand, his face unreadable. "Family," he said finally, his voice gruff. "Protecting the ones I love, no matter the cost."

I felt a pang as I saw a glimpse of the man beneath the cartel prince facade.

"That's admirable," I said, gently squeezing his arm. "Not many people would be willing to make that kind of sacrifice."

Dante let out a humorless laugh. "You have no idea." He paused, his eyes searching mine. "But enough about me. What about you, Eva? What are your priorities?"

The question caught me off guard, and I felt my carefully constructed mask begin to slip. "I, uh..." I stammered, cursing myself for my lack of composure.

Dante's lips morphed into a small, knowing smile. "Don't worry, babe. I'm not looking for some big, dramatic declaration." He reached up, his fingers gently tracing the line of my jaw. "I just want to know you. The real you, not this polished, perfect version you show the rest of the world."

"Dante, I..." I trailed off, unsure of what to say. How could I possibly act real for Dante?

"Shh," he said, his thumb brushing across my lower lip. "It's okay. You don't have to say anything." His gaze darkened, the air between us crackling with undeniable tension. "Just let me in, Eva. Let me see you."

Before I could react, his mouth was on mine, his kiss searing and possessive.

I melted into his embrace, my hands fisting in the front of his shirt as I returned his kiss with a fervor that surprised even me. Everything else faded away - the mission, the lies, the guilt. All that mattered was Dante and how he made me feel alive in a way I hadn't experienced in years.

When we finally broke apart, both of us panting, I knew I was in far deeper than I ever could have imagined. Dante Reyes had wormed his way under my skin, past my defenses, and into the very core of me. And I had no idea how I would find the strength to pull myself back out.

"We should probably head back to the house," I managed. "Dinner will be served soon."

Dante's hand found mine, and our fingers intertwined, fitting together perfectly. As we walked back to the house, the gravel path crunching beneath our feet, I marveled at how my skin tingled at his touch, a silent testament to his power over me.

SIXTEEN

DANTE

I stood in front of the mirror, adjusting my tie with more precision than was necessary. My mind kept drifting back to the stolen moments with Eva in the stables. The way her body molded perfectly against mine, the taste of her lips, the soft sighs that escaped her as our kisses deepened... it was all I could think about. A heady rush of desire coursed through me at the memories.

I ran a hand through my hair, attempting to regain my composure. This was absurd. I was Dante Reyes, a man known for his ironclad self-control and focus. And yet, here I was, utterly captivated by a woman I barely knew.

A sharp rap on the door snapped me out of my reverie. "Come in," I called out, steeling myself and giving my appearance one last critical once-over.

The door opened, and my sister, Sofia, breezed in, her face lit up with a radiant smile. "Dante, are you ready for dinner? You won't believe the fantastic afternoon Eva and I had riding horses!"

My heart twisted at the bitter tang of jealousy as I imagined Eva enjoying herself without me. "Oh, really?" I forced a casual tone, attempting to conceal my interest. "Do tell, sis."

Sofia enthusiastically launched into a play-by-play of their horseback-riding adventure, her hands gesturing vividly as she spoke. She described the breathtaking scenery, the sense of freedom they felt riding across the open fields, and how Eva had quickly overcome her initial nervousness.

"She's incredible, Dante," Sofia gushed, her eyes sparkling with excitement. "I can already tell we're going to be best friends."

As Sofia rambled on, my mind took off, galloping into a deliciously naughty daydream. I pictured Eva and me cantering through the trails, her hair whipping in the breeze like a damn banner of lust. We'd discover some secret clearing, just the two of us, and that's when I'd make my move. I'd yank her off the horse and have my wicked way with her, my fingers exploring every inch of her delectable body.

Man, I'd take my sweet time undressing her, teasing her like a fucking master of foreplay. I'd kiss and nibble my way down her neck, her breasts, and her stomach until she was a quivering mess. And then... then I'd dive in. I'd taste her like she was a goddamn ice cream cone on a sweltering day, savoring every inch of her silky skin.

She'd be moaning, begging for more, and I'd give it to her.

I'd slam her against a tree or lay her down on the soft grass. Either way, I'd be inside her, our bodies grinding like they were made for each other, losing ourselves in a frenzy, our moans drowned out by the ocean waves as we fucked like animals in heat, our passion as old as time itself.

I was snapped out of my daydream by the shrill ringing of my phone, interrupting my X-rated thoughts. I lunged for the device, nearly knocking over a stack of papers in the process. Clearing my throat, I answered, striving for a professional tone.

"Dante here," I said, my voice edged with irritation at the interruption.

"Boss, it's Marco," came the familiar gravelly voice. "We've got a fucking situation. It's Raul."

Fuck. I didn't have time for more of Raul's bullshit. Shooting an apologetic look at Sofia, I said, "Duty calls, sis. Sorry, but I need to handle this."

She rolled her eyes good-naturedly and stood up. "Fine. I'll catch up with you later." With a playful wave, she strolled out of my room.

I turned my attention back to Marco, my voice clipped. "What's the issue now?"

"The fifty kilos weren't at the drop point, boss. That son of a bitch Raul must be trying to renegotiate our deal again." Marco's voice was tight with frustration.

A surge of anger coursed through me, chasing away the last remnants of my desire-fueled haze. "The hell he thinks he's doing? We had a clear agreement with those Colombians."

"I know, Dante. But the coke wasn't there. Raul's playing games." Marco's tone was weary, reflecting the weight of our shared frustration.

I clenched my jaw, fighting the urge to smash something. That greedy Colombian bastard was pushing us, testing our limits. "And the payment we made? Gone too?"

"All of it, boss," Marco sighed. "What's your call?"

I began pacing the length of my room. There was only one way to handle this. Raul needed to be put in his place, once and for all.

"I'm coming back to Miami," I growled, my voice laced with determination. "Let's pay Raul a visit and teach him some manners."

Marco didn't argue. He knew better than to try and change my mind once it was set. "Understood, boss. I'll make the necessary arrangements."

I ended the call, my finger hovering over the 'end' button a moment longer than necessary, my jaw clenched so tight it throbbed. This wasn't just about money or power; it was about respect. I'd be damned if I let some cocky Colombian punk like Raul Moreno disrespect me and the Reyes name.

It was time to remind that lowlife exactly who he was dealing with.

THE ESCALADE TORE through the streets, my knuckles white as I gripped the steering wheel, anger coursing through me.

"Easy, Dante," Marco cautioned from the passenger seat, his voice a rumble. "We need to keep our heads straight, man."

I shot him a withering glare, my jaw clenched tight. "That snake Raul is trying to play us, Marco. I just know it."

Marco nodded, a grim look on his face. "I hear you, boss. But we have to be smart about this. Charging in half-cocked ain't going to do us any favors."

I knew he was right, but the rage burning inside me was damn near blinding.

When we arrived at the warehouse for the meeting, I expected a heavy confrontation with Raul over the missing shipment. I hadn't anticipated that Raul would insist he'd already handed over the product to one of my men.

"Dante, I swear on my mother's grave, I gave the shipment to your guy," Raul said, his voice steady despite the sweat beading on his brow.

At first, I thought he was full of shit, trying to weasel his way out of our deal with some lame excuse. I stepped closer, my eyes narrowing as I searched his face for any sign of deceit. "You expect me to believe that? You think I'm some fool, Raul?"

Raul held up his hands. "I'm telling you the truth, Dante. I wouldn't dare cross you. This isn't on me."

The more he spoke, the more it became clear that we

had been played—and Javier Cruz was the only one with the audacity and resources to pull off such a daring scheme.

"Cruz," I spat, the name leaving a bitter taste in my mouth. "That sneaky bastard."

Marco's eyes widened as realization dawned on him. "He must have someone on the inside who knew our protocols and had access to our credentials."

That arrogant prick had infiltrated my crew. He must have impersonated one of my men to take possession of the shipment from Raul. It was a calculated move designed to sow discord between us and our Colombian suppliers while lining Cruz's pockets with primo products.

I clenched my fists, the rage building inside me like a volcano ready to erupt. "I'm going to get to the bottom of this," I growled. "And when I do, Cruz is going to pay for this. That's a promise."

There was no frickin' way I'd let my old man's order to leave Cruz alone stand any longer. But I had to play this smart. Barging into Cruz's turf without a solid game plan would be too dangerous. But first, I would get Papi to back the hell off and let me off the leash.

As I raced down the highway toward Palm Beach, my mind churned with the revelations of Cruz's betrayal. The bastard had stolen from us, and now he was hiding behind my father's protection. It didn't make sense. Why would Papi shield a rival like Cruz?

An hour later, I pulled the Escalade into the mansion's driveway, slamming it into park with a satisfying jolt. The tires kicked up a rooster tail of gravel as I stormed across the courtyard, my strides long and purposeful.

Inside, I flung open the study doors, scanning the room for any sign of my father. But it was empty, the silence broken only by the ticking of the antique grandfather clock in the corner.

"Where the hell is he?" I growled to no one in particular.

"Dante?"

I spun at the sound of my mother's voice. Isabella Reyes stood in the doorway, her eyes wide with concern as she took in my disheveled appearance.

"Where's Papi?" I demanded, my tone clipped and harsh. "I need to speak with him. Now."

My mother's brow furrowed, her lips pursing into a tight line. "Your father had some business," she said, calm but firm. "He won't be back until tomorrow."

I let out a frustrated growl, raking a hand through my hair. Of course, the old man would be conveniently absent when shit hit the fan. Typical fucking power move, leaving me to deal with the fallout on my own.

"What's going on, mijo?" my mother asked, her tone gentler now as she approached me. "Talk to me."

I hesitated momentarily, considering whether to burden her with the details. But in the end, I knew better not to. "Nothing I can't handle, Mami."

She regarded me for a long moment, her gaze searching mine. Finally, she gave a curt nod. "Do what you need to do, mijo," she said, resolute. "But be careful."

I pulled her into an embrace, drawing strength from her unwavering support. "I will, Mami. I promise."

With a final squeeze, I released her and strode from the father's study.

Exhausted and frustrated, I shut myself in my room, struggling to rein in my emotions. I grabbed a whisky glass and filled it with enough Macallan to make the damn bottle weep.

I drowned half of it in one gulp and could almost think straight again.

A knock on the door made me tense. My hand instinctively moved to the small of my back, where my sidearm rested in its holster. "Who is it?" I barked.

"It's me, Dante." The soft, melodic tones of Eva's voice drifted through the door, instantly sparking a different kind of fire within me.

I wrenched the door open to find her standing there, a vision of temptation in a flowing, almost see-through dress, living little to the imagination. Her dark hair tumbled in glossy waves over her shoulders, framing a face that Michelangelo could have sculpted.

"Eva," I breathed, my voice husky.

She favored me with a slow, sultry smile that threatened my self-control. "I heard voices. I figured you were back," she said, her eyes roaming over me in a way that made my skin prickle with awareness. "I wanted to make sure everything was alright."

I studied her for a moment, but as always, Eva was an enigma, her face giving nothing away.

"Everything's fine," I lied, forcing a casual shrug. "Just some business I had to take care of."

As I let her inside and closed the door, I could see the curiosity burning in her fathomless eyes. "Business, hmm?"

I barked out a harsh laugh, shaking my head. "Yeah, baby. Just some bullshit with a rival crew. Nothing I can't handle."

Eva took a step closer, her body heat radiating off her in waves that had me fighting the urge to pull her flush against me. "You seem tense, Dante," she purred, her fingers trailing along the taut muscles of my forearm. "Maybe I can help you... relax."

Christ, the way she said that last word in a lustful caress that promised all manner of delicious sins. I felt my cock stir, straining against the confines of my pants as desire coiled hot and heavy in my gut.

"Is that so?" I growled, my gaze dropping to those full, tempting lips. "And what exactly did you have in mind to help me relax, Eva?"

She leaned in closer, her breath a warm whisper against my skin. "Oh, I have all sorts of ways," she said, her fingers tracing a slow, teasing path up my arm. "Ways that would make you forget all about your... business troubles."

I groaned, my resolve crumbling like a sandcastle in the tide. Grabbing her by the waist, I hauled her against me, our bodies melding together in a perfect, scorching fit.

"You're playing a dangerous game, Eva," I rasped, my mouth hovering a hairs breadth from hers. "But fuck, I can't resist you."

A wicked smile played upon her lips, her eyes sparkling with desire. "Then don't," she breathed, and then she was kissing me, her mouth hot and demanding against mine, as her fingers expertly unbuttoned my pants, freeing my cock.

"Fuuuck," I groaned as she dropped to her knees before me, her hands planted on my thighs. "You're something else, you know that?"

Her eyes sparkled with mischief as she looked up at me, her lips curving into a sultry smile. "I know," she said, her tongue peeking out to lick her lower lip. "And I think you'll enjoy this."

With that, she leaned in, her lips wrapping around the head of my cock like the filthy angel she was, her tongue swirling around the sensitive tip. I hissed, my hips jerking as her mouth engulfed me, the sensations threatening to overload my brain.

Eva went to town, sucking, licking, and teasing like a pro. Her hands gripped my thighs, her fingers digging into the muscles as she took me deeper into her throat. Her tongue swirled and teased, her cheeks hollowing as she sucked me like she hadn't eaten in days. Groaning, I tangled my hands in her hair, guiding her head as I thrust gently into her mouth.

"Such a good girl," I growled, my hips picking up the pace as she devoured me. "Take it all, Eva. Show me what a dirty little cock whore you are."

Her only response was a throaty moan as she took me deeper. I could feel the head of my cock bumping against the back of her throat, and I knew she was taking me to the limit, making me beg for more. The sounds of her little whimpers drove me to the edge of sanity.

My balls tightened, the coil of pleasure winding tighter as I felt my orgasm approaching like a freight train. "Eva, baby," I rasped, my hips stuttering as I tried to hold off the inevitable. "I'm gonna come."

She moaned, the vibrations shooting straight to my cock as she hollowed her cheeks and went down on me one last time, her nose buried in my trimmed pubes. That was it. With a harsh groan, I gripped the back of her head, my hips slamming forward as I emptied myself into her mouth. Rope after rope of hot cum coated her throat, and she swallowed greedily, milking me dry with a soft hum of satisfaction.

I collapsed against the door, panting like crazy. Eva looked up at me with those smoldering eyes, a string of cum connecting her lips to my softening cock.

"Well, I think that did the trick," she purred, her eyes dancing with amusement and something more.

I barked out a laugh, feeling the tension coiled so tightly in my body finally begin to ease.

I gently lifted her and kissed her neck. I was just getting started.

SEVENTEEN
NATALIA

My jaw was aching after giving Dante the hottest blowjob ever, but as his mouth trailed hot kisses down my neck, sending electric shocks to my throbbing core, I couldn't give a damn about a bit of jaw pain.

I arched into him, my hands clawing at his hair, silently begging for more. His fingers found my zipper in my back, dragging it down with a maddening slowness that had me whimpering like a bitch in heat. My dress fell to the floor, leaving me in nothing but my skimpy lingerie and fuck-me heels.

"Goddamn, you're a masterpiece," he growled, his eyes raking over me like he wanted to devour me whole. The raw, animalistic hunger in his gaze made me feel like the sexiest woman alive. I grabbed him, ripping at his shirt, desperate to feel his bare skin against mine. He let out a low, rumbling chuckle that vibrated through my entire being and obliged, revealing the chiseled planes of his chest and abs.

Dante's hands were like fire on my skin, sending shivers of need racing through me as he expertly undressed me. His lips trailed a path down my neck, his teeth nipping at my sensitive flesh, and I arched into him, moaning his name. This man had a hold on me, and I couldn't escape. Frankly, I didn't want to.

He effortlessly pinned me against the wall, my bra dangling from one finger like a trophy. Fuck me, this guy's got some hidden magic talent!

With each flick of his tongue, Dante's lips danced over my hard nipples. I damn near blacked out and would've slid to the floor in a quivering puddle if it weren't for his vice-like grip.

"Dante, I want your cock!" I panted, digging my nails into those rock-hard shoulders of his. A dark, dangerous chuckle escaped his lips, and he just smirked.

"All in good time, sweetheart," he growled, then did the unthinkable. He dropped to his knees, yanking down my panties with one swift motion.

"First, I have to return your little favor," he said, and before I could even form a witty comeback, his warm, wet mouth was on me, lapping at my folds like a man possessed.

"Fuck, Dante, you animal!" I screamed, my back arching against the wall. He was like a goddamn sex-crazed lion, and I was his juicy piece of prey.

"Do you like that, kitten?" he purred, grazing his teeth against my swollen clit.

"Yes! Fuck, yes, more!" I mewled. "Dante," I panted, my voice a desperate whimper. "I need you now."

He chuckled low and deep, the vibrations sending shivers. "My pleasure, mi reina." His hands slid down my hips, gripping my ass roughly as he hoisted me upward. My legs wrapped around his waist without a second thought, locking me in place as he positioned himself at my entrance.

"Are you ready?" he breathed, the heat of his arousal infusing every syllable.

"Damn, <u>Dante</u>," I gasped, my back arching into him as he teased my entrance with the swollen head of his massive, throbbing cock. "I can't wait any longer."

"So impatient, mi reina," he purred, his voice dripping with desire before he plunged into me in one deep, relentless thrust.

White-hot pleasure ripped through me as if I were being cleaved in two - in the most delicious way imaginable. His thick, hard cock filled me to the core, making my toes curl and my vision blur. The wall beneath us vibrated with our frenzied movements, our ravenous moans reverberating off the walls. He was everywhere at once, inside and out, claiming every inch of me as his own.

"Dios mío," he growled against my ear as our bodies collided feverishly. "It feels so fucking good the way your cunt clenches around my cock."

I clung to him, my nails raking down his back as we lost

ourselves in the age-old dance of pleasure and release. Dante's muscular body pressed against mine, his skin slick with sweat as he moved within me. Each thrust sent waves of ecstasy coursing through my veins, and I couldn't help but cry out, my voice mingling with his guttural moans.

"Eva," he breathed, his lips brushing against my ear. "You're incredible."

I responded by capturing his mouth in a searing kiss, pouring all my passion and desire into the act. The world around us faded into nothingness, leaving only the two of us and the connection that transcended the physical realm. As we both came simultaneously, I knew that this was more than just sex; it was a merging of souls, a surrender to the magnetic pull that had drawn us together from the very beginning.

Afterward, as we lay tangled in each other's arms, the familiar pang of guilt was nagging at me. My mission, my whole reason for being here, popped into my head. I was tasked with taking down the very guy who had just made me feel more alive than anyone else ever had. As Dante's breathing steadied and his fingers trailed lazily on my back, I started questioning everything I thought I knew.

"What are you thinking about?" Dante said, his fingers still dancing along my spine.

I hesitated, unsure of how to put my thoughts into words. "I... I'm just trying to make sense of all this," I admitted. "Of us."

He propped himself up on one elbow, his blue eyes searching mine. "What do you mean?"

Could a man like Dante Reyes indeed be the monster I had been led to believe? Or was there more to him than his family's criminal empire suggested?

I didn't have the answers; truth be told, I wasn't sure I wanted them. All I knew was that I was in much deeper than I ever intended.

"Nothing," I said, forcing a smile. "Just basking in the moment."

Dante grinned. "Then let's keep basking."

I snuggled closer, breathing in his scent. My lips brushed against his chest as I spoke, my voice a soft murmur. "I sure hope that got your mind off your Javier Cruz problems."

The words were out of my mouth before I could stop them, and I felt Dante's body go rigid beneath me. His fingers stilled on my skin, and I could sense the tension radiating from him.

Shit. Eva Morales wouldn't know about Dante's problems with Javier Cruz.

Dante's hand slid up my back, his fingers tangling in my hair as he tilted my face to meet his gaze. His blue eyes were intense, searching mine for answers I wasn't sure I could give. "I never told you about Javier Cruz, querida." His voice had a dangerous edge to it.

"I- I overheard your phone call." I fumbled for an explanation, hating the lie even as it tumbled out. "I just assumed."

Dante's touch on my skin raised gooseflesh. "People who assume, angel," he whispered, quoting an old adage, "they make an ass out of u and me." His eyes darkened as Dante moved his hand further down. "I'm afraid I'll have to punish you now."

I shivered as his hand cupped my ass. The words hung in the air, a mix of warning and desire, the look in his eyes promising a storm.

"Oh?" I purred, arching my back ever so slightly. "And how exactly do you plan on punishing me, Mr. Reyes?"

Dante's grin was nothing short of wicked as he flipped me onto my stomach, pinning my wrists above my head with one hand while his other hand trailed down my back. "Let me show you," he growled, his voice husky with need.

The first smack landed on my left cheek, a stinging sensation that bloomed into heat. A moan escaped my lips as Dante's hand connected with my skin, again and again, alternating between my cheeks. Each smack was just enough to leave a tingle without crossing the line into painful territory. Somehow, he knew exactly how much I could take – and how much I secretly craved.

"You like that, huh?" he teased, running his fingers over the pinkening skin before delivering another playful smack.

"Mmm," I moaned into the sheets, arching my hips back against him in invitation. "More."

Dante chuckled darkly before obliging me, upping the intensity just enough to leave me gasping. Heat pooled between my thighs as he continued to spank and caress me in equal measure, driving me closer to the edge with each swat of his hand on my sensitive flesh.

"You're so wet for this," he growled.

"God, Dante," I panted, my hips grinding against the mattress as the heat between my legs grew more insistent with each smack. "I... I can't... I'm so close."

His hand stilled for a moment, his breath hot in my ear. "Tell me what you want, Eva."

"I want... I want you," I moaned, my cheeks flushing as I admitted my desire for him.

With a growl of approval, Dante's hand slid between my thighs, his fingers finding the slick folds of my pussy. He teased me mercilessly, circling around my clit before dipping a finger inside me just enough to make me whimper.

"Say it again," he demanded, his voice rough with need. "Tell me who you belong to."

"You," I gasped out. "I'm yours, Dante."

That was all it took. With a groan of satisfaction, Dante plunged two fingers inside me while his other hand continued to spank and caress my ass in time with his thrusts. The sensations were almost too much to bear as the pleasure built within me like a tidal wave crashing onto the shore.

"That's it," he encouraged, his breathing ragged in my ear. "Come for me, mi reina."

The orgasm hit me as I cried out Dante's name into the pillow below me. My entire body shook with the force of it as wave after wave of ecstasy washed over me.

As the intensity of my release subsided, Dante wrapped his arm around me, pulling me closer to his chest as he nuzzled my neck with his nose. "Mmm... Mi carino," he mumbled sleepily in my ear, his even breathing soon filling the room.

I lay there for a moment, my heart still pounding as I processed the night's events. Javier Cruz, the spanking, and now here we were – tangled together in a mess of sheets and each other's limbs. A small smile crept onto my lips as I traced the tattoos on Dante's bicep absently. How had my life come to this?

Slowly, exhaustion crept up on me, too, lulling me into a hazy state between wakefulness and sleep. My last thought before drifting off was how much I hated myself for loving this life – the danger, the adrenaline rushes, and most of all... him.

I WOKE UP WITH A START. For a moment, I was unsure of my surroundings. Then the memories of the previous night came rushing back – the heated passion, the tangled sheets, Dante's body against mine—my sore ass.

I rolled over, expecting to find him beside me, but the space was empty, the sheets cool to the touch. It was Sunday morning, and despite it still being the weekend, he must have slipped out early, no doubt attending to the myriad responsibilities of running a criminal empire. Those kinds of people don't take time off.

I snuck out of his room, my bare feet silent against the plush carpet of the hallway as I made my way to the guest room. Once inside, I locked the door behind me and quickly showered. My mind was a whirlwind of conflicting emotions, but I pushed those thoughts aside. I couldn't afford to dwell on them now.

I dressed in comfortable travel clothes, a casual sundress and sandals. With my suitcase in hand, I took one last look around the opulent guest room and headed downstairs to bid farewell to the Reyes family.

Sofia was already up, and the sight of her with her coffee cup paused midway to her lips would have been comical under different circumstances. Her disappointment at my imminent departure was clear, her eyes wide and mournful like a kicked puppy.

"You can't leave so soon," she protested, pouting as she returned her cup to the saucer. "We haven't even had a chance to plan our next girls' day out."

I offered her a small, apologetic smile as I sat opposite her at the breakfast bar. "I'm sorry, Sofia," I said, my tone sincere. "Work calls."

She sighed dramatically but nodded in understanding. "I get it, duty and all that," she said, her playful smile returning. "But promise we'll get together this week, Eva."

"It's a date," I assured her, mirroring her smile. "I'll text you as soon as I'm back in the city."

With a last round of hugs and well-wishes from Sofia, I found myself back in my car, the Reyes estate receding in my rearview mirror as I drove back to Miami. The further away I got, the tighter the knot of anxiety in my stomach grew.

I couldn't stop replaying the scene from last night, Dante's piercing gaze as he questioned my knowledge of Javier Cruz. I had managed to deflect his suspicion—for now—but deep down, I knew the clock was ticking on my cover.

It was past noon when I unlocked the door to Eva's apartment. I dropped my bag and fired up my laptop, taking a deep breath as the secure video link established our connection.

"Ramirez," Agent Morrow's gruff voice greeted me, his grizzled face filling the screen with its usual stern look on his face. "How'd it go?"

The debriefing was thorough as I relayed the details of my weekend at the Reyes compound. I outlined the layout of the house, the security measures, and the interactions between Dante and his family, painting a vivid picture for my handler.

But the sensitive information I had uncovered in Ricardo's study had Morrow sitting up a little straighter in his chair, his eyes narrowing as he processed the gravity of my discovery. "A shame you got interrupted before you could photograph it all, but you did good, Natalia," he said, giving me a curt nod of approval.

As I sent the photos through our secure server, Morrow's eyes roamed over the documents I had managed to capture in Ricardo's office.

"What do they mean?" I asked, leaning forward in anticipation. "Can they help us bring down their operation?"

He held up a hand, his gaze still locked onto the screen as he navigated through the images, his brow furrowing in concentration. "These are promising," he said, his tone carefully measured. "But it's not enough yet. We need more concrete evidence. This is a good start, though."

"And what if my cover gets blown before I find that proof? What if Dante...?"

Morrow's gaze snapped up to meet mine, the hardened edge in his eyes softening just enough to offer me a crumb of reassurance. "You're a good agent, Natalia," he said firmly, his voice steady and confident. "You're smart, resourceful, and most importantly, you've got instincts that money can't buy."

He paused, his gaze never wavering from mine. "You've got a good thing going with Eva's character. It's believable, it's alluring, and it's got Dante's attention. Keep that up, and keep him close. Just remember—"

"Don't get too close," I finished for him with a weary sigh, repeating the mantra that had been drilled into me since day one of my training. But it was easier said than done, especially when dealing with Dante Reyes.

Morrow nodded, giving me a stern look of warning. "Exactly. Keep your head on straight, and keep us in the loop with anything—and I mean anything that could be even remotely useful. If you feel like things are getting too hot, pull back and regroup."

I nodded in understanding as I thought about the implications of this latest development. "Yes, sir. I won't let you down."

After that, the conversation shifted to more mundane matters - updates on the team, check-ins on my safety and well-being, and reminders of protocol and procedure.

As the video link went dark, I slumped back in my chair, releasing a slow, steadying breath. The path ahead was fraught with danger, pitfalls, and temptations at every turn.

But at least my cover was still safe.

EIGHTEEN
DANTE

SINKING BACK AGAINST THE PLUSH RED VELVET couch, I narrowed my eyes as I scrutinized the dancers rehearsing on the small stage. Something was off with their timing, their movements lacking the seamless precision I demanded in my club.

"Again, from the top," I barked, the sharp edge of my voice cutting through the thumping bassline. "I want to see some real fire, ladies. This is Diablo, not some rinky-dink strip joint off the interstate." I took a sip of my whisky and plunked the glass down hard.

The dancers exchanged glances but obediently reset their positions and began the routine anew. As the music swelled, their bodies moved in tandem, hips swaying, muscles rippling beneath glistening skin.

I nodded, satisfied that the message had been received. Perfection was the minimum expectation here – anything less was unacceptable.

My phone buzzed in my pocket, the vibration jolting me from my intense focus. A glance at the screen revealed Sofia's name and smiling face.

"What is it, sis?" I answered gruffly, my attention still divided between her call and the performance unfolding before me.

"Dante!" Her voice, bright and cheerful as ever, pierced through my darkening mood. "You, Eva, Allen, and I—dinner on Friday. There's a new fusion place on Ocean Drive I'm eager to try."

Hearing Allen's name, an image of his smarmy face flashed before me, instantly grating on my nerves. That guy was the epitome of a pompous ass, oozing an air of entitlement. The very definition of a jerk, the type I made it a point to avoid.

"I thought I made it clear to stay away from him. He's nothing but trouble." My voice held an edge, a warning.

I could almost feel her steeling herself over the phone. "I don't care, Dante. Eva encouraged me to be more assertive. So, that's what I'm doing. Standing my ground with you and Allen."

I opened my mouth to protest, but the words died on my lips as a stray movement on stage caught my attention. One of the dancers, a willowy blonde with endless legs, had abandoned the routine and was now making her way toward me, her hips swaying hypnotically.

"What the–" I sputtered, my phone nearly slipping from my suddenly nerveless fingers as the dancer planted her topless body on my lap, her large breasts mere inches from my face.

"Dante?" Sofia's voice crackled through the speaker, tinny and distant. "Are you still there?"

The dancer smirked, her tongue darting out to trace the shell of my ear as she undulated against me, her movements slow and sinuous. I bit back a groan as I desperately tried to regain control of the situation.

"Yeah, uh... dinner sounds great, Sof," I managed to choke out, my voice strained. "Count us in."

I barely registered Sofia's delighted response before ending the call, tossing the phone aside as I surrendered to the dancer's sensual assault. My hands found her hips, guiding her motions as she rolled and gyrated in my lap, her fingers tangling in my hair.

The rehearsal was supposed to be an opportunity to fine-tune our performances for the club. But this dancer changed everything when she latched onto the sensitive spot below my ear. This was so very crossed-lines territory.

As the song ended, reality smacked me in the face, and gently, I pushed her off my lap, my better judgment returning. I croaked out my thanks as she practically purred in disappointment. With a sultry saunter, she walked away, hips swaying back to the stage, leaving me to breathe and regroup.

I couldn't deny the rush of pure, carnal lust that had surged through me during our little impromptu lap dance, but I had Eva on my mind – constantly.

Eva's face was seared into my brain, those smoldering eyes and full lips promising untold pleasures. But what about the mystery surrounding her, the secrets I knew she was keeping?

That little slip-up the other night, her casual reference to my business with Javier Cruz, caught my attention, and I was already planning to do something about it.

The shrill ringing of my phone cut through the thumping bass, shattering my reverie. I snatched it up, not even glancing at the caller ID before barking a curt, "Yeah?"

"Hey, Boss." Marco's gruff voice crackled through the line. "We're still good for our little surveillance op tomorrow?"

A slow grin spread across my face. The prospect of finally getting answers about the woman consuming my thoughts lit a fire inside me.

"Absolutely," I said, leaning back in my chair as I motioned for the dancers to take five. "Pick me up in the morning."

I ended the call and leaned back in my chair. Part of me felt like a sleazebag, putting my girlfriend under such intense scrutiny. But a bigger part of me, the part that had been raised in the cartel world, knew this was necessary.

Trust was a luxury I couldn't afford, not when there were so many unanswered questions surrounding Eva. And if she was somehow involved with Javier Cruz in a scheme against me, against my family... well, let's just say that would be a shame.

A sharp whistle from the stage jolted me from my thoughts. The dancers had reassembled, their bodies poised and ready to continue the rehearsal.

"Alright, ladies," I called out, pushing aside my concerns. "Let's take it from the top. And this time, I want to see some heat."

———————

THE TINTED windows of the Escalade provided a one-way mirror into the glitzy, upscale side of Miami's streets. My eyes narrowed as I watched Eva slip out of a fancy apartment complex, wearing a T-shirt and jeans. It was not what I'd expected after always seeing her in heels and dresses, but maybe it was her work clothes.

I ducked in the seat, signaling Marco to start the engine as she emerged.

"What do you make of it?" Marco asked, his gruff voice slicing through the tense silence.

I shook my head slowly, my jaw clenched. "I don't know, man. But something about Eva just ain't sitting right with me."

We followed discreetly as Eva's sleek Porsche merged onto the highway towards the city's heart.

"What's the plan here, Dante?" Marco's voice pulled me from my thoughts. "We can't just tail her forever. Eventually, she's gonna catch on."

I exhaled slowly, raking a hand through my hair. He was right, of course. But confronting Eva head-on, demanding answers, and showing my hand too early was not an option. There had to be a more discreet way to find some answers.

"Let's go back and check out that apartment she left. I have a hunch about that place."

Marco nodded and turned the car around.

We stopped out front and waited a few minutes, watching her apartment windows for any movement. When we were sure nobody was inside, we made our move.

The lock on the apartment door was no match for Marco's skilled hands. He grinned at me as he showed me a tiny piece of clear tape between the door and the frame, creating a makeshift seal. Yep, something was up with Eva, alright.

Marco opened the door, and we were inside, stepping into the opulent living room.

As we moved through the rooms, it all felt a little staged—hardly any pictures or personal touches.

But it was the closet that caught my attention. It was filled with boxes stacked haphazardly on top of each other. I pulled them aside.

Hidden in the back was a large black duffel bag.

With trembling hands, I unzipped the bag. I gasped, my breath hitching in my chest as I saw what was inside. Police riot gear, heavy and black, with the word "DEA" emblazoned across the back.

Suddenly, the memories came flooding back. The raid

on the warehouse, the chaos and gunfire, and the woman I had encountered, the one I had let live—the woman in the gear.

Eva.

I felt like somebody had punched me, the air rushing out of my lungs in a strangled gasp. Everything about her, about us, had been a lie. She had infiltrated my life and my family, all in the name of bringing me down.

Rage coursed through me, hot and bitter. I searched the rest of the apartment for any shred of evidence, anything that would confirm what I already knew in my heart.

I found it in a drawer by the bed—a police badge gleaming silver in the dim light. Next to it was an ID card with her picture and real name.

Natalia Ramirez. DEA.

She looked different in this picture, but there was no doubt. Natalia and Eva were the same person. I stared at the badge, my mind reeling. How could I have been so blind, so fucking stupid? I had let her into my life, my heart, and all the while, Natalia had been plotting against me.

I thought of all the moments we had shared, the steamy encounters and hot sex. Her words and the way she looked at me made me feel like I was the only man in the world. It was all an act, a carefully crafted deception designed to confuse and make me trust her.

The worst part was that it had worked. I had fallen for

her hard and fast. I had let my guard down and allowed myself to hope for a future with her. And all the while, she had laughed at me, mocking me for my foolishness.

As the initial shock began to wear off, a new emotion took root—a cold, calculated determination. If Natalia thought she could manipulate me, she had another thing coming. It was time to turn the tables and regain control of this twisted game she had started.

A slow, predatory grin spread across my face as a plan began to take shape.

Marco's voice snapped me back to reality. "We should get going."

I nodded, and we set about erasing any sign of our intrusion, returning every item to its precise location. Marco ensured the front door looked untouched, buffing the lock and re-sealing it.

Silent as ghosts, we descended the stairs and blended into the hustle of the street outside, heading for our car. As we drove away from Eva's apartment, the weight of our discovery hung heavy in the air. Marco's eyes flicked between the road and me, concern etched across his face. I knew he was waiting for me to speak, to give some direction on how to proceed with this explosive information.

Finally, I turned to him, my voice low and serious. "Marco, what we found out today... about Eva, about her real identity as Natalia... it can't leave this car. Do you understand?"

Marco's brow furrowed, his grip tightening on the steering wheel. "Dante, man, this is big. Your father—"

"Especially not my father," I cut him off, my tone sharp. "Ricardo can't know about this. Not yet."

He shot me a skeptical look. "Are you sure about this? He's going to be pissed if he finds out we kept this from him."

I leaned back in my seat, running a hand through my hair. "I know, but trust me on this. We need to play this smart. If Ricardo finds out about Natalia being DEA, he'll have her killed without a second thought. And right now, she's our best chance at figuring out what's really going on."

Marco nodded slowly, processing my words. "So what's the plan?"

"We keep her close, feed her false information, and try to figure out who else might be involved. There's no way she's working alone on this."

"And what about you?" Marco asked, his voice tinged with concern. "I've seen how you look at her, Dante. Can you handle playing this game?"

I clenched my jaw, pushing down the surge of emotions threatening to overwhelm me. "I have to. It's the only way to protect the family and get to the bottom of this mess."

Marco was silent for a moment before speaking again. "Alright, I'm with you. But be careful, man. This is dangerous territory we're treading into."

I nodded, grateful for his loyalty. "I know. That's why I need you to have my back on this. Not a word to anyone, especially Ricardo. Promise me."

"You have my word," Marco said solemnly.

As we drove on through the Miami night, I steeled myself for the challenge ahead. The woman I thought I knew was a lie, but the game was far from over. It was time to show Natalia—and whoever else was pulling the strings —that they had severely underestimated Dante Reyes.

NINETEEN
NATALIA

I MUST'VE BEEN OUT OF MY MIND WHEN I DECIDED IT was a great idea to sneak in an afternoon of freedom. But I needed a break.

Sure, ditching my cover for a few hours was a gamble. Still, the need to reconnect with Natalia—the woman I was before the boundaries of my real self and my alter ego began to smudge—was too overwhelming. Plus, the thought of Valentina's radiant smile and upbeat vibe lifted my spirits instantly. That sunshine girl was the antidote to cure my darkness. So when she called me for a coffee date, telling me she had gossip so sinister it could only be said in person, the temptation was too strong.

I peeled off the form-fitting dress, the fabric sighing as it slipped to the floor. I kicked away the agonizing heels that had carried me through the cartel's difficult terrain.

I slipped into my trusty t-shirt and jeans, and fuck, it felt like pure bliss, the soft fabric a warm embrace from my true self that this undercover op had slowly been smothering.

As I strolled down the apartment stairs in my comfortable jeans and T-shirt, I felt liberated. But as I came out the front, my cop senses started tingling. Parked across my building was a black Escalade with tinted windows—nothing out of the ordinary—except for the fact that I'd never seen that car parked here before the entire two months I'd lived here. Now it was, and my instincts were screaming at me to pay attention.

I tried to tell myself I was being paranoid, that it was just a coincidence. But something about that car set my teeth on edge. So, I jumped in my car and did what any self-respecting DEA agent would do: I changed my route, doubling back and taking the long way to the cafe downtown.

I spotted the same Escalade a few cars behind me, but after several detours, I no longer saw it—false alarm.

When I finally arrived at the cafe, Val was already waiting for me with two cups of strong Cuban coffee and a stack of pancakes that would put any Instagram influencer to shame.

"Dios mío, I've missed this," I sighed, taking a sip of the coffee and letting the familiar taste wash over me. "How are you holding up, Val?"

She shrugged, her dark eyes watching me closely. "Better now that you're here. I've been worried sick about you, Nat. This undercover gig of yours is killing me."

I smiled at her, grateful for her concern, even as I felt a

pang of guilt. "I know, and I'm sorry. But I promise, I'm okay. This operation is just... a little intense." I wasn't quite ready to share details with Val, remembering Morrow's warning that everything had to go through him.

We spent the next few hours laughing, catching up on all the crazy things that had happened since we last saw each other. It was like old times, like nothing had changed. But, of course, everything had changed. Matt was killed, and I was deep undercover with the fucking cartel.

As we polished off the last of the pancakes, I noticed Val seemed off, like something was bothering her that she wasn't telling me.

"Hey, are you okay?" I asked, reaching across the table to squeeze her hand. "You seem..."

She hesitated, her eyes darting away from mine. "It's nothing, really."

"Talk to me, Val. What's going on?"

"I met Jason at a party, totally drunk, and he totally hit on me," Val told me, searching my face for a reaction.

"Jason?" The mention of his name hit me hard, even months later. But, I'd moved on, shoved him into a tiny box labeled "trash," and buried it deep.

"Yeah, that loser." Val rolled her eyes, shaking her head. "I swear, he's even more of a slimeball than I remembered. He was all over me like a cheap suit, and I had to practically threaten to break his arm to get him to back off."

"The very memory of that assclown makes my fists itch," I said through gritted teeth.

"Dude's a total waste," Val agreed, her eyes narrowing.

"And he's still digging himself a deeper hole, by the sounds of it."

I arched an eyebrow, curiosity getting the better of me. "Oh, yeah? What's he done now?"

"Served himself a big old slice of karma, that's what," she snorted derisively. "Turns out his little 'fling' didn't appreciate being treated like a piece of meat. Melissa dumped his sorry ass, and now he's sofa surfing, probably still trying to snake his way between some poor girl's sheets."

"Couldn't happen to a more deserving douche," I said, feeling a savage delight in his downfall. "Guess his charm offensive ran out of gas."

"Damn straight," Val laughed, taking a slug of her coffee. "Just goes to show, Nat, that you dodged a bullet there. That guy was a walking, talking disaster."

I nodded, the coffee suddenly tasting like victory. "You can say that again. Love may be blind, but I should've seen that coming. My gut was telling me to run, but no, I had to learn the hard way."

"Love?" Val scoffed. "That waste of space wasn't worth a single tear, let alone a heartbreak. He can rot in the bed he made."

Her loyalty never failed to bring a smile to my face. "You're damn right, and I'm thankful that toxicity is out of my life."

Taking another bite of the pancake, I soaked in the comfort of the food and Val's unwavering friendship. She was the sharp-tongued, honest-as-hell guardian angel on my shoulder, keeping me from stepping into the same pile of shit twice.

"Anyway, enough about that asshole." She waved her hand in dismissal, her eyes softening. "You didn't come here to talk about him. So girl, dish, any hunky guys falling for your sexy fake-ass undercover persona?"

A slow smile spread across my face as I thought of Dante. "Maybe," I teased, enjoying the playful moment.

Val's eyes widened, and she sat up straighter, her face mixed with excitement and concern. "Ooh, la la! Spill the beans, girl! Any sparks?"

I practically cackled, leaning across the table with a devilish glint in my eye. "Oh, there's sparks, alright. More like a full-blown fireworks show. But, that's all I can say for now." I shot a quick glance at my phone, the time glaring back at me like a neon sign. Crap, it was late. Better leave before playing with fire – getting caught by Dante or Sofia in this cozy cafe was a big no-no for my secret agent life.

I stood and hugged Val like it might be the last time. "Keep your ear to the ground for any Jason whispers, will ya?" I said, not quite ready to admit that our next chat could be ages away, potentially lost in the abyss of months.

The bright sunlight assaulted my eyes as I burst out of the diner. I fetched my sunglasses and scanned the street, my gaze darting from car to car, searching for any sign of the black Escalade that had set my nerves on edge.

Luckily, the street was clear, the sidewalks bustling with the usual midday crowd: no mysterious vehicles, no shadowy figures lurking in doorways. I paused momentarily, trying to calm the adrenaline coursing through my veins.

I drove back to the apartment, but instead of taking my usual route, I drove through side streets and alleys, doubling back and changing course at random intervals. It was a habit I had picked up in my early days with the DEA, a way to shake any potential tails and ensure I wasn't being followed.

After reaching my building, I took the stairs two at a time, my keys already in hand as I approached my door. A glance confirmed that the lock was undisturbed, the tiny piece of tape I had placed as a makeshift seal still intact.

I slipped inside, locking the door behind me and leaning against it heavily. My apartment was just as I had left it, with every item in its place and no sign of intrusion or disturbance. But as I scanned the familiar space, I couldn't shake the unease that had settled deep in my bones.

I collapsed onto the couch, my head falling into my hands. What was wrong with me? Why was I seeing threats around every corner, jumping at shadows like a paranoid conspiracy theorist? I had always prided myself on my level-headedness and ability to keep calm under pressure. But now, it felt like that facade was crumbling, the cracks in my armor widening with every passing day.

A nagging voice in the back of my mind whispered that this job was wearing me down and that the constant vigilance and deception were taking their toll. I had been undercover for weeks now, living and breathing the persona of Eva Morales. But with each passing day, the lines between Natalia and Eva blurred a little more, until I wasn't sure where one ended and the other began.

And then there was Dante, who had started as just another target, another steppingstone on the path to bringing down the cartel. But somewhere along the way, he had become something more—a temptation.

TWENTY

DANTE

My mind was a whirlwind of tension and anger. The name "Natalia" tasted like ash in my mouth, a stark reminder of the betrayal that had festered inside me since I discovered her real identity. Eva—or rather, Natalia Ramirez—had played me for a fool, and tonight, I intended to turn the tables.

I checked my reflection in the mirror, adjusting my tie for the umpteenth time. The man staring back at me was a portrait of calm composure, but beneath the surface, I was a mess of conflicting emotions. I was about to engage in a high-stakes game of cat and mouse, and I was determined to come out on top—or at least not make a complete ass of myself.

The drive to the restaurant was a blur, my thoughts consumed by the woman who had infiltrated my life under false pretenses. The irony wasn't lost on me. Here I was, the son of a notorious cartel leader, lamenting a lack of honesty in my personal life. If my father could see me now, he'd probably laugh himself into an early grave.

As I stepped out of my car and handed the keys to the valet, I spotted Eva—no, Natalia—waiting for me at the restaurant entrance. She looked stunning, her dark hair cascading over her shoulders in loose waves, her body hugged by a sleek red dress that left little to the imagination. For a moment, I allowed myself to appreciate her beauty, to remember the passion that flared between us. Then I reminded myself of her deception, and I plastered on my best "I'm-totally-not-onto-you" smile.

"Eva," I greeted her, my voice a mix of charm and feigned nonchalance. "I see you've dressed for the occasion. I hope you're not expecting me to behave myself tonight."

She raised an eyebrow, a hint of a smirk playing on her lips. "Behave? I didn't think that word was in your vocabulary, Dante."

I chuckled, playing along. "Oh, it's in there hiding. Right next to 'boring' and 'early night.' Two other concepts I'm not familiar with."

"Is that so?" she replied, her eyes twinkling with mischief.

I offered her my arm, feeling the warmth of her body as she pressed against me. "You know, that dress has me wondering what secrets you're hiding underneath. Any sexy lingerie I should know about?"

Eva laughed, a sound that was both musical and

dangerous. "A girl's got to have some mysteries, Dante. You'll just have to use your imagination."

"Trust me, it's working overtime," I quipped, guiding her towards the restaurant entrance. "Shall we go inside? I'm dying to see if the food here lives up to the hype. And who knows? Maybe I'll get some answers about that lingerie situation over dessert."

We entered the restaurant, a trendy new spot on Ocean Drive that my sister had been so eager to try. The hostess led us to our table, where my Sofia and her pompous boyfriend, Allen, were already seated. The sight of Allen, with his smug grin and overly styled hair, was like a splinter under my fingernail, irritating and impossible to ignore.

"Ah, the man of the hour!" Allen exclaimed, raising his glass in a mock salute. "Good to see you, Dante."

I forced a nod, and my jaw clenched tight. "Allen," I grunted, taking the seat next to Natalia. I could feel her gaze on me, assessing, maybe questioning, but I kept my attention focused on the menu in front of me, deliberately avoiding her eyes.

After we ordered food, Allen's behavior grew increasingly intolerable. He dominated the conversation, regaling us with tales of his financial prowess and material wealth, all while making lewd remarks and inappropriate gestures towards Sofia. My sister laughed, oblivious to her boyfriend's bad manners, and I felt a surge of protective anger on her behalf.

Ever the strategist, Natalia attempted to steer the

conversation toward safer waters. Still, Allen was like a dog with a bone, unable or unwilling to recognize the discomfort he was causing. Each suggestive comment, each unwanted touch, stoked the flames of my fury, and I found myself gripping my wine glass so tightly I feared it might shatter in my hand.

When Allen's attention shifted to Natalia, making a thinly veiled pass at her right in front of me, that was the last straw. I felt a red haze descend over my vision, my instincts screaming at me to defend what was mine—or at least, what he thought was mine.

"That's enough," I said. I fixed Allen with a hard stare, my hand curling into a fist beneath the table. "Show some respect."

Allen blinked at me, his brow furrowing in confusion—or perhaps it was feigned ignorance. "What's the matter, Dante?" he asked, the smirk still playing on his lips. "Can't take a little joke?"

I leaned forward, my eyes never leaving his. "This isn't a joke. Keep your hands and comments to yourself, or you'll find out exactly what I'm capable of."

A tense silence settled over the table, the atmosphere thick with hostility. Natalia touched my arm, a cool counterpoint to the rage boiling within me. "Let's just enjoy our meal," she said, her voice barely audible over the sound of my heartbeat thundering in my ears.

Allen scoffed, shaking his head in disbelief. "Jesus, Dante, lighten up. I didn't realize you were so sensitive."

Sofia interjected before I could respond, her voice shaky but firm. "Enough, both of you!"

Everybody was quiet all of a sudden, and my sister continued.

"Dante, I know you disapprove of Allen, but he's my boyfriend, so will you behave for just one night? You too, Allen."

Allen shrugged, draining the last of his wine before refilling. "Fine by me, honey, as long as your gangster brother can keep his gun in his pants."

I was almost out of my seat and in Allen's throat when, luckily, the waiter brought our food.

We all dug into the food, and as I sat there, watching Natalia and Sofia laugh and chat like they'd known each other since childhood, a part of me felt a twinge of... something. Jealousy? No, that wasn't it. It was something else, something deeper and far more unsettling.

Just a few days ago, the sight of my sister smiling and genuinely enjoying herself with her new friend would have filled me with fucking joy. But, after uncovering who Eva's truly was, it all changed.

The knowledge that everything about her was fake—her laughter, warmth, and apparent fondness for Sofia—itched under my skin like a goddamn parasite. There she was, playing the part of the perfect friend with such convincing ease that it made my blood boil.

Sofia was too trusting, too innocent to see through Natalia's deception. She had no idea that the woman she was confiding in, the woman she had invited into our lives, was an enemy working to bring us down.

But I kept my mouth shut, plastering a smile on my face as I watched the charade unfold before my eyes. I played the part of the attentive boyfriend, the protective brother, all while my mind raced with plans and strategies.

Eva—Natalia—had no idea that I was onto her. As far as she knew, her cover was still intact, her secret still safe. And I intended to keep it that way, at least for the time being.

The more she trusted me, the deeper she dug her own grave. I would give her inaccurate information and lead her down a path of my own making, all while keeping a close eye on her every move.

I watched as she charmed the waitstaff, listened attentively to Sofia's stories, and subtly deflected Allen's misogynistic behavior and insults. She was good; I had to give her that. If I hadn't discovered the truth about her, I would have been fooled into believing she was exactly who she claimed to be.

As the evening was winding down and the last dessert plates cleared away, the tension at the table had gone from my worst nightmare to something...almost not insufferable.

Natalia leaned in close. "It's not exactly bedtime for me just yet," she purred, her hand sliding along my thigh, her fingers tracing a teasing path sending a jolt of desire straight to my cock. "Maybe we could do something..."

I felt a slow, predatory grin spread across my face as I turned to meet her gaze. "Is that so?" I said, my hand covering hers, pressing her palm more firmly against the rapidly growing bulge in my pants. "And what exactly did you have in mind, querida?"

Her eyes sparkled, a playful smile tugging at the corners of her luscious lips. "Why don't you take me back to your place, and I'll show you?"

My cock twitched at her words as I imagined all the delicious ways I could make her scream my name tonight. Maybe add a bit of extra spice...as payback.

We said our goodbyes to Sofia and Allen, the latter of whom was still shooting me wary glances after our little confrontation earlier in the evening. But I didn't give a fuck. All that mattered was getting Natalia alone to my place.

The drive back to South Beach was a blur of neon lights and throbbing bass, the city's energy matching my own as I navigated the familiar streets with practiced ease. Natalia's hand rested on my thigh, her touch a brand through the fabric of my pants.

We stepped into the private elevator that would take us up to my penthouse above Club Diablo, and I could feel the anticipation building, a tangible force that hummed in the air between us. Natalia stood beside me, her eyes locked onto mine, a silent promise of the pleasure that awaited us both.

The doors slid open, revealing my home's opulent luxury. I watched Natalia's face as she took in the sleek, modern decor, the floor-to-ceiling windows offering a breathtaking view of the Miami skyline. But it was the bedroom that I was most eager to show her.

I led her through the penthouse, my hand at the small of her back, guiding her toward the room that held my most intimate secrets. The door swung open, and I watched her closely as she stepped inside, her eyes widening as she took in the sight before her.

The room was a testament to my darkest desires, a place where I could indulge in the taboo pleasures of dominance and submission, roleplaying, and bondage. The walls were lined with velvet-draped hooks, tools, and toys designed to bring my partners to the very edge of ecstasy. A massive four-poster bed dominated the center of the room, its posts equipped with sturdy restraints and its sheets a bright, enticing red.

Natalia turned to face me, her gaze filled with curiosity and desire. "So, this is where the real magic happens, huh?" she quipped, her voice a soft, sultry whisper that made my cock ache with need.

I stepped closer, crowding her against the wall, my hands on either side of her head. "You have no idea, my queen," I growled, lowering my mouth to hers in a searing kiss that left no doubt about who was in control tonight.

I could feel her body yielding to mine, her breath hitching as I ground my hips against hers, letting her feel the full extent of my arousal. I wanted her to understand what she was getting herself into tonight.

With a swift, decisive movement, I reached for the zipper of her dress, dragging it down and peeling the fabric away from her body, revealing the black lace lingerie beneath. She was a vision of hot temptation, her curves on full display, and I couldn't wait to explore every inch of her.

I led her to the bed, my hands at her waist as I lifted her onto the mattress, watching as she sank into the plush duvet, her dark hair fanning out around her head like a halo. I reached for the restraints, my fingers deftly securing her wrists and ankles, spreading her wide for my pleasure.

Natalia tugged at the restraints, a thrill of excitement flashing in her eyes as she tested her bonds. "What's the matter, querida?" I teased, my hands skimming over her body, my touch light and teasing. "Feeling a little... bound?"

She bit her lip, her gaze locked onto mine as she gave another experimental tug. "Maybe I like it," she said, her voice breathy.

I chuckled darkly, my fingers tracing the delicate lace of her bra, my thumbs circling her hardened nipples through the fabric. "Oh, I have a feeling you're going to like this a lot," I promised, reaching into a nearby drawer and withdrawing a long, slender feather.

Natalia's eyes widened as I trailed the feather along her skin, starting at her collarbone and slowly working my way down, watching goosebumps erupt. I took my time, exploring every dip and curve of her body, reveling in the way her breath caught each time the feather grazed her sensitive flesh.

By the time I reached the waistband of her panties, she

was practically squirming on the bed, her body arching towards my touch, her cheeks flushed with arousal. I could see the need in her eyes, the desperate plea for her release that she barely managed to contain.

But I wasn't done with Natalia yet. Not by a long shot.

I set the feather aside and reached for a silk blindfold, watching her face as I covered her eyes, plunging her into darkness. "Do you trust me, Eva?" I said as I leaned in close, my lips brushing against her ear.

She nodded, her breath coming in short, shallow gasps as she awaited my next move. I reached for another toy, a small, buzzing bullet vibrator that I knew would drive her wild. I pressed it against the thin fabric of her panties, grinning as she bucked against the sudden sensation.

"Dante, please," she moaned, her voice laced with need. "I need you inside me."

"Patience, mi reina." I silenced her with a kiss, my tongue delving into her mouth as I continued to tease her with the vibrator, my fingers deftly slipping beneath the side of her panties to stroke her slick, wet folds. She was soaked, her body practically vibrating with need, and I couldn't resist the urge to taste her.

I kissed down her body, my lips and tongue leaving a wet, tingling trail in their wake as I settled between her legs, my hands gripping her hips as I pulled her towards me. Pushing her panties aside, I buried my face in her pussy. I lapped at her, my tongue circling her clit, my teeth grazing the sensitive bud as I drove her higher and higher until she was teetering on the edge, her entire body trembling with the force of her impending orgasm.

And then, just when she was about to come, I pulled back, denying her the release she so desperately craved. She whimpered in frustration, her body arching off the bed, but I was merciless, my fingers and tongue working in tandem to keep her hovering on the brink of ecstasy without letting her fall over the edge.

"Please, Dante," she begged, her voice a hoarse, desperate whisper. "I need to come."

I chuckled darkly, my lips and chin glistening with her arousal. "And you will," I assured her, my voice a low, seductive purr. "But not until I say so."

I positioned myself at her entrance, the head of my cock pressing against her slick, wet heat. I looked down at her, my gaze raking over her bound, blindfolded form, and I felt a surge of raw, primal lust.

"Are you ready for me, Eva?" I growled, my hands gripping her hips as I prepared to thrust inside her.

She nodded, her lips parting on a silent moan as I pushed forward, filling her in one long, slow stroke. She felt like heaven, her tight, wet pussy gripping me like a fist, and I knew I wouldn't last long.

I set a punishing rhythm, driving into her again and again, each thrust more forceful than the last, my hips slamming against hers as I fucked her with all the pent-up frustration and anger that had been building since I discovered her real identity. I could feel her muscles tightening around me, her body coiling like a spring as she neared the precipice again.

"Come for me, Eva," I commanded, my voice a harsh, guttural rasp as I reached between us, pressing the vibrator against her clit once more. "Let go, mi reina. I want to feel you come undone. Hear you scream my name."

At my words, she shattered, her entire body convulsing as waves of pleasure crashed over her, her pussy clamping down around my cock as she cried out my name, her voice echoing off the walls of the bedroom. I followed her over the edge, my orgasm barreling through me like a freight train, my body shuddering with the force of my release.

For a long moment, we lay there, our bodies slick with sweat, our breaths ragged and uneven. I reached up, removing the blindfold and releasing Natalia from the restraints, my hands gently massaging her wrists and ankles as I brought her back down to earth.

Playing the role of the perfect boyfriend, I rolled onto my side, pulling her into my arms. Her body fit perfectly against mine as I pressed a kiss to the top of her head. "You are incredible, Eva," I said, my voice filled with admiration and a hint of something more, something deeper.

She snuggled closer, her hand resting over my heart as she looked up at me, her eyes shining with satisfaction and affection. "You're not so bad yourself, Dante Reyes," she said, her voice soft and sleepy as she drifted off to sleep in my arms.

I held her as she slept, keenly aware I was flirting with disaster. I kept reminding myself that Eva—or Natalia—

was a DEA agent, a woman who'd wormed her way into my world with a false identity, no doubt collecting dirt to topple my family's empire.

Make no mistake. I'd neutralize the threat, likely torpedoing her career and future in the process.

Yet, gazing at her now, raven locks cascaded over the pillow, lips parted in a breathy sigh, part of me almost pitied her. Could there be more to her than this undercover ruse? Buried beneath the lies, was there a chance at something genuine between us? Some naive shred of me almost dared to hope.

TWENTY-ONE
NATALIA

I was barely through my apartment door before I powered up my laptop, my fingers flying over the keys as I initiated the secure video link to Agent Morrow. Despite my A-plus performance between the sheets last night, I still couldn't shake the gnawing worry that my slip-up with Dante at the Palm Beach estate might have jeopardized everything. Something was different about him at the dinner.

The screen flickered to life, revealing Morrow's grizzled face. His steely gaze seemed to bore right through me, assessing and analyzing with the precision of a man who had seen far too much in his years with the DEA.

"Ramirez," he greeted me, his voice gruff with the remnants of sleep. "Talk to me. What's happened?"

I launched into a detailed account of what had happened last night on my date with Dante. As I relayed the story, I fixated on how Dante looked at me, maybe a slight suspicion lurking in his piercing blue eyes.

Morrow listened intently, his face impassive as he absorbed the information. "Getting too close to these people... it's a risky move, Natalia," he warned, his tone grave. "You're playing a dangerous game."

"I know, sir," I said, my voice steady despite the knot in my chest. "But I'm confident that I can handle Dante. I've got him eating out of the palm of my hand."

Morrow arched an eyebrow, the ghost of a smile tugging at the corners of his mouth. "Natalia, listen to me," Morrow said, his voice firm. "I understand the importance of gaining Dante's confidence, using your...assets, but you need to be careful. Dante is not a naive college kid."

I bit my lip, the gravity of his statement settling over me. "I will, sir. I promise."

Morrow sighed, pinching the bridge of his nose as he considered his next words. "Alright," he finally said, his gaze locking onto mine. "You're a fine agent, and I trust your judgment. But you need to be more vigilant. And, no more slip-ups, you hear me?"

"Loud and clear, sir."

"Good. Tell me what else you've learned since the last debriefing, and we'll strategize how to use that information to our advantage."

I spent the next twenty minutes detailing everything. Afterward, Morrow leaned back in his chair, a thoughtful expression on his face.

"This is solid work, Natalia," he said, his tone grudgingly admiring. "But to build a case that'll stick, we need concrete evidence—names, dates, specific locations of drop points."

I nodded, my mind spinning with plans and strategies for extracting the information. "I'll get it, sir. I'll make sure of it."

"See that you do," Morrow said, his eyes hard. "But remember, you pull the plug the instant you feel you're over your head. No case is worth your life."

"Understood."

We ended the call soon after, the screen going dark as I was left alone with my thoughts. The magnitude of my task felt overwhelming at times, but I was determined to see it through.

THE FOLLOWING week was a blur of meetings and covert surveillance. I shadowed Dante as he went about his daily business. I stood by his side and watched him charm investors at swanky restaurant openings and broker multi-million-dollar real estate deals in high-rise boardrooms. I saw the respect he commanded from his underlings and the fear he inspired in his rivals.

And each night, when we lay tangled in each other's arms, I listened intently as he spoke of his plans to legitimize the family business, to transform the cartel into an untouchable empire that would span generations.

It was during one of these late-night confessions that I hit the jackpot.

"We've got a shipment coming in tomorrow," Dante said, his voice filled with satisfaction. "It's bigger than anything we've done before, and it's going to open many doors for us."

My heart began to race, the adrenaline coursing through my veins. This was it—the break we had been waiting for. "Oh, yeah?" I said, trying to keep my tone casual. "And what exactly is in this... shipment?"

Dante chuckled, his arms tightening around me. "Let's just say it's not Bibles, querida," he said, his voice a low rumble against my ear. "And it's going to make us a lot of money."

I feigned sleepiness, snuggling closer to him as I pressed for more information. "Mmm, sounds dangerous. Are you sure it's worth the risk?"

"It's always worth the risk," he said. "Especially when the payoff is this big."

We fell silent after that, and I lay there for hours, my mind racing with the implications of Dante's revelation. If I could alert Morrow in time to intercept the shipment, it could potentially deal a crippling blow to the cartel's operations and provide invaluable evidence for building our case.

But to do that, I needed to know where and when the exchange would occur. And convincing Dante to share that information with me... well, that would be a challenge.

THE OPPORTUNITY PRESENTED itself the following day as Dante and I shared a brunch at an upscale café in the heart of Miami. As we sipped our cocktails and nibbled on our tapas, I casually broached the subject of the shipment, trying to appear only mildly interested in the intricacies of his illicit activities.

"I've been thinking about what you said last night," I began, carefully watching his reaction. "About the big shipment coming in. It must be quite an operation."

Dante studied me for a moment, his gaze probing yet unreadable. "It is," he confirmed, his tone guarded. "But it's not something you need to worry about, mi reina."

I reached across the table, my fingers tracing idle patterns on the back of his hand. "You know you can trust me, right, Dante?" I said, allowing vulnerability to creep into my voice. "I would never do anything to jeopardize what we have."

He captured my hand in his, his thumb rubbing circles on my skin. "I know," he said softly, the tension in his shoulders seeming to ease. "It's just... this is a complicated business, Eva. It's not something I like to discuss outside of the... inner circle, you know?"

I nodded, giving his hand a reassuring squeeze. "I understand," I said, playing the role of the devoted girlfriend to perfection. "But if there's anything you can share with me... I want to feel like I'm part of your world, Dante."

For a long, agonizing moment, he didn't speak. I could see the internal battle behind his blue eyes, the warring desires to protect and trust me. And then, slowly, he began to talk.

He outlined the plan in broad strokes, careful not to divulge too much sensitive information. But it was enough —enough for me to piece together the where and when of the impending drug deal. The shipment was scheduled to arrive at midnight, offloaded from a cargo ship docked at a private marina on the city's outskirts.

I hurried through the rest of the brunch with Dante, thinking about the crucial details he had just revealed about the impending shipment. This was the break I had been waiting for.

As Dante rambled about some mundane business detail, I nodded absently, my thoughts consumed by the plan already taking shape. I should get back to my place and alert Morrow as soon as possible, giving his team enough time to mobilize and intercept the shipment before it could be offloaded and dispersed.

"Eva? Are you listening to me?" Dante's voice broke through my reverie, his brow furrowed in concern.

I blinked, forcing myself back to the present moment. "Of course," I lied smoothly, offering him a warm smile. "I was just thinking about how much I'm looking forward to our plans later tonight."

A slow, predatory grin spread across his face, and he reached across the table to trail his fingers along the inside of my wrist. "Is that so?" he purred, his voice a low, seductive rumble. "What exactly did you have in mind for tonight, querida?"

I leaned forward, my lips curving into a coy smile. "Oh, I think you know exactly what I have in mind," I said, letting my gaze drift meaningfully down to the bulge straining against the front of his pants. "You, me, and your little playroom. And I can promise you, it'll be... unforgettable."

Dante's eyes darkened with desire, and for a fleeting moment, I felt a twinge of guilt for the deception I was about to perpetrate. But I quickly pushed those thoughts aside, reminding myself of the bigger picture and the mission.

After settling the check and bidding Dante a temporary farewell, I hailed a cab and directed the driver to my apartment building. My heart was pounding with a heady mix of anticipation and trepidation as I ascended the stairs, my mind already formulating the best way to relay the information to Morrow.

Once inside, I powered up my laptop using the secure video link. Morrow's grizzled face appeared on the screen.

"Ramirez," he greeted me, his voice gruff. "What have you got for me?"

I steadied myself before launching into a detailed account of my conversation with Dante over lunch. I outlined the shipment's specifics – the location, the time, the magnitude of the operation – my words tumbling out in a rush, fueled by the adrenaline coursing through my veins.

As I spoke, I observed Morrow's face, gauging his reaction. I could see he was already strategizing and formulating a plan of action.

When I finished, he paused, his gaze thoughtful. "This is it, Natalia," he said, his voice heavy. "This could be the break we've been waiting for."

I nodded, my throat tight with a mix of anticipation and apprehension. "I know, sir," I said, my voice steady despite the maelstrom of emotions swirling within me.

Morrow's eyes hardened. "Once this operation is in motion, there's no going back. Your undercover operation ends after this."

My mind flashed back to the moments I had shared with Dante – the stolen kisses, the heated embraces, the nights spent tangled in his sheets. Memories that, until recently, had been nothing more than a means to an end, a way to further my cover and gain his trust.

But now, as the prospect of seeing him arrested – or worse – loomed before me, I couldn't deny the twinge of sadness that tugged at my heart. I had to remind myself that Dante Reyes was a criminal, a man who had built his empire on a foundation of violence and corruption. And yet, in the quiet moments we had shared, I had glimpsed a different side of him – a vulnerability, a longing for something more than the life he had been born into.

I shook my head, banishing those thoughts from my mind. Now was not the time for sentimentality or second-guessing. I was a DEA agent, and my duty was clear.

"I understand, sir," I said, my voice firm and resolute.

Morrow nodded, seemingly satisfied with my response.

"Alright, then. I'll mobilize the team and coordinate with local law enforcement. This could be our one shot."

With that, the video call ended, leaving me alone with my thoughts. If everything went according to plan, the Reyes cartel would be dealt a devastating blow, their operations crippled, and their leadership potentially facing lengthy prison sentences.

But at what cost?

I shook my head, steeling my resolve. This was the path I had chosen, the life I had dedicated myself to. There could be no room for sentiment, no matter how genuine the connection might have felt.

Tonight would be the last night as Eva Morales, the last time I would share Dante's bed.

A single tear traced its way down my cheek as I bid farewell to Eva Morales, to the life I had so carefully constructed, and to the man who had stolen a piece of my heart.

TWENTY-TWO
DANTE

THE HEAVY BAG SWAYED WITH EACH THUNDEROUS blow, the rhythmic thud of my fists echoing through the gritty, dimly lit boxing gym. Sweat poured down my face, stinging my eyes, but I didn't falter, my focus unwavering as I channeled my frustrations into every punch. The worn leather felt like a second skin against my wrapped knuckles, each impact reverberating through my arms and into my core.

The gym was a relic from another era that felt frozen in time and the perfect place to burn off the calories from my lunch with Natalia, not to mention the fucking tension.

I sensed Marco's presence before I saw him, his familiar footsteps approaching the ring with a purposeful stride. I threw one last vicious combination, my fists connecting with the heavy bag in a rapid-fire succession of lefts and rights, sending it swinging wildly on its chain. Satisfied with my handiwork, I turned to face my friend and confidant, a wolfish grin spreading across my face as I wiped the sweat from my brow with the back of my hand.

"I hope you're here to spar and not just to admire the view," I quipped, my eyes glinting with challenge as I took in Marco's amused grin on his face.

Marco chuckled, shaking his head as he ducked under the ropes and into the ring with a fluid grace that belied his size. "And risk messing up this pretty face? Not a chance, hermano. I'll leave the masochism to you."

I tossed him a pair of focus mitts, grinning as I rolled my shoulders, preparing for another round. "Then shut up and hold these for me. I've got some steam to blow off."

Marco obliged, slipping on the mitts and bracing himself for the onslaught. As I unleashed a flurry of jabs and crosses, the satisfying smack of leather against leather filling the air, we fell into our familiar rhythm, the conversation flowing as quickly as the punches.

"So, about this DEA agent," Marco began, his dark eyes searching mine for any hint of uncertainty. "Are you sure you know what you're doing, Dante? That is some serious shit we're talking about."

My jaw tightened, my punches coming faster and harder as the anger surged through me like a tidal wave. The thought of Natalia infiltrating my world and threatening everything I had built made my blood boil. But I couldn't let Marco see the cracks in my armor or let him know just how much she had gotten under my skin.

"I've got it under control," I gritted out, my breath coming in sharp bursts as I punched the mitts with renewed vigor. "Natalia thinks she's playing me, but I'm holding all the cards. I'm feeding her just enough bullshit to keep her on the hook but not enough to do any real damage."

Marco grunted as he absorbed a particularly vicious left hook, his brow furrowing with concern. "And what about your father? If he finds out about her..."

I felt my blood run cold at the mention of my father, my fist connecting with the mitt with a resounding crack. Ricardo Reyes was not a man to be trifled with, and if he discovered that I had been harboring a DEA agent right under his nose... well, let's just say it wouldn't be pretty.

"He won't because you're not going to tell him. No one is. We've already been over this once." My voice was low and dangerous, the unspoken threat hanging heavy between us. I held Marco's gaze, my eyes boring into his with an intensity that left no room for argument. "This stays between us, understand?"

Marco held up his hands in a gesture of surrender, the mitts making a soft thud as they collided. "Hey, you know I've always got your back, hermano. If you say this is the best way to handle it, then I trust you."

I nodded, my lips pressed into a thin line. "Good. Because we've got bigger fish to fry than some DEA chick with a hard-on for playing spy games."

Marco's eyes narrowed, his head cocked to the side as he regarded me with a knowing look. "Speaking of fish, what's the deal with your sister's boyfriend? I haven't found shit on that pendejo. How about you?"

I shook my head, not admitting I've been too busy fucking a DEA agent to investigate Sofia's new beau. "Not a damn thing. But I know there's something off about him, Marco. I can feel it in my gut."

Marco nodded. "Want me to dig deeper? See if I can shake loose any skeletons in his closet?"

"Fuck, yeah. Do it," I told him, my tone hushed. "Bring Pedro into the mix if that's what it takes. Just keep it on the DL. Sofia's already so far up in my ass I can taste her goddamn perfume. The last thing I need is her pressing me with a million fucking questions."

Marco grinned, his teeth flashing white against his tanned skin. "Discreet is my middle name, hermano."

As Marco left the gym, I shifted my focus back to the punching bag, my hands pounding out a storm of punches. I had this gut sense that the coming days would demand every scrap of power and precision from me. Growing up in the cartel had taught me one thing: appearances were never to be trusted. There was always more beneath the surface.

Exhausted, I peeled off my gloves as sweat dripped down my face, each drop a testament to the grueling workout I had just endured.

A text notification caught my attention.

I grabbed my phone from the bench and noticed Eva's name flashing across the screen.

Looking forward to tonight. Any hints on where you're taking me? ;)

A slow grin spread across my face as I tapped out my response.

Wear something you can dance in, querida. Trust me, you'll want to be comfortable.

I hit send and slipped the phone back into my pocket, already looking forward to the night ahead. Natalia had no idea what was coming.

"BUCKLE UP, baby, because tonight's gonna be one wild ride," I said, flashing a grin as I pulled my sleek ride up to Club Salsa Fuego, the hottest spot in South Beach. "Forget those lame-ass clubs packed with 'roided out douchebags and dry humping plastic bimbos."

Natalia raised an elegant eyebrow, her full lips twisting into a mysterious smile as she surveyed the club's exterior. Lights illuminated the vibrant red façade, pulsing to the rhythm of a sensuous salsa melody that drifted through the open doors. "And what will I find here, Dante?"

I stepped out of the Maserati, my eyes never leaving hers, and opened the passenger door for her. "A real taste of Latin flavor, mi reina. Are you ready to show me your moves?"

She took my hand, her touch sending a jolt of electricity through my body as she gracefully exited the car. Her emerald dress hugged her curves in all the right places, and her hair fell in loose waves around her shoulders, enhancing her exotic beauty. My dick twitched in anticipation as I imagined those dark locks cascading over my pillow later tonight.

As we approached the entrance, the bouncer gave us a nod of recognition and stepped aside, letting us bypass the eager crowd waiting to get in. I felt Natalia's hand tighten in mine as we stepped into the club's dazzling lights and swirling colors.

The energy was electric, with vibrant salsa beats thumping through the speakers, moving bodies in perfect harmony. I led Natalia through the crowd, eager for what was to come.

I recognized a familiar waiter from my frequent visits. He caught my eye and gave a subtle nod, leading us to a secluded booth at the back. I knew this would be the perfect place for my plans.

"Would you like a drink?" I asked, sliding into the booth.

"A mojito, please," Natalia said, her eyes sparkling.

I ordered two mojitos and leaned back, taking in the lively atmosphere. "Are you ready to dance, Eva?" I asked, reaching for her hand across the table.

She gave my hand a gentle squeeze. "I'd love to, Dante, but it's been a long time since I danced salsa."

The waiter returned with our drinks, and I took a refreshing sip before setting the glass back on the table. "In that case, let's warm up with a slower song. I wouldn't want to lead you into a fast-paced dance and have you realize I've lost my rhythm."

Natalia laughed, her eyes dancing with mischief. "I have a feeling you haven't lost your touch, Dante."

The music shifted to a slower, more romantic salsa tune, setting the perfect tone for our dance. I placed my hand on the small of her back, feeling her body mold to mine as we stepped onto the dance floor.

I guided Natalia through the basic steps, our bodies moving in perfect harmony with the rhythm. Despite her claimed rustiness, she followed my lead with fluid grace, her hips swaying seductively to the music.

The initial apprehension faded as we surrendered to the music, our steps growing more confident, our movements more daring. Our gazes locked, our eyes never wavering as we danced, the electricity between us crackling like the candles flickering on the nearby tables.

As the DJ played an up-tempo salsa song next, I spun Natalia gracefully, her dress floating around her like an emerald cloud. Near the song's end, I pulled her close, our bodies moving in sync with the frantic rhythm. On the song's final note, I dipped her, eliciting a gasp from her lips. I brought her back up, and our mouths collided in a passionate kiss fueled by the adrenaline of the dance.

The crowd erupted in applause and whistles, but I barely heard them. All I felt was the heat of Natalia's body against mine, the taste of her lips on mine. She melted against me, her hands roaming my back as our kiss deepened, hot and urgent.

Breaking away, breathless and flushed, I said in her ear,

"Let's get out of here, mi reina. The night is still young, and I suspect it's about to get even hotter."

With a secret smile, Natalia took my hand, and we made our way through the cheering crowd, our steps never losing the salsa rhythm. I opened the door of the Maserati for her, and she slid inside, her scent lingering in the air as I walked around to the driver's side.

The engine roared to life, and my mind was already spinning with the erotic possibilities that awaited us.

That dance was just the beginning.

TWENTY-THREE

NATALIA

THE SALSA RHYTHMS STILL RAN THROUGH MY BODY, perfectly syncing with my racing heart as Dante practically dragged me into his swanky penthouse. There was something wild and feral in his eyes, a hunger he could barely control. It set every nerve ending in my body on fire with a heady mix of "fuck yes" and "oh shit."

We crashed through the front door, and Dante was on me in a flash, his mouth devouring mine like a man possessed. His hands groped me with a crazed urgency that was equal parts hot as hell and mildly terrifying. I could feel his rock-hard cock pressing into my hip as we stumbled toward Dante's kinky playroom, and a delicious shiver of anticipation raced through me.

Still, I couldn't shake the sadness that clung to me like an octopus wrapping its tentacles around my heart. This was our last time. After tonight, nothing would be the same. And, damn it, I had fallen hard for Dante Reyes. It wasn't supposed to happen. He was the target, a means to an end. But somewhere along the way, he had become so much more.

I forced the melancholy from my mind, steeling my resolve. This was for Matt. I owed it to him and to his poor mother, who had spoken so highly of me at the funeral, to see this through to the end. Ricardo Reyes had to pay for the lives he had destroyed, and this was the only way.

But that didn't mean I couldn't give Dante one last night he would never forget. I would burn every moment into my memory, savoring the heat and passion that had consumed me during this undercover op.

"Mi reina, what's wrong?" Dante asked, his eyes searching my face as we entered the dimly lit playroom. "You're trembling."

I forced a smile, my heart hammering in my chest. "Nothing's wrong, Dante," I said, reaching up to gently cup his cheek. "I'm just feeling a little overwhelmed, that's all."

Before he could respond, I stepped back, my hands moving to the zipper of my dress. With a swift motion, I tugged it down, the fabric sliding off my shoulders to pool at my feet. I followed with my panties, leaving me naked before him.

"Tonight, I'm entirely yours, Dante," I purred, my voice husky with desire. "Do with me as you please."

A wild light sparked in Dante's eyes as his gaze raked over my naked body. "That's what I like to hear, my queen," he growled, his voice thick. "And I intend to take full advantage of that offer."

He took my hand, his touch sending a jolt of electricity through me, and led me to the padded wall with the heavy-duty restraints. Without a word, he turned me to face the wall and secured my wrists and ankles in a spread-eagle position, the soft leather cuffs biting into my skin just enough to heighten my senses. I felt deliciously vulnerable, completely at his mercy, and the adrenaline rush made my skin prickle with awareness.

Dante paused momentarily, his eyes never leaving mine as if seeking my silent consent. I gave a subtle nod, and my heart surged with anticipation. A slow, predatory grin spread across his face, and he moved to the toy box, reaching inside to retrieve a flogger.

Dante's eyes never left mine as he approached me, his intentions clear. I swallowed hard, excitement and apprehension warring within me. This was new territory for me, but I trusted Dante. He would know my limits and respect them.

The first strike landed on my upper back, the sensation a sharp sting that sent a thrill of pleasure through me. My body tensed as I waited for the next blow.

Dante took his time, landing each strike with precision, his eyes never leaving mine. The flogger danced across my skin, each contact a caress that raised goosebumps in its wake. I arched my back, my breath coming in sharp gasps as the sensations intensified.

"You like that, don't you, Eva?" Dante growled, his

eyes dark with desire. He leaned in close, his lips brushing my ear as his hand trailed a teasing path down my body. "You like being at my mercy, knowing I'm in control."

I whimpered, my body aching for more. "Yes, Dante," I whispered, my voice barely above a breath. "Please, don't stop."

At my words, he chuckled, the vibrations reverberating through me. "As you wish." He brought the flogger down in a swift, firm motion, striking the sensitive skin of my inner thighs. "Count for me, Eva. I want to hear the numbers fall from your beautiful lips."

"One," I gasped, my eyes clenching shut as the burn radiated through me.

He brought the flogger down again, this time on the curve of my ass, the sensation sending a jolt of pleasure straight to my core. "Two," I moaned, my body arching towards him.

Dante continued his assault, each strike a perfect blend of pleasure and pain, pushing me closer and closer to the edge. "That's it, Eva," he purred, his lips brushing my ear as his fingers trailed down my body. "You're so wet for this, mi reina. Your body is begging for more."

"Yes, Dante, please," I begged, my inhibitions melting away under the onslaught of sensations. "Don't stop."

He chuckled darkly, his breath hot against my skin. "Anything for you, mi reina." He brought the flogger down in rapid succession, the strikes landing on my ass and thighs, sending waves of pleasure coursing through me. "Keep counting, angel," he said, his voice a low, seductive purr. "I want to hear you lose yourself in the numbers."

"Ten, eleven, twelve," I moaned, my body bucking against the restraints as my mind clouded with pleasure. "Dante, please, more."

At my words, Dante paused, admiring his handiwork, the pink stripes crisscrossing my skin. I felt his fingers gently tracing the marks, soothing the soreness with feathery light touches. "So beautiful," he said, his eyes dark with longing. "You take pain so well."

I whimpered, my skin tingling with the aftermath of the flogging. "Please, Dante," I pleaded, my body aching for release. "I need more."

A slow, predatory grin spread across Dante's face as he moved behind me, his fingers gently probing at my slick folds. "Oh yes, you do," he growled, his lips brushing my ear as he teased my entrance with the tip of his finger. "You want to be filled, don't you, mi reina? Stretched and fucked until you scream my name."

"Yes," I moaned, my body quivering with need. "Please, Dante, fuck me."

I felt him position himself at my entrance, the head of his cock teasing me with a gentle pressure. "Oh, I'm gonna fuck you, baby," he growled.

With one swift, forceful thrust, he plunged into me, filling me. I cried out, my back arching as the delicious stretch sent a wave of pleasure radiating through me. Dante set a punishing pace, his hips slamming into mine, our bodies colliding in a frantic rhythm.

The restraints dug into my skin, the leather biting into my wrists and ankles as Dante pounded into me relentlessly, each thrust driving me closer to the edge. I could feel the orgasm building inside me, coiling tighter and tighter until I thought I might explode.

"Come for me, Eva," Dante commanded, his voice harsh with need. "Let go, mi reina. Give yourself to me."

At his words, I shattered, my entire body convulsing with the force of my release. My cry echoed off the walls of the playroom as wave after wave of pleasure washed over me, my vision tunneling down to a pinpoint of light.

Dante groaned, his hips stuttering as he followed me over the edge, his body shuddering with the force of his release. We hung suspended in the aftermath for a long moment, our bodies slack and sated.

Dante gently released me from the restraints, his hands soft and gentle as they undid the leather cuffs. He gathered me in his arms, my naked body molding to his as he carried me through the doorway of the playroom and into the bedroom beyond.

He laid me down on the bed, his touch gentle as he pulled the covers over us. As we lay there, tangled in each other's arms, I knew this would be our end. But for now, I allowed myself to fall into the fantasy, to pretend that this could be real.

Dante pulled me closer, his lips trailing kisses along my shoulder. "That was incredible," he said, his voice husky. "You are one hell of a woman."

I snuggled closer, my eyes drifting closed as I relished

the feel of his arms around me and his body's warmth against mine. "And you are one hell of a man, Dante Reyes," I whispered, my voice soft and sleepy.

He chuckled, his breath tickling my skin. "Get some rest, mi reina. You're going to need your strength for what's to come."

I felt the rumble of his words more than I heard them, his breath already evening out as he succumbed to sleep. But my mind continued to race, my thoughts swirling with the implications of what was to come.

The comfortable warmth of the bed and the steady rise and fall of Dante's chest lulled me into a restless sleep, my dreams haunted by dark, shadowy figures and faceless enemies.

TWENTY-FOUR
DANTE

THE SCENT OF FRESHLY BREWED COFFEE WAFTED through the air, mingling with the aroma of sizzling bacon and eggs as I navigated my penthouse's sleek, modern kitchen. The sun was just beginning to show, casting a warm, golden glow over South Beach. It was a view that never got old, a constant reminder of the empire my father had built from the ground up.

But this morning, my thoughts weren't on business or the cartel. They were on her—Eva, or rather, Natalia. Last night had been... unexpected.

The memory of her naked body, the way she had surrendered to me in the playroom, sent a jolt of lust coursing through me. I adjusted the waistband of my low-slung sweatpants, willing my cock to behave. There would be time for round two later. Right now, I had breakfast to prepare.

I was just plating the food when I heard the soft pad of

footsteps against the marble floor. I turned to see Natalia emerging from the bedroom, her long, dark hair cascading over her shoulders in a tousled, just-fucked mess that made my dick twitch with interest. She was wearing one of my dress shirts, the fabric hanging loosely on her frame, and the sight of her in my clothes did something dangerous to my insides.

"Good morning," she said, her voice soft and sleepy as she approached me with a shy smile. I could tell she was still trying to reconcile the man she thought she knew with the one who had taken her to the edge of pleasure and pain.

"Morning, mi reina," I said, my voice gruff with a mixture of desire and something else, something that felt suspiciously like tenderness. "I hope you're hungry."

Her eyes flicked to the plates of food on the counter, and she nodded, her smile widening as she sat at the breakfast bar. "Starving, actually. You didn't have to go to all this trouble, though."

I shrugged, pouring her a cup of coffee just as she liked it—black, no sugar. "It's no trouble at all. Besides, I figured you might need some fuel after last night."

Her face turned beet red when I brought up last night's raunchy romp, and I felt like a smug motherfucker knowing I was the one who made that sexy vixen blush.

We flirted shamelessly over breakfast, cracking jokes. It was a rare glimpse of a goofy side that I usually kept under lock and key. But with Natalia, it was different. She never judged me or talked down to me. She was the perfect woman for me.

Too bad it was all a fucking lie.

My thoughts were interrupted by a sharp knock at the door. I frowned, glancing at the clock on the wall. It was early for unexpected visitors, especially ones who didn't bother to call first. Natalia's eyes flicked toward the door, and I could see the wheels turning behind those dark orbs.

"I'll get it," I said, setting down my coffee mug, my muscles tensing as I moved towards the door.

I pulled it open to find my sister standing in the hallway, her usual carefree expression replaced by a deep crease between her brows, and her eyes searched my face for reassurance. I felt a surge of protectiveness, an instinctive need to shield her from whatever had her on edge. "Sofia? What's wrong?"

"Dante," she breathed, eyes darting past me to Natalia, who watched us from the kitchen. "Thank God you're home. I must talk to you."

I guided her inside, closing the door behind her. "Everything okay?"

Sofia took a deep breath, her shoulders rising and falling with the action. "I think I was wrong about Allen."

"What do you mean?" My protective instincts kicked into overdrive at the mention of her boyfriend. "Did he do something?"

She shook her head, eyes darting nervously between Natalia and me. "No, not exactly. But last night, he asked me all these questions about Dad and the family, and it felt... weird."

My jaw clenched at the mention of my father and the cartel, and I felt Natalia's gaze on me, sharp and assessing. "What kind of questions?" I asked, doing my best to keep my voice casual.

"He was asking about our family history, our businesses, and Dad's associates," Sofia explained, her eyes wide with concern. "I tried to brush it off, but he kept pressing like he was digging for something."

"The guy is a dick, always has been," I growled, more pissed off than I cared to admit. "Don't worry, I'll find out his deal, okay?"

Sofia relaxed a little, relief flooding her features. "You think he could be hiding something?"

"I don't know, but I sure as hell intend to find out." I gave her a reassuring squeeze on the shoulder. "You did the right thing by coming to me, Sof."

Sofia chewed her lip, worry still evident in her eyes. "He can't know anything, Dante. He just can't."

"He won't, sis," I promised, giving her shoulder a final squeeze. "Now, go on, get some rest. I'll take care of this."

Sofia nodded, her eyes drifting to Natalia, who stood quietly by the breakfast bar. "Oh, hey, Eva," she said, her face brightening slightly. "Are you free this morning? Do you want to go shopping with me? I could use some retail therapy after all this."

Natalia shook her head, her eyes apologetic. "Thanks, Sofia, but I have to work. I'm already late."

Sofia pouted but didn't push the issue. "Another time, then," she said, quickly hugging Natalia. "It was so much fun last time we hung out. We should do it again soon."

"Definitely," Natalia agreed, returning the hug.

As I closed the door behind Sofia, Natalia gave me one last sultry look before she disappeared down the hallway to get dressed, my mind awhirl with thoughts of what just happened.

The thought of Allen using my sister to get information on our family had me more riled up than I cared to admit. Good thing I had Marco looking into the asshole already. I just couldn't shake the feeling there was something we weren't seeing, something bigger at play here.

But at the same time, I felt bad for Sofia. My sister had no clue that I was already looking into her boyfriend or that her new best girlfriend was an undercover DEA agent. Her little safe world was nothing but lies and deception.

Natalia returned fully dressed, her eyes warm, and before I knew it, she was pulling me into a heated embrace, her lips crashing against mine. I felt her tongue tease mine in a promise of future delights.

When we finally parted, Natalia's cheeks flushed. "That was amazing," she said, her tone light.

"It was," I replied, a smile tugging at my lips.

After Natalia had left, I stood at the window, watching the Miami sunrise paint the sky in hues of pink and gold. A strange sense of calm washed over me. Despite the storm raging inside, I couldn't deny the spark of hope that flickered in my chest.

Natalia Ramirez. DEA agent. My enemy. And yet, the woman who had somehow managed to burrow her way into my heart.

I closed my eyes, remembering the feel of her in my arms, the sound of her laughter, the fire in her eyes when she challenged me. It was all real – I could feel it in my bones. And that realization hit me like a freight train.

Maybe, just maybe, there was a way out of this mess. A path that didn't end in bloodshed and betrayal, but in something... more.

I turned away from the window, my mind racing with possibilities. What if I could use this situation to our advantage? What if, instead of seeing Natalia as a threat, I could turn her into an ally?

It was a dangerous game, full of risks and potential pitfalls. But as I poured myself another cup of coffee, I felt a surge of determination. I was Dante Reyes, after all. I'm building an empire on taking risks and turning impossible situations to my advantage.

This would be my greatest challenge yet – navigating the treacherous waters between love and duty, trust and betrayal. I couldn't deny I felt a glimmer of excitement, as I imagined the hauntingly beautiful face of the woman who had managed to capture my heart despite all odds.

Natalia Ramirez.

Eva Morales.

My enemy.

My lover.

My undoing.
My hope.

TWENTY-FIVE
NATALIA

I PACED THE CONFINES OF MY SPARSE APARTMENT, MY mind a whirlwind of anxiety and uncertainty. The seconds ticked by with agonizing slowness, each stretching out like an eternity as I waited for word from Morrow about the bust.

I imagined the events of the past few hours in my mind–the frantic preparations, the tense briefing with the tactical team, the anticipation of finally dealing a devastating blow to the Reyes cartel's operations. I should have heard back by now.

But... nothing. Radio silence.

I chewed my lip, my fingers drumming an erratic rhythm against my thigh as I struggled to maintain my composure. What could have gone wrong? Had the operation been compromised somehow? Or was it simply a false lead, another dead end in this twisted game of cat and mouse?

The questions swirled in my mind, each more unsettling than the last. And at the center of it all was Dante, his piercing blue eyes and cocky grin burned into my memory. Had he played me from the start, given me false information to keep me off balance and protect his precious cartel?

The thought made my blood boil, but I forced it down, refusing to let doubt take root. Dante was many things – a criminal, a liar, a master manipulator – but deep down, I didn't believe he was capable of such calculated deception. Not with me.

Or was that just wishful thinking on my part?

I shook my head, banishing the thought before it could take hold. I couldn't afford to let my emotions cloud my judgment, not now. Not when so much was at stake.

With a frustrated growl, I switched on my laptop and punched in Morrow's code, my fingers trembling with barely contained impatience. The connection rang and rang, each unanswered tone like a dagger to my heart.

Just as I was about to give up and try Valentina, the screen flickered to life, Morrow's stern face filling the screen.

"Ramirez," he greeted me, his voice tight with tension. "We have a situation."

My heart plummeted, and my worst fears were confirmed in those three simple words. "What happened?" I demanded, my voice clipped and professional despite the maelstrom of emotions raging within me.

Morrow sighed, his eyes betraying weariness. "The place was empty, not a single trace of drugs or cartel members. They must have gotten wind of the raid and changed locations."

A cold chill ran through me as his words sunk in. "Do you think Dante knew?" I asked, my heart hammering in my chest. "And he purposely gave me bad info?"

Morrow held up a hand, his voice steady. "Now, hold on, we don't know that. The cartel could've just moved the shipment as a precaution. It's not uncommon for them to switch locations at the last minute."

I blew out a breath. I was relieved that my cover wasn't blown but disappointed that we'd lost our opportunity to seize the shipment.

"So what now?" I asked, forcing my voice to remain steady.

Morrow's gaze hardened, his jaw set in a firm line. "Now, you stay the course, Ramirez. It was just a minor setback, a bump in the road. You need to keep pushing, keep digging for information that can help us take these bastards down for good."

"And if Dante knows? If he's been playing me all along?"

Morrow's eyes bored into mine. "Then you do what you must do, Natalia. But until we know for sure, you keep your head down and your eyes open. Understood?"

I nodded, my jaw clenched with determination. "Understood, sir."

With a curt nod, Morrow ended the call. I sank onto the couch, my head falling into my hands as I tried to make sense of the tumultuous emotions swirling within me.

The failed raid was a setback, but somehow, the thought of continuing my assignment—of staying close to Dante and sharing his bed—sent me a thrill of anticipation coursing through me.

THE WARM MORNING did little to thaw the icy knot of dread that had taken root in the pit of my stomach. As the previous night's events replayed in my mind, that nagging suspicion I had began to take hold—the suspicion that Dante had played me.

If that were the case, my cover was undoubtedly blown, and I was in more danger than I could fathom.

I flopped onto the edge of the bed and ran a hand through my hair as I wrestled with the implications. Had Dante known all along? Had he been stringing me along, keeping me close while feeding me just enough lies to keep me off balance? The thought made me shudder, but deep down, a part of me refused to believe it.

There had been moments, fleeting as they were, when I had glimpsed something genuine in Dante's eyes—a vulnerability, a longing for something more than the life he had been born into. Could it all have been an act, a masterful deception orchestrated by a man whose very existence was rooted in lies and deceit?

I glanced at my phone and found last night's text to Dante. His response had been curt, a stark contrast to the usual playful banter we shared.

Busy night at the club. Talk later.

I stared at the words, my brow furrowing in frustration. There was no explanation or hint as to whether Dante knew my real identity. It was just a brush-off that told me nothing and everything all at once.

With a sigh, I tossed the phone aside. I needed answers, and I needed them soon. If Dante knew the truth, then every second I remained undercover was a risk—not just to myself but to the entire operation. And if he didn't... well, then I had a chance to salvage this and continue my mission.

But how could I know for sure? How could I gauge Dante's level of suspicion without tipping my hand and putting myself in even greater jeopardy?

The answer came in the form of a text message from Sofia. My heart leapt into my throat as I read the words, a plan beginning to take shape in my mind.

Hey girl! Lunch today? I need to vent about Allen.

A slow smile spread across my face as I typed out my response, my fingers flying over the keys with renewed determination.

Absolutely! I could use some girl time myself. How about that little café on Ocean Drive?

Sofia's response was immediate, a flurry of celebratory emojis and exclamation points that brought a genuine smile to my face. Despite the constant threat of danger that loomed over me, there was something refreshingly pure about my friendship with Sofia. She was a beacon of light in the darkness that had consumed my life, a reminder of the innocence I had long since sacrificed in the name of duty.

As I showered and dressed, my mind whirred with possibilities. If I played my cards right and convinced Sofia of my true intentions, I could enlist her help turning Dante. He had often spoken of his desire to take the cartel in a more legitimate direction, to shed the blood and violence that had defined his family's legacy. This could be his chance—our chance—to start anew.

When I arrived, the café was bustling, the air thick with the aroma of freshly brewed coffee and buttery pastries. Sofia was already seated at a corner table, her dark hair pulled back in a sleek ponytail, her eyes scanning the menu intensely.

"Hey, girl!" she greeted me with a warm smile, setting the menu aside as I slid into the chair opposite her. "You look fabulous, as always."

I returned her smile, the weight on my shoulders lifting ever so slightly. "So do you," I said, reaching across the table to gently squeeze her hand. "Now, tell me what's going on with Allen. Did he do something stupid again?"

Sofia rolled her eyes. "Doesn't he always?" she sighed, launching into a tale of Allen's latest mishap.

As she spoke, I studied her closely, taking in the subtle nuances of her expressions, the way her eyes would light up when she spoke of her family, the way her lips would quirk into a half-smile whenever Dante's name passed her lips. She was an open book; her emotions laid bare for the world to see, and in that moment, I knew what I had to do.

"Sofia," I interrupted gently. "There's something I need to tell you."

She fell silent, her eyes widening as she registered the gravity in my tone. "What is it?" she asked, her brow furrowing with concern.

I took a deep breath, steeling my resolve. This was it—the moment of truth. "I'm not who you think I am," I began, my voice steady despite the tremor of nerves coursing through me. "My name isn't Eva Morales. It's Natalia Ramirez, and I'm a DEA agent."

The words hung in the air between us, heavy and charged with tension. Sofia's eyes widened, her mouth parting in a silent gasp as the truth washed over her.

"I know this must be a shock," I pressed on. "But you've got to believe me when I say my feelings for you are genuine. I never meant for things to go this far, but..."

My voice trailed off as I searched for the right words to convey the depth of my emotions, the conflicting loyalties that had torn me apart from the inside.

"But what?" Sofia whispered, her eyes shimmering with unshed tears. "You're telling me that everything we've shared, every moment we've spent together, has been a lie?"

"No," I insisted, reaching across the table to grasp her hand. "Never that. The opposite. My friendship with you and how I feel about you and your brother are real, Sofia. More real than anything I've ever known."

She shook her head, her lips pressed into a thin line as she struggled to process the truth. "I don't understand," she said, her voice trembling. "Why are you telling me this now? What do you want from me?"

I paused, my heart hammering in my chest. This was the moment, the crossroads where everything could change.

"I need your help, Sofia," I said, my voice steady and resolute. "I need you to help me convince Dante to turn against your father, to bring down the cartel once and for all."

Sofia's eyes widened, her hand slipping from mine as she recoiled in shock. "You can't be serious," she breathed. "Dante would never betray our family like that."

"But he wants out, Sofia," I pressed, leaning forward in my seat. "He's told me how much he wants to leave the violence and corruption behind to build something legitimate for himself. Becoming a state witness against Ricardo is his chance, your chance, to start over."

Sofia shook her head, her eyes glistening with tears. "I don't know what kind of game you're playing, Eva... or Natalia, or whoever you are," she said, emotion choking her voice, making it raw and unsteady. "But I won't be a part of it. I won't betray my family."

With that, she rose from her seat, her movements jerky and uncoordinated as she fumbled for her purse. "Stay away from me," she warned, her voice trembling. "And stay away from my brother, or I swear to God, I'll make you regret ever crossing our path."

Her words landed like a blow, knocking the wind out of me and leaving me reeling. And then she was gone, disappearing into the bustling crowd of patrons. As reality sank in, I felt the first tendrils of despair creeping into my heart.

If Sofia couldn't be swayed, if she refused to see the truth, then what chance did I have of convincing Dante? And if he knew the truth about my identity, I was well and truly alone, a lamb sent to slaughter in the heart of the lion's den.

As I sat there, I wondered if I had made a grave miscalculation. Had I pushed too hard, too fast, in my desperation to bring Dante to my side? Or had I simply underestimated the depth of loyalty that bound the Reyes family together, a bond forged in blood and reinforced by generations of ruthless ambition?

One thing was sure—I was fucked.

TWENTY-SIX
DANTE

I stared at the stack of paperwork on my desk, the words blurring together as my mind drifted back to the events of the past weeks. Javier Cruz, the bastard that my dad wouldn't let me have a go at; then there was Allen, my sister's boyfriend, also a prick; and finally, the revelation that Eva—my Eva, the woman I had let into my heart and my bed—was Natalia Ramirez, a fucking DEA agent.

I raked a hand through my hair, letting out a frustrated growl as my phone buzzed to life on the desk. Sofia's name flashed across the screen, and a pang of guilt twisted in my gut. My sister remained in the dark about the lies and betrayal enveloping her. She had no clue that the woman I had welcomed into our lives, the one she called her new best friend, was nothing but a carefully crafted illusion.

With a heavy sigh, I swiped to answer the call, steeling myself for whatever fresh hell awaited me.

"Hey, sis," I greeted her, my voice carefully neutral. "What's up?"

"Dante," Sofia said, her voice tight with tension. "I need to talk to you. It's important. Can you meet me for coffee?"

I glanced at my watch, my mind racing as I tried to calculate how long it would take me to get to the café she frequented. "Yeah, sure. Give me an hour."

"Okay," she breathed, a sigh of relief audible over the line. "I'll see you then."

Hanging up the phone, I couldn't shake the feeling that something was off. Sofia always sounded strong, never this vulnerable. I pushed back from the desk, my thoughts churning as I tried to piece together the fragments of the puzzle.

As I always did, I paused by the window, gazing out over the streets of South Beach, my playground, for as long as I could remember. This was the world I had been born into, where loyalty was everything, and betrayal was a death sentence.

The hour ticked closer, and I grappled with the decision weighing on me. Should I tell Sofia the truth about Natalia and risk losing my sister's trust forever? Or should I keep silent, clinging to the hope that this twisted situation could somehow be salvaged?

The drive to the café passed in a blur, my mind consumed with endless doubts and uncertainties. By the time I arrived, Sofia was already waiting as she nursed a steaming cup of coffee.

"Hey," I greeted her, sliding into the chair across from her. "What's going on?"

Sofia's eyes met mine, and I saw a depth of pain and betrayal that cut me deep. "I know something about Eva," she said. "She's not who you think she is."

The air left my lungs in a rush as her words sank in. "How...?" I began, but the question died on my lips, rendered irrelevant in the face of the truth.

Sofia shook her head, her eyes glistening with unshed tears. "She told me herself," she said, her voice trembling. "She's a DEA agent, Dante. Her name is Natalia Ramirez, and she's been lying to us this whole time."

I opened my mouth to respond, but no words came. What could I say? How could I explain I already knew?

"You knew," Sofia spat, her face a mask of betrayal. "You knew who she really was, yet you let her into our lives. My life? I believed she would be my best friend, Dante."

"I..." I tried to speak, but the words choked me.

Sofia's eyes narrowed with bitterness. "You used me."

I reached across the table, my hand closing over hers in a desperate bid for understanding. "It's not that simple, Sof," I pleaded, my voice raw with emotion. "There's more to this than you know."

She jerked her hand away, her face hardening. "Save it, Dante," she said. "I don't want to hear your excuses."

As she rose from her chair, her movements jerky and uncoordinated, a wave of panic washed over me. "Sofia, wait," I called out, desperation clawing at my throat. "Please, let me explain."

But she was already out the door.

I bolted from the cafe, my pulse thundering in my ears as I scanned the bustling street for any sign of Sofia. I couldn't let her walk away, not like this – not with this hanging between us like a suffocating shroud.

"Sofia!" I called out, my voice strained as I pushed through the throngs of people. "Sof, wait!"

She didn't slow her pace, her steps quickening as she rounded the corner and headed towards a bus. I cursed under my breath, my legs propelling me forward as I fought to catch up with her.

"Sofia, please!" I begged, my hand closing around her arm as she stepped onto the bus. "Just give me a chance to explain."

She whirled around, her eyes blazing with a fury I had never seen directed at me before. "Explain what, Dante?" she hissed. "How you have been lying to me this whole time? How you let that... that woman into our lives, knowing full well who she was and what she was doing?"

I cringed at the sharpness in her words, but I didn't release my grip on her arm. "It's not like that, Sof," I pleaded, my voice strained. "I never meant to hurt you."

The bus driver cleared his throat, his impatient gaze flickering between us. "Either get on or get off, folks. We're holding up the line here."

Sofia moved to board the bus, but I tightened my grip,

desperation clawing at my insides. "Wait, just... just let me tell you my plan," I blurted out, the words tumbling from my lips before I could stop them.

She paused, her eyes narrowing with skepticism. "Your plan?"

I nodded as I formulated the idea that could potentially save my relationship with my sister – and my life. "Yeah, my plan for Natalia," I said, emphasizing her real name.

Around us, the other passengers shifted in their seats, their gazes flickering towards us with curiosity and annoyance.

Sofia glanced at the captive audience we had inadvertently attracted. "Dante, maybe we should take this somewhere else," she said, her cheeks flushing.

I nodded. Without another word, I tugged Sofie off the bus, ignoring the stares from the other passengers as we stumbled onto the sidewalk and walked into an empty alley.

"You got one minute to explain," Sofia demanded, her arms crossed over her chest as she fixed me with a pointed stare. "And this time, try not to broadcast it to the entire city."

I paused to gather my thoughts. "I've been playing Natalia since I found out who she was," I began. "I have given her just enough information to keep her hooked, but nothing that could hurt the family."

Sofia's brow furrowed, her eyes searching mine for any

hint of deception. "But why?" she pressed. "Why go through all this trouble? Why not just expose her?"

I stared at Sofia, her words hanging in the air between us. She was right, of course. Exposing Natalia was what I should do. However, my father wouldn't hesitate to put a bullet in her head. The thought made my stomach churn, and a cold sweat broke out on my brow.

"I... can't," I said.

"You're playing with fire, Dante," she warned, her voice tense. "And I don't just mean with Natalia, I mean with Dad." She paused, her lips set in a thin line before continuing. "And even if you somehow manage not to get yourself killed for this... this infatuation, what happens once she gets what she needs from you? Have you thought about that, huh?"

Part of me wanted to bark at her, tell her to mind her own fucking business, but the concerned glint in her dark eyes held me back. Sofia was right: I was gambling with Natalia's life... and my own. My reckless emotions had landed me in dangerous territory, where the irony was undeniable – as a Reyes, I should have been the hunter, not the hunted. Yet, here I stood, willingly ensnared by a woman who might ultimately betray me.

I ran a frustrated hand through my hair and shot my sister a warning glare. "This... infatuation, as you call it, runs deeper than you know." My voice was huskier than I intended. "I care about Natalia, and I have no intention of watching our father's henchmen put a bullet through her head."

Sofia gasped, her hand flying to her mouth as the full weight of what Natalia would face if our father learned she was a DEA agent hit her. What began as a strategic move had shifted dramatically – I was falling for the captivating DEA agent who had come into my life. I couldn't let the woman I was falling in love with become another casualty of Ricardo Reyes' ruthless pursuit of power.

Sofia moved closer, her usually vibrant eyes dull with fear and worry. She reached out and clasped my hands in hers – a silent plea for reason. "Then cut her loose, Dante," she urged me earnestly. "Convince her to start a new life far away from our father before it's too late."

I ran a hand through my hair, frustration, and desperation warring within me. "I know, Sof, I know," I said, my voice strained. "But it's not that simple."

Sofia shook her head. "It is that simple, Dante. You have to end this. Cut her loose before it's too late. Tell her to stay away from us, from the cartel."

The words hung in the air. Natalia was a threat, a liability, and in our world, liabilities were eliminated – swiftly and without mercy.

But I knew I couldn't bring myself to do what she asked. Because deep down, beneath the layers of lies and deception, I'd fallen for Natalia. A part of me saw her as more than just a DEA agent, more than just another pawn in the twisted game we were playing.

"I can't do that, Sof," I said, my voice low and resolute. "I won't."

Sofia's eyes widened, her mouth parting in a silent gasp

of disbelief. "Dante, please," she whispered, her voice thick with emotion. "Don't do this. Don't throw everything away for her."

I shook my head, my jaw clenched with determination. "You don't understand, Sofia. Natalia... she's different. She's not like the others."

A bitter laugh escaped Sofia's lips, her eyes glistening with unshed tears. "That's what you think, Dante," she said, her voice trembling. "But she's playing you, just like she's been playing me all along. Can't you see that?"

I opened my mouth to protest, but Sofia held up a hand, cutting me off before I could speak.

"No, listen to me," she said, her voice urgent. "This can only end one way, Dante. Either you cut her loose, or she ends up dead. And if you don't do it, if you don't make her leave, then Dad will find out."

Her words hit me like a punch to the gut, their implications clear and undeniable.

"There's another way," I said, the words tumbling from my lips before I could stop them.

Sofia's brow furrowed, her eyes narrowing. "What are you talking about?"

I drew a deep breath, steeling my resolve. "I could turn myself in," I said, my voice barely above a whisper. "Become a witness against Dad and the cartel."

Sofia's mouth parted in a silent gasp of shock and disbelief.

"You can't be serious," she breathed. "Dante, that's... that's betrayal. Dad would never forgive you."

I shrugged, my expression hardening into a mask of determination. "Maybe that's the point, Sof," I said, my voice low and resolute. "Maybe it's time for a change. Teach him a lesson for once."

TWENTY-SEVEN
NATALIA

THE TEARS BURNED HOT TRAILS DOWN MY CHEEKS AS I gripped the steering wheel, my knuckles turning white from the sheer force of my grip. The streets of Miami blurred past in a kaleidoscope of neon lights and honking horns, but I barely registered them.

How could I have been so stupid, so naive? To think that I could convince Sofia to turn against her own family, to betray the bonds of blood and loyalty that ran deeper than any undercover mission. I had played my hand too soon and pushed too hard, and now the consequences threatened to unravel everything I had worked for.

The rational part of my mind tried to cling to the hope that Sofia wouldn't tell her father a word about this, that she would keep my secret if only to protect her brother. But the doubts swirled like a whirlpool, whispering insidious thoughts that chilled me.

What if she told Dante? What if she revealed the truth

about my identity, shattering the delicate web of lies and deception I had so carefully woven?

I had become too invested, too emotionally entangled in this assignment. Dante Reyes was supposed to be a means to an end, a steppingstone on the path to bringing down the cartel that had claimed the life of my partner and so many others. But somewhere along the way, the lines had blurred, and I had allowed myself to become seduced by the promise of something more.

Gritting my teeth, I forced myself to focus on the road ahead. As my apartment building came into view, I felt a surge of relief. The prospect of shedding the persona of Eva Morales and retreating into the safety of my true self offered a glimmer of solace in the darkness.

I barely remembered parking the car, my movements fueled by pure muscle memory as I made my way up the stairs and into the sanctuary of my apartment. The door had barely closed behind me before I was kicking off the high-end heels.

I powered up my laptop by shaking my hands and initiated the secure video link to Morrow. His stern face appeared on the screen.

"Ramirez," he greeted me. "You look like you have been through hell and back. What happened?"

I willed my voice to remain steady as I recounted the disastrous encounter with Sofia. As the words tumbled from my lips, I felt a strange sense of detachment, as if I were narrating someone else's story, someone else's failure.

Morrow's brow furrowed, his eyes narrowing as he

absorbed the implications of my actions. "You went off-book, Natalia," he admonished, his tone sharp and disapproving. "You know the protocols, the rules. We don't involve civilians, not unless it's necessary."

I flinched at the reprimand, my cheeks burning with shame. "I know, sir," I said. "I made a mistake, a lapse in judgment. I thought I could turn Sofia and convince her to help us bring Dante in."

Morrow shook his head. "And now, you've put the entire operation at risk. If Sofia tells Dante the truth, if he finds out who you are, or worse, if their father finds out..."

His voice trailed off, the unspoken threat hanging between us. We both knew the consequences, the brutal retribution that would be exacted upon me if Ricardo Reyes discovered my real identity.

"I know," I whispered, my throat constricting with emotion. "I screwed up, sir. I let my emotions cloud my judgment, and now I've jeopardized everything."

Morrow's gaze softened, his features etched with concern and resignation. "It's time to pull the plug, Natalia," he said, his voice grave. "This operation has gone too far and become too compromised. I'm calling you in."

The words hit me like a physical blow, stealing the air from my lungs as his decision sank in. "But... sir," I protested, my voice trembling with desperation. "We're so close. Suppose I can get Dante to trust me and open up about the cartel's operations. At least give me one shot. We don't even know; maybe Dante wants to escape the cartel."

"It's too late and risky for that, Ramirez," Morrow cut

me off, his tone leaving no room for argument. "Your cover is blown, and your life is at risk. We can't afford to lose another agent, not to these bastards."

I opened my mouth to protest, but the words died on my lips as a strange expression flickered across Morrow's face. It was fleeting, barely perceptible, but in that moment, I saw something in his eyes that I had never seen before – uncertainty, perhaps even fear.

"Sir?" I ventured, my brow furrowing with concern. "Is everything alright?"

Morrow blinked, his mask of stoic professionalism slipping back into place. "Everything's fine, Ramirez," he assured me, his voice firm and steady. "Just focus on getting out of there safely. We'll debrief once you're back at headquarters."

But even as he spoke, I couldn't shake the feeling that something was off, that there was more to this decision than he was letting on. Before I could press him further, however, my phone buzzed to life on the table beside me, the screen lighting up with a text from Valentina.

"Urgent! Meet at the usual place in an hour."

"Sir, I have to go," I said, gaze flicking back to Morrow's image on the screen. "But we're not done discussing this. I need to know what's going on."

Morrow's jaw tightened ever so slightly. "Just focus on getting out of there, Ramirez," he reiterated. "We'll handle the rest."

The video call ended, and I closed my laptop, feeling a growing sense of unease. I stripped off the last remnants of my Eva Morales persona, trading the designer dress and jewelry for a simple T-shirt and jeans.

Something wasn't right. Morrow's evasiveness, his sudden insistence on pulling me out before even approaching Dante with an offer of immunity for his testimony – it all felt off, like pieces of a puzzle that refused to fit together no matter how hard I tried. And then there was Valentina's urgent summons, a lifeline amid the chaos that threatened to consume me.

As I stepped into the sunshine, a surge of determination coursed through me. I had to uncover the truth, no matter what. The mission and sacrifices I had made couldn't all be for nothing because that would mean Matt died for nothing.

With a deep breath, I climbed into my car and set off towards the cafe, speculating about the possibilities and unanswered questions. Whatever was going on, whatever secrets were being kept from me, I was determined to uncover the truth.

The cafe was nestled in a quiet corner of Miami, unassuming and discreet – the perfect place for a meeting of this nature.

I scanned the dimly lit interior, quickly finding Valentina tucked away in a secluded booth at the back. She looked up as I approached, her dark eyes glinting with relief.

"Nat," she greeted me, her voice a low murmur as I slid into the booth opposite her. "Thank God you're alright. I was starting to worry."

I managed a tight smile as I took in the tense set of her shoulders, the way her fingers drummed an erratic rhythm against the tabletop. "What's going on, Val?" I asked. "Your text sounded urgent."

Valentina leaned forward as she glanced around the cafe, checking for potential eavesdroppers. "I don't know how to say this, Nat," she began. "But... there's a mole within the DEA."

The words hit me like a physical blow, stealing the air from my lungs. "A mole?" I echoed, my mind reeling with the implications. "Are you sure?"

Valentina nodded. "I wish I weren't," she said. "But I've been digging, and the pieces just don't add up."

She reached into her bag and withdrew a thick manila envelope before sliding it across the table towards me. "Take a look at these."

With trembling fingers, I opened the envelope, my eyes widening as I took in the contents – a stack of surveillance photos, grainy but unmistakable, showing members of the Reyes cartel engaged in what appeared to be a routine drug deal.

"This was taken two days before the raid on the warehouse," Valentina explained. "Notice anything off?"

I studied the photos, furrowing my brow as I tried to understand what I saw. At first glance, everything appeared routine—the cartel members exchanging packages and conducting their business as usual. But then, something caught my eye, a subtle detail I almost missed.

"The location," I breathed as the realization hit me.

"This isn't the warehouse we raided. It's somewhere else entirely."

Valentina nodded. "Exactly. And that's not all." She reached into the envelope again, producing a bundle of documents – surveillance logs, phone records, and other intel that had been gathered in preparation for the raid.

"Look at the dates," she instructed her voice tight with barely contained fury. "These logs, these phone records – all point to the cartel operating out of the warehouse we raided. But these photos prove otherwise."

My mind raced, the pieces falling into place with a sickening clarity. "Someone tipped them off," I whispered in disbelief. "Someone at HQ leaked the raid's location, and that's why the warehouse was empty of drugs."

Valentina's jaw clenched as she nodded. "And that's not even the worst part," she said. "You know, the intel that led us to that warehouse in the first place. Can you guess what I found out?"

I shook my head as a sense of dread settled over me.

Valentina's eyes shimmering with unshed tears as she reached across the table to grasp my hand. "I'm so sorry, Nat," she said. "But it looks like Matt was set up, and a mole in our department was behind it."

I felt the world spinning around me, a flood of emotions threatening to overwhelm me as the truth sank in. Matt's death, the raid that had gone so wrong – it wasn't the Reyes cartel's doing, not entirely. Someone within our ranks had betrayed us and sold us out to the people we were trying to bring down.

Anger and grief had consumed me after Matt's death, but now they sharpened with this revelation. I had spent all this time blaming Dante, blaming the cartel for my partner's loss.

Even as this newfound knowledge threatened to crush me, clarity surged within me, reigniting my determination to see this through. One thing was clear: Dante Reyes was not the true enemy here.

No, the real enemy was the corruption that had taken root within the organization I had sworn to serve, the rot that had plagued and spread, claiming the lives of good men like Matt. And if I had any hope of bringing those responsible to justice, honoring Matt's memory, and ensuring that his sacrifice was not in vain, then I needed to act – but not as I had initially envisioned. Because with the knowledge that a mole had been working against us all along, the game had changed.

If I could convince Dante to turn against his father and help me expose the mole within our ranks, then perhaps there was a chance – a chance for redemption, for justice, for a future that didn't involve bloodshed and betrayal.

As I looked into Valentina's eyes, I saw the same resolve reflected at me, a steely determination that burned brighter than the flickering candles that adorned our table.

"We have to stop them, Val," I said. "All of them – the cartel, the mole, whoever is behind this. We must bring them down, no matter what it takes."

Valentina nodded, her grip on my hand tightening as a

slow smile spread across her face. "You know I'm with you, Nat," she said. "To the end."

DRIVING BACK TO THE APARTMENT, I gripped the steering wheel tightly as my thoughts turned to Valentina's shared revelations. A mole within the DEA, someone who had been feeding information to Ricardo Reyes, someone who had likely compromised my cover and put my life at risk.

The implications were staggering. But even as the anger and betrayal threatened to consume me, a part of me clung to the hope that Dante's feelings for me were genuine. The moments we had shared, the passion and vulnerability he had shown me – could it all have been an act, a carefully orchestrated deception designed to keep me under his thumb?

I shook my head, banishing the doubts from my mind. Now was not the time for second-guessing.

As I pulled into the parking lot of my apartment complex, my mind was made up. I couldn't walk away, not now, not when I was so close to unraveling the truth behind the corruption. And if that meant confronting Dante, laying all my cards on the table, and allowing him to choose a side, then so be it.

I knew I was going against Morrow's orders, but now, I had little choice. If the DEA had been compromised, if there were traitors in our midst, then I couldn't trust anyone but myself, Valentina – and perhaps, Dante.

But I had no idea how Dante would react when laid bare the lies and deception that had brought us to this point. What if he didn't already know? Would he lash out in anger, consumed by the betrayal and the desire for vengeance? Or would he see the truth, the opportunity for redemption that lay before him?

My number one priority was dictating the terms of our confrontation and ensuring that I remained safe no matter what.

I would choose the battleground and set the stage on my terms.

A slow smile spread across my face as the beginnings of a plan took shape.

TWENTY-EIGHT
DANTE

I STUMBLED THROUGH THE DIMLY LIT PARKING LOT, my body heavy with exhaustion. The familiar weight of my car keys jingled in my hand as I approached my sleek black Maserati, the promise of a few hours of respite calling to me like a siren's song.

But just as I reached for the door handle, a prickling sensation crawled up my neck, a sixth sense honed by years of living on the razor's edge of danger. I tensed, my muscles coiling like a spring as I whirled around, ready to face whatever threat lurked in the shadows.

Too late.

A sharp sting pierced the side of my neck, and before I could react, a wave of dizziness washed over me, my vision blurring and my limbs growing heavy. I tried to fight it and lash out at my unseen attacker, but my movements were sluggish and uncoordinated, as if moving through a thick, dense haze.

Then the world tilted on its axis as my knees buckled, my body crumpling to the unforgiving pavement. I struggled to stay conscious, to cling to the rapidly fading threads of awareness, but it was a losing battle.

The last thing I saw before the darkness claimed me was a pair of scuffed boots advancing toward me with a slow, deliberate stride.

WHEN I CAME TO, I was in the trunk of a car, at least by the smell of it. My limbs felt like lead as I tried to piece together what the hell just happened. Motherfucking Javier Cruz, this had to be his work. It reeked of the desperate, back-alley tactics that asshole loved. Well, he picked the wrong fucking guy to mess with this time.

My head was still cloudy when the car lurched to a stop. I could hear muffled voices outside. I tried to make out what they were saying, but with the buzz in my ears, it all sounded like underwater shit. My heart pounded, fear of what was coming next gripping me.

I gasped for air as the trunk lid opened, and blinding light from a flashlight pierced the darkness. As my eyes adjusted, I found myself staring up at... Natalia? What the hell? Her expression was a mix of determination and something else – something I couldn't quite place.

"Dante," she said, her voice steady, betraying none of the turmoil I knew must be raging within her. "We need to talk."

I struggled to sit up, my limbs still heavy and uncoordinated from the effects of the sedative. "Talk?" I rasped, my throat dry and aching. "Is that your word for kidnapping, special agent Natalia Ramirez?"

Natalia's eyes narrowed, her jaw tightening ever so slightly. "Don't play the victim, Dante," she countered, her tone sharp and unyielding. "You knew what you were getting into when you gave me those false leads."

I felt a surge of anger course through me, pushing past the lingering haze of the drugs. "And you knew what you were doing when you lied to me and manipulated me with your undercover shit," I shot back, my voice rising with each word. "So, let's not pretend like either of us has the moral high ground here."

A flicker of something like regret passed across Natalia's features. "You're right," she conceded. "We've both played our parts, deceived each other in our own ways. But that's not why we're here, Dante."

I arched an eyebrow, curiosity, and caution warring within me. "Then why are we here, Natalia?" I asked, emphasizing her real name. "What's this all about?"

She inhaled deeply, her eyes never leaving mine. "It's about the truth, Dante. The truth about the DEA and your father, about the corruption that runs deeper than we could have imagined."

I felt my heart skip a beat as her words sank in. "What are you talking about?" I demanded.

Natalia's eyes blazed with anger and determination. "The raid on the warehouse that went wrong," she began.

"It was a set-up, Dante. Someone within the DEA tipped off the cartel and compromised the entire operation. Killed my partner, Agent Matt Bennett."

I shook my head, my mind reeling with the implications of her revelation. "That's impossible," I breathed. "No one knew the details except for..."

My voice trailed off as the realization hit me, a sickening weight settling in the pit of my stomach. "My father," I said, the words tasting like ash on my tongue. I remembered him telling me that he had moved the product. However, I'd never imagined an informant within the DEA had told him. "He set me up, used me as bait to get your partner killed. But why?"

"Maybe Matt was getting too close. No matter what, the cartel had a mole in the DEA for a long time."

"I swear to you, I had no part in that setup," I rasped. "I'm not proud of everything I do, but I'm not a murder..."

She held up a hand, silencing me with a gentle shake of her head. "I know, Dante," she said, her eyes shimmering with sadness and resolve. "I wouldn't have brought you here if I thought otherwise."

I searched her face as I tried to make sense of it all. "So, what are you saying, Natalia?" I asked. "What do you want from me?"

She leaned in closer, her face mere inches from mine. "I want you to help me take down your father," she said.

I narrowed my eyes. "I had a feeling. Maybe we can discuss that later, but first, there's a little matter we need to clear up."

"I'm listening," she said cooly.

"You stuck a fucking needle in my neck," I breathed in her face.

She didn't flinch. "You spanked me twice. I think we're even."

Before I could utter a comeback, Natalia's lips crashed against mine, her kiss fierce and hungry. I melted into her embrace, my hands tangling in her hair as I surrendered to the emotions that threatened to consume us both.

A pointed cough from behind Natalia broke the spell, and we parted, breathless and flushed. I noticed the other woman standing a few feet away, her arms crossed over her chest.

"As touching as this little reunion is," she drawled, "maybe we should take this somewhere else."

Natalia flushed, her cheeks coloring with embarrassment as she straightened, her composure slipping back into place. "You're right, Val," she said, her gaze flickering back to me. "We have much to discuss, and this isn't the ideal location."

I nodded. "Lead the way," I said. "Preferably a place with alcohol. I need a fucking drink."

———

I NURSED my tequila as we settled into a secluded booth at the back of the dimly lit Cuban joint Valentina had suggested. The mouthwatering scent of spices and sizzling meat wafted through the air, a sharp contrast to our uneasy vibes.

"So," Valentina began, her dark eyes flickering between Natalia and me. "We all know why we're here. The question is, what's the plan?"

I took a sip of my drink, letting the fiery liquid burn down my throat before responding. "The plan is simple," I said. "We take down my father and anyone else loyal to him."

Natalia nodded. "Easier said than done, Dante," she pointed out. "Your father is a powerful man with deep resources and connections. We can't just waltz in there guns blazing."

"She's right," Valentina chimed in, her brow furrowed in thought. "We need to be smart about this, play our cards close to the chest until we have enough evidence to make a case that'll stick."

I leaned back in my seat, my mind whirring with possibilities. "Then that's where I come in," I said, a slow smile spreading across my face. "I can spy on my father, snoop around a bit, and find out what he knows about the mole in the DEA."

Natalia's eyes widened, a flicker of concern passing across her features. "Dante, that's too risky," she protested, her voice tinged with worry. "If your father even suspects that you're working with us, he won't hesitate to eliminate you as a threat."

I reached across the table, my fingers brushing against hers in a gentle, reassuring gesture. "I know the risks," I said. "But this is our best shot, our only shot at bringing down the cartel and exposing the mole."

Valentina nodded. "He's right, Nat," she said. "We can't take down the cartel without insider information, and Dante is our best chance at getting that."

Natalia's jaw tightened, her eyes burning with emotions – concern, determination, and something else that I couldn't quite place. "Alright," she conceded.

I squeezed her hand, my thumb tracing soothing circles against her skin. "I promise I'll do whatever it takes to keep us both safe."

We spent the next hour hashing out the details, our voices hushed as we strategized and planned our next moves. Valentina would continue digging into the mole, using her contacts and resources to uncover any evidence that could lead us to the traitor. Natalia would deal with Agent Morrow to discover what he was hiding; *if* he was hiding anything at all.

Meanwhile, I would play the part of the devoted son and try to uncover information about his dealings with the mole and the events surrounding Agent Bennett's death.

As the night deepened and the tequila flowed, laughter replaced the initial tension. Natalia's hand brushed mine, fingers lingering a moment too long, sending shivers down my spine. Her gaze met mine, eyes dark with desire, and I felt the heat rising between us, undeniable and electric.

Ever the voice of reason, Valentina was the first to call it a night. "Alright, lovebirds," she quipped, her eyes twinkling with mischief as she slid out of the booth. "I'll leave you two to... reconnect."

Natalia flushed, but her gaze never wavered from mine. Her eyes burned with a mix of desire and vulnerability that sent my heart racing.

As Valentina disappeared into the night, I turned to Natalia, my hand finding hers beneath the table. "So, mi reina," I said, my voice a low, seductive purr. "What do you say we take this reunion somewhere a little more... private?"

Natalia's lips stretched into a slow, sultry smile, her fingers tightening around mine. "I thought you'd never ask, Dante," she purred, her voice thick with promise.

TWENTY-NINE
NATALIA

As we left the Cuban restaurant, Dante's hand found the small of my back, guiding me toward the waiting cab with a delightful possessive touch.

The instant the car doors closed behind us, our pent-up desire exploded into a raging inferno. Our mouths crashed together in a desperate, hungry kiss, and our hands roamed and explored with a frantic urgency that spoke of pent-up longing.

Dante's fingers tangled in my hair, his lips trailing a scorching path along my jaw and down the column of my throat. I arched against him, a soft moan escaping my lips as his teeth grazed the sensitive skin of my pulse point.

"Ahem."

The driver's pointed cough shattered the moment, and we sprang apart, breathless and flushed with desire. Dante shot the man a withering glare, his eyes blazing with frustration.

"Where to, folks?" the driver asked, his tone hinting at amusement, which only fueled Dante's irritation.

Before I could respond, Dante leaned towards me, his voice low. "We can't go back to my place," he said, his breath hot against my ear. "Not until this is all over. Too many eyes, too many potential threats."

I nodded, understanding the implications of his words. The familiar comfort of his penthouse and the allure of the playroom beckoned me, but I resisted their siren call, knowing that we couldn't gamble with so much on the line.

Dante's lips morphed into a slow grin, his eyes sparkling with mischief. "I have a better idea," he purred, his voice a low, seductive rumble. "Our family yacht. Nobody is ever using it. We can lay low there for a few days."

I tried to play it cool, but the possibility of sneaking away with Dante on a private yacht made my heart flip. He flashed me a knowing smile before turning to the driver, telling him to head to the marina.

As the cab merged into the flow of traffic, Dante's hand found mine, his fingers lacing through my own in a gesture that was equal parts possessive and reassuring. "It'll take at least twenty minutes to get there in this traffic," he said. "Maybe we should continue our... reunion? Give two fucks about what the driver thinks?"

As I leaned in, a slow smile spread across my face, my lips brushing against his in a teasing caress. "I like that idea, Dante," I breathed, my fingers trailing a searing path along the hard planes of his chest.

Dante growled low in his throat, his arm snaking around my waist and pulling me flush against him. Our mouths collided, tongues tangling and dueling for dominance as our world faded into a hazy blur.

My hands were all over his body, reacquainting myself with the hard, muscular contours that I had come to crave like a drug. Dante's fingers deftly undid the buttons of my blouse, his touch searing a path along my heated skin as he pushed the fabric aside to expose my lace-clad breasts.

I gasped into his mouth as his calloused fingers traced the delicate curves, his thumb brushing over the taut peak of my nipple through the thin lace. The sensation was electric, sending sparks of pleasure shooting straight to my core.

"Dante," I breathed, my voice a desperate plea as I arched against him, silently begging for more.

He chuckled, the sound low and wicked as his lips trailed a blazing path along the column of my throat. "Patience, mi reina," he said, his breath hot against my skin. "We'll have all the time in the world on the yacht."

And in that moment, lost in the heady haze of desire and the promise of what was to come, I realized he was right. There was no longer a time limit to our relationship, no longer a need to rush to capture every bit of deliciousness he continuously emitted. For the first time, the constant threat of danger and betrayal faded into the background, replaced by a singular focus—Dante and the undeniable connection that bound us together.

As the car slowed to a stop, Dante's hand found mine,

his fingers intertwining with my own as he led me out of the vehicle and into the marina.

My breath caught in my throat as we stepped onto the yacht's gleaming deck, my eyes widening as I took in the sheer luxury.

"Welcome aboard, mi reina," Dante said, his voice a low, seductive purr as he slid an arm around my waist, pulling me flush against his side. "What do you think?"

"It's... incredible," I breathed, my gaze sweeping over the expansive deck and the glittering view of the ocean that stretched before us. "I've never seen anything like it."

Dante chuckled, his chest rumbling against my back as he pressed a lingering kiss to the curve of my neck. "It's my father's," he admitted, his voice laced with something dark and complex. "He doesn't even like being on the water, but he had to have the biggest, most ostentatious yacht money could buy."

I arched an eyebrow, turning in his embrace to face him. "And you?" I asked. "Do you enjoy being out on the open water?"

A genuine smile spread across Dante's face, his eyes crinkling at the corners in a way that made my heart skip a beat. "I do," he confessed, his fingers trailing a feather-light path along my jawline. "This is the only place I can truly escape, the only place where the weight of the cartel, of my father's legacy, doesn't seem quite so suffocating."

I nodded. It made sense. For a man like Dante, born into a life of violence and corruption, the open sea must have represented a rare taste of freedom, a fleeting glimpse of something beyond the confines of the world he knew.

"So, where's the playroom?" I teased, my voice dropping to a sultry murmur as I traced his chest with the tip of my finger. "Or do you have some other... special accommodations in mind?"

Dante's eyes darkened with desire, his lips curving into a wicked grin. "Sadly, mi reina, my father's yacht lacks the amenities we've grown accustomed to," he purred, his fingers tangling in my hair as he pulled me closer. "But I assure you, we can improvise."

I bit back a moan, my body thrumming. "Is that so?" I breathed, my fingers curling into the fabric of his shirt as I fought to maintain my composure.

He leaned in, his lips brushing against my ear as his breath danced across my skin. "I'm quite skilled with knots, you know," he said, his voice a sultry promise that sent a delicious ache pulsing between my thighs.

"Well, in that case, I can't wait to see what you have in store for me, Dante Reyes."

His grin widened, his eyes glinting with desire. Without another word, he backed me towards the entrance to the cabin below.

The gentle hum of the yacht's engines vibrated beneath our feet, the rhythmic pulse resonating with the pounding of my heart.

We went down the staircase to the master suite, and the lavish decor took me aback. Plush cream carpeting, polished mahogany furniture, and floor-to-ceiling windows that offered an unobstructed view of the starlit sky created an atmosphere of refined luxury. But it was the massive king-sized bed that dominated the room, its sheets a pristine white that beckoned like a siren's call.

Dante turned to face me, his eyes burning with an intensity that made my knees weak. "Are you sure about this?" he asked, his voice filled with a raw vulnerability that belied his usual confident demeanor. "Once we cross this line without pretending, there's no going back. This is real. You'll be mine in every sense of the word."

This wasn't just about the physical act of submission; it was about laying myself bare, offering him a part of myself that I had guarded fiercely. But as I looked into his eyes, I knew there was nowhere else I would rather be, no one else I would rather be with.

"I'm sure," I whispered, my voice steady despite my emotions swirling. "I trust you, Dante."

A predatory grin spread across his face, and his eyes darkened with desire as he closed the distance between us. "Such pretty words," he said, his fingers tracing the contours of my face in a gentle, reverent caress. "But actions speak louder than words, don't they?"

Before I could respond, he captured my lips in a searing kiss, his tongue delving into my mouth with a possessive hunger that left me breathless.

He broke the kiss, his breath coming in sharp bursts as he stepped back, his gaze raking over me with raw, primal hunger. "Clothes off, mi reina," he commanded.

I complied without hesitation, peeling off my clothes

with a sense of urgency that bordered on desperation. I stood before him, naked and exposed, my body trembling.

Dante's eyes drank in the sight of me, his gaze lingering on my breasts, my stomach, the juncture of my thighs. "So beautiful," he whispered. "You take my breath away."

He reached into his pocket, withdrawing a length of silk that glinted in the dim light. "Hands," he ordered, his voice firm and authoritative.

I extended my arms, my breath hitching as he wrapped the silk around my wrists, securing it with intricate knots. The fabric was soft against my skin, yet it held me fast, a tangible reminder of my surrender, my trust in him.

Dante led me to the bed, his hands guiding me gently as he positioned me on my back, my bound wrists resting above my head. He reached into the bedside table drawer, withdrawing a black satin blindfold that matched the restraints.

"Trust me, Natalia," he purred as he covered my eyes, plunging me into darkness.

I nodded, my senses heightened as the world around me faded into a hazy blur. I was acutely aware of every sound, every movement, every breath that passed between us. I could feel the heat of his body as he moved over me, his gaze as it swept over my exposed flesh.

His lips brushed against mine, a featherlight caress. "I'm going to make you feel like you've never felt before," he promised in a seductive whisper that made my heart race.

I felt Dante's strong hands on my ankles, guiding

them apart before securing my legs to the bedposts with what felt like the same silk material he'd used on my wrists. My heart pounded in anticipation, a delicious thrill coursing through me as I lay there, vulnerable and exposed.

"Tonight," he purred in my ear, "I'm going to show you my world, take you places you've never been before. But first, we need a safe word."

I hesitated for a moment. This was it; there was no turning back now. I needed a word that would snap me out of any fantasy we might venture into, in case... "Um... strawberry?" It was the first thing that came to mind, and I immediately regretted it.

Dante chuckled softly, his laughter low and sensual. "Strawberry it is." He pressed a feather-light kiss to my neck before moving downward. "Now, try to remember that tonight is about trust and pleasure."

Before I could respond, a sharp pain lashed out at my inner thigh, making me gasp in surprise. My eyes flicked behind the blindfold as I realized it was a whip or some-thing similar. The stinging quickly faded into a delicious burn that traveled through my body straight to my core.

"That little snap was just so you know who's in charge," he said matter-of-factly as if he'd just commented on the weather. He continued his journey upwards along my thighs, each strike leaving behind a trail of fire in its wake.

"Have you ever tried a butt plug, mi reina?" he asked.

I shook my head as I remembered fantasizing about

him taking me like this. "No," I replied, unable to hide my excitement.

"Well, then, I think it's time we changed that, don't you?"

I bit my lip as I nodded.

A noise sounded like Dante was getting something from the bedside table drawer. "I think we should start with the smaller one," he said. "Just to get you used to the sensation."

My breath came in short, shallow gasps as his fingers brushed the sensitive skin of my inner thigh, sending a shiver of anticipation racing through me. "Relax," he said, his lips brushing against my ear as his fingers trailed a teasing path toward my core. "I'm going to make you feel so good."

I moaned softly as his fingers found my slick entrance, teasing and probing with a gentle pressure that had me squirming beneath him. "That's it, mi reina," he purred, his voice a low, seductive rumble. "Let me hear how much you're enjoying this."

He eased a slick finger inside my butthole, his touch gentle and patient as I adjusted to the sensation. "Oh, Dante," I breathed as he added a second lubed finger, stretching me open.

I whimpered, my body thrumming with need as Dante prepared me, his touch both tender and commanding.

"You like that, don't you?" he growled, his breath hot against my skin. "Feeling so full, so pleasured."

"Yes," I whispered, my body arching against him as a

coil of tension began to tighten within me. "More, please, Dante. I need more."

Dante chuckled, the sound sending a thrill of anticipation racing through me. "As you wish," he purred, withdrawing his fingers, and I heard him reaching for something.

I felt him slick the butt plug with lube, his fingers teasing and probing at my entrance, stretching me open as he slowly inserted the toy. I gasped at the sensation, my body tensing momentarily before relaxing into the fullness.

"How does that feel, mi reina?" Dante asked, his voice a sultry murmur as he began to slowly thrust the plug in and out, sending waves of pleasure coursing through me.

"Oh, God," I moaned, my hips bucking against him as the coil of tension within me tightened. "It feels incredible, Dante. Please, don't stop."

Dante's breath was hot against my skin as he continued to thrust the plug in and out, his fingers teasing and caressing my sensitive flesh. "I can tell you like feeling full in your tight virgin ass, so satisfied."

"Yes," I whimpered, my body arching off the bed as a wave of pleasure washed over me, threatening to consume me. "More, Dante. Please, fuck my ass."

Dante chuckled, withdrawing the butt plug and reaching for something else from the drawer. "Not sure you're ready for my cock yet. Let's try this first."

I felt a blunt pressure at my entrance, the tip of a lubed-up dildo pushing gently against me. "Relax, mi reina," Dante said softly, easing the toy inside me. "Just breathe and let it happen."

I nodded, my breath coming in short, sharp gasps as the dildo stretched my ass open, filling me in a way I'd never experienced before. Dante began to move the dildo in and out, his thrusts slow and measured, his free hand teasing and caressing my clit.

I whimpered, my body thrumming with pleasure as Dante continued to stroke me with the dildo, his touch both gentle and commanding. "Oh, Dante," I breathed, my hips arching off the bed as a coil of tension began to tighten within me. "Please, I need it now."

Dante removed the dildo. "You ready for me?" he asked and positioned the tip of his cock against my anus.

"Yes," I whispered, my body aching for him as he eased inside my ass, stretching me open in a way that was both familiar and new.

Dante set a slow, torturous pace, his hips moving in and out with a steady rhythm that had me squirming beneath him. "Take it, mi reina," he purred, his hands gripping my hips, guiding our movements. "Take it all; feel me fill you."

I could feel my body thrumming with pleasure like I'd never felt before. "Oh, Dante," I gasped as his thrusts became more insistent, more urgent. "Please, don't stop."

Dante growled as he took control, one hand gripping my hips while he flicked my clit with the thumb of his other. "That's it, mi reina. Let go, come for me again."

His words were like a trigger, sending me tumbling

over the edge again. I cried out, my body convulsing with the force of my release as Dante followed me over the edge, his release flooding my body as he called out my name.

We collapsed on the bed, and as we lay tangled together, our hearts pounding and our breaths mingling, Dante removed my blindfold. I looked at him, my eyes soft. "Dante," I whispered, tracing the contours of his face with my finger.

He captured my hand and brought it to his lips, placing a tender kiss on my palm. "Natalia," he murmured, his voice thick with emotion.

At that moment, I knew that what we had was powerful enough to overcome any obstacle.

THIRTY

DANTE

THE MASERATI'S ENGINE ROARED AS I TORE DOWN THE winding drive towards my father's palatial estate in Palm Beach. The manicured lawns and meticulously pruned hedges blurred past my window, starkly contrasting the storm of emotions within me.

Last night with Natalia had been... transcendent. The way she had surrendered herself to me, the trust and vulnerability in her eyes as I bound her wrists and took her to new heights of pleasure. It had awoken something primal within me, a possessive need to claim her, to make her mine in every sense of the word.

But more than that, it had unlocked a part of me buried beneath my father's suffocating patrimony. For the first time I had felt truly alive, free from the shackles of the life I had been born into.

And now, as the imposing silhouette of my father's

mansion loomed before me, I felt that newfound freedom slipping through my fingers like grains of sand. The mere thought of facing my father, looking into those cold, calculating eyes, pretending to be the dutiful son he expected, made my stomach churn with a potent mix of rage and disgust.

How could I play the part? How could I cozy up to the man who had so callously used me as a pawn in his twisted game of power and deception, endangering not only my own life but that of the woman I loved?

Natalia.

Her name was like a soothing balm, a reminder of why I was doing this, the reason I had to swallow my pride and play along with my father's charade. If I wanted to overpower him and expose him, I had to keep my emotions in check; I needed to be the master of deception that my father had groomed me to be.

The iron gates parted before me, and I eased the Maserati onto the winding drive that led to the main house.

I pulled to a stop in the circular drive in front of the imposing entrance, my heartbeat galloping as I killed the engine and stepped out onto the intricately designed pavers.

The massive front doors swung open before I could reach for the ornate knocker, and a familiar face emerged.

"Dante," Marco greeted me, his voice a low rumble as he stepped aside to let me pass.

I nodded, jaw clenched as I brushed past him and into the cavernous foyer.

"He's in the study," Marco called after me. "Be careful, hermano."

I acknowledged his words with a curt nod, my steps faltering before I forced myself onwards.

As I approached the doors, the muffled sound of voices reached my ears—my father's deep baritone punctuated by the occasional higher-pitched response of one of his henchmen. I steeled myself, straightening my shoulders and schooling my features into a mask of impassivity before reaching for the brass handle and pushing the door open.

My father sat behind his massive mahogany desk, his imposing frame silhouetted against the windows overlooking the manicured grounds. "Dante," he greeted me, his voice a low rumble. "I was beginning to wonder if you'd forgotten your way home, hijo."

I felt Tony's eyes upon me, his gaze sharp and assessing as he took in my every move. Tony had been by my father's side for decades, the enforcer who helped build the Reyes cartel into the sprawling criminal empire it was today.

"Never, Father," I said, my voice steady despite the turmoil within me. "I've simply been... preoccupied with matters of business."

Ricardo's eyes narrowed, his lips curving into a humorless smile that didn't reach his eyes. "Ah, yes," he drawled, leaning back in his chair. "Your little... side ventures. Tell me, Dante, how is that strip club of yours faring these days? Still not turning a profit?"

M. S. PARKER

The barb was deliberate, a not-so-subtle jab at my efforts to distance myself from the cartel's more unsavory activities. But I refused to take the bait, refused to let my father see the chink in my armor his words were designed to exploit.

"Club Diablo is doing just fine, Father," I said evenly. "I've been exploring new avenues for expansion, some legitimate business opportunities that could prove quite lucrative."

Ricardo's brow arched. "Legitimate, you say?" he scoffed, his fingers drumming the polished surface of his desk. "And what would the heir to my empire want with legitimate businesses?"

I was done with his manipulation games. "I am not here to discuss the club or my other business ideas. I am here to discuss your mole in the DEA."

My father tried to hide his surprise, but I could read him like a book. He nodded to his lieutenant. "Tony, we can continue our business later. I need to have a word with my idiot of a son here."

Not until Tony was out of the room did my father look at me again. "What makes you think I have a mole in the DEA, son?" he asked, studying me intensely.

I leaned over his desk. "Because I know you had Natalia's partner killed because he was getting too close," I breathed.

A flicker of surprise crossed his features, quickly masked by that infuriatingly calm demeanor he always adopted. "Our little Agent Ramirez has been filling your head with stories." He leaned back, steepling his fingers as he regarded me with a predatory gaze. "So what if I had? That misguided pup stuck his nose where it didn't belong. He got what was coming to him."

The callous disregard in his tone made my stomach churn. I knew my father was nothing but a ruthless monster who placed no value on innocent lives, all in the name of protecting his precious empire, but to go against his own blood.

"You son of a bitch," I growled, taking a menacing step forward. "You set me up as bait to draw them in, knowing full well people would die."

Ricardo's smile widened, cold and predatory. "Of course I did, mijo. This is war, and in war, there are always casualties." He spread his hands in a mock gesture. "Sacrifices must be made for the greater good of our organization."

"Sacrifices?" I spat the word like a curse, my hands balling into fists. "You mean cold-blooded murder."

He waved a dismissive hand, that maddening smirk never wavering. "Call it what you will. The fact remains that your little DEA girlfriend and her partner made the mistake of crossing me."

Something in me snapped, the last thread of respect I'd harbored for the man who had sired me fraying and unraveling. I lunged forward, slamming my palms down on his desk with enough force to make the heavy oak shudder.

"You lying, manipulative bastard," I snarled, leaning across the expanse of polished wood until our faces were mere inches apart. "You used me as a pawn in your twisted game. Put me in the crosshairs without a second thought."

Ricardo met my gaze unflinchingly, his cold, dead eyes betraying not a shred of remorse. "I did what was necessary to protect our interests, our legacy. If a few expendable pawns had to be sacrificed along the way, so be it." His lips curled into a sneer. "Don't try to act so high and mighty, Dante. You're cut from the same ruthless cloth as the rest of us. It's in your blood."

I recoiled as if he'd struck me, his words hitting me like a physical blow. Was he right? Had the poison of this life, this brutal existence, corrupted me so thoroughly that I was no better than him—a soulless monster concerned only with power and self-preservation?

No. I refused to believe that. Not after everything I'd seen, everything Natalia had shown me about honor and justice and doing the right thing, no matter the cost.

"You're wrong," I rasped. "I'm not like you, old man. Not anymore."

He leaned back in his chair, steepling his fingers again as he studied me with cold calculation. "I must say, I'm surprised seeing you jeopardize everything we stand for, all for a piece of ass with a badge."

White-hot fury lanced through me at his dismissive words, his utter disregard for the woman who had shown me there was more to life than this twisted world of violence and depravity.

"Watch your fucking mouth," I snarled, my body

coiled tight with barely contained rage. "Natalia is worth more than you could ever comprehend, you soulless prick."

A cruel smile twisted Ricardo's thin lips. "Such passion," he mocked. "Tell me, does she know what you're capable of? The atrocities you've committed in service of this 'twisted world'?" He tisked again, his eyes glittering with malicious glee. "I'd be careful if I were you, mijo. Wouldn't want your little girlfriend to see the real Dante Reyes, now would we?"

I clenched my fists, my nails biting into my palms as I fought to maintain my composure despite my father's taunts. "You don't know a damn thing about Natalia," I ground out. "She's more special than you could ever imagine, old man. Stronger than both of us."

A cruel chuckle rumbled from deep within his chest, the sound grating on my frayed nerves. "We'll see about that, won't we?" He leaned forward, his eyes glittering with malice. "I'm going to enjoy watching her break."

White-hot rage surged at the implied threat, boiling my blood. I saw red, focused on a primal urge—to wipe that smug grin off my father's face with my bare hands.

In a blur of motion, I lunged across the desk, my fingers closing around the starched collar of his shirt as I hauled him bodily out of his chair. Ricardo's eyes went wide with shock and fear as I slammed him against the wall, the heavy thud reverberating through the room like a gunshot.

"You listen to me, you twisted piece of shit," I snarled, my face mere inches from his. "If you so much as breathe in Natalia's direction, I'll put you in the ground myself. Do you hear me?"

For the first time in my life, I saw a flicker of genuine fear in my father's eyes. Gone was the cocky bravado, the unshakable confidence that had allowed him to commit atrocity after atrocity without a shred of remorse. At that moment, he was just a sad, pathetic old man staring down the barrel of his mortality.

"You wouldn't dare," he rasped, his voice thin and reedy. "I'm your father, your blood."

A bitter laugh tore from my throat, harsh and mocking. "Blood? Is that what you think binds us together, old man? All I see when I look at you is a twisted, soulless monster who would sell his offspring to the devil if it meant clinging to his precious power for a little while longer."

Ricardo opened his mouth to spew more of his venomous rhetoric, but I cut him off with a vicious shake that snapped his head back against the wall.

"Not another word," I growled. "From this moment on, you and I are done. This whole bloody empire you've built on a foundation of lies and corpses—it's over. I'm going to burn it all to the ground, and there's nothing you can do to stop me."

His eyes widened, the tendons in his scrawny neck straining as he fought for breath. "You ungrateful whelp," he choked out. "After everything I've done for you, for this family-"

"This isn't a family!" I roared, giving him another vicious shake. "It's a goddamn crime syndicate, a blight on the face of humanity! And I will be the one to put it in its grave once and for all."

With a snarl of disgust, I released my grip, letting the withered husk of the man who had once struck fear into the hearts of entire cartels crumple to the floor in an undignified heap. My father coughed and sputtered, his blood-shot eyes swimming with rage as he glared up at me.

"Mark my words, boy," he gasped, his voice a rasping croak. "You turn your back on everything we've built, and there will be consequences. Dire ones. I'm coming after you."

I met his gaze without flinching, my jaw set in a hard line. "I'm counting on it."

Turning on my heel, I strode from the office without a backward glance, the taste of liberation mingling with the bitter tang of regret on my tongue. There was no going back now - I had crossed the Rubicon and burned the bridges that had once bound me to this life of violence and depravity.

As I emerged into the hallway, I caught sight of Marco waiting for me, my oldest friend, and my brother in all but blood.

"Dante," Marco's voice rumbled. "You alright, bro? You look like you've just come face-to-face with a ghost. So much for your plan of playing his good son to find proof, huh?"

A laugh escaped me, raw and humorless. "New plan," I said, my voice a taut wire ready to snap. "That bastard just confirmed my worst fears – he threw me to the wolves in that warehouse sting. He made me a sitting duck for the DEA. And that's not even the worst of it. He ordered that DEA agent's death."

Marco's face hardened, a shadow passing over his features. "Motherfucker," he hissed under his breath, his disgust palpable. "But what's his game? Why gamble with your neck and risk drawing the heat from the DEA?"

I scrubbed a hand over my face. "My father's got a rat in the DEA's ranks, someone who's been keeping him in the loop, helping him dodge the feds for decades. He wanted to keep his precious mole around, so when Natalia's partner got close to the mole, Ricardo ordered him killed."

"You're fucking kidding me," Marco blurted, his disbelief etched across his face.

"There's no going back now. I'm taking down my father. Are you with me?"

Marco's resolve solidified, his eyes blazing with the unwavering loyalty born from a lifetime of shared battles. "Whatever it takes, I'm with you. To the bitter end."

I clasped his shoulder, gratitude surging through me. "Thanks, Marco," I said, my eyes sweeping over the gilded cage of my father's mansion. "Let's bounce from this shithole."

With a nod, Marco's grin returned, slow and full of promise. "No need to say it twice, hermano," he said, gesturing toward the exit. "I've got the perfect thing to take your mind off this and rethink our new plan."

Half an hour later, the familiar scent of gunpowder

and oiled metal filled my nostrils as Marco and I stepped into the private shooting range. The rhythmic pop of gunfire echoed through the cavernous space, a sound that once filled me with a sense of purpose and belonging. Now, it just reminded me of the life I was trying to leave behind.

Marco clapped me on the shoulder, his voice cutting through the noise. "Alright, hermano. Time to blow off some steam and clear that head of yours."

He handed me a sleek Beretta 92, its weight a comforting presence in my hand. We took our positions on the firing line, and I slammed the magazine home, racked the slide, and chambered a round with practiced ease.

"Fire at will," Marco barked, and I squeezed the trigger.

With each successive shot, I felt the tension ebb from my body, anger and frustration bleeding away with every spent casing that hit the concrete floor. It was cathartic, a release valve for the maelstrom of emotions threatening to consume me.

As we paused to reload, Marco turned to me, his eyes narrowed in concentration. "So, what's the new plan, Dante? We can't just sit around waiting for your old man to make his move."

I exhaled slowly, considering our options. "We need proof, Marco. Hard evidence of my father's illegal dealings that we can hand over to the feds."

Marco nodded, a thoughtful expression crossing his face. "You know, I've been thinking. Your father's been spending a lot of time at that new office building down-town lately. Something's going on there, I can feel it."

My interest piqued. "What kind of something?"

"Not sure," Marco admitted. "But he's been real secretive about it. Extra security, restricted access. It's not like him to be so paranoid."

A plan began to form in my mind, the pieces falling into place. "You thinking what I'm thinking?"

A slow grin spread across Marco's face. "Break-in?"

I nodded, feeling a surge of adrenaline at the prospect. "If there's anything incriminating, it'll be there. We get in, find the evidence, and get out."

"It's risky," Marco warned, but I could see the excitement in his eyes. "Your old man's security is no joke."

"That's why I've got you, brother," I said, clapping him on the shoulder. "There's no one I'd rather have watching my back."

Marco's grin widened. "Alright, let's do this. But we'll need to plan carefully. Surveillance, security systems, entry points – we need to cover all our bases."

I nodded, feeling a renewed sense of purpose. "We'll start tonight. Scope out the building, figure out the weak points."

As we turned back to the targets, squeezing off another round of shots, I felt a glimmer of hope. This was it – our chance to bring down my father's empire and maybe, just maybe, find a way out of this mess.

With each bullet that found its mark, I imagined I was chipping away at the walls of lies and deceit that had surrounded me for so long. And for the first time in days, I allowed myself to believe that there might be a light at the end of this dark tunnel – a future where Natalia and I could be together, free from the shadows of my past.

"Ready for another round?" Marco asked, breaking me from my thoughts.

I nodded, a determined smile playing on my lips. "Let's do it. We've got work to do."

THIRTY-ONE
NATALIA

I GAZED AT MY REFLECTION IN THE YACHT'S BATHROOM mirror. The memory of last night with Dante still lingered on my skin, a delicious ache that reminded me of the passion we'd shared. I closed my eyes, savoring the recollection of his hands on my body, his lips trailing fire across my skin...

"Focus, Natalia," I muttered, shaking off the haze of desire. As much as I longed to lose myself in thoughts of Dante, I had more pressing matters to attend to.

Val's revelation about a mole in the DEA had turned my world upside down, leaving me questioning everything I thought I knew. The idea that someone within our ranks had been feeding information to Ricardo Reyes for years made my stomach churn. How many operations had been compromised? How many lives had been lost because of this traitor?

And then there was Ted Morrow, my handler and the

man I'd trusted implicitly since joining the DEA. The grizzled veteran had always been a steadfast ally, a rock in the tumultuous sea of undercover work. But now, doubt gnawed at the edges of my certainty. Could he be involved? Did he know more than he was letting on?

I grabbed my purse, double-checking that my gun was securely holstered inside. As I made my way across the yacht's deck, the Miami sun beating down on me, I steeled my resolve. I was going to get answers, one way or another.

The drive to the restaurant where I was meeting Morrow seemed to take an eternity, my mind racing with possibilities and scenarios. I rehearsed what I would say, how I would approach the subject without tipping my hand. If Morrow was involved, I couldn't risk alerting him to my suspicions.

As I pulled into the parking lot of the upscale bistro, I spotted Morrow's beat-up sedan parked near the entrance. Taking a deep breath, I stepped out of my car and made my way inside, my heart pounding in my chest.

Morrow was already seated at a corner table, his weathered face creased with concern as he caught sight of me. "Ramirez," he greeted me, his voice gruff but warm. "Glad you could make it."

I slid into the seat across from him, forcing a smile that didn't quite reach my eyes. "Wouldn't miss it, sir," I replied, my tone carefully neutral. "It's been a while since we've had a chance to catch up face-to-face and not just a zoom call."

Morrow nodded, his eyes searching my face with an

intensity that made me wonder if he could sense the turmoil roiling beneath my calm exterior. "Something's up with you," he said, leaning in closer. "You pulled the plug on the operation like I said, right?"

I hesitated, weighing my words carefully. I wasn't ready to reveal Dante's willingness to help take down his father. "Actually, sir, I came upon something," I began, my fingers toying with the edge of my napkin. "I've uncovered some information that could have serious implications for the entire investigation."

Morrow's brow furrowed, his expression a mixture of curiosity and concern. "What kind of information, Ramirez?" he pressed, his voice low and urgent.

I took a deep breath, steeling myself for what I was about to say. "There's evidence to suggest that there's a mole within the DEA," I said, my eyes never leaving his face as I watched for any sign of recognition or guilt. "Someone who's been feeding information to the Reyes cartel for years."

Morrow's reaction was immediate and visceral. His face paled, his eyes widening in shock as he leaned back in his chair. "Jesus Christ," he muttered, running a hand through his thinning hair. "Are you sure about this, Ramirez?"

I nodded, my gut clenching at the raw emotion in his voice. Either Morrow was a damn good actor, or he was genuinely blindsided by this revelation. "I have reliable intel," I confirmed, keeping my voice low to avoid being overheard. "It explains a lot of our failed operations, including the warehouse raid that got Matt killed."

At the mention of my former partner, Morrow's expression darkened, a flash of pain and anger crossing his features. "Goddamn it," he growled, his fist clenching on the table. "If that's true, if someone in our ranks is responsible for Matt's death..."

He trailed off, his eyes meeting mine with a fierce intensity. "We need to tread carefully here, Ramirez," he said, his voice low and urgent. "If there really is a mole, we can't trust anyone. Not even our own people."

I nodded, a small part of me relaxing at his words. If Morrow was involved, he was putting on one hell of a performance. "What do you suggest, sir?" I asked, leaning in closer.

Morrow's eyes darted around the restaurant, as if checking for potential eavesdroppers. "We need to keep this under wraps for now," he murmured. "Continue your operation with Reyes, see if you can uncover any more information about who might be feeding them intel from our side."

I hesitated, a flicker of doubt crossing my mind. "Sir, with all due respect, shouldn't we bring in Internal Affairs? If there's a traitor in our midst..."

Morrow shook his head vehemently. "Not yet," he insisted, his voice brooking no argument. "We don't know how deep this goes, Ramirez. For all we know, the Internal Affairs could be compromised too. No, we need to handle this ourselves, at least until we have more concrete evidence."

I nodded, my mind racing with the implications of his words. Was Morrow truly looking out for the integrity of the investigation, or was he trying to cover his own tracks? The doubt that had taken root in my mind refused to be silenced, even as I wanted desperately to believe in the man who had been my mentor and ally for so long.

"Understood, sir," I said, forcing a note of conviction into my voice. "I'll keep digging, see what else I can uncover."

Morrow reached across the table, his weathered hand closing over mine in a gesture of reassurance. "Be careful, Ramirez," he said, his voice gruff with emotion. "You're in deep with some dangerous people. If they get even a whiff of suspicion..."

I nodded, a lump forming in my throat at the genuine concern in his eyes. "I know the risks, sir," I assured him. "I'll watch my back."

As we finished our lunch, making small talk about inconsequential matters to avoid arousing suspicion, I couldn't shake the feeling that I was standing on the edge of a precipice. The ground beneath my feet felt unstable, shifting with every new revelation and unanswered question.

Walking back to my car, I felt the weight of the world pressing down on my shoulders. Who could I trust? Dante, the man I was falling for despite my better judgment?

Morrow, my mentor and ally? Or was I truly alone in this fight against corruption and betrayal?

One thing was certain – I was going to get to the bottom of this, no matter the cost. For Matt, for justice, and for my own peace of mind. The truth was out there, and I was going to find it, even if it meant burning everything I thought I knew to the ground.

THE ELEVATOR DOORS SLID OPEN, and I stepped out onto Valentina's floor, my mind still reeling from the day's events. The hallway stretched before me, a gauntlet of identical doors that seemed to mock my confusion and frustration. Before I knew it, I was standing in front of Val's apartment, rapping my knuckles against the wood in the familiar rhythm.

Moments later, the door swung open, revealing Valentina's smirking face. Her dark hair was pulled back in a messy bun, and she wore an oversized NYPD t-shirt that hung off one shoulder – a souvenir from our academy days.

"Well, well, if it isn't Miami's most notorious under-cover hottie," she drawled, leaning against the doorframe. Her eyes narrowed as she took in my tense posture and the shadows under my eyes. "Damn, chica. You look like you've been through the wringer. What's up?"

I didn't waste time with pleasantries, just pushed past her into the apartment. "We've got a problem, Val. A big one."

Her brows furrowed, but she didn't miss a beat, shutting the door behind me with a firm click. "Alright, lay it on me. But first, you look like you could use a drink."

Before I could protest, Val was already moving towards her kitchen. I paced the length of her living room, my fingers twisting nervously as I tried to organize my thoughts. The apartment was quintessentially Val – a mix of sleek modernity and controlled chaos. Case files were scattered across her coffee table, and a half-eaten pizza sat on the counter, evidence of another late night poring over evidence.

Val returned with two glasses of amber liquid, pressing one into my hand. "Okay, spill. What's got you wound up tighter than a two-dollar watch?"

I took a deep breath, then launched into my story. The words tumbled from my lips in a rush as I filled her in on Morrow's infuriating dismissal of my suggestion to bring the information about the potential mole to Internal Affairs. I told her about my growing suspicions, the nagging feeling that something was very wrong with him.

By the time I finished, Val's eyes were blazing with righteous fury. She slammed her glass down on the coffee table, sending case files scattering. "That asshole," she hissed, her fingers curling into tight fists. "If there's a mole in our midst, we need to smoke them out and make them pay. Not sit on our asses and continue as if nothing had happened. What the fuck!"

I nodded grimly, grateful for her unwavering support.

"Exactly. But we need to be smart about this, Val. We can't just go in guns blazing."

She snorted, rolling her eyes. "Since when have you been the cautious one, Ramirez? Where's that badass spirit that used to get us into so much trouble back in the day?" A mischievous grin spread across her face. "Remember that time as rookies we snuck into the evidence locker to 'borrow' that fancy tech for our off-the-books stakeout?"

Despite the gravity of the situation, I couldn't help but crack a smile at the memory. "Yeah, and I remember spending the next month on desk duty as punishment. But this is different, Val. We're talking about uncovering a mole, a traitor who could be embedded deep within the agency. One wrong move and we're fucked, or worse."

Val's face sobered, her fiery bravado tempering into something more focused, more strategic. She flopped down onto her couch, patting the spot next to her. "Alright, so what's the plan? And don't give me any of that 'we should wait and see' bullshit. I know you've got something cooking in that devious mind of yours."

I sank down beside her, running a hand through my hair. "We start by feeling out our contacts, the ones we know we can trust implicitly. See if they've noticed anything off, any whispers or rumors that could point us in the right direction."

"I've already gone through all of them," Val interjected, frustration evident in her voice. "Nothing, zip, nada. It's like trying to catch smoke with your bare hands."

I leaned forward, elbows on my knees. "Okay, so we

need to dig deeper. What about our CI network? Anyone been acting strange lately? Suddenly flush with cash or nervous about meeting?"

Val's brow furrowed in concentration. "Now that you mention it, there's this one guy – Julio. He's been a reliable informant for years, but lately... I don't know. Something's off. He's been dodging my calls, and when I do manage to get him on the phone, he sounds... scared."

My pulse quickened. "That could be something. We need to talk to him, face to face. But we've got to be careful. If he is connected to our mole, we can't tip our hand."

Val nodded, her eyes gleaming with the thrill of the hunt. "I've got an idea. There's this dive bar downtown where Julio likes to hang out. We could 'accidentally' run into him there, keep things casual."

"Good thinking," I agreed. "But what about Morrow? That stubborn jackass is just going to keep stonewalling us, isn't he?"

Val's face darkened. "Fuck Morrow. If he's not going to help us, we'll do this on our own. We don't need his permission to do our jobs."

I hesitated, torn between my instinct to follow protocol and the burning need to uncover the truth. "I don't know, Val. Part of me still wants to believe he's on the level, that he's just being overly cautious. But the other part..." I trailed off, shaking my head. "I don't know who I can trust anymore."

Val reached out, gripping my hand tightly. "Hey, you

can trust me, chica. Always. We're in this together, no matter what. Partners, remember?"

I squeezed her hand back, feeling a wave of gratitude wash over me. "Partners," I echoed. "And that's why I need you to have my back on this, Val. We're going to have to play this close to the vest, keep our cards hidden until we know exactly who we're dealing with."

Her eyes glinted with determination, a feral grin tugging at the corners of her mouth. "Just say the word, Ramirez. I'm locked and loaded. We'll find this mole and make them wish they'd never even thought about betraying the badge."

A small smile tugged at my lips as I nodded, already feeling the burden shifting, becoming more manageable with Val at my side. "Alright, let's get to work. We've got a traitor to catch and a whole lot of asses to kick."

Val stood up, cracking her knuckles with an exaggerated gesture. "Now that's more like it. So, what's our first move, partner?"

I rose to join her, feeling a renewed sense of purpose coursing through my veins. "First, we need to have a talk with Julio. If he's our link to the mole, we need to know who he's talking to, where he's going. Then we hit that bar, see if we can't loosen his tongue a bit."

Val grinned, already moving towards her bedroom. "I'll grab my gear. You know, for a minute there, I was worried you'd gone soft on me, Ramirez. But this? This is the badass partner I know and love."

As Val went to gather our equipment, I stared out her

window at the Miami skyline. Somewhere out there, a traitor was hiding in plain sight, threatening everything we'd worked for.

"Ready to raise some hell?" Val called, emerging with a duffel bag slung over her shoulder.

I turned to her, a determined smile playing on my lips. "Let's do this. We've got work to do."

THE NEON SIGN of "The Rusty Anchor" flickered dimly in the humid Miami night. Val and I sat in her beat-up Chevy, watching as Julio stumbled into the seedy bar.

"Showtime," Val muttered, killing the engine. "Remember, we're just two gals out for a drink. Nothing suspicious."

We sauntered into the bar, the stench of stale beer and desperation hitting us like a wall. Julio was nowhere to be seen.

"I'll check the back," I murmured to Val. "You take the bar."

I pushed through the crowd, my eyes scanning for our target. As I approached the restrooms, I caught a glimpse of Julio slipping into the men's room.

I signaled to Val, who nodded and made her way over. "Ladies' room's full," she announced loudly. "Guess we'll have to use the men's!"

We burst into the bathroom, catching Julio mid-snort, a line of white powder disappearing up his nose.

"Jesus Christ!" he yelped, stumbling backward.

Val's hand shot out, grabbing him by the collar. "Hello, Julio. Fancy meeting you here."

His eyes darted between us, panic setting in. "I-I can explain—"

"Save it," I cut him off. "We need to talk."

For the next twenty minutes, we grilled Julio mercilessly. He babbled about drop-offs and coded messages, but nothing we didn't already know or suspect.

"Come on, Julio," Val growled, her patience wearing thin. "There's got to be more. Who's the mole?"

Julio's bloodshot eyes widened. "The mole? I-I don't know anything about a mole!"

I leaned in close, my voice low and dangerous. "Think harder, Julio. Your freedom depends on it."

He swallowed hard, his Adam's apple bobbing. "I swear, I don't know who it is. But..." he hesitated.

"But what?" I pressed.

"There's this agent I've seen snooping around a lot. More than usual, you know? Always asking questions, making deals."

My heart rate quickened. "Who, Julio? Give me a name."

He licked his lips nervously. "Agent Morrow. I've seen him all over the place lately. It's like he's everywhere, man."

The words hit me like a punch to the gut. Morrow? It couldn't be. And yet...

I exchanged a shocked glance with Val, whose face had gone pale.

"You're sure about this, Julio?" Val asked, her voice barely above a whisper.

He nodded vigorously. "Yeah, yeah. Morrow's been all over the place. It's weird, you know?"

The implications of what Julio was saying crashed over me like a tidal wave. Morrow, my handler, the man I'd trusted with my life... could he really be the mole?

As we left Julio trembling in the bathroom, my mind was reeling. If Morrow was the mole, it explained his reluctance to pursue the lead, his insistence on maintaining the status quo. But it also meant that my entire operation, my cover, everything I'd worked for, was compromised to the enemy himself, Ricardo Reyes.

Val gripped my arm as we stumbled out into the night air. "Nat," she said, her voice tight with concern. "What are we going to do?"

I stared out into the street, my world tilting on its axis. "I don't know, Val," I whispered. "But if Morrow is the mole... we're in deeper trouble than we ever imagined."

THIRTY-TWO

DANTE

THE FLUORESCENT LIGHT OVERHEAD FLICKERED, casting an eerie, staccato glow over the rows of filing cabinets that stretched out before us. I could hear the distant hum of the city outside, but here, in the belly of my father's downtown office building, time stood still, suspended in a web of secrets and lies that had sustained my family's empire.

Marco's dark eyes met mine, a silent nod was all the confirmation I needed that we were in this together, two brothers in arms against the most formidable adversary of all – my own flesh and blood. Ricardo Reyes, the man who had raised me, the man whose legacy I was determined to dismantle, one incriminating document at a time.

I thumbed through the files, my eyes scanning the pages with ruthless efficiency. Numbers, transactions, ledgers – a tangled web of financial deceit that painted a vivid picture of my father's illicit dealings. Money laundering, bribery, extortion – it was all there in black and white, a testament to the ruthless ambition that had fueled the Reyes cartel's rise to power.

"Jackpot," I said, a grim smile tugging at the corners of my mouth as I snapped a photo of yet another damning piece of evidence.

Marco didn't respond, too focused on his own task, his fingers flying over the keyboard of a desktop computer as he accessed my father's encrypted financial records. The man was a wizard with technology, able to navigate firewalls and decrypt passwords with an ease that bordered on the supernatural.

I was about to suggest we wrap things up when a prickling sense of unease set my every nerve ending on high alert. I had learned long ago to trust my instincts.

"Marco," I hissed. "We've got company."

His head snapped up, his gaze meeting mine with an intensity that spoke volumes. "How much time?"

I cocked my head, straining to pick up any sound that might betray the presence of an uninvited guest. "Not much. Maybe a minute, tops."

Marco didn't hesitate, his movements swift and precise as he began to shut down the computer, covering our digital tracks with the same efficiency he applied to everything in his life. "We need to move. Now."

I nodded, tucking the last of the files back into place before following Marco towards the exit. We had almost reached the door when the unmistakable sound of footsteps echoed down the hallway, growing louder with each passing second.

"Fuck," I muttered under my breath, as I weighed our options. There was no way we could make it out of the building without being seen, not unless we could find another way out.

Marco seemed to read my thoughts, his eyes flickering towards the window at the far end of the room. "The ledge," he whispered, already moving towards the window. "We can hide on the ledge until they're gone."

I didn't need any further convincing, falling into step behind him as we opened the window. The sound of voices grew louder as Marco climbed onto the ledge, the security guards no doubt conducting a routine sweep of the premises.

My heart hammered against my ribs, not from fear of being discovered, but from a sheer, primal refusal to end up as a smear on the pavement fifty feet below. I gripped the windowsill, my knuckles white as I gritted my teeth and hauled myself onto the tiny ledge, barely wide enough to accommodate our feet, my back pressed against the building.

"Shit," I muttered under my breath, my voice barely audible over the distant sounds of traffic. "I fucking hate heights."

Marco, the bastard, had made it look effortless. "Having second thoughts, hermano?" he quipped, an indulgent smirk on his face as he took in my less-than-graceful struggle.

The answer was a resounding yes, but I wasn't about to give him the satisfaction of hearing it. "Don't be an asshole," I shot back. "Just keep a lookout."

Marco's smirk widened, his eyes glittering with silent laughter. "Sure thing, bro," he said, pivoting on the ledge with an almost casual grace of a cat burglar that I knew was calculated to irritate the hell out of me.

I tried to focus on anything but the dizzying drop beneath my feet, but my mind kept conjuring images of plummeting to the unforgiving concrete below. My palms were slick with sweat, and I could feel my heart pounding in my ears.

"Hey, Dante," Marco said, his voice uncharacteristically gentle. "Remember that time in Cancun when we climbed that ancient Mayan temple?"

I managed a weak chuckle. "You mean when I got stuck halfway up and you had to talk me through it?"

Marco nodded, a fond smile playing on his lips. "That's the one. You made it to the top then, didn't you? This is no different. Just focus on my voice and take deep breaths."

I closed my eyes, concentrating on Marco's words and the steady rhythm of my breathing. Slowly, the panic began to subside, replaced by a tentative calm.

"There you go," Marco encouraged. "You're doing great, hermano. Just a little longer."

Peering cautiously through the window, I scanned the room we had just vacated, my brow furrowing as I caught sight of the guards. They moved with a practiced efficiency, their movements crisp and purposeful as they swept the space for any signs of disturbance.

But it wasn't the presence of security guards that set my pulse racing – it was their tattoos, an unmistakable insignia, a symbol that I'd seen many times before.

"Marco," I hissed, my voice a taut whisper. "Those aren't my father's men. That's Javier Cruz's crew."

Marco's eyes narrowed, his jaw tightening as he processed the implications of my words. "You're sure?"

I nodded grimly. "Positive. I'd recognize that tattoo anywhere."

A silent understanding passed between us, a realization that this was no mere coincidence. Javier Cruz's men, moonlighting as security guards in my father's own building – it was a not-so-subtle reminder that my father was up to something big.

As the guards moved on, their footsteps fading into the distance, Marco signaled the all-clear, and we carefully hauled ourselves back through the window and into the relative safety of the room.

"What the hell is going on, Dante?" Marco demanded, his voice a low growl as he scanned the space for any signs of tampering. "Since when does your old man let Cruz's goons roam free in his own backyard?"

I shook my head, my mind whirring with possibilities, each one more unsettling than the last. "I don't know, hermano," I admitted. "But I intend to find out. Something important must be hidden here if Cruz's men are watching."

With a renewed sense of purpose, we turned our attention to scouring every nook and cranny of the building for anything that might shed light on the unholy alliance between my father and Javier Cruz.

As we searched, Marco couldn't resist one last jab. "You know, for a guy who owns a nightclub and a penthouse on the top floor of a skyscraper, you sure are a wimp when it comes to heights."

I shot him a glare. "Shut up and keep looking."

Our banter was cut short as we stumbled upon a hidden panel in the wall, cleverly disguised to blend in with the surrounding decor. Marco's nimble fingers made quick work of the lock, and as the panel swung open, we found ourselves face to face with a sight that made my blood run cold.

Hidden behind the false wall, nestled in the shadows like a serpent coiled and ready to strike, was a sight I'd never expected – a fully equipped methamphetamine lab, complete with rows of glassware and bubbling beakers filled with noxious-looking chemicals.

The moment I stepped inside, the pungent chemical stench hit me. My eyes watered at the assault, but I pushed through the discomfort, taking in the sight that unfolded before me.

I counted fifteen large barrels, each one filled with a bubbling, fluorescent green liquid that churned and swirled, sending noxious fumes wafting through the air. Beakers, flasks, and other lab equipment were strewn across every available surface, along with plastic bags filled with a white, crystalline substance that I recognized all too well.

"What the actual fuck?" The words escaped me in a stunned whisper as the truth washed over me. "A meth lab?"

I felt the air leave my lungs in a rush, a wave of disbelief crashing over me as I took in the scene before me. This wasn't just some side hustle, some petty criminal enterprise – this was a full-blown meth operation, the kind of high-stakes game that could topple empires and leave entire cities in ruins.

"Madre de Dios," Marco breathed, his eyes wide as he surveyed the lab. "Your old man has really gone off the deep end this time, hasn't he?"

I could only nod, my throat constricted with a potent mix of anger and betrayal. All this time, my father had been keeping me in the dark, feeding me scraps of information while he plotted and schemed behind my back. And now, to discover that he had been working together with Javier Cruz, the very man who had disrespected me and threatened everything I held dear – it was a bitter pill to swallow.

Despite my father's deception, I felt a new resolve taking root, a steely determination that burned brighter than my anger.

"Marco," I said, my voice low. "Get the camera. We're going to document every inch of this place."

My friend didn't hesitate, springing into action with the same efficiency that had seen us through countless operations. Together, we methodically photographed and cataloged every piece of evidence, every damning detail that could link my father to this illicit operation.

As we worked, my mind raced, piecing together the puzzle that had eluded me for so long. It all made sense now – the reason my father had been so adamant about protecting Javier Cruz, the reason he had refused to let me go after the snake for his disrespectful behavior. They were partners, co-conspirators in a dangerous and twisted game.

With pictures taken of every detail, we found a fire escape and hightailed it out of there, as fast as we could. The clock was ticking, the guards were bound to come back to check the room again.

I tried to focus on the present, to concentrate on not slipping on the fire escape as my shoes gripped the metal stairs with every step, but my mind kept wandering back to that fucking meth lab. Dammit. How could I have been so blind, so fucking clueless? Right under my damn nose...

"Take it easy there, hermano. Breathe," Marco called out, two steps above me. "We're almost home free."

I did, the cool night air filling my lungs. Freedom tasted sweet, even though the reality of it all was bound to come crashing down sooner rather than later. I could feel it in my bones, the stakes getting higher with each passing minute.

Finally, we scrambled into the car, the engine roaring to life as we tore out of the parking lot, tires squealing. We didn't say a word for a few minutes, both of us lost in our own thoughts. But eventually, my buddy just couldn't hold it in anymore.

"Damn, Dante. Who would've thought the old man was running a damn meth lab in the office building?"

I gripped the wheel tighter, the muscle in my jaw twitching. "I know, man. It's a whole new level of fucked up."

Marco's eyes darkened, his jaw grinding from side to side as he stared out the tinted window. "What the hell are we gonna do, Dante? Cruz... That bastard's gotta pay, man, and now."

I nodded, feeling the same coiled anger thrumming in my veins. "He will, hermano. But first, we need to do this right. We have the evidence we need to bring my father down. But I want to make damn sure his pet snake Cruz also goes down for this."

Marco's dark eyes met mine, an unspoken pact passing between us that needed no words.

As we drove toward the marina, the weight of our discovery settled over us like a shroud. The game had changed, the stakes raised to a level neither of us had anticipated. But one thing was certain – there was no going back now.

I thought of Natalia, of the promise of a future we'd dared to dream of, and I knew that this was our chance. With the evidence we'd gathered tonight, we could bring down not just my father, but an entire criminal empire. It was a dangerous gambit, one that could cost us everything, but it was a risk I was willing to take.

For Natalia. For a chance at redemption. For the hope of a life free from the shadows that had haunted me for so long.

As we pulled up to the yacht, I turned to Marco, my voice filled with grim determination. "Tomorrow, we figure out our move, and we end this once and for all."

Marco nodded, his eyes glinting with the same fierce resolve. "I'm with you, hermano. To the bitter end."

I welcomed the fresh air as it washed over me, cleansing away the sour taste of the meth lab from my mind, if only for a moment. Marco gave me a curt nod and drove into the night.

Back on the yacht, I opened the laptop and studied the pictures we'd taken at my father's office building. My grip tightened as I scrolled through the images, each one a nail in my father's coffin. There was no denying it anymore—Ricardo Reyes had lost his fucking mind getting knee-deep in the meth trade, playing with fire and putting everyone at risk.

The gentle rocking of the boat did nothing to calm the storm brewing inside me. Each photo was a stark reminder of the betrayal, the lies, and the danger that now loomed over us all. I zoomed in on a particular image—a close-up of the meth lab's setup—and felt my stomach churn. The sheer scale of the operation was staggering.

I ran a hand through my hair, feeling the weight of responsibility settling on my shoulders. How the hell was I going to navigate this mess? How could I protect the people I cared about and still bring down my father's empire?

Suddenly, I felt Natalia's presence behind me, her footsteps soft and silent on the teak deck. "Dante," she said, her voice like warm honey as she slid her arms around my waist. "What's wrong?"

I tensed at her touch, my inner turmoil battling with my longing for her. The laptop screen glowed accusingly, and I quickly closed it, shielding the incriminating photos from her view. "It's nothing," I lied, my voice tight as I turned to face her.

Natalia's eyes, those beautiful, perceptive eyes that seemed to see right through me, searched my face. She didn't buy my bullshit for a second. "There's something you're not telling me," she said softly, her hand coming up to cup my cheek. "Did you and Marco find anything tonight?"

I blew out a breath, my shoulders sagging under the weight of it all. The urge to confide in her, to share the burden of what I'd discovered, was almost overwhelming. But the thought of putting her in danger, of potentially compromising her position, held me back.

"Not now, Natalia," I said, my voice barely above a whisper. "I'll tell you everything tomorrow, I promise. But tonight..." I pulled her close, breathing in the scent of her, my anchor amid the storm. "I need you," I said against her hair, my lips brushing her ear. "More than I've ever needed anything."

Natalia's arms tightened around me, her lithe body

molding against mine. "I'm right here, Dante," she murmured, her breath warm against my skin. "Always."

I captured her lips in a fervent kiss, my hands tangling in her hair as I poured every ounce of my desire, every unspoken word, into that kiss. Natalia melted against me, her soft moans fueling the fire within me. In that moment, I wanted to lose myself in her, to forget about the impending storm and just exist in this bubble of passion and comfort.

With gentle, practiced ease, she began to unbutton my shirt, her lips trailing a searing path along my jaw, down my neck. Each touch was electric, sending shivers down my spine and igniting a fire in my core.

I groaned, my desire for her overwhelming every rational thought. "Natalia," I breathed, my resolve crumbling in the face of her insistent touch. "Let's get in bed."

A seductive smile played at the edges of her lips, her eyes burning with a raw intensity that made my heart race. "As you wish, Dante," she purred, her fingers dancing over my bare skin as she led me away from the couch and towards the bedroom.

The yacht's master suite was bathed in soft, ambient light, casting a warm glow over Natalia's skin as she slowly undressed. I watched, mesmerized, as she revealed herself to me, each inch of exposed skin a work of art that I longed to explore.

The crisp white sheets whispered against my skin as I pulled Natalia close, the smell of her perfume enveloping me, a comforting balm to the turmoil raging within me.

Her soft curves fit against me perfectly, her breath teasing my neck as her hands roamed with a purposeful intent.

Her lips found mine again, her kiss urgent and passionate, tasting of wine and something sweeter, something uniquely her. I gave in to the hunger, the need that had been growing inside me. Our tongues dueled, our hands exploring with a frantic urgency as the world around us faded.

"Mi reina," I whispered hoarsely, my fingers tangling in her hair. "Get ready."

She didn't need to be asked twice, her body arching against mine as she tightened her grip, drawing me closer in a decisive movement. I felt her smile against my skin, a sensuous trail of heat that only fueled my desire further.

With a primal growl, I plunged into her, our bodies uniting with a perfect, exquisite harmony. Natalia moaned, her fingers digging into my back as I began to move, a primal rhythm taking over as I drove myself deeper and deeper into her welcoming heat.

I felt her nails dig into my skin, her breath hot and ragged against my neck. "Don't hold back, Dante," she whispered, her voice thick with desire.

I obliged, my movements growing more urgent, more insistent, each thrust pushing us further towards the precipice. The evidence, my father, the looming threat of Javier Cruz—it all faded into the background, swallowed by my intense pleasure and the overwhelming love I felt for the woman in my arms.

Natalia's body arched against mine, her breath coming

in short gasps as she clung to me, her nails biting into my skin. "Yes, Dante," she moaned, her voice a mixture of pleasure and desperation. "Right there. Harder."

I groaned, pushing myself deeper, our bodies moving in perfect synchronicity. The tension built, a coiling spring of pleasure threatening to snap at any moment. Natalia arched her back, her fingers tightening in my hair as she pulled me closer, her moans echoing in my ear.

And then, with one final, powerful thrust, I felt the world shatter around us, the pleasure exploding in an all-encompassing rush. Natalia cried out, her body convulsing against mine as the waves of ecstasy washed over us. I held her close, my arms tight around her slender frame as the aftershocks rippled through us.

For a moment, we lay there, our breaths mingling, our hearts pounding in time. The gentle lapping of waves against the yacht's hull created a soothing rhythm, a stark contrast to the tempest of emotions swirling within me.

Natalia stirred, her soft lips brushing against my ear. "I love you, Dante," she whispered, her voice filled with a tenderness that made my heart ache.

I pressed a gentle kiss to her temple, inhaling the sweet scent of her hair. "I love you too, mi reina," I said, tightening my embrace as our challenges began to settle over me once more.

Because I knew, as we lay there, entwined in the aftermath of our passion, that the coming days would test our love and loyalty like never before. The evidence hidden in my laptop, the secrets I was keeping from her—they all weighed heavily on my conscience.

As Natalia's breathing evened out, signaling her drift into sleep, I found myself wide awake, staring at the ceiling. The euphoria of our romp slowly gave way to the cold reality of our situation. Tomorrow, I would have to tell her everything. Tomorrow, we would have to face the storm head-on.

But for now, in the quiet of the night, with Natalia's warm body pressed against mine, I allowed myself a moment of peace. Whatever challenges lay ahead, whatever dangers we would face, I knew one thing for certain: my love for this woman was the one constant in my life, the one thing I could always count on.

With that thought, I closed my eyes, letting the gentle rocking of the yacht lull me into a fitful sleep, my arms still wrapped protectively around Natalia.

THIRTY-THREE
NATALIA

THE FIRST LIGHT OF MORNING SEEPED THROUGH THE bedroom cabin's porthole, bathing it in a soft, warm radiance. I stirred, fighting off the lingering haze of sleep. Dante lay beside me, lost in peaceful slumber, his face untroubled and serene - a welcome change from last night's emotional turmoil.

I untangled myself from the sheets and Dante's arms, moving with slow, purposeful care to let him rest undisturbed. God knows he needed it after the last few weeks.

Checking my phone, I saw a text from Valentina lighting up the screen.

"Stuck at HQ all day, chica. You're on your own. Stay safe."

Disappointment flared, but I pushed it aside. If Val was tied up today, then it was on me to unravel the mystery of the DEA mole.

I thought of Morrow, the way he'd dismissed the idea,

refused to even consider it, and what Julio had said about him - it set off warning bells in my head. Morrow was hiding something, I was sure of it. Maybe even actively trying to fuck us over.

A plan formed in my mind. I'd tail Morrow all day, keep tabs on his every move, hoping to catch him slipping up. It was a gamble that could royally fuck me over if he made me, but I had no other play. I needed the truth, whatever it took.

Determined I grabbed my shit and headed for the bathroom, ready to start the day with a much-needed shower.

As hot water poured over me, steam swirling around, the heat melted away the tension from yesterday's bullshit.

Lost in thought, I didn't catch the door opening or the quiet steps of Dante sneaking in. Suddenly, his arms were around my waist, his breath hot on my neck, making me jump.

"Morning, my queen," he whispered, his voice a seductive growl that made me shiver with want.

I sank back against him, my back fitting perfectly against his hard chest. "Dante," I gasped, my voice catching as his lips scorched a path over my shoulder. "Didn't hear you come in."

He laughed, the sound vibrating through me as his hands explored my slippery skin, igniting sparks everywhere they touched. "I can be pretty sneaky when I want," he purred, fingers drawing teasing patterns along my breasts.

I bit back a moan. "Is that so?" I managed, my voice breathy as I arched into him, silently pleading for more.

Dante's response was a low, sensual growl as he spun me around, his hands sliding down my body, a deliberate possessiveness that stole my breath away.

"Dante," I whimpered, my plea swallowed by his consuming kiss. His tongue plundered my mouth, a carnal invasion that buckled my knees.

Greedy hands pawed at my breasts, igniting my desperation with each squeeze and caress. I ground against him, my craving spiraling out of control. His fingers delved between my slick folds to circle my entrance, stoking my frenzy.

"Please," I gasped, my spine bowing under his touch. "Fuck me. Right now."

Dante's fierce grip on my hips sent a jolt through my core as he hoisted me up, my back slamming against the wall. I locked my legs around him, clinging to his neck as he plunged into me with one decisive stroke.

A guttural moan tore from my throat, my nails clawing into his shoulders as he stretched me to the limit, igniting every nerve with exquisite pleasure. Dante's ragged breaths mingled with mine as he started to move, his fingers digging into my flesh as he pounded into me with reckless abandon.

"Dante," I panted, our bodies crashing together with each relentless thrust, the water creating delicious friction. "Fuck me harder."

He ramped up the intensity, his strokes turning

desperate and demanding, our rhythm syncing in perfect carnal harmony as the steamy shower enveloped us. Ecstasy overtook me, my head lolling back as I teetered on the brink of oblivion.

"Surrender to it," Dante commanded, his gravelly voice dripping with lust. "Come on my cock."

An earth-shattering climax ripped through me, my body shuddering violently as I cried out his name like a prayer, clinging to him for dear life. Dante followed me over the edge, a deep groan reverberating in my ear as he spilled himself inside me, his thrusts slowing as he nestled his face into my neck.

For a moment, we stood there, locked in an embrace, our hearts pounding in time, our breath mingling with the steam that surrounded us. "Te amo," he whispered, his lips brushing my shoulder.

I tightened my arms around him. "I love you too, Dante," I said.

Reluctantly, we parted, the water growing cooler as the steam dissipated. I felt Dante's gaze on me, his eyes dark and intense as he took in my flushed skin, his hands reaching out to brush a stray lock of wet hair behind my ear.

"So beautiful," he whispered. "Especially with my mark on you."

A slow smile curved my lips as I raised a hand to touch the spot on my throat where he had marked me, a silent brand that spoke of our connection, our undeniable bond. "I'm yours," I said. "Always."

I SIGNALED the barista for another hit of caffeine, my gaze flicking to the clock. Four hours had crawled by since I'd planted myself here, a glorified statue, while Morrow was tucked away in the building across the way.

Just as I turned to head back to my table, there he was —Morrow, emerging from the building heading out. My coffee splashed onto the floor, forgotten, as I bolted from the cafe, my focus locked on reaching my car before Morrow vanished.

But as I approached, I let out a curse. " Shit!" A parking boot was clamped onto my front wheel, courtesy of the city's vigilant parking patrol. Seriously?

Salvation came in the form of a passing cab, and I waved it down with the frantic energy of someone on the brink.

Tumbling into the backseat, I didn't waste a second. "Follow that car!" I thrust a finger toward Morrow's retreating sedan, the command spilling from my lips in a rush of adrenaline.

The cab driver, a wiry man with a thick gray beard and a pair of aviator sunglasses, arched a bushy brow at me in the rearview mirror. "Which one, miss? There's about a million of 'em out there."

I craned my neck, scanning the flow of traffic for Morrow's black sedan. "The dark one, two blocks ahead. The one that's about to turn onto 5th Avenue."

With a grunt of acknowledgement, the cabbie

slammed his foot down on the gas pedal, the taxi's engine roaring to life as we lurched forward into the stream of oncoming traffic. Horns blared and brakes squealed as we wove through the chaos with a prowess that could only be described as masterful.

"You've done this before, haven't you?" I asked, as I gripped the edge of the seat, my knuckles turning white.

The cabbie chuckled, his eyes never leaving the road. "You could say that, miss. I've been driving these streets for more years than I care to count. There ain't a car in this city that can outrun me."

I nodded, a small smile tugging at the corners of my mouth. "Good. Because the man we're following? He might just lead us to the key to solving one of the biggest cases of my career."

The cabbie's eyes flicked to mine in the rearview mirror, a spark of curiosity lighting up his weathered face. "Is that so? Well, in that case, miss, you just sit back and let me do the driving."

True to his word, the cabbie maneuvered through the streets and after a tense and twisting chase through the city, Morrow's sedan finally came to a stop in front of an old office building nestled in the heart of downtown Miami. I watched as Morrow entered the building, disappearing from sight.

The cabbie pulled over a safe distance away, his eyes flicking to mine in the rearview mirror.

"This is your stop, miss," he said. "You sure you wanna go in there?"

I nodded, my gaze fixed on the entrance of the building where Morrow had just disappeared. "I have to. It's my job."

The cabbie grunted, his lips pressing into a thin line as he studied me. "Well, in that case; when you're done in there, I'll be waiting right here for you."

I thanked him, throwing a wad of cash onto the front seat before slipping out of the taxi and into the night. As I approached the building, I felt a chill, a sense of foreboding that permeated the very air around me.

The structure was an architectural relic from a bygone era, its brick facade and arched windows reminiscent of the film noir detective movies I had loved as a child.

With a quick glance over my shoulder to ensure I hadn't been followed, I slipped inside the building, my footsteps silent on the worn carpet as I ascended the stairs to the second floor.

The hallway was dimly lit, the air heavy with the musk of mildew and neglect. I moved with practiced stealth, my ears straining for any sound that might betray the presence of an unseen observer.

I found an office at the end of the hall, its door ajar as if inviting me to step inside. This must be Morrow's office. I hesitated for a moment, weighing the potential consequences of my actions, before finally giving in to the irresistible pull of curiosity.

I pushed the door open and slipped inside, my eyes quickly adjusting to the gloom as I took in my surroundings. The office was small and sparsely furnished, with a worn wooden desk, a filing cabinet, and a couple of mismatched chairs.

Morrow was nowhere in sight.

I moved towards the desk, my fingers brushing over the scattered papers and files that littered its surface.

I opened the top drawer and felt my breath catch as I caught sight of a series of cryptic notes scrawled on a yellow legal pad. The handwriting was unfamiliar, but the implications of what I was seeing were crystal clear.

The notes contained coded references to various DEA operations, including the botched warehouse raid that had resulted in Matt's death. There were also several mentions of a mysterious individual referred to only as "The Benefactor," alongside a series of bank account numbers that I recognized as being tied to the Reyes cartel.

My gaze landed on the computer screen, still glowing with the light of Morrow's open email. With trembling fingers, I slid into the chair and navigated to the secure drive I knew he kept for sensitive operations. My fingertips flew over the keys, decrypting the files with a swiftness that belied my inner turmoil.

Whatever was in those files had to be the proof I needed. I grabbed a USB flash drive I had found in Morrow's desk drawer and plugged it into the computer. I began the process of transferring the files, my eyes flicking nervously towards the door as I waited for the progress bar to fill.

But just as the final file was about to finish, I heard a toilet flush. *Fuck*. Morrow was in the adjoining bathroom.

The door handle rattled, and my heart damn near jack-hammered out of my chest. I scrambled to stash the flash drive in my bra and hastily tried to rearrange Morrow's desk to look like I never touched anything.

I didn't finish before the door swung open, and there stood Marrow himself in all his rumpled glory.

"Natalia," he drawled, eyeing me. "Looks like someone's been snooping where she shouldn't."

I froze, my mind searching for an excuse, an alibi, anything to get me out of this clusterfuck. But Morrow just shook his head and closed the door behind him.

"Save it, Ramirez," he said gruffly. "I know what you were doing in here."

Shit. Here it comes - the clink of handcuffs, the cold steel of a holding cell. I prepared myself for the inevitable, squaring my shoulders and meeting his gaze head-on. If I was going down, it would be on my own terms.

But the arrest never came. Instead, Morrow sunk into his chair with a weary sigh, suddenly looking every bit his age.

"You weren't the only one sniffing around where you shouldn't," he admitted, rubbing a hand over his craggy face. "I found something, too. Something big."

I edged closer, eyeing him warily. "What are you talking about, Morrow?"

He let out a humorless chuckle, opened his desk drawer, and lifted up a false bottom. He reached underneath and when his hand emerged, he was clutching a slim folder.

"See for yourself," he said, tossing the folder onto the desk.

I snatched it up eagerly, my fingers trembling ever so slightly as I flipped through the pages. Reams of encrypted data, coded transmissions, a damning trail of breadcrumbs leading straight to the biggest rat of them all: Chief Reynolds. The head of the DEA. That backstabbing, degenerated scumbag. He was the one feeding information to Ricardo himself.

"How did you get..." I began.

Morrow shrugged, his mouth set in a grim line. "I found it stashed in Reynolds' private safe, along with a few other...incriminating items."

Anger surged through me. I wanted to scream, to rage against the sheer injustice of it all. But I swallowed it down.

Morrow watched me carefully. For once, there was no hint of judgment or condescension in his eyes. Just a weary sort of understanding, the kind that can only come from years of wading through this same cesspool of corruption and deceit.

"What's the pl—"

The sound of approaching footsteps in the hallway cut me off mid-quip, and we both tensed, ears perked like a pair of feral cats.

Morrow jerked his head toward the window and handed me the folder. "Now you know why we couldn't go to the Internal Affairs. If anything happens, take this to the DA. He's the only guy who can nail the Chief."

I tucked the folder under my jacket, gave a nod and made for the window. One foot was already out when I turned back to Morro. "See you on the other side." Then, with a wink and a two-fingered salute, I disappeared.

I hit the pavement hard, tucking into a roll to bleed off the momentum. As I dusted myself off and made sure the folder was intact, I glanced back up at Morrow's window one last time. The grizzled old warhorse was nowhere to be seen.

I patted the folder under my jacket and turned on my heel, my mind whirring a mile a minute. So Reynolds was the big bad wolf, huh?

All those years, all those lives sacrificed on the blood-soaked altar of his greed and ambition. Made me want to put my fist through something—preferably his smug, self-satisfied face.

I paused, fishing the stolen flash drive out of my bra with a grimace. Thank god I sprung for the industrial-strength underwire.

My fingers traced the outline of the innocuous little device as I weighed my options. I could take this straight to the DA, blow the lid off this whole rotten conspiracy in one fell swoop. But I should wait to hear back from Morrow.

This needed to be handled delicately.

I tucked the drive together with the envelope and turned my focus to locating my cab driver.

I had barely made it a few steps down the alley when a black sedan screeched to a halt in front of me, blocking my path like a brick wall. The tires squealed against the pavement, making my heart leap into my throat.

Before I could even think about making a move, two cops burst out of the car, guns drawn and pointed right at me. The sight of those barrels aimed my way made my blood run cold.

"Natalia Ramirez, you're under arrest!" one of the cops barked, his voice cutting through the sticky heat of the day.

Well, fuck me sideways. This was not how I saw my afternoon going.

Questions pounded in my head as the cops manhandled me into the backseat, slamming the door shut behind me with a finality that made my stomach churn.

With my hands cuffed behind my back all I could do was hold on for the ride.

THIRTY-FOUR
DANTE

I COULDN'T KEEP THE SLY GRIN FROM MY FACE AS I walked down the hallway of Alessandro's building. This morning's steamy rendezvous with Natalia in the shower was still fresh in my mind, leaving me with a spring in my step and a satisfied smirk stuck to my face.

That woman had a way of making my troubles melt away, at least for a little while.

A sharp whistle interrupted my train of thought, followed by Alessandro's booming voice. "Hey there, Dante! Good to see you, my friend!"

I snapped out of my reverie, shaking hands with Alessandro as he greeted me with his usual exuberance. The man was like a bulldozer wrapped in a tailor-made Italian suit, his larger-than-life persona filling the room.

He ushered me towards the conference room, his hand resting on my shoulder in a familiar gesture. "You're looking well. Life treating you good, eh?"

I flashed him a cocky grin, unable to contain my smug satisfaction. "Something like that," I said.

As we entered the conference room, a sudden worry crept in at the sight that greeted me. There she was, Alessandro's sexy-as-sin secretary, Vanessa, perched on the edge of the table like a cat ready to pounce. Her legs were crossed, the hem of her skirt riding high on her thigh, and her eyes sparkled with mischievous intent.

The last time we had a meeting, she had made it more than clear that she was interested in a little extracurricular activity with me. And from the looks of it, that offer was still very much on the table.

"Dante," she purred, her red lips curving into a knowing smile as she took in my appearance with a predatory gaze. "It's been too long."

I took a seat across from her, letting my eyes roam appreciatively over her curves. I couldn't deny that Vanessa was a damn fine woman, with her dark hair, sultry eyes, and body that could stop traffic. But lately, my heart —and other parts of me—only had eyes for one woman: Natalia.

"Vanessa," I drawled, letting my gaze linger just a beat too long before meeting her eyes. "Looking as stunning as always."

She leaned forward, her fingers caressing up my arm. I could feel the heat of her touch, and a tiny part of me wondered what it would be like to give in to her advances. After all, she was offering exactly what I usually wanted: no strings attached.

But then I thought of Natalia, and my resolve strengthened. I gently removed Vanessa's hand, my fingers brushing against hers for just a moment before I withdrew.

She pouted, but there was a challenge in her gaze, a silent promise that she wasn't giving up so easily.

I returned to the reason why I was there. "Great to see you again, Alessandro. I trust you've been well?"

He gave a hearty laugh, rubbing his hands together as he took a seat at the head of the table. "Never better, my friend. Business is booming."

I settled back into my chair, a confident smile on my face. "That's good to hear. I have some exciting updates to share about our potential partnership as well."

Vanessa poured coffee for us, her movements smooth and deliberate.

I launched into my pitch, laying out the potential benefits of our business deal with a confidence that I knew would appeal to Alessandro. I outlined the financial gains, the expanded market reach, and the synergies between our organizations.

As I concluded my presentation, Alessandro leaned back, steepling his fingers as he regarded me with a calculating gaze. "Impressive, Dante. Very impressive."

I allowed myself a satisfied smile, relishing the compliment coming from a man of Alessandro's stature. "Thank you. I believe this deal could be mutually beneficial, and I'm confident we can make it a success."

Alessandro nodded, his face turning somber. "Unfortunately, Dante, I'm going to have to decline your offer."

My smile faltered, confusion washing over me as I tried to make sense of his words. "I don't understand. What's changed?"

Alessandro's eyes flickered to Vanessa, who offered him an almost imperceptible shake of her head. "It's not you, Dante. It's... circumstances beyond my control."

I felt a spark of annoyance igniting within me, a burning need to understand what had caused this sudden change of heart. "Circumstances? What circumstances?"

Alessandro shifted uncomfortably in his seat, his gaze dropping to the table. "It's your father, Dante. He... paid me a visit."

My blood ran cold at the mention of my father, a bitter taste rising in my mouth. So, even here, he found a way to sabotage my plans.

"What did he say?" I bit out.

Alessandro hesitated, his eyes flicking to Vanessa before returning to mine. "He made it very clear that he does not approve of our business venture, and he has... asked me to walk away."

A snarl built in my throat, an animalistic growl that rattled the fragile fragments of my self-control. How dare my father try to interfere? Again. Always my fucking father, standing in the way of my dreams, casting his long, dark shadow over my life.

"I'll handle my father," I said, my hands clenched into fists on the tabletop. "You have my word, Alessandro. This deal will go through."

Alessandro shook his head. "I'm sorry, Dante. I can't

risk it. My family – they're my priority. I can't afford to get caught up in your family's... issues."

I could feel Vanessa's eyes on me, watching the scene unfold. But I barely registered her presence, anymore.

"I understand, Alessandro," I said, my voice cold. "Family is everything, after all. Even when they're the ones fucking you over."

I pushed back from the table, my movements smooth and controlled despite the turmoil raging within me. "Thank you for your time. I'll see myself out."

I didn't look back as I walked away, my mind already spinning with plans. My father thought he could control me, could dictate the terms of my life with threats and intimidation. Fuck that.

The elevator doors closed behind me, and I slammed my fist against the wall, the force of the impact reverberating through my body. I wanted to scream, to unleash the rage that was building inside me.

I stabbed at the buttons for the lobby, the elevator descending with excruciating slowness. I wanted to get the hell out of this building, breathe some fresh air and clear my fucking head.

As the doors slid open, I strode out into the opulent lobby. Fuck! I really wanted to see Natalia, to lose myself in her embrace and wash away the bitter taste of my father's betrayal.

I needed her in a way I couldn't ignore.

The rush of the street welcomed me as I emerged from the building, the afternoon sun warming my face. I pulled out my phone, my thumb hovering over Natalia's contact for a moment before I pressed the call button.

It went to voicemail. "Natalia, it's me. I need to hear your voice. Call me back when you get this."

Next, I hit the speed dial for Marco, the phone to my ear as I strode towards my Maserati. This was the only way to re-center, get my head back in the game after the biggest potential business deal went down the drain because of my asshole father.

The phone rang twice before Marco's voice cracked through the line. "Dante, what's the word?"

"The deal with Alessandro is off," I muttered, the disappointment bitter on my tongue. I filled Marco in on the details, my voice tight with frustration.

On the other end of the line, I could practically hear Marco's scowl. "Fuck Ricardo. Don't worry, Dante. We'll find a way. We always do."

His words did little to ease the knot in my stomach. My dreams of creating a life outside the cartel, of building something legitimate that my father couldn't touch, seemed to be slipping further and further out of reach.

As I slid into the driver's seat of my car, Marco's next words stopped me cold. "Hey, Dante, I almost forgot. Remember that guy you asked me about? Allen Hawkes, your sister's beau?"

"What about him?" I asked, my curiosity piqued despite my foul mood.

"Well, Pedro found something. Turns out he's been

spotted with none other than our favorite cartel scumbag, Javier Cruz."

I swore under my breath, the mention of Javier's name sending a surge of anger through me.

"It gets worse, hermano," Marco continued. "Allen was spotted at one of Javier's known stash houses. Looks like he owes Javier some serious cash, and our friend is making sure he pays up."

My grip tightened on the steering wheel as I considered the information. "We need to pay this Allen asshole a visit. Find out once and for all what the deal is with him."

Marco didn't hesitate. "Say the word, Dante. I'll meet you at his place in 20."

Marco gave me Allen's address and twenty minutes later, we were standing outside Allen's posh apartment, the sun glinting off the glass and steel facade. The doorman gave us a wary glance but let us up without asking questions, probably scared shitless by our dark suits and stony expressions.

I knocked on the door, my fist poised to deliver a second, more insistent knock when the door swung open. Allen stood there, his eyes widening at the sight of us, his carefully constructed mask of arrogance slipping just a fraction.

Before he could even muster a greeting, I had him by the collar, hauling him into the apartment. Marco followed close behind, letting the door click shut with a finality that punctuated the seriousness of the situation.

"What the fuck, man," Allen sputtered, his eyes flicking between us. "What do you want?"

I slammed him against the wall with a satisfying thud. "We want answers, you little weasel," I growled, my voice cold and dangerous. "Why were you at Javier Cruz's stash house? What does he have on you?"

Allen's eyes went wide, the fear in them unmistakable. "I...I don't know what you're talking about! Let me go!"

I tightened my grip, relishing the fear in his eyes. "Oh, I think you do, Allen. You owe Javier a shit ton of money, don't you? What did you lose it all on, huh? Stocks? Crypto? Cocaine?"

Allen whimpered, a sheen of sweat appearing on his forehead. "I-... just made a bad investment, that's all. I don't know anything about Javier Cruz."

I leaned in close, my lips inches from his ear. "Javier Cruz isn't the kind of guy you want to owe money to, Allen. He's the kind of guy who'll make you wish you were never born."

Marco stepped forward. "Start talking, asshole. Tell us what you know, or so help me God, I'll make sure you regret ever crossing paths with Javier Cruz."

Allen's eyes darted between us, his chest rising and falling rapidly as he tried to form a coherent sentence. "Okay, okay! I'll tell you! I lost the money. It was bad timing, that's all. I'm paying Javier back, I swear."

"Oh, you're paying him back all right," I growled, slapping him hard across the face. "Giving him information about me and my family."

"Wait!" Allen yelped, his voice cracking. "No, I swear. I haven't told him shit!"

I was about to hit him harder when the sound of the door opening made me freeze. Suddenly, Sofia stood in the doorway, her eyes wide, her hand still on the doorknob as if she were prepared to flee.

She took in the scene before her: me with my hands on Allen, Marco looming behind me, Allen cowering against the wall. "Dante?" Her voice was small, quivering, as if the very foundations of her world were crumbling beneath her feet.

I dropped my hands from Allen, straightening up as I turned to face Sofia. "Sofia, I..." I began, struggling to find the words to explain.

But she didn't give me a chance. "Get out," she whispered, her voice shaking. "Get out, Dante. Now."

I took a step towards her, hoping to explain, to make her understand. But Sofia just backed away, shaking her head. "No, don't. Just... don't. I don't ever want to see you again, Dante. Stay away from me."

Her words hit me with the force of a wrecking ball. I opened my mouth to protest, to try and reason with her, but she was already gone, her footsteps retreating down the hallway.

I stood there, numb and hollow, as the weight of what I'd done settled over me. Marco put a hand on my shoulder. "I think it's time to go, hermano. We got what we needed."

I nodded, my thoughts swirling as the realization of

what I'd done struck me. I had come here intending to help Sofia, to protect her from the scumbag who was dragging her into the cartel world. But instead, I had become the villain, the embodiment of the violence and brutality I had wanted to shield her from.

The ride back to my yacht was torture, every mile an agonizing journey into the depths of my own personal hell. Sofia's words echoed in my mind, slicing through me with a sharp pain that no amount of liquor or women could dull.

As I stepped into the boat, the opulent surroundings felt like a mockery of the life I had built, the illusion of control and freedom crumbling around me. I went down into the cabin area and sank into the nearest chair, my head in my hands as I tried to make sense of the chaos whirling through my mind.

Natalia wasn't here to greet me and she never returned my call. Maybe she finally wised up and saw me for who I really was. I pulled out my phone, my finger hovering over the call button for Natalia. But a dark laugh escaped me, harsh and humorless. "You're no different, Dante. No different from your father." The words felt sour as they left my mouth. I tried to get rid of the unpleasant aftertaste of self-loathing that lingered. Today, I had proven it to myself. I had resorted to violence and intimidation, letting my anger take control and cloud my judgment.

The voice of reason in my head, the one that had been whispering to me for weeks, grew louder, drowning out my attempts to justify my actions. You're just like him, Dante.

It's in your blood, in your very genes. There's no escaping it.

I dropped my phone and poured myself a drink, the liquid burning a path down my throat as I collapsed onto the couch.

It was no use. No use trying to escape, to fight against the darkness etched into my very DNA. I was my father's son, after all.

Perhaps it was time to accept my fate, to stop fighting against the inexorable pull of the life I was born into, and to give up the dream of a better life, a life away from the cartel and its inescapable violence.

I poured another drink, numb to the burn as the liquor slipped down my throat. The darkness was calling to me, a familiar embrace that promised to smother the pain, to drown out the relentless whispers of my own inadequacies.

THIRTY-FIVE
NATALIA

I sat in the stark, sterile interrogation room, my wrists bound by cold steel handcuffs that bit into my skin with every futile attempt to free myself. My heart pounded in my chest, a relentless drumbeat that echoed the fear and uncertainty coursing through my veins.

They had taken everything from me – my badge, my weapon, the folder, and the flash drive containing the evidence that could have brought down Chief Reynolds and exposed the rot festering within the DEA. I was a rat in a maze, trapped and helpless, with no clear path to freedom.

The room was a sensory deprivation chamber, designed to break the will of anyone unfortunate enough to find themselves within its oppressive confines. The walls were a bland shade of gray, devoid of any warmth. A single light bulb hung from the ceiling, casting a stark, unforgiving light that leached the color from everything it touched.

I had lost all sense of time, my mind adrift in a sea of troubled thoughts, when the door creaked open, and Chief Reynolds stepped inside. The very sight of him spiked my adrenaline.

In his hands, he held a file – the file I had risked everything to obtain.

"Natalia Ramirez," Reynolds began, his voice charged with false sympathy as he took a seat across from me, "You've really dug yourself into a hole this time, haven't you?"

I glared at him, my jaw clenched tight. "You won't get away with this, Reynolds," I spat, the venom in my voice belying the fear that twisted in my gut. "Morrow knows the truth. He has evidence that will expose you for the corrupt piece of shit you are."

Reynolds chuckled, a low, rumbling sound that filled the room with its mocking cruelty. "Ah, yes. Ted Morrow," he mused, leaning back in his chair, his eyes glinting with malicious amusement. "Unfortunately, your dear friend suffered a tragic accident earlier this evening."

A sense of dread coiled in the pit of my stomach. "What did you do?" I whispered, my voice barely audible.

"Nothing that hasn't been done before," Reynolds said with a dismissive wave of his hand. "In this line of work, accidents happen. Especially to those who stick their noses where they don't belong."

His words hit me like a physical blow, stealing the air

from my lungs. Morrow – my mentor, my ally – was gone, his life snuffed out, all to protect Reynolds' twisted version of the truth.

"You're a monster," I hissed, my eyes burning with rage. "A soulless, power-hungry monster who will stop at nothing to protect his own corrupt ass."

Reynolds shrugged, unperturbed by my outburst. "I'm a survivor, Agent Ramirez," he corrected, opening the file and spreading its contents across the table like a macabre fan of cards. "And in this game, there are winners and losers. It's really quite simple."

I stared at the photos and fabricated communications spread out before me, each one a lie designed to paint me as the traitor within our ranks. There I was, shaking hands with Dante, whispering in the ear of a known cartel member, accepting a thick envelope that was no doubt meant to represent a payoff.

"This isn't real," I protested, my voice wavering ever so slightly as I struggled to maintain my composure. "It's a setup, a desperate attempt to divert attention from your own misdeeds."

Reynolds merely smiled, his eyes gleaming with satisfaction. "Is it, though?" he asked. "Because from where I'm sitting, it looks like you've been playing both sides for quite some time now, Agent Ramirez."

I shook my head as I tried to piece together a coherent argument that could dismantle the narrative Reynolds had so carefully constructed. "You won't get away with this. There's evidence to prove your involvement with Ricardo Reyes. It shows that you were the mole."

"Ah, but you see, that evidence no longer exists," Reynolds said, his voice smooth and untroubled. "It's been destroyed. Burned to ashes, just like your credibility and your career."

My heart sank, the crushing weight of despair pressing down on me as the reality of my situation took hold. I was alone, without allies, without hope, ensnared in a trap of Reynolds' own making.

As if on cue, two officers appeared in the doorway, their faces devoid of emotion as one of them gestured for me to rise. "Time to go, Ramirez."

I stood on shaky legs, the handcuffs rattling as I moved. Reynolds watched me with a smug, self-satisfied grin that I longed to wipe off his face with my fist. But I was powerless, just another casualty in his relentless quest for power and control.

I was marched down a series of dimly lit corridors, the fluorescent lights casting long, ominous shadows that mocking my predicament. My mind was a whirlwind of fear and rage.

I'll be honest. Getting tossed into a cell like some two-bit criminal stung more than I'd like to admit. After they removed my handcuffs and the bars clanged shut behind me, I shot a venomous glare at the two smirking MDPD officers Reynolds had in his back pocket.

"You guys do realize you're making a huge mistake,

right?" I snarled, gripping the cold metal bars. "I'm one of the good guys here!"

The taller officer, a beefy meathead with a pencil-thin mustache, just chuckled. "That's what they all say, sweetheart. Enjoy your new digs and your cell mates."

I resisted the urge to flip him off as they walked away, no doubt congratulating themselves on bagging such a dangerous "criminal mastermind." Please. If these glorified mall cops knew what I was really up against, they'd probably soil themselves.

I leaned back against the grimy wall, barely noticing the other two women in the cell, and ran a hand through my disheveled hair. How the hell had things gone so sideways? One minute, I was closing in on that weasel Reynolds and his shady cartel ties, and the next, I was the one being treated like public enemy number one.

I'd been so close to nailing that bastard, to getting justice for Matt and exposing the whole rotten system. But Reynolds had an airtight frame job.

Worse, with that fake file he'd cooked up, any attempt to blow the whistle on his twisted dealings would just look like a desperate, defensive ploy. The bastard had made sure of that, crossing every T and dotting every I to craft the perfect illusion of my culpability.

I snorted bitterly, picturing Reynolds as he watched me get hauled off. He was probably polishing his precious medal collection, congratulating himself.

I sank down onto the cold, hard bunk, staring at the cracked cement walls of my new "accommodations." For the first time since this whole mess started, I felt a twinge of hopelessness creep in. How the hell was I supposed to clear my name when I was trapped in this dingy cell?

The sound of shrill laughter broke me from my pity party. "Well, well, looks like the new fish is having a rough first day!"

I rolled my eyes, not in the mood for whatever fresh hell this was. "Can it, Trailer Trash, before I shove my foot so far up your–"

"Easy there, chica," the voice cut me off with a wheezy chuckle. "I'm just tryin' to welcome you to the joint in a friendly way."

Despite my foul mood, I had to smirk at the woman's ballsy attitude. "Yeah, well, your 'friendly' could use some work."

As twisted as this whole clusterfuck had become, I had to admit, my current predicament was almost impressive.

I settled back on the creaky bunk.

Reynolds might have thought he'd won by tossing me in here, but this wasn't over by a long shot.

THIRTY-SIX

DANTE

I JOLTED AWAKE, THE REMNANTS OF A NIGHTMARE still clinging to the edges of my consciousness. My body was coated in a sheen of sweat, the sheets twisted and tangled around my legs as if I had been thrashing in my sleep.

Beside me, the bed was empty, the sheets rumpled and cold, a silent testament to Natalia's absence. I reached out, my fingers brushing against the pillow, and a sense of unease settled over me like a shroud.

She should have been here on the yacht with me, her warm body pressed against mine, her soft breath tickling my neck as she slumbered peacefully in the aftermath of our lovemaking. But the space beside me was painfully empty, a void that echoed with a thousand unspoken questions.

I grabbed my phone from the nightstand, my thumb

hovering over Natalia's number as I debated whether to call her or not. It wasn't like her to disappear without a word, especially after the passion we had shared yesterday morning.

With a frustrated sigh, I tapped the screen, my pulse elevated as the line began to ring. One ring, two rings, three... and then her voicemail picked up, her familiar voice sending a pang of longing through me.

"Natalia, it's me," I said, my voice saturated with worry. "Where are you, mi reina? Call me back as soon as you get this."

I ended the call and tossed the phone aside, scrubbing a hand over my face as I tried to make sense of the unease that had taken root in the pit of my stomach. Something wasn't right, I could feel it in my bones, a primal instinct that had been honed over years of navigating the treacherous waters of the cartel world.

With a grunt, I hauled myself out of bed and padded across the carpet to look out the cabin window. The first rays of dawn were painting the horizon in hues of orange and pink but I couldn't appreciate the splendor of it.

As I stood there, my mind began to wander, sifting through the events of the past few days, searching for any clue that might explain Natalia's sudden disappearance. Had I done something to upset her? Said something that had pushed her away? No, that didn't make sense. Our connection had been stronger than ever, our bond forged in the fires of passion and trust.

I forced myself to get ready, to go through the motions of my morning routine while my thoughts remained fixed on Natalia. I showered, dressed, and tried to call her again, each unanswered ring fueling the fire of my growing concern.

It wasn't until I got a call from Valentina, Natalia's closest confidant at the DEA, that I got the first real lead on her disappearance. Valentina's voice was tight with worry.

"Dante, it's not good," she said. "Natalia's been arrested."

Arrested.

"What the fuck do you mean, she's been arrested?" I growled, my grip tightening around the phone. "For what?"

Valentina hesitated, her breath hitching as she prepared to deliver the blow. "They're saying she killed Ted Morrow."

My blood ran cold at the mention of Morrow's name. Ted Morrow was Natalia's mentor. The idea that she could be responsible for his death was ludicrous, a twisted joke that wasn't even remotely funny.

"That's bullshit," I hissed. "Natalia would never hurt Morrow."

Valentina sighed, a sound heavy with regret. "I know, Dante. But you know how these things go. They need a scapegoat, and Natalia's the perfect fit."

I ended the call with Valentina, my mind already

whirling with a plan of action. The mission was simple. Get Natalia out of that hellhole, clear her name and expose the real culprit behind Morrow's murder. And there was only one man I trusted to handle a job of that magnitude.

Johnny "The Fixer" Flynn was a shark in a suit, a defense attorney with a reputation for getting his clients out of even the stickiest situations. He was also one of the few people in this world who owed me a favor – a big one.

I dialed his number, my voice steady and composed. "Johnny, I need you to spring someone from lockup. It's urgent."

Johnny didn't even hesitate, his voice a low growl as he took in the details of Natalia's predicament. "Consider it done, Dante," he assured me, his tone leaving no room for doubt. "I'll have your girl out before lunchtime."

I disconnected the call, a small spark of hope igniting within me. If anyone could navigate the treacherous waters of the criminal justice system, it was Johnny "The Fixer." But as I grabbed my keys and headed for the cabin door, I couldn't shake the feeling that time was running out.

I SLAMMED my fist against the steering wheel as a snarl of rage tore from my throat. Fucking hell, this was a mess – a goddamn clusterfuck of epic proportions.

Natalia, my fierce, indomitable queen, had been arrested. Hauled off like a common criminal, accused of the most heinous of crimes, murdering her own mentor, Ted Morrow.

The very notion was absurd. Natalia, a cold-blooded killer? The woman who had shown me the path to redemption, who had ignited a spark of hope within my jaded soul that there was more to life than the endless cycle of violence and retribution?

Impossible.

My phone vibrated in my pocket, jolting me from my vengeful reverie. A quick glance at the screen revealed the name I had been waiting for.

"Talk to me, Johnny," I growled.

"Easy there, tiger," came Johnny's smooth, unflappable drawl. "I've got a handle on things. Bail hearing's been set for an hour from now."

I blinked, taken aback by the swiftness of his actions. "An hour? Shit, Johnny, you really do live up to your nickname."

A rich, self-assured chuckle crackled over the line. "You know me, Dante. When it comes to greasing the wheels of justice, I'm the best damn mechanic in town."

I felt a grudging smile tug at the corners of my mouth. Johnny Flynn was many things – arrogant, smarmy, and more than a little morally flexible – but he was also a master of his craft, a legal virtuoso who could navigate the treacherous waters of the justice system with an ease that bordered on the supernatural.

"Alright, Johnny, I'm on my way to the station now," I

said, my grip tightening on the wheel as I wove through the midday traffic. "Don't start the party without me."

"Wouldn't dream of it, amigo," he drawled, the faint clink of ice cubes against glass punctuating his words. "Just try not to cause too much of a ruckus when you get here, huh? These cops get awfully touchy when you start throwing your weight around."

I snorted, my lips curving into a wolfish grin. "No promises, counselor. These bastards have my queen locked up on some bullshit charges. They're lucky if I don't burn the whole damn station to the ground."

Johnny's laughter echoed through the speaker, rich and untroubled. "That's my boy," he purred. "Fiery as ever. Just don't do anything too rash. You got it? I'd hate to have to bail your ass out next."

With a roll of my eyes and a muttered curse, I ended the call, tossing my phone onto the passenger seat as I gunned the engine. The Maserati surged forward, devouring the asphalt as I weaved through the snarled traffic with a reckless abandon that would've made lesser men quake in their boots.

As the police station loomed ahead, I felt a surge of resolve coursing through my veins. They could throw every charge, every accusation in the book at Natalia, but it wouldn't matter.

I would move heaven and earth to see her free, to unleash the full fury of my resources and influence upon the system that dared to cage my queen. The wheels of justice might grind slowly, but I would be the wrench that jammed them, the unyielding force that ground their machinations to a halt.

With a grin and a gleam of determination in my eyes, I pulled into the station's parking lot, the tires of my Maserati leaving streaks of rubber on the pavement as I brought the car to a screeching halt.

It was time to get my queen.

THIRTY-SEVEN
NATALIA

FEAR WAS HEAVY IN THE AIR AS I PACED THE CONFINES of the holding cell, my mind a whirlwind of thoughts and memories.

The seconds ticked by like leaden footsteps, each one dragging me deeper into the brutal reality that was my new life. I was trapped, ensnared in a web of lies and deceit that tightened around me with every passing minute.

But it wasn't just the threat of a lengthy prison sentence that had my heart palpitated wildly. It was the knowledge that, once my affiliation with the DEA was exposed, my life would be worth less than nothing in this place. Every face that surrounded me, every hardened criminal locked away in this concrete hell, would see me as the enemy. And in a place like this, the enemy didn't last long.

I could feel their eyes on me, their gazes like daggers

boring into my back as they whispered amongst themselves. They may not have known exactly who I was yet, but it was only a matter of time. And time was a luxury I didn't have.

I tensed, my back against the cold, unforgiving wall as a crew of newly arrested women swaggered into the cell, their eyes scanning the room like predators on the hunt. My gaze locked with the leader, a hulking, tattooed woman with a scar across her cheek that spoke of a thousand violent altercations.

"You," she rumbled, her voice laced with the same Southern twang I remembered all too well. My heart sank as the pieces clicked into place. Kayla Hayes. We'd put her brother away last year for running drugs. "I know you, pig. You and your narc buddies locked up my brother last year."

Shit. Shit. Shit.

The memories flashed through my mind: a raid on a seedy motel, Kayla's brother cuffed and spewing curses as we hauled him off, and now, his sister standing before me, eyes glittering with a cold, calculating fury. I didn't stand a chance against her and her crew. Not here, not now.

This was bad. I'd gone weeks before Dante figured me out, yet in here, I get made within the first day. It wasn't a coincidence. Someone, probably named Reynolds, made sure to put Kayla in here with me.

I straightened my spine, willing myself not to show a shred of weakness as they advanced, their steps deliberate and menacing.

Kayla advanced on me, her crew falling into step behind her, their intentions clear in the predatory smiles that twisted their lips.

I braced myself, my muscles coiling like a spring as I prepared to fight for my life. I might have been outnumbered, might have been defenseless against the storm that was about to break, but I'd be damned if I went down without a fight.

The first punch was a blur of motion, a blinding flash of pain as it connected with my jaw. I staggered back, tasting blood as the metallic tang filled my mouth. But I didn't go down. I wouldn't give them the satisfaction.

I lashed out with a swift kick to Kayla's midsection, catching her off guard as she grunted in surprise. For a moment, the tables were turned, but it was a fleeting victory. The rest of her crew was on me in an instant, a flurry of fists and feet that had me hitting the ground with enough force to knock the wind from my lungs.

I curled into a ball, protecting my vital organs as the blows rained down on me. I could feel my consciousness wavering. But I refused to surrender, refused to let them see my fear.

And then, just when I thought my life was over, the onslaught stopped. I lay there, gasping for breath, as the sound of the commotion slowly receded into the background. I could hear the guards shouting, their voices muffled by the ringing in my ears.

I rolled over onto my back, wincing as pain lanced through my body. My vision was blurred, and I could feel the warm trickle of blood running down my face from a bloody nose. But I was alive, and for now, that was all that mattered.

"Ramirez! You made bail. Let's go. Someone's waiting."

I didn't hesitate, surging forward with a gratitude that was almost overwhelming. I owed that guard my life, literally. And maybe one day, I'd find a way to repay that debt. But for now, all I could do was keep putting one foot in front of the other, following the guard out of the belly of this beast and towards whatever waited on the other side.

My mind raced as I was escorted down the corridor. Was this an extraction by my DEA team? Or was it something else, something more complicated and potentially risky?

As we rounded the final corner, the answer came into view. There he was, Dante Reyes, looking disheveled, his eyes burning with a thousand unspoken words. In that moment, seeing him felt like the first breath of fresh air after being trapped underwater, a lifeline that tethered me to the world I knew.

I felt Dante's arms tighten around me, his embrace a refuge from the storm that had threatened to consume me. As I clung to him, burying my face in the crook of his neck, I could feel the tension radiating off him in waves, an energy that spoke volumes about the depths of his concern.

"How did you know?" I whispered, my voice hoarse with emotion. "How did you find me?"

Dante pulled back, cradling my face in his hands as he searched my eyes. "Valentina called me. She told me everything."

I nodded, tears pricking at the corners of my eyes as I realized just how close I had come to losing everything.

"Natalia," he said. "What happened in there? Who did this to you?"

I pulled back, my gaze meeting his, and I saw the raw fury simmering in those dark, intense eyes. It was a look I had seen before, a look that spoke of a barely restrained violence, a primal urge to protect and avenge that burned deep within his soul.

"It's nothing," I tried to reassure him, my voice a little shakier than I would have liked. "Just a misunderstanding with some of my other cell mates."

Dante's jaw clenched, his fingers ghosting over the bruise that was beginning to blossom across my cheekbone. "Nothing?" he growled. "Natalia, you're hurt. Badly."

I winced as his touch probed the tender flesh, a sharp ache radiating through my skull. "It's just a bloody nose, Dante," I insisted, trying to downplay the severity of my injuries. "I've had worse."

His eyes narrowed, and I could see the muscle twitching in his jaw as he fought to rein in his emotions. "That's not the point, mi reina," he said. "You could have a concussion or worse. We need to get you checked out."

I opened my mouth to protest, but the look on his face stopped me cold. His eyes showed a fierce determination, and I wasn't about to argue with him. At that moment, I realized just how deeply his concern ran and how much he cared for my well-being.

"Alright," I relented, my shoulders sagging as the adrenaline that had been fueling me began to dissipate. "But I don't know if I can trust a hospital right now, Dante. Not with everything that's going on."

He nodded as he brushed a stray lock of hair from my face. "I know, mi reina. That's why I have someone else in mind. Come on, let's go get you signed out and get your belongings."

With a gentle hand on the small of my back, he guided me towards the sleek, black Maserati that was parked at the curb. I slid into the passenger seat, wincing as the movement sent a fresh wave of pain lancing through my body.

As Dante pulled away from the station, his gaze kept flickering towards me, a silent assessment of my condition that spoke volumes about his concern. "Dr. Sanchez is an old friend," he explained, his voice cutting through the heavy silence that had settled over us. "He's discreet, and he owes me a favor or two. He'll be able to take a look at you without raising any red flags."

I nodded, leaning back against the plush leather seat and closing my eyes. The adrenaline crash was hitting me hard, leaving me feeling drained and utterly exhausted. But even through the fog of pain and fatigue, I could feel the warmth of Dante's presence beside me.

Without thinking, I reached out, my fingers seeking his, and he responded in kind, his hand enveloping mine in a gentle embrace. The simple gesture was like a balm to my frayed nerves, a reminder that I wasn't alone in this fight, no matter how bleak things seemed.

THIRTY-EIGHT
DANTE

I STIRRED, THE DAWN'S SOFT LIGHT SEEPING THROUGH the cabin windows, illuminating the angelic face of my Natalia. I loved to watch her sleep, her breath soft and steady, her skin luminous in the morning light.

I gently pulled her closer, her warmth seeping into me as I basked in the simple joy of waking up beside her. I knew that peace wouldn't last; the chaos of our lives would intrude eventually. But for now, in this tranquil moment, I wanted to savor the feeling of her body nestled against mine, the rise and fall of her chest as she breathed.

As my eyes adjusted to the soft light, the purpling bruises on her face came into view, a silent reminder of the assault she had endured in that holding cell. Thank God for Dr. Sanchez; his steady hands and quiet clinic had checked her well and concluded there was no concussion or permanent damage.

The memory of seeing her coming out of the holding

cell, beaten and bloodied, still haunted me. How could anyone lay a hand on her, try to snuff out the light that burned so fiercely within her?

My thoughts must have stirred something in her because her eyelids fluttered, her lashes casting delicate shadows on the curves of her cheeks. I watched as she blinked herself awake, the sleep slowly fading from her eyes to be replaced by consciousness and awareness.

A soft smile curved her lips as she met my gaze, a silent message passing between us that needed no words.

"Good morning, mi amor," I said, my voice a low rumble as I tucked a lock of hair behind her ear.

"Mmm," she responded as she stretched, her body arching against mine. "What time is it?"

"Early," I said, my lips finding the sensitive spot on her neck, eliciting a soft sigh from her. "We have time."

I could feel the smile in her kiss as she responded with a passion that bordered on desperation. Perhaps it was the lingering fear that life was too damn short or the sheer relief that she had escaped that hellish cell relatively unscathed. Or maybe it was the consuming, all-encompassing love that burned between us, demanding to be satiated. Whatever it was, I was swept away in it.

The rest of the world fell away as our mouths fused, our breath mingling in a desperate hunger that had us both on the brink. My lips never broke contact with her skin as I trailed kisses down the column of her neck, relishing the taste of her.

Her hands roamed over my back, her fingernails gently

scraping against my skin as she urged me closer, her hips arching against mine. I chuckled, the sound vibrating against her skin, and I deepened the kiss.

She moaned, her fingers tangling in my hair as she pulled me closer, our bodies moving in perfect unison, caught in the relentless current of our shared passion. I mapped her curves with my hands, worshipping her like the goddess she was.

"Dante," she panted, her breath coming in short gasps as I moved within the orbit of her heat.

I entered her, our flesh joining as one, and she cried out, her nails digging into my back as I filled her. I relished her moans, the way her body arched against mine, matching my rhythm with a feverish intensity.

I lost myself in the heady fusion of our bodies, in the exquisite pleasure that erased all thoughts, all worries, all doubts.

As the waves of passion ebbed, I held her close, our breath mingling in the aftermath. "I love you, Dante," she whispered, as she tightened her arms around me.

"Te amo, mi reina," I said against her hair, my lips pressing a gentle kiss to her forehead. "Always."

We lay entwined, our breath and heartbeats slowly syncing, our bodies still joined in the languid aftermath of our lovemaking. Her soft curves molded against mine, her head resting on my shoulder as she played with the hairs on my chest.

I could stay like this forever, just the two of us, suspended in this bubble of tranquility. But the reality of our situation wouldn't be denied. It lurked in the corners of the room, a shadow waiting to pounce the moment we lowered our guard.

Natalia stirred, her breath catching as if she, too, sensed the approaching storm. "Dante," she whispered. "What are we going to do about Reynolds and your father?"

I kissed the top of her head, my lips lingering on her silky hair. "I don't know, mi vida. But we will figure something out. Together."

She nodded, her body tensing against mine. "Before Reynolds framed me, Morrow told me to take the file he had found on Reynolds to the U.S. Attorney's Office. Their prosecutors can indict Reynolds if they have enough evidence."

I sat up, propping myself on one elbow as I turned to face her. "That's good news, baby. Where's the file now?"

Pain flashed in her eyes, and I knew the answer before she spoke. "Gone. When I got arrested, Reynolds took it and probably had it destroyed."

A growl built in my throat as I imagined getting my hands around Reynolds' scrawny neck, watching the light fade from his cold, dead eyes.

Natalia must have seen the murderous thoughts crossing my mind because she laid a gentle hand on my chest. "What's on your mind, Dante?" she asked, reading me like an open book. "Spill it. Did something happen with your father?"

I grimaced at the mention of Ricardo, my stomach

churning at the thought of the monster who had raised me. "What if I'm turning into him?" I blurted out before I could stop myself.

Her eyebrows shot up in surprise at my outburst. "What?"

I ran a hand through my hair, struggling to put my jumbled thoughts into words. "I... I almost beat the shit out of that sleazebag Allen yesterday. And Sofia walked in on it. She hates me now, Natalia. I saw it in her eyes. Jesus, I'm just like my dad. A violent, impulsive brute."

Natalia placed her hand over mine. "No, Dante," she said firmly, her eyes locking with mine. "You are not like him, and you never will be. You're nothing like your father."

Her voice was confident and unwavering, and for a moment, I let her conviction wash over me. But the doubts wouldn't be denied. "How can you be so sure? Who's to say I won't turn into another Ricardo, dragging my family through the mud of danger, violence, drugs, and murder?"

Natalia's eyes softened, her hand squeezing mine in reassurance. "Because I know you, Dante. I see the real you, the man you are deep down." She paused, searching for the right words. "Underneath all that anger and pain, you have a heart of gold. Yes, you may have a bit of a temper, and you've done some questionable things. But it's different. You're not cold and ruthless like Ricardo. You're not evil. You're passionate and loyal. You feel things deeply, and you care about your family, maybe too much. You'd never intentionally hurt them."

Her words settled over me, a soothing balm to my troubled soul. "I hope you're right," I said, unable to keep the doubt from creeping back in. "But what if I'm only fooling myself, lying to you and everyone else, pretending to be someone I'm not?"

Natalia's eyes flashed with determination, and she propped herself up on one elbow, leaning closer. "You're not lying, Dante. I know you. I see the real you, and you are absolutely nothing like your father."

Her gaze was steady, her conviction unshakeable, and I felt the tension within me begin to ebb. I wanted—needed—to believe her. "But what about Sofia?" I asked. "I failed her, and I hurt her. How can I make it up to her?"

"We'll talk to her, Dante," Natalia said, her voice calm and reassuring. "We'll explain that you only wanted to protect her, and she'll understand. I won't let her hate you, Dante. Not when I know how much you love her."

Natalia's faith in me was unwavering, an anchor in the tempest at hand. I cupped her face, my thumb gently brushing her cheek. "You're right, mi vida," I said. "You always are. Thank you."

We snuggled close for a minute then suddenly Natalia jerked. "Holy shit, Dante, wait. I just remembered something. Morrow might have had a copy of the file."

My eyes widened at the prospect, hope sparking within me. "What? Where?"

Excitement flashed in her eyes, and she sat up. "Every time I would zoom call Morrow, I noticed the painting behind him was always at a slightly different angle. Like it's been moved and then put back. Maybe that sly old dog was hiding something behind that painting."

"Then we need to take a look," I said, reaching for my pants.

Natalia's eyes flicked to my bare chest, a mischievous smile playing on her lips. "Can it wait?"

But before I could say a word, Natalia pounced on me, her hungry lips crashing into mine. I groaned, my hands roaming her body, desperate to feel her silky skin and every luscious curve.

"I think that can be arranged," I managed to say, my lips still glued to hers as my hands traveled down her back.

Natalia found her way to my hardening cock. "Because I believe there's a very important file right here that needs my... close examination."

Her laughter was like music, a symphony of joy in the middle of the chaos around us. And in that moment, as her warm mouth engulfed the tip of my cock, I knew that no matter what came next, nothing would compare to this.

THIRTY-NINE
NATALIA

"A RE WE SURE ABOUT THIS?" I WHISPERED, GIVING Dante a sidelong glance as we prowled through the deserted parking lot. The July heat was like a hairy wool blanket, smothering and suffocating, but my pulse was what made me sweat.

Lips pressed in a hard line, Dante didn't answer, and his silence spoke volumes. We were about to violate the sanctity of a crime scene, but police procedure didn't factor in our ticking clock. We had to do this.

Before I could second-guess myself into paralysis, Dante had a bump key out, ready to pop the lock on Morrow's apartment. It only took a gentle click and a deft twist of his wrist, and we were in. The place looked exactly like it did when I was here last: austere, impersonal, and reeking of scotch and cigars.

As I stepped into the living room, the seriousness of

what we were doing hit me. We were breaking and entering, tampering with evidence, all in a desperate bid to clear my name and expose Reynolds for the corrupt bastard he truly was.

"Over here," Dante's voice cut through the silence, drawing my attention to the far wall where the painting hung, its frame slightly askew.

I moved towards it, my fingers tracing the ornate edges of the frame as I studied it closely. I was right – there was definitely something off about the way it hung, like it had been moved and replaced countless times.

"Help me with this," I said, as I gestured for Dante to grab the other side of the frame.

Together, we carefully lifted the painting away from the wall, revealing a hidden compartment concealed behind the drywall. My heart leaped into my throat as I caught sight of the weathered manila envelope tucked inside, the words "Reynolds" scrawled across it in Morrow's familiar handwriting.

"Bingo," I breathed, my fingers trembling as I pulled the envelope free and checked the insides.

Dante's arm snaked around my waist, his body warm and solid against my back as he peered over my shoulder. "Is that it? The file on Reynolds?"

I nodded, my throat tight with emotion as I clutched the envelope to my chest. "Yeah, this is it. Our smoking gun."

A tense silence settled over us as we stood there. This

was it – the key to exposing Reynolds' corruption, and bringing down the man who had orchestrated this entire nightmare.

"We need to get out of here," Dante said, as he guided me towards the door. "Before someone shows up and catches us red-handed."

I didn't need to be told twice, and my feet carried me forward with a renewed sense of purpose. We slipped out of the apartment, retracing our steps with the same stealth that had brought us here, and made our way back to the safety of Dante's yacht.

As the familiar surroundings of the cabin enveloped us, I felt a weight lift from my shoulders. We were safe, at least for the moment, and we had the evidence we needed to bring Reynolds to his knees.

With trembling fingers, I opened the envelope and pulled out the contents to show Dante. This was it. It was all here – copies of encrypted communications, financial ledgers detailing offshore accounts and wire transfers, coded records of meetings and transactions, a damning dossier that laid bare Reynolds' decades-long tenure as a cartel mole.

"Holy shit," he said, his voice barely audible as I flipped through the pages, each one more incriminating than the last.

Dante's arm tightened around my waist as he continued to study the documents over my shoulder. "We need to move fast," he said. "As soon as Reynolds catches wind that there's a copy of the file, he'll stop at nothing to bury it."

I nodded as I met his gaze. "We go straight to the US Attorney's Office. Get them to issue a warrant and watch the dominoes fall."

A fire burned bright within me, a fierce, unquenchable blaze that would consume everything in its path. Reynolds had made a grave mistake in underestimating me, in thinking that he could silence me with threats and intimidation.

He was about to learn just how wrong he was.

MY HEART RACED AS DANTE, and I strode through the imposing doors of the US Attorney's Office, Morrow's file heavy in my hands. This was it – our one chance to clear my name and bring Reynolds and the entire corrupt edifice crumbling down around him.

The receptionist eyed us warily as we approached, no doubt taking in our disheveled appearance and the grim determination etched into our faces. "Can I help you?" she asked, her tone politely skeptical.

"We need to see the head prosecutor. Immediately," I stated, my voice firm. "It's a matter of national security."

She opened her mouth to protest or demand some form of identification, but the look on Dante's face must have given her pause. She picked up her phone, and a minute later, with a curt nod, she gestured towards the elevators. "Fourth floor. They'll be expecting you."

The ride up to the fourth floor was tense, the silence punctuated only by the soft hum of the elevator's machinery. Dante's hand found mine, his fingers intertwining with my own in a silent show of solidarity. I drew strength from his touch, from the unwavering conviction that burned within him.

The doors slid open, revealing a bustling office area filled with cubicles and the frenetic energy of legal professionals hard at work. A stern-faced woman in a crisp pantsuit approached us, her gaze appraising us with a thinly veiled disdain.

"This way," she said, her voice clipped and businesslike as she led us down a maze of corridors and through a set of heavy oak doors.

The conference room was a study in understated opulence, with plush leather chairs and a gleaming mahogany table that seemed to stretch on forever. Seated at the head of a table full of prosecutors was a man I recognized immediately – Elliot Granger, the US Attorney for the Southern District of Florida.

Granger rose to his feet as we entered and gestured for us to take a seat. "Miss Ramirez, Mr. Reyes," he began, his voice carrying the weight of a man accustomed to being obeyed. "I must admit, I was surprised to receive your request for a meeting. Especially under such... unusual circumstances."

I squared my shoulders, steeling myself for the battle

ahead. "I appreciate you agreeing to see us, Mr. Granger," I said, my voice steady despite the butterflies that had taken up residence in my stomach. "What we have to share with you is of the utmost importance, and it concerns not only the integrity of the DEA but the very fabric of our nation's justice system."

Granger arched an eyebrow, his expression one of polite skepticism. "That's quite a bold claim, Agent Ramirez. Especially coming from someone who is currently facing charges of murder and corruption."

Beside me, I felt Dante tense, his jaw clenching as he fought to maintain his composure. "Those charges are a sham, and you know it," he growled. "Natalia is being framed by the very man who orchestrated this whole goddamn mess – Chief Reynolds."

A murmur rippled through the assembled prosecutors, their expressions ranging from disbelief to outright scorn. But before any of them could voice their protests, I slid the file across the table towards Granger.

"This is the proof," I said, my voice ringing with conviction. "Everything you need to bring Reynolds down, to expose his decades-long tenure as a mole for Ricardo Reyes."

Granger eyed the file warily, as if it might suddenly sprout fangs and bite him. But after a moment's hesitation, he flipped it open, his eyes scanning the contents with a furrowed brow.

The room fell silent. I could see the disbelief on

Granger's face slowly giving way to grim realization as he pored over the damning evidence in the file.

Finally, he looked up, his gaze flickering between Dante and me. "This... this is incredible," he said. "If what you're saying is true, if this evidence is legitimate..."

"It is," I assured him, my voice unwavering. "And that's not all. Dante has information, insider knowledge that could help bring down Ricardo Reyes himself."

Granger regarded Dante with suspicion. "Is that so, Mr. Reyes? And what, pray tell, would compel the heir to one of the most powerful criminal empires in the city to turn on his own family?"

Dante met Granger's gaze unflinchingly, his eyes burning with a fierce intensity that took my breath away. "Because I'm done with the lies, the violence, the corruption that has defined my family's legacy for generations," he said. "I'm done watching good people suffer at the hands of monsters like my father, like Javier Cruz."

He paused, his gaze sweeping over the assembled prosecutors as if daring them to challenge him. "I won't lie to you – my hands are far from clean. I've done things, terrible things, in service to the cartel. But I'm willing to lay it all on the table to give you everything I have on my father's operations, financial dealings, and criminal infrastructure In return, I want immunity for me and my men."

A hush fell over the room, Dante's words hanging heavy in the air. I could see the doubt, the suspicion flickering across the faces of the prosecutors like shadows dancing in candlelight.

But then, with a slow, deliberate motion, Dante reached into his jacket and withdrew a thick manila envelope, sliding it across the table towards Granger. "This is just the beginning," he said. "I can get you everything you need to dismantle my father's cartel, his entire operation from the ground up."

Granger eyed the envelope warily, his fingers drumming against the polished wood of the table as he considered the implications of what we were offering. Finally, after what felt like an eternity, he looked up, his gaze steady and resolute.

"Very well," he said. "We'll convene an emergency grand jury and begin the process of issuing indictments and arrest warrants. But make no mistake, Mr. Reyes – if you're lying to us, if this is some sort of elaborate ruse, you'll be the first one we come after."

Dante nodded. "I understand, Mr. Granger. And you have my word – I'm in this for the long haul. No more lies, no more games. It's time to burn this whole fucking thing to the ground."

As Dante and I exited the conference room, the impact of our actions enveloped me. We had just laid our cards on the table, gambling everything on the hope that justice would prevail, that the truth would finally come to light.

Elliot Granger's words echoed in my mind, a solemn vow that hung in the air like a promise. "We'll convene an emergency grand jury and begin the process of issuing indictments and arrest warrants," he had said.

I felt a flicker of hope, a spark of optimism that threatened to ignite the fire of my determination. This was the chance to expose Reynolds as the corrupt, power-hungry monster he truly was.

We stepped into the elevator, the doors sliding shut behind us with a soft, muffled thud. The silence was deafening, the only sound the soft hum of the elevator's machinery as it carried us back down to the lobby.

"Let's head back to the yacht and get changed before heading out for dinner," Dante suggested.

Dante led me to his Maserati, the sleek, black vehicle gleaming under the harsh glare of the sun. He opened the passenger door for me, his gaze lingering on my face as if to reassure himself that I was alright.

As he pulled away from the curb, I allowed myself a moment of quiet reflection. While the outcome was far from certain, I knew that we had made the right decision.

"Are you okay?" Dante's voice broke through my thoughts, his tone one of concern.

I turned to face him, my gaze meeting his in a silent exchange of understanding. "I'm fine," I assured him, my voice steady despite the whirlwind of emotions that threatened to consume me. "Just... processing everything, I guess."

He nodded, his eyes fixed on the road ahead as he navigated the crowded streets with practiced ease.

We drove in silence for a while, each of us lost in our

own thoughts as the cityscape whizzed by in a blur of color and motion. It wasn't until we pulled into the marina that I noticed a familiar figure standing on the dock by Dante's yacht.

My heart nearly stopped when I saw Sofia, her body slumped against the setting sun. She looked so fragile, so broken. The mascara stains on her face made it obvious she'd been crying her fucking eyes out.

Dante bolted from the car, running to his sister and wrapping her in his arms like he could shield her from the world. I stood back, giving them space to talk.

"Sofia, what the hell happened?" Dante asked, his voice cracking with worry as he held her close.

She clung to him desperately, like she was drowning and he was her only lifeline. "I fucked up, Dante. I should've believed you from the start."

He pulled away, searching her face for answers. "What are you talking about? Just tell me."

Sofia glanced at me for a split second before focusing back on her brother. "It's Allen. That sleazeball has been working for Javier Cruz all along, just like you said."

I could see Dante's jaw clench, the rage boiling under the surface.

"How did you...?" he asked, his voice dangerously calm.

With shaking hands, she pulled out a sleek black phone. "I found this hidden in Allen's jacket. It's a burner phone, and it's full of messages from Javier."

Dante snatched the phone, his grip so tight I thought he might shatter it. "What kind of messages?"

Sofia steadied herself. "Allen made a deal with the devil. He's been spying on you, feeding Javier intel on your every move. And in return? Javier agreed to wipe out Allen's debt. Seventy-five-thousand dollars."

A low, guttural growl rumbled in Dante's throat. I could see the rage building behind his eyes, the barely contained fury.

"That bastard," he snarled, his grip tightening around the phone until his knuckles turned white.

Sofia nodded, her eyes glistening with unshed tears. "According to the messages, Allen's information led to Javier being able to trick Raul into thinking he was one of your men."

A tense silence fell over us with Sofia's revelation hanging heavy in the air. I could see Dante was mulling it over, all the pieces of the puzzle finally falling into place. His gaze softened as he looked at his sister. "Thank you, Sofia," he said, pulling her into another embrace. "For trusting me."

Sofia clung to him, her slender frame trembling. "I'm just sorry it took me so long to see the truth," she whispered, her voice muffled against Dante's shoulder.

Dante pulled back, his hands cupping Sofia's face. He looked into her eyes with a fierce conviction. "Go home and be with mami. Something's about to go down and I don't want her to be by herself. Soon it will all be over." he vowed. "No more lies, no more violence, no more cartel business. From now on, everything we do will be above board and legal."

Sofia's lips morphed into a tentative smile, her eyes shining with hope. "I believe you, Dante," she said, her voice soft but unwavering.

As I watched the two siblings embrace, I felt a surge of love and admiration for them. Despite the darkness that had surrounded them and the legacy of violence and corruption that had threatened to consume them, they had found the strength to break free to chart a new course for themselves.

FORTY

DANTE

THE ESCALADE PURRED SOFTLY, A STEADY RUMBLE that did little to soothe my raging storm within. My fingers tapped erratically on the wheel, matching the pounding of my heart.

Beside me, Marco checked his gun for the third time, the familiar metallic click of the magazine sliding home. "This is it, brother," he said quietly. "Time to show that snake Javier what happens when you fuck with Dante Reyes."

I nodded tightly, jaw clenched as I stared at my old man's office building. The glass and steel tower loomed over the street, a monument to the empire Ricardo built on blood and fear.

But tonight, it wasn't my father I was after. No, while the DEA and Natalia were focused on bringing in Ricardo and Reynolds, I had a different target in mind.

Javier fucking Cruz. That bastard had been a thorn in

my side for months, jacking my product and disrespecting me at every turn. He was a cancer that needed to be cut out before he infected everything I held dear.

My old man had forbidden me from touching him, claiming Javier was too valuable, that his connections made him untouchable. Yeah right, turns out they were cooking meth together.

But now? The gloves were off. No more playing nice, following orders like a good soldier. It was time for some payback.

"Remember the plan," I said. "We get in, find Javier, and end this. For good."

Marco grinned, a predatory thing that would've sent lesser men running. "With pleasure, boss."

I hadn't told Natalia or the DEA about the meth lab Marco and I had discovered. It was a secret I had kept close to my chest, a trump card that I had been waiting to play at just the right moment.

And that moment was now. Because I knew that if Javier was going to be anywhere, it would be there, in that hidden room deep in the bowels of my father's building. He would be trying to grab as much product as he could before he ran like the coward he was.

We watched in silence as a sleek black car pulled up to the building, and a lone figure emerged from the shadows. Javier Cruz, in the flesh, and surprisingly, he was alone. There was no crew and no backup. Just a man on the run, desperate to save his own skin.

"Showtime," I muttered, slipping out of the car and

motioning for Marco to follow. We moved like shadows, silent and deadly, as we made our way into the building, our guns drawn and ready.

The lobby was deserted, and the only sounds were the soft hum of the air conditioning and the distant ding of an elevator. We took the stairs toward the secret room where I knew Javier would be.

But he must have spotted us because all hell broke loose the moment we stepped through the door to the floor. Gunfire erupted, the sound deafening in the enclosed space. The acrid smell of cordite filled the air, mingling with the coppery tang of blood.

I dove for cover, my heart hammering in my chest as I returned fire. Beside me, Marco grunted in pain, his hand clutching his shoulder as blood seeped between his fingers.

"Fuck," he hissed, his face contorted in a grimace. "I'm hit."

I spared him a glance, my jaw tightening at the sight of my best friend, my brother, wounded and unable to fight. But there was no time to dwell on it, no time for anything but the battle at hand.

"It's just a flesh wound. Go on. Get the motherfucker for me," Marco said and managed a thumbs up. "I'll wait back here."

That rat bastard Javier was always one step ahead, laughing as he darted through the shadows like a goddamn ghost. Bullets screamed past me, close enough I could feel their heat kissing my skin. But I didn't flinch. Couldn't.

Not with Marco bleeding out back there, trusting me to finish this.

Javier had to die. No mercy, no quarter for disrespecting and stealing from me. And for hurting my people? The ones I loved most? Oh, he'd pay. I'd make damn sure of it.

But the slippery fuck was too quick. He led me on a wild chase, always just out of reach. And then, in a flash of movement, he was behind me, gun pressed to the back of my skull.

"Drop it, Dante," he growled, voice dripping venom. "Or I'll paint these walls with your brains."

I had no choice. Heart hammering so loud, surely he could hear it, I slowly let my gun fall. The metal clattered against the concrete floor. But this wasn't over. No way.

"You're too easy, chico. Just like your girlfriend's DEA partner," Javier said, his words casual, almost conversational. "Matt, wasn't it? He was getting too close to our operation, sticking his nose where it didn't belong. So I put a bullet in his head."

My blood ran cold at his words, a wave of fury washing over me.

"And that little bitch of yours, Natalia?" Javier continued, his voice taunting. "I saw how you spared her that night, how you let her live. I almost killed her myself, you know. Would have, too, if I hadn't heard the sirens."

He laughed, a cruel, mocking sound that made my skin crawl. "I should have pulled the trigger on both of you. Then, Ricardo would have gotten what he wanted."

I closed my eyes, my thoughts on Natalia. The memory of her bloodied and beaten in that jail cell, her eyes haunted and her spirit broken, was seared into my mind, a nightmare that would never fade.

But then, Javier's words sank in, and a cold, creeping dread settled in the pit of my stomach.

"Ricardo?" I asked, my voice hoarse. "What did my father want?"

Javier chuckled, the sound low and menacing. "Oh, Dante. You really are naive, aren't you? Your father wanted the two DEA agents dead and you to take the blame for it. He gave me the order himself. And, it would have worked brilliantly if you just had shot that fucking bitch."

I felt like a freight train had slammed into me, the air rushing out of my lungs in a single, painful exhale. My own father, the man who had raised me, who had molded me into the man I was today, had wanted me gone, framed for murdering cops?

Javier raised his gun, taking aim at my head. "And now, I get to fulfill half of his order. Goodbye, Dante Reyes."

I braced myself for the end, for the searing pain of the bullet tearing through my skull. I thought of Natalia, of the life we could have had together, of the love that burned so brightly between us. I thought of my sister, Sofia, of the promise I had made to protect her from the darkness that had consumed our family.

And I thought of my father, of the man who had betrayed me in the most ultimate way possible. In that moment, I felt a hatred so pure, so all-consuming, that it threatened to swallow me whole.

But the end never came. Instead, a single shot rang out, the sound like a thunderclap in the stillness of the room.

Javier crumpled to the ground, his gun clattering uselessly beside him. Blood blossomed on his shoulder, a red stain that spread across the white fabric of his shirt.

I spun around, expecting to see Marco standing there, his gun still smoking. But it wasn't Marco.

It was Natalia.

Her gun was raised, and a look of fierceness etched onto her face. Without hesitation, she strode forward, her weapon trained on Javier's prone form.

"You killed Matt," she snarled, her voice trembling with barely contained rage. "You murdered my partner in cold blood."

Javier laughed, a sick sound that bubbled up from his throat. "And I'd do it again," he spat, his eyes gleaming with malice. "Just like I should've killed you and your boyfriend here when I had the chance."

Natalia's finger tightened on the trigger, her jaw clenched tightly. I could see the war raging within her, the primal desire for vengeance battling against her sense of justice.

"Natalia," I said softly. "Don't. He's not worth it."

For a moment, I wasn't sure if she heard me, her gaze still fixed on Javier's sneering face. But then, slowly, she lowered her gun, her shoulders slumping as the fight drained out of her.

"You're right," she said, her voice hoarse with emotion.

The sound of sirens filled the air, growing louder with each passing second. I helped Natalia secure Javier, my mind still reeling from the revelations he had unleashed about my father setting me up.

As the police flooded into the building, I watched as they hauled Javier away, his face contorted in a mask of hatred and defiance. Marco was loaded into an ambulance, his wound more serious than he had let one, but not life-threatening. I told him I'd check in on him tomorrow, and off he went.

And then it was just me and Natalia, standing amidst the chaos and destruction, our bodies trembling with the aftermath of the adrenaline rush.

"How did you find me?" I asked, my voice rough with emotion.

She shook her head, a wry smile tugging at the corners of her mouth. "I'm a DEA agent, remember? It's my job to track down dangerous criminals."

I couldn't help but laugh at that, the sound bubbling up from somewhere deep within me. "Is that what I am now? A dangerous criminal?"

Natalia reached out to cup my cheek. "No, Dante. You're a man who's trying to do the right thing, even when the whole world seems to be against you."

I leaned into her touch, my eyes fluttering closed as I savored the warmth of her skin against mine. "I don't know what I would do without you, mi reina," I said.

She pressed her forehead against mine, her breath

ms

mingling with my own. "You'll never have to find out, mi amor. I'm not going anywhere."

We held each other, soaking up that closeness, that intimacy, like it was our goddamn life force while the shit-storm kept raging all around us. But eventually, we had to break apart, all the crap we still had to deal with crashing down on us again.

"C'mon, let's head back to the boat," I said, my voice shot to hell. Natalia gave me a nod, but then this devilish grin spread across her face. "Or we could go to your place instead. No more sneaking around. And I'm jonesing for some quality time in the playroom if you know what I mean."

Fuck, just the thought had me rock hard in seconds. "I'm all yours, baby. Let's go." We started heading to my place, but then Natalia's phone started buzzing. She took one look at the screen, and her eyebrows shot up. It was Valentina calling.

"Val, what's up?" she asked, putting the phone on speaker so I could hear.

"We got him, Nat," Valentina's voice crackled through the line. "Reynolds is in custody. The evidence you provided was enough to secure an arrest warrant."

Relief washed over me like a tidal wave, the weight of the world lifting from my shoulders. Reynolds, the corrupt bastard, was finally where he belonged - behind bars.

"Holy shit, Val, that's incredible," Natalia said, her voice wavering with the intensity of it all. "But what about Ricardo? Did they get him too?"

The loaded silence from Valentina's end said it all. "Yeah, about that, Nat," she finally responded. "When our guys busted into the Reyes compound, Ricardo was already gone. Somehow, he caught wind of what was coming and disappeared before we could get our hands on him."

My heart sank, a cold, creeping dread settling in the pit of my stomach. My father, the mastermind behind everything, was still out there, a specter of violence and corruption that would stop at nothing.

"What about my mother?" I asked, my voice hoarse with fear. "Is she safe?"

"She's okay, Dante," Valentina assured me, her voice softening with sympathy. And your sister, Sofia. They were both at the compound when we moved in but not under arrest. We'll need to question them, though, to see what they know about your father's whereabouts."

I nodded, my jaw clenching with determination. "I need to see them, Val. I need to make sure they're alright."

"Of course," she said with understanding. "I'll arrange for them to be brought to the DEA offices. You and Natalia can meet them there."

We ended the call, a silence settling over us as we absorbed the news. Ricardo was still out there, a threat that loomed over everything we had fought so hard to build.

But as I looked at Natalia, her hand clasped tightly in my own, I knew that we would face this challenge together, just as we had faced every other obstacle that had been thrown our way.

"We'll find him, Dante," she said, her voice fierce with determination. "We'll bring your father to justice, no matter what it takes."

I nodded, drawing strength from her unwavering conviction. "I know we will, mi reina. But first, let's get to Sofia and my mother. Make sure they are safe."

We made our way to the DEA offices and found Sofia and my mother in a small room huddled together on a worn couch. They looked up as we entered, their eyes wide with fear and uncertainty.

"Dante," Sofia breathed, rushing forward to embrace me. "Thank God you're alright. We were so worried."

I held her close. "I'm okay, hermana," I said. "I'm just glad you and Mama are safe."

My mother stood, her face drawn and tired, but her eyes were filled with a fierce love that took my breath away. "Mijo," she whispered, pulling me into her arms. "What have you done? What have you gotten yourself into?"

"I had to do it, Mama," I said. "I couldn't let Father destroy everything. You and Sofia."

She nodded, her eyes shimmering with unshed tears. "I know, mijo. I know. But now, we must be strong. We must face whatever comes next together, as a family."

I looked at Natalia, her hand still clasped tightly in my own, and I knew that she was a part of that family now, too. She had stood by my side through everything, had risked her life and her career to help me bring down my father.

And now, as we faced the future, I knew that she would be there with me every step of the way, a constant reminder of the love and the hope that had brought us this far.

"We'll get through this," I said, my voice ringing with conviction. "Together, we'll find a way to make things right, to build a new life free from the violence and the corruption that has haunted us for so long."

As I looked around at the faces of the people I loved most in this world—my sister, my mother, and the woman who had captured my heart—I knew that no matter what the future held, we would face it together.

EPILOGUE

NATALIA

IT HAD BEEN TWO MONTHS SINCE DANTE AND I brought down his father's cartel, and I couldn't believe how much our lives had changed. Ricardo Reyes was not in charge of the cartel, and Dante was a changed man, hell-bent on creating a legitimate empire that had nothing to do with his father's criminal past.

And tonight, standing in the heart of his newest venture—a soon-to-open nightclub in South Beach—I could see the fire in his eyes. It wasn't the dangerous, volatile flame that used to burn so fiercely within him, but a steady, unwavering passion that fueled his ambition.

"This place is going to be incredible, mi reina." His voice was filled with excitement as he gave me a tour of the massive space that would soon become Miami's hottest new nightclub.

I looked around, taking in the sleek, modern design, the

state-of-the-art sound system, and the multiple dance floors that would soon be packed with guests. "I can't wait to see it all come together," I said. "Especially this dance floor." I nudged him towards the center of the room, where a gleaming hardwood floor awaited the rhythmic stomps of salsa dancers.

Dante smiled, his eyes sparkling with mischief. "Oh, we can't have a brand new club without breaking it in properly." Before I could ask what he meant, he pulled out his phone and I watched as he opened an app. With a few taps on the screen, salsa music sprang to life and he took my hand in his, his fingers entwining with mine as he pulled me closer. "Dance with me?"

My pulse quickened, and a smile spread across my face as I stepped into his embrace. Our bodies moved in sync, our footsteps echoing across the empty club as we lost ourselves in the music. Dante's lips brushed my ear, his breath hot against my skin as he whispered, "You're breathtaking, mi amor."

I leaned into him, my body fitting perfectly against his as we moved in perfect unison. "You're not so bad yourself, Mr. Club Owner." I flashed him a flirtatious smile, our eyes locking for a heated moment before we continued our dance.

As the final notes of the song echoed through the empty nightclub, Dante twirled me one last time, the movement sending a thrill racing through me. He pulled me into his grasp, his arms tightening around me in a possessive embrace. "Now, what did you have in mind for this dance floor, mi reina?" His voice was low and playful, his eyes glittering with desire.

I bit my lip, feeling a familiar warmth pool between my legs. "Well, I was thinking..." I paused, trailing my fingers up his chest, savoring the feeling of his heart thundering beneath my touch. "We could christen it properly."

His eyes darkened. "Oh, really?"

I nodded, a mischievous smile playing on my lips. "Absolutely."

Before he could respond, I felt the vibration of his phone buzzing in his pocket. He let out a soft curse, his hands lingering on my waist as he reluctantly reached for his phone. "Hold that thought, mi amor. It's Marco. I'll be right back."

I pouted, but I knew better than to get in the way when it was business. "Fine, but hurry up," I called out as he walked away, already immersed in conversation with his partner in crime—literally.

I took a moment to catch my breath, fanning myself with my hand as my heart rate slowly returned to normal. I scanned the room admiring the decor that fit flawlessly with Dante's vision of an elite club. It was perfect. As I continued to take in the large club space, my eyes landed on a door marked "Staff Only."

A smile curved my lips as an idea took shape in my mind. Why not take advantage of the club's many features? I made my way towards the restricted area, feeling a familiar rush of adrenaline as I pushed open the door and stepped into the dimly lit hallway beyond.

At the end of the hall, I pushed open another door, stunned as I stepped into a luxurious VIP room.

The space was designed for ultimate privacy and indulgence, with plush couches, a fully stocked bar, and a flickering fireplace. I ran my fingers over the soft fabric of the couch, my mind already spinning with possibilities.

"Like what you see, mi reina?"

I whirled around at the sound of Dante's voice, my heart hammering in my chest. "Very much so," I said, my voice playful. "Especially these VIP rooms. They're amazing."

He chuckled, his eyes scanning the room as he took a step towards me. "They are quite something, aren't they? But I think we can make them even better."

My eyebrows shot up in surprise. "Oh?"

Dante nodded, his eyes glittering with mischief. "I was thinking we could add a few... enhancements." He strode towards me, his hands reaching for the sash of my dress. "Perhaps a Saint Andrew's cross over here, a bed over there..."

I laughed, heat spreading through my body as his fingers deftly untied the sash, letting my dress fall open to reveal my lace lingerie beneath. "Is that so?"

"Absolutely," he purred, his lips brushing against my ear as his hands slid down my back. "But first, we should thoroughly test the... amenities."

I shivered at the feel of his breath against my skin, a rush of desire coursing through me as his lips found mine in a searing kiss. My hands roamed his broad chest, and I could feel his heart pounding beneath my touch as his mouth devoured mine.

"Mr. Club Owner, I do believe you're trying to take advantage of me," I said between kisses, my lips curving into a teasing smile.

Dante pulled back, his eyes darkening as he took in the desire pooling in my eyes. "Only if you let me."

I leaned in, my lips brushing his ear as I whispered, "Then I might just let you. But only if you promise to show me all the exclusive VIP perks."

His eyes glinted with desire, his hands possessively roaming my body as he drew me closer. "I promise, mi amor. We'll test every inch of this room until we get it just right."

Our kisses grew more urgent, our bodies pressing together as we sank onto the plush couch, the cushions swallowing our moans as we lost ourselves in each other. The satin and velvet textures brushed against my skin, the flickering fire casting an amber glow over our flushed bodies.

And in that moment, as Dante's hands explored my curves with eager fingers, I knew that no matter what challenges the future might hold, we would face them together, our love burning brightly to guide us through the darkness.

But for now, all I could think about was enjoying the

perks of being with the club owner, especially those in the VIP rooms. Oh, the perks most definitely included Dante's talented hands and mouth on me.

THE END

The Reyes Cartel series continues in Book 2.

ABOUT THE AUTHOR

M. S. Parker is a USA Today Bestselling author and the author of the Erotic Romance series, Club Privè and Chasing Perfection.

Living in Las Vegas, she enjoys sitting by the pool with her laptop writing on her next spicy romance.

Growing up all she wanted to be was a dancer, actor or author. So far only the latter has come true but M. S. Parker hasn't retired her dancing shoes just yet. She is still waiting for the call for her to appear on Dancing With The Stars.

When M. S. isn't writing, she can usually be found reading– oops, scratch that! She is always writing.

For more information:
www.msparker.com

ACKNOWLEDGMENTS

First, I would like to thank all of my readers. Without you, my books would not exist. I truly appreciate each and every one of you.

A big "thanks" goes out to all the Facebook fans, street team, beta readers, and advanced reviewers. You are a HUGE part of the success of all my series.

I would like to give a special thanks to Jillian Haworth who helped me with the final edits of the book. You rock, girl.

Printed in Great Britain
by Amazon